Also by Dara Horn

ALL OTHER NIGHTS

THE WORLD TO COME

IN THE IMAGE

W. W. NORTON & COMPANY

New York • London

More Praise for *A Guide for the Perplexed*

"Intricate and suspenseful, *A Guide for the Perplexed* is both learned and heartfelt, an exploration of human memory, its uses and misuses, that spans centuries in a twisty braid full of jaw-dropping revelations and breathtaking reversals. An elegant and brainy page-turner from a master storyteller."

—Geraldine Brooks, Pulitzer Prize winner and author of *Caleb's Crossing*

"It's not every day you come across a genuinely page-turning kidnapping story that is also replete with historical, psychological, and interpretive insights into Maimonides, envy, and motherhood, not to mention replicating the narrative structure and central themes of the biblical story of Joseph. *A Guide for the Perplexed* is Dara Horn's most ambitious, audacious, edifying, and entertaining novel yet."

—Elif Batuman, author of *The Possessed: Adventures with Russian Books and the People Who Read Them*

"Riveting. . . . This is extraordinary material, emotionally resonant and intellectually suggestive, and Horn's portraits of the sisters are wonderfully ambiguous. . . . [Horn] interweaves historical and contemporary tales to create intriguing echoes and layers of metaphor. . . . Horn's searing family drama easily encompasses whole worlds of political, philosophical and moral conflicts. . . . Beautifully written and overwhelmingly sad."

—Wendy Smith, *Washington Post*

"Horn moves seamlessly back and forth in time."

—*Entertainment Weekly*

"An intriguing and readable novel."

—Laurie Muchnick, *Bloomberg News*

"Computer science and medieval philosophy mesh in Dara Horn's accomplished novel about digital dangers and the nature of memory."

—Barbara Kiser, *Nature*

"Yes, the novel is as intricately constructed as Joseph's coat of many colors, and, yes, it echoes the thematic density of the philosophical work after which it is named, but beneath all that beats the living heart of a very human drama, one that will have readers both caught up in the suspense and moved by the tragic dimensions of the unresolved dilemma at the core of the story." —*Booklist*, starred review

"Ms. Horn makes all characters, the heroic and the evil, all too human and all too real. . . . To call this novel an international thriller seems to diminish it. Yet at the same time Ms. Horn has pushed the genre into newer and stranger places."
—Karl Wolff, *New York Journal of Books*

"Dara Horn's fourth, and best [novel]. . . . Her funniest work yet. . . . Horn frames a contest between predetermination and free will in which her characters are each humbled, a religious dialogue taking the form of this humane, erudite novel."
—Saul Austerlitz, *Boston Globe*

"[An] intense, multilayered story. . . . [Horn's] writing comes from a place of deep knowledge. . . . Horn is rigorously, impressively devoted to theme, and all of her novel's threads are in service of it. No detail is out of place. . . . I admired Horn's intensity and integrity, much as I admired the same qualities in her characters." —Jami Attenberg, *New York Times Book Review*

"A work marked by brilliant conceits and clever plotting."
—*Kirkus Reviews*

"Horn is embracing her own, livelier brand of Jewish history, embodied in the joys of discovering—and creating—the past anew." —*Tablet*

"And as I keep insisting to anyone who will listen, Dara Horn is the China Miéville of literary fiction and her newest book, *A Guide for the Perplexed*, proves it. It's a philosophical treatise, cyberthriller, family story, kidnapping, and quest for the Information Age's Holy Grail—universal archiving—all in one."

—Jenn Northington, Tor.com

"Readers will be taken in by this literary thriller's fast-paced plot and complicated but well-imaged characters."

—*Library Journal*

"[A] stunning work of the imagination that enlightens as it entertains." —Sidney Offit, *Moment* magazine

"Horn's novel—which is loosely based on the biblical story of Joseph—is one of immense intellectual ambition, and yet it pulls off the impressive feat of maintaining a fast pace and vivid imagery without sacrificing the nuances of its existential explorations. . . . This novel [is] as culturally significant as it is entertaining." —Hannah Sheldon-Dean, *Bookslut*

"Astoundingly well researched, ambitious as all get-out, and utterly absorbing." —Jenn Northington, Book Riot

"Dara Horn gives a modern twist to the discovery of the Cairo Genizah, one of the most important cultural finds in Jewish history. . . . [A] gripping story." —Nicole Levy, *Jewish Journal*

"Horn's literary energies are generated cumulatively through plot, moral weight, and elegant thematic architectures built from the storehouses of Jewish culture. . . . She is first, and foremost, a storyteller, yet these stories carry Horn's readers higher and further than many of her contemporaries do with dazzling prose." —Michael Weingrad, *Jewish Review of Books*

"Dara Horn not only writes about topics in which she is well versed, but she further researches each topic to authenticate her subject, even in a fictional interpretation. . . . Horn did a fantastic job unveiling the constraints of memory, regardless of how realistic they may seem." —*Damian Daily*

"A multi-layered meditation on memory that weaves its way through history, politics and sisterly rivalry while keeping the pages turning with a blockbuster-worthy kidnapping plot."
—Judith Basya, *HEEB*

"An engaging blend of historical fiction and contemporary thriller. . . . [A]n ambitious and philosophical novel. . . . [I]ntriguing. . . . *A Guide for the Perplexed* will greatly appeal to readers looking for a unique and contemplative adventure."
—Sarah Rachel Egelman, Bookreporter.com

"A novel of astonishing imagination and profound meaning."
—*Jewish Book World*

"Horn explores sibling rivalry, memory, free will, the paradox of hope assuming God is all powerful, and quantum physics, no less. *A Guide for the Perplexed* is a return to form for this challenging, marvelous writer. Her intellectualism and religious exploration create a thought-provoking read that won't soon be forgotten." —Kelly Roark, *Newcity Lit*

"Wondrous. . . . [A] richly layered novel. . . . Horn has magically summoned the wisdom of the ages to address a most contemporary dilemma. How ought one live a meaningful life in a world that perpetually disappears before our eyes? . . . [W]hat makes *A Guide for the Perplexed* Horn's finest novel is its riveting and suspenseful quality as the narrative unfolds. . . . A novelist at the height of her powers." —Andrew Furman, *Miami Herald*

Dara Horn

A Guide for the Perplexed

a novel

Printed in the United States of America
First Published as a Norton paperback 2014

For information about special discounts for bulk purchases,
please contact W. W. Norton Special Sales
at specialsales@wwnorton.com or 800-233-4830

Manufacturing by Courier Westford
Book design by Ellen Cipriano
Production manager: Devon Zahn

Library of Congress Cataloging-in-Publication Data

Horn, Dara, 1977–
A guide for the perplexed : a novel / Dara Horn. — First Edition.
pages cm
ISBN 978-0-393-06489-6 (hardcover)
1. Sisters—Fiction. 2. Kidnapping—Egypt—Fiction. I. Title.
PS3608.076G85 2013
813'.6—dc23
2013009456

ISBN 978-0-393-34888-0 pbk.

W. W. Norton & Company, Inc.,
500 Fifth Avenue, New York, N.Y. 10110
www.wwnorton.com

W. W. Norton & Company Ltd.,
Castle House, 75/76 Wells Street, London W1T 3QT

1 2 3 4 5 6 7 8 9 0

For Maya, Ari, Eli, and Ronen—

who will forget what I remember,

and who will remember what I forget

A Guide
for the
Perplexed

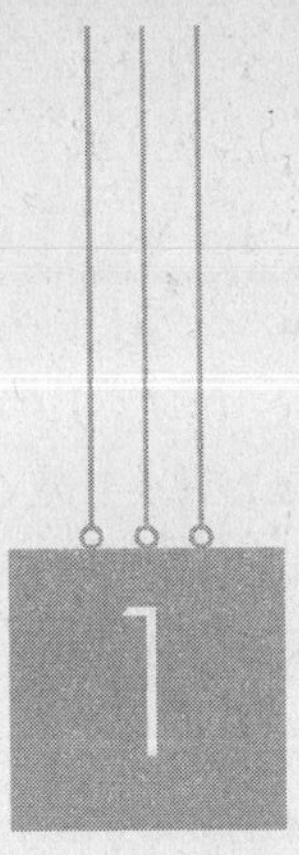

WHAT HAPPENS TO DAYS that disappear? The light fades, the gates begin to close, and all that a day once held—a glance, a fight, a taste of bread, a handful of braided hair, thousands of worries and triumphs and regrets—all of it slips between those closing gates, vanishing into a dark and silent room. When Josephine Ashkenazi first invented Genizah, all she wanted to do was open those gates.

At least, that was how it started. In its earliest versions, the program Josie invented was little more than a variant on dozens of others. But then the software grew, unfolding before her like a prophetic dream. By the time she was twenty-four years old, Genizah was a vast platform, password-protected and accessible from anywhere, that saved not only material that its users deliberately created, but essentially everything else they did too, running recording components on devices the users already owned and then employing natural language processing and facial recognition to catalogue worlds of data according to the users' habits—which the software learned from the users themselves. By the time she was twenty-six, Genizah didn't merely store data, but tracked it, showing past trajectories and using them to predict the users' future. By the time she was twenty-seven, she had married the company's chief engineer, had been the subject of a nationally televised documentary, and had a baby. By the time she was thirty-three, her six-year-old daughter Tali's every moment was recorded forever. But Tali knew nothing about it until one morning when, almost by accident, Josie showed her the archive of her life.

"I can't find my shoes, Mommy," Tali had announced as she finished her breakfast. "I looked and looked, but they're nowhere."

"That's impossible," Josie told her. Josie was throwing things into her own bag, checking messages, noting the time. In half an hour she would be at her office, meeting her sister Judith, who had been working at the company for the past seven years—ever since Josie had taken pity on her unemployed sister and parked her in the company's public relations office. Every day Josie dreaded seeing her; every day Josie wished she could find a way not to dread it, to pretend her sister was someone different from who she was. But it was impossible. The thought of Judith made Josie unreasonable, illogical. And Tali—the girl whose resemblance to her mother ended at the roots of her long black hair—made her feel the same way. "They're somewhere. Probably somewhere obvious. Where did you take them off yesterday?"

"I don't remember," Tali said, losing interest. She was dressed, as always, entirely in orange, which she claimed was for "safety." Now she was dipping the ends of her hair into her milk, painting the table white.

Josie scaled the stairs and quickly glanced around Tali's bedroom, checked her closet, dropped to the floor to check under her bed, returned downstairs to look in the kitchen, then by the TV. To Josie's chagrin, Tali seemed to be correct. The shoes were nowhere.

"Now I can't go to school," Tali proclaimed, with obvious delight.

Josie sucked in her breath. She stepped to the kitchen counter and grabbed her tablet, entering passwords with a few quick taps. Under "local panoramic search," she typed in "Tali," then "shoes." In an instant an image appeared—poor quality, she noted with disgust—of Tali's new sneakers, mid-drop, as they descended from Tali's feet to the floor of Josie's car. "There they are," Josie said, and tipped the screen toward Tali. "You must have taken them off on the way home."

Tali gaped, then ran to the garage. Josie smiled as she tucked the tablet into her bag and followed Tali, opening the rear car door. Josie watched as her daughter's eyes bulged at the sight of the shoes on the car's floor. Tali shoved her sneakers on and then climbed into the seat, still gaping. "How did you do that?" Tali asked.

Josie took the tablet out of her bag and turned it toward her daughter. "I have everything from your life in here," she said. It was hard to repress the pride in her voice. "That picture was pulled off the camera on my phone, from when the phone was in that holder between the seats, facing you."

Tali was baffled. "How did the camera know to take a picture?"

"It happens automatically," Josie said. "The camera is running all the time. Then the pictures get saved in a—a program I made that collects everything and sorts it." She was surprised by how difficult this was to explain to someone who was six years old. She pointed to the screen. "Anything you ever want to remember, it's here."

Tali stared at the screen, stunned. Her dark hair shone in the car's dim interior light. "Really? Like what?"

"Like everything," Josie said. "Here's what happens when I search for your shoes, for instance." She tapped in keywords as images of doors flashed on the screen, little animated doors opening to reveal hundreds of photos and video clips. "See, these are the first shoes you ever wore, when you were about a year old." Josie looked at the picture and felt a sudden shiver as she saw her daughter at eleven months—Josie could still remember guessing when old photos had been taken, but here the date and time appeared automatically—balancing on unsteady legs. Was that fat little baby the same person as the stringy six-year-old who was now staring at the screen? How was it possible? She recalled reading that nearly all of a person's cells are replaced every seven years, and wondered if it were true. If it were, then this Tali was only about 15 percent of the baby Tali in the picture, if that. Josie shook away the thought and tapped out more words on the screen, silencing the breath of eternity over her shoulder. "And here's when we bought you those shoes last week," she said.

Josie glanced at the picture of Tali's feet in the shoe store, and then at Tali, anticipating her delicious awed expression again. She was surprised to see Tali grimacing, avoiding her eyes.

"When you got mad at me," Tali muttered.

Josie frowned. She hadn't remembered that, though now it occurred to her that the shopping trip had been unpleasant—that she had been distracted by a message from her office while Tali tried on the shoes, and Tali, in a bid for her attention, had knocked over a large cardboard display case, sending sneakers flying across the store. Josie returned the tablet to her bag and slid into the driver's seat, unsettled. She started the car, glancing at Tali in the rearview mirror. Her daughter was twisting a long lock of dark hair around her finger, and Josie realized she had forgotten to brush it, much less wash out the milk. She wondered if she should apologize for her inattention in the shoe store last week, or if Tali ought to have apologized to her. Or was it better to pretend it hadn't happened, to avoid ruminating over the past? Which would make Tali feel better? Or—the question she knew she should be asking instead—which would make Tali *become* better? Josie had no idea. She was about to speak, to conjure up something soothing and inevitably false, when Tali spoke again.

"Is everything from when you were little in there too?" Tali asked.

"No, actually," Josie admitted, and began backing the car out of the garage, relieved to have left the scene in the shoe store behind. "I hadn't invented it yet then."

"Lucky you," Tali said.

Josie paused, pressing the brake as the car emerged into daylight. "Lucky? Why?"

"Because you get to remember everything the way you want, instead of how it really happened."

Josie laughed. "That's how everyone remembers things anyway, with or without the pictures."

Tali turned to look out the window as the car backed onto the road. Josie remembered what awaited her at work: her sister Judith. She glanced again at Tali in the rearview mirror, and felt a rush of relief that Tali was still an only child. The moments Josie remembered best were usually those she preferred to forget.

▪ ▪ ▪

On that cool spring morning in 1896, the two sisters appeared before Solomon Schechter like ghosts, looking exactly as he once imagined ghosts might look: almost human, but slightly faded, with some aspect of them uncanny, carrying with them an unmistakable shadow of eternity. What was uncanny about the two women who had just stopped him on King's Parade was that they were identical.

"Mr. Schechter!"

"Mr. Schechter!"

Solomon Schechter was walking alone on King's Parade, through a dense mist rising from the river along the backs of the colleges on the road. When he had first arrived at Cambridge from Jews' College in London in 1894, people had backed away from him as he walked down the street, stepping aside to stare at this short strange man who, with his blue eyes, his red beard, his waistcoat covered with cigarette ash, and his accent none of them could place, seemed to wear his flapping college robes as though they were a shoddy disguise. Two years later, the merchants in the row of shops opposite the Gothic college buildings knew better than to disturb him as he walked down King's Parade with his face in a book. This time he was immersed in a German journal article describing a new translation of Maimonides, following an argument about the incorporeality of God.

The mist off the river was thick that morning, enveloping him as he read. As he glanced up from his journal, he thought of one of the nursery rhymes he had heard his younger daughter reciting: *One misty moisty morning, when cloudy was the weather, I chanced to meet an old man, clothed all in leather.* And then the one about London Bridge collapsing, and the other one about birds flying out of a pie. It was unredemptive nonsense, an insult to the adult brain. His siblings at home in Romania were grandparents already, but at forty-six years old, he was new to nursery rhymes. His wife, Matilda, thought they were important. "You don't want them going to school without knowing what their classmates know," she scolded him when he tried to hide his children's *Mother Goose* collection. "How will they play with the other children if they don't know the rhymes?"

Schechter had learned verses as a child, too: *The earth was formless and void, and darkness was over the face of the deep, and the wind of God fluttered over the water. And Cain said, "Am I my brother's keeper?" And Abraham stretched out his hand and took the knife to slaughter his son. And the brothers said to one another, "Here comes Joseph, that dreamer! Come now, let us kill him and throw him into one of the pits. Then we shall see what will become of his dreams."* The words were seared into his mind like a brand on the body. Forgetting them was more than impossible; it would be like forgetting his own hand. Yet when he heard his daughter singing her English nursery rhymes, something haunted him, an imperceptible loss, the way that running a fingertip across his own cheekbone made him recall pressing his fingers into his cheek, touching the forgotten hairless smoothness of his own face, as he once leaned over a book as a boy in Romania. Only rarely did it return to him, in his adult life on this fogged island far from any home: not merely the words of childhood, but their sensation—the awareness of how, for a child, words are living things, with colors and smells and textures completely independent of their meaning. For his daughter, someday, hearing those nonsense words *one misty moisty morning* would be all she required to remember what it was like to be young. But for Solomon Schechter, Reader in Rabbinics at Cambridge University's Faculty of Oriental Studies, the words of childhood and adulthood were the same, and because of that his past was lost, his own private memory fallen into a pit of words from ancient days, invisible and unreachable. He breathed in the fog and thought of another verse from childhood, from the sage Ben Sirah: *Wisdom came forth from the mouth of the Most High, and covered the earth like a mist.* He returned his eyes to the journal in his hand and read the medieval philosopher's words: *I have shown you that the intellect which flows from God to us is the link that joins us to God. You have it in your power to strengthen that bond, if you choose to do so, or to weaken it gradually until it breaks.*

"Mr. Schechter!"

"Mr. Schechter!"

"Good morning," he stammered as the two women approached him. They were older and taller than he was, their twinned heads of bunned gray-blond hair towering above him. He slipped the journal awkwardly under his arm.

Now he recognized the spectral twins. They were Mrs. Agnes Lewis and Mrs. Margaret Gibson, Scottish lady adventurers, world-famous of late for their discovery in the monastery at Mount Sinai of the oldest manuscript of the Gospels. It was the only known version of the Christian Bible written in Syriac, the language Jesus spoke—the Lewis Codex, it was now called, after Agnes Lewis published her translation of it. All of Cambridge lauded the twins, despite the fact that they didn't have so much as a ladies' seminary diploma between them. They had just gone off to Egypt again, hunting for more Bibles. Matilda knew them both well, confided in them, relished their company on Saturday afternoons. Schechter knew them too.

Yet after two years in Cambridge he still could not tell them apart.

"Mrs. Lewis, Mrs. Gibson," he said vaguely, careful to look at both of them as he said each name. "Welcome back!"

"We're so glad we've found you, Mr. Schechter," one of the twins exclaimed. "Professor Taylor told us we ought to see you immediately."

"Without delay," said the other. "We were just our way to the Faculty, but—"

"But imagine, here you are, on King's Parade, as if you knew we were looking for you! It's all too astonishing."

One twin turned to the other. "Margaret, bumping into Mr. Schechter on King's Parade is hardly astonishing. He's probably on his way from the library to visit Professor Taylor at St. John's."

Schechter began to nod, but the sisters were looking at each other as though he had disappeared.

"But Agnes, it *is* a bit coincidental, isn't it?" the other twin replied. "That it would be precisely now?"

"Margaret, you've spent too much time with those fatalistic monks. They've affected your brain."

"I spent precisely as much time with those fatalistic monks as you did, Agnes."

"But I did not allow them to affect my brain." The twin turned back to him. "Don't indulge her, Mr. Schechter. It is hardly astonishing to meet you here, particularly compared with what we have to show you."

"Professor Taylor advised that we ought to speak to you at once, about some manuscripts we purchased in Cairo."

"No one seems able to identify them."

"He thought perhaps you could help."

Their voices, too, were identical. They spoke in a kind of Greek chorus, echoing each other's thoughts. The doubled voices made Schechter anxious. Since his parents died, it had become painful for him even to open letters from his sister and brothers at home. But now a door in his mind opened, and he saw himself from the outside, long ago: Shneur Zalman, the boy he once was, and his identical twin brother Srulik, whom everyone once mistook for him. Two redheaded boys, standing next to each other with their heads nearly touching, perched over the same lectern, studying from the same book—Shneur Zalman arguing on behalf of God, and Srulik prosecuting against him. It always happened when he encountered other identical twins: the uncanny jolt of recognition, the reminder that he was living only half a life. Fourteen years earlier, Srulik had moved to Palestine, where he now called himself Yisrael ben Yitzhak. Shneur Zalman had moved to England, where he called himself Solomon Schechter. As Schechter stood before the twins, he felt an unexpected pang of longing. It had been years since he had even seen a photograph of Srulik. Did they still look alike? Or had his brother shaved his beard, tanned his skin, aged his mind—his body and soul so altered that the two brothers were no longer identical at all?

"We bought the manuscripts from one of the Hebrew merchants there, in the souk," one of the twins continued.

"Near the Hotel d'Angleterre. We used to stay at Shepheard's, but only tourists go there now."

"The salesman actually followed us into the hotel. He claimed to have hundreds of manuscripts like the ones we bought."

"Literally hundreds, if we wanted to purchase more."

"There was a limit to what we were willing to purchase with our own funds."

"We didn't want to invest in something whose value we could not ascertain. But now it's clear that they are authentic. We—"

One of them reached into a fold of her long black cloak and withdrew a scrap of leathery parchment, slightly smaller than her hand. Its color was a very dark brown, a sheath of hide, but the black ink on it was eminently legible. Schechter bent slightly to see it, bowing his head. The letters were Hebrew.

"You can see they aren't forged. The orthography looks to be twelfth-century or so."

"Or thirteenth, perhaps. If you look here, you'll see that this is a copy of *Dalalat al-Ha'irin—Guide for the Perplexed*."

"The first Hebrew translation from the Arabic, at any rate. *Moreh Nevukhim*. This is just the introductory bit."

Schechter leaned closer as one of the twins held the parchment up in the fogged morning light. His journal slipped from under his arm and tumbled into the gutter. He didn't pick it up. His eyes were fixed on the tiny paper, on the handwritten scrawl of Hebrew letters. He edged closer. *In the name of God, Lord of the Universe,* he read, *to R. Joseph, may God protect him, son of R. Judah, may his rest be in Paradise . . .*

"Put that away, Agnes. The humidity will destroy it. We shall show Mr. Schechter everything back at the house."

"Quite right, Margaret. I just wanted to be sure that Mr. Schechter understood what sort of material we've collected."

"Oh, I understand," Schechter pleaded. "I do." He could barely restrain himself from grabbing the paper out of the woman's hands. He inwardly mourned as her long fingers folded back around the parchment, concealing it in some hidden pocket of her long black cloak.

"The introductory bit is mainly letters and the like," she said, patting her cloak with her pale hand. "Lots of 'My dear pupil, I shrivel at your feet, in the name of the munificent Lord,' and on and on, and then rhymed prose. Oh, endless horrid rhymed prose."

"Agnes can't bear rhymed prose."

The women glanced at each other, sharing an identical grimace.

"I can bear rhymed prose, Margaret. Just not horrid rhymed prose."

"Agnes, it is hardly appropriate for you of all people to judge the quality of twelfth-century rhymed prose. Mr. Schechter would surely agree, as an academician. What seems horrid to you may well have been—"

"Margaret, you've fallen for the monks again, plain and simple. You've a weakness for musty rituals. But I for one am not afraid to declare that any rhyme that compares a lady's lips to a 'wine-dark cloud upon the moon' is horrid, no matter in what century it was composed."

"But what about the bit with the gazelle? I rather liked it."

"That was horrid too."

"Did you really think so? 'My soul leaps like a young gazelle,' that bit?"

"Trite."

"But in the twelfth century, it wasn't yet trite."

"Yes, it was. Its triteness is timeless."

Schechter inched backward. He listened in a kind of rapture, unable to believe what he was hearing. It was as if he had happened upon his children engrossed in a discussion of the incorporeality of God. He stood before them with his mouth hanging open, his red beard brushing his academic robes.

The women looked at him and laughed.

"Please," one of them said, "come with us."

Without a word, he did, proceeding past the medieval colleges on King's Parade in the misty morning light, listening as the twins continued to argue the merits of rhymed prose.

THE UNCANNY TWINS LIVED at Castlebrae, an enormous Tudor-style palace near Clare College, which they had built for themselves on the occasion of one of their marriages to a Cambridge librarian. The twins had money; Schechter assumed it came from one of their dead husbands. Not from the dead librarian's salary, of course, but presumably from some sort of ancient inheritance, going back to whichever ancestral barbarians had most efficiently sacked the outposts of Rome. No one in Cambridge ever seemed to need to earn a living; making money was considered beneath the dignity of men of ideas. Among such people money was a novelty item, contemplated from behind glass. The entrance hall of Castlebrae was filled with display cases showing the deceased librarian's vast coin collection. As Schechter followed the twins down the hall, he slowed to marvel at the ancient coins. He quickly spotted the one he remembered from his first visit to Castlebrae: a silver shekel minted in Jerusalem in the first century of the common era—or, as the coin itself declared, Year 5 of the Jewish revolt against Rome.

"I've never fully understood how the two of you came to find the Codex," Schechter ventured as they proceeded down the cavernous hallways of the house. He was itching for the manuscripts, but by now he had learned the unwritten code of the British upper classes: the elaborate dance of pleasantries, flattery, tea, liquor, remarks about the weather, more pleasantries, more flattery, more tea, more liquor—and only then, with perseverance and luck, could one enter an unlocked door to the inner vault of the mind. Already a servant had collected his coat. The twins were now gesturing him onto a velvet couch in one of the half-dozen sitting rooms, signaling to another servant to prepare tea. The two of them sat opposite him on a modern green velvet sofa, a happy couple in their lovely home. They were like a husband and wife.

"How did you even begin to learn Syriac, and all of the

other languages that would have been required?" Schechter asked, though his wife surely could have told him. Flattery was required now, he knew. He would never have made it from a starved Jewish town in Romania to Christ's College at the University of Cambridge if he hadn't known, intuitively, in every country and in every city and at every footfall along the way, which language was required.

"Our late father was a barrister in Aberdeen," Mrs. Lewis said. Or was it Mrs. Gibson? The one who hated rhymed prose, whichever she was. It did not help that their widow's frocks, as far his untrained eye could tell, were as identical as they were. "We didn't have any brothers," she continued, "so he raised us like sons."

"He started us on Latin when we were six years old, and then we went on to Greek and Hebrew, so that we could read the word of the Lord," the other twin said. "Of course I don't need to tell you, Mr. Schechter, that Hebrew is rather simple once one masters the verbs. But oh, one could slit one's throat over the verbs!"

"Especially the *hufal* conjugation," her sister added. "It generated many a private *hapax legomenon* when we were ten years old."

The sisters laughed aloud as though this were a brilliant joke. Schechter remembered one of his university classes on biblical scholarship in Berlin, where he had first encountered the term *hapax legomenon*. It meant any word that only appeared once in the Bible, and which no one could therefore fully understand. He had laughed when he learned it; he had noticed such words since he was a child. Rashi and Abraham ibn Ezra and Onkelos—his dearest friends, scattered across centuries and continents but always gathered at the margins of his favorite books—had never failed to explain them.

"Our father was quite wealthy," one twin continued.

"Not at first," the other interjected.

"A distant cousin of his passed away, and it happened that this cousin had inherited a vast fortune from his brothers in America. When he died, he had no one else on whom to bestow it. Once our father inherited the money, he offered to take us on holiday to any country we liked, on the condition that we were willing to learn its language first."

"French and German are required merely to qualify as being alive."

"But Agnes was dying to go to Italy, and I wanted to go to Spain, so we learned Spanish and Italian as well."

The servant had returned to the room with a teapot and teacups now, but Schechter declined. He was hypnotized. He knew the lure of languages; learning them had come to him, too, like an addiction. In Berlin ten years earlier, he had learned English solely in order to read George Eliot, and then French solely to read Voltaire. George Eliot had been well worth the language, but Voltaire had been a taunt, a wrenching at his soul. "You have surpassed all nations in impertinent fables, in bad conduct and in barbarism," wrote Voltaire—father of the Enlightenment, creator of the modern mind, diamond in the crown of Western civilization—of Schechter and his family. "You deserve to be punished, for this is your destiny." And another *bon mot* from the *philosophe* on the Jews: "They are, all of them, born with raging fanaticism in their hearts, just as the Bretons and Germans are born with blond hair." This raging fanaticism left the red-haired Shneur Zalman (for in reading Voltaire, he once again became Shneur Zalman) wishing he had followed his twin brother to Palestine to drain a malarial swamp. To purge the university libraries of Europe of disease would be impossible.

Instead, he inoculated himself with Torah. He was not the first Jewish instructor at Cambridge, but he was among the first to take up his post without breaking the covenant with God. He walked down King's Parade with his head covered in humility before the king of kings, never entered the glorious college chapels, and arranged dispensations for the handful of unconverted Jewish students who would otherwise be required to kneel and bow before their professors in order to receive their degrees. At Christ's College, where Schechter's patrons had hosted him in 1894, the manciple in charge of formal dinners had trained the cooks in preparing kosher food. One of the twins, forgetful, was now offering him a plate of biscuits from the servant's tray, likely baked with lard. "No, thank you," he said. And, not wanting to embarrass her: "I've just had tea at home."

"Yes, perhaps better we should skip tea," the other twin said. "We don't want any damage to the manuscripts."

"The manuscripts," Schechter repeated, hoping they would notice. But the sisters were proceeding with their story, unimpeded by his boiling curiosity. He leaned forward, clutching his knees to keep himself from jumping out of his chair.

"More recently Agnes learned Syriac on her own."

"With some help from Mr. Kennett at the Faculty. Privately of course, since apparently it would be absurd for a woman to attend lectures."

"And we both learned Arabic years ago, so that we could travel without a dragoman."

"The first dragoman we used on the Nile was horrid. He was a Maltese, and he called himself a Christian, though he hardly would have qualified as one in the eyes of Christ. He had no thought but to drain our pocketbooks."

"Learning Arabic is actually easier than finding a trustworthy guide in the Levant."

"Lately Margaret has been reading the Koran, while I've been working through some of the Hebrew philosophers and poets. Ibn Gabirol and so forth."

"We've had considerable trouble with the Judeo-Arabic dialect, though."

"Perhaps simply because the rhymed prose is so horrid," said one of them—the one, he had thought, who liked the rhymed prose. Were they joking? Or was he confused? The twin sisters laughed. On the velvet couch in the grand sitting room, Schechter sensed an absence beside him, longing seeping into his body like a forgotten smell. He remembered sitting at a wood-planked table in the hovel that was once his home, long ago: studying with Srulik, arguing with Srulik, laughing with Srulik, hearing his own laughter echoed in Srulik's laugh.

"When our father passed away, we were only twenty-three, and neither of us had married," one of the twins said. "Normally his estate would have been held in trust until at least one of us secured a son-in-law to inherit it from him. But our father was very frightened that a husband might someday take advantage of either of us. In his will, he stipulated that the two of us would inherit all of his wealth, but only on the condition that we never live apart from each other."

"And we never did."

"Even when we were married, though unfortunately our husbands predeceased us."

They were like duplicates, Schechter thought, a cosmic error. They had lived together since the womb. If he and Srulik were ever reunited, would they become one person again? Or had they been severed from each other forever, each condemned to live only half a life? He thought of one of Srulik's letters, written in a Hebrew that he still recognized as his identical twin's voice: *Shneur Zalman, here's a story for you! Last week I was digging an irrigation ditch for the groves in the new town we just founded, Zikhron Yaakov. I stopped to rest, and then the ground opened beneath my feet and I fell into a hole in the earth. When I managed to light a match from my pocket, I saw that I was in an ancient cistern, with smooth stone walls and dark rings marking the water levels. I made a torch out of an olive bough that I found on the floor, and then I could even see the chisel marks where the cistern had been carved from the rock. Hours passed before someone found me and pulled me out. While I was waiting to be rescued, I wondered how old the cistern must have been. On the floor I found the answer: a bronze coin from the time of the Maccabees, lying at my feet. I'm sure you make all kinds of important discoveries in your fancy library every day,* his identical twin wrote in Hebrew script, *but I doubt you will ever fall through a hole in the floor and land in the memory of God.*

"After our father died we were quite distraught, and we decided it would lift our spirits to go to Egypt," one of the twins continued.

"And our dragoman was so horrid that we had to learn Arabic."

"Margaret, we already explained about the horrid dragoman."

"Did we? He was a Maltese, and called himself a Christian, but—"

"The point, Mr. Schechter, is that when Margaret's husband passed away, we decided to fulfill our dream of going to Mount Sinai, to the monastery there. Because we had heard wonderful things about their manuscript library."

"The manuscripts—" Schechter tried to interject. But the twins had abandoned him at the door of the present, entering the past as though it were a tastefully appointed room in Castlebrae.

"We knew modern Greek, you see, so the monks befriended us quite quickly. They didn't see us as instruments of the Empire, as everyone else sees Britons in the Levant."

"Though in fact we *were* instruments of the Empire, in a manner of speaking."

"In no manner of speaking, Agnes! We didn't even take the manuscripts back with us! That German professor von Tischendorf did, and they called him a thief. They told us he was no better than Lord Elgin, the one who took the sculptures from the Parthenon for the British Museum. The monks are all Greek, you see, so they are quite sensitive about the Elgin Marbles."

"The blasted Elgin Marbles," the other sister groaned. "As if anyone had even glanced at them in the twenty centuries before they arrived in London."

"Mr. Schechter, you know Professor Rendel Harris at the Faculty, of course. He told us that the monks at St. Catherine's had a closet full of manuscripts in Syriac that he hadn't had time to see. When he heard we were planning to return, he taught us how to use the photographical equipment, and he also told us precisely where we ought to look."

"In a great big wooden chest in the abbot's bedroom. Rather intimate, in fact, although Father Galakteon was surprisingly welcoming. He even kissed Margaret's hand. Quite shocking for an Orthodox monk."

"Don't believe her, Mr. Schechter. He was a lovely gentleman, and entirely respectful."

"Margaret, you and your monks! Good gracious, Mr. Schechter, she positively swooned at them. You see, Margaret's late husband was a minister."

"I fail to see how that is relevant, Agnes."

"It is quite relevant, Mr. Schechter. Because it was the monks' fondness for Margaret, as the distraught widow of a man of faith, that made them so willing to share the manuscripts with us."

"That is untrue, Agnes. They simply appreciated that we spoke Greek. And that Agnes could read Syriac."

"Can you imagine, Mr. Schechter? None of them read Syriac, even though they live inside the greatest archive of Syriac manuscripts in the world. Would it have been so hard for them to learn Syriac? Honestly! What else are they doing with their time?"

"Agnes, you forget that not everyone is so gifted with languages."

"Nonsense. It's a mere lack of will. I myself would have offered them a correspondence course, simply to prevent them from destroying the treasures they had in that place. They were using manuscripts as kindling."

"Yet your main method of befriending them was to make disparaging remarks about the Pope."

The pleasantries phase of British upper-class conversation, Schechter had learned, generally attained terminal velocity when someone mentioned the Pope. His patience had run out.

"So what manuscript did you want me to see?" he finally asked.

The twins jumped from their sofa. One of them hurried to a cabinet near the window, from which she withdrew a small leather briefcase.

"My sister and I recommend that you read the manuscript yourself," she said.

The other twin seated Schechter at a card table, as the first twin began drawing out long strips of parchment from the leather case and laying them before him. It was a poem, he saw, written in a clear Hebrew script:

The blessing of a father settles the root,
But the curse of a mother plucks up the plant.
For he who despises his father deals presumptuously
And he who curses his mother angers his Creator . . .
Seek not that which is hidden from you!
What is permitted, think thereupon,
But you have no business with the secret things.

The letters were inscribed in dark brown ink. As he read them, they burned in his brain like black fire on white fire. Was it possible?

"This is puzzling," he admitted aloud.

"We agree."

He drew in his breath. "If I were forced to conjecture—"

"We force you to conjecture," a twin interrupted.

"Conjecture!" the other cried.

"If I were forced to conjecture," he repeated, "I would say that this is a Hebrew version of part of the biblical Apocrypha—the book that Christians call Ecclesiasticus. The Wisdom of Ben Sirah." He gave the final *h* the guttural it deserved. He enjoyed making the sound; his Gentile students could never quite do it.

"Precisely, Agnes. Just as I said!"

"Margaret, I believe I noted it first."

"No, you thought it was a much later translation from the Greek."

"That was only a supposition, Margaret, based on what is known to exist of Ben Sirah." She pronounced the guttural *h* precisely.

The two women turned back to him. "At any rate, Mr.

Schechter, we are in complete agreement," the other twin announced. "My sister and I concur that this is the original Hebrew version of Ben Sirah." The guttural, once again, was exact.

Schechter looked again at the script, bending down over it, breathing in its letters. "But that would be impossible," he said. "It's a book that doesn't exist."

The twins laughed.

"Books that don't exist, Mr. Schechter," one of them said, "are our favorite sort of books."

"Books that don't exist are invariably better than those that do."

"That's why we kept looking for the Syriac Gospels. Surely the language Christ spoke would have been better than the Greek. One must admit that the Greek of the Gospels is really rather horrid."

"Heresy, Agnes!"

"Margaret, it is hardly heretical to note that a warmed-over and poorly executed version of a literary text is horrid, when it clearly is. One simply cannot deny that the Syriac Gospel is in every aspect superior to the Greek from a literary point of view."

"I would agree, Agnes, except that the Syriac text says that Joseph begat Jesus. I consider the omission of the virgin birth to be a rather significant deviation from the Greek."

"Well, I suppose that is one demerit in the Syriac text."

"That, and the fact that the Syriac version omits Christ's resurrection."

"Oh, Margaret, must you always be so negative? It isn't *omitted*, Mr. Schechter. The text simply terminates with Mary Magdalene entering Christ's tomb and finding his body missing."

"Precisely, Agnes—implying that Christ's tomb was merely robbed. There is no suggestion whatsoever of Christ rising from the grave."

"It's quite possible that the text was fragmented. Most likely it was a scribal error."

"*Scribal error?* The very next line reads, 'Here endeth the Gospel of Mark'!"

"Margaret, please, take the long view for once, would you? We've discovered the greatest biblical manuscript in church history, and here you are harping on the details."

"Forgive me, Agnes, but I do not consider the resurrection of Christ to be a detail. The text we found suggests that there was no virgin birth, and no resurrection. You've become so enamored of our grand discovery that you scarcely seem to have read it. Do you not find it even slightly disturbing that this manuscript we found in the Sinai, which is surely older and closer to the lives of the apostles than every other version of the Gospels in existence today, gives almost no indication of the divinity of Christ?"

"I think the poetry of Christ's teachings in Syriac is utterly unsurpassed."

"If all we care for are Christ's teachings, then we might as well be bloody Jews!"

Schechter coughed. The twins looked at him, one with a deep blush creeping into her wide pale face. He tried to think like Matilda, to say something that would put others at ease.

"I don't think you need to be concerned about the Lewis Codex replacing the Christian Bible," he finally said, his tone carefully managed. He made a point not to say "New Testament." He heard his little daughter singing a nursery rhyme in some rear bedroom of his mind: *Make new friends, but keep the old—one is silver and the other's gold!* His daughter's perfect native

English was his own family's newest friend. He considered the words of the rhyme, and the testaments old and new. *Halevai*, he thought in Hebrew. *If only.*

"Agnes would surely be delighted if the Lewis Codex replaced the Gospels," the blushing twin remarked. Schechter noted to his relief that her complexion was returning to its usual pallor.

"Margaret, you must admit that the poetry is unsurpassed."

"Unsurpassed," the other woman sighed. "And blissfully devoid of any mention of gazelles."

Schechter leaned over the table, examining again the shred of parchment before him. No matter how many times he read it, his conclusion was inescapable. But it was impossible, simply impossible. He read it again, pondering the blessing of the father, the curse of the mother, the probability of angering the Creator. *Seek not what is hidden from you . . . You have no business with the secret things.*

"Ben Sirah is quoted in the Talmud quite a few times," he declared, as if he were giving one of his lectures at the Faculty—though it was clear that these women could teach at the Faculty themselves.

"Of course, we're familiar with his work in Ecclesiasticus," one twin remarked.

"Yes. He's a woman-hater."

Schechter smiled. "But no one has ever seen a copy of Ben Sirah's original text. Even the Greek versions of it are corrupt. In the original Hebrew it no longer exists."

"Our favorite kind of book," one of the twins said. The women shared a smile.

But Schechter didn't notice; he was still staring at the Hebrew letters on the table before him. "Professor Margoliouth at Oxford gave his inaugural lecture about Ben Sirah," he muttered. "He argued quite forcefully that the Syriac version *was* the original, that the man had never written completely in Hebrew at all."

In the past few years Professor David Margoliouth had burrowed into Schechter's mind, a grain of sand caught uncomfortably in his consciousness around which he formed pearls of thought from a slick of envy. Margoliouth was Schechter's new twin in his new life, the chaired professor of Hebrew at Oxford. Margoliouth was appointed at a far higher level than Schechter, and naturally enjoyed much higher esteem. Margoliouth's parents were Jews who had converted to Christianity, the father even becoming a missionary, and they had raised their son in the Anglican Church. Professor Margoliouth was ensconced among the enlightened.

"Perhaps Professor Margoliouth was insufficiently informed," one of the twins offered.

"Perhaps all of us are insufficiently informed," her sister said.

Schechter remembered the translated words he had dropped in the gutter on King's Parade: *You have it in your power to strengthen that bond, if you choose to do so, or to weaken it gradually until it breaks.*

"Where did you find this," he said, his voice low. He tried to make it a question, but couldn't. His hands were shaking.

"Cairo," one twin offered, though this was well beyond obvious. Except with each other, they were impeccably polite.

"Yes, yes, certain," stuttered Schechter. Was it the adjective "certain," like the Yiddish *zikher*? Or should it have been "certainly"? He was forgetting his English now, flustered. He was never flustered. He had reverted to thinking in Yiddish, in Hebrew, in Syriac. "But—but from whom? How?"

"As we mentioned, Mr. Schechter, we purchased them from

a Hebrew gentleman in the souk," one said, without the slightest trace of impatience. The twins' courtesy was bottomless, reverberating in the depths of their souls.

"He had a stall around the corner from Shepheard's," the other twin added. "An antiquarian merchant."

"Antiquarian merchant, indeed. Goodness, Agnes, the man wouldn't even let us leave without buying a rug."

Schechter interrupted. "You bought these on the street?"

"In a manner of speaking," one of the twins replied.

"Agnes, it isn't a manner of speaking. Yes, Mr. Schechter, we did buy them on the street. Or at least from a street merchant who later followed us back to our hotel."

"'Margaret, really. 'On the street' suggests that the merchant was disreputable. There was absolutely nothing disreputable about Mr. Maimoun."

"A reputable merchant of antiquarian manuscripts would not have insisted that we also purchase a handmade rug for eleven pounds sterling."

"But it's such a lovely rug."

A nursery rhyme of Schechter's youth returned to him: *God suspended the earth upon a void.* The manuscript was in his hand now, floating on air.

"Did Mr. Maimoun say where he found this?" he asked.

"He was rather coy about it. His entire enterprise was quite dodgy, no matter what Agnes might suggest."

"He implied that he was the manuscripts' sole proprietor. He told us quite clearly that we could search all of Cairo and would find no one else with access to such manuscripts as his."

"Agnes, you know perfectly well that was rubbish. He just wanted us to buy more manuscripts. And preferably another rug."

Schechter was ignoring them now, contemplating the script

in his hand. "Archibald Sayce," he said, thinking aloud. "Sayce brought back something like this."

"Professor Sayce at Oxford?" one of the twins asked. Sayce was another Hebraist, a Christian one, and an expert on Apocryphal texts. There was no one, and perhaps nothing, the twins did not know. "What do you mean?"

"He recently came back from Egypt with nine leaves of a Ben Sirah manuscript," Schechter said. "He's about to publish an article about them in *Britannica*. Professor Robertson Smith showed me a draft of his translations, to ask me if there were any errors he had missed. In the introduction Sayce said he had bought them from an antiquarian in Cairo."

The twins laughed, snorting identical snorts. "Mr. Maimoun has been very busy, I see," one of them said.

"I suspect that Professor Sayce is now the proud owner of a lovely new rug."

One twin stopped laughing, pointedly. "Oh, but Mr. Schechter, Mr. Maimoun was an honest man. Really, he was. He even told us he was a beadle at one of the synagogues there."

Schechter frowned. "A beadle," he repeated.

"Yes. He used the Hebrew term, *shamash*. I imagined it was rather like being an altarboy."

"More like a custodian," Schechter said.

"He said the synagogue where he worked was built on the site where the infant Moses was placed in the basket and floated down the Nile," her sister added. "The building is over a thousand years old."

"He offered to take us there, but at that point we no longer had much time, and it didn't seem worthwhile. And in any case I simply didn't trust the man, even if Agnes did."

"If he'd only been a monk, you'd have believed his every word!"

Outside the twins' palace it had begun raining in earnest. One of the twins produced a matchbook and lit a lamp on the wall above Schechter's head. The smell of the match struck in the dimming room, the edged scent of phosphorus and ash, ignited a memory that had long darkened in his mind: his father lighting a tall woven multi-wicked candle and holding it aloft in the darkness in their tiny three-room house in Romania, watching, entranced, as each of the wicks ignited, one by one, from the first flame. A thought entered his mind, a match struck in a darkening room.

"Every synagogue has a storeroom in it called a *genizah*—a hiding place," Schechter said. "A place for keeping damaged books and papers that contain the name of God."

The twins looked at him, their blue eyes alert, eager. He had reached the border of a new country: this was something they did not know.

"An archive, you mean?" one of them tried.

"Like the one the monks were maintaining at St. Catherine's," the other mused.

"You mean like the one the monks *weren't* maintaining at St. Catherine's," her sister huffed. "Mr. Schechter, do you know why we decided to look for Hebrew manuscripts in Cairo to begin with? Because we had seen them at St. Catherine's. The monks were using them in the refectory as butter plates."

But the other twin remained transfixed. "*Every* synagogue has one of these?" she asked. "How on earth do they manage it? Wouldn't that require every congregation to have its own librarian?"

Schechter shook his head. "No, no, nothing like that. These books are rubbish, you see. Complete rubbish. Torn, worn, burned, damaged by water or smoke, illegible in too many places—and also irreparable. And in the case of printed matter, replaceable. You must understand the importance of documents in the Jewish world. In the case of the Pentateuch, the physical parchment itself must be perfect, undamaged in any respect, or else the text itself is no longer considered functional. I'm referring to books and scrolls and papers that can no longer be used."

"So why keep them at all?" one sister asked.

"There are rabbinic laws that forbid the destruction of any object inscribed with the name of God, in observance of the commandment against taking the name of God in vain."

"That seems rather extreme, doesn't it?"

Years earlier, Schechter might have cringed. He had winced at his first dinner at Christ's College two years before, when the college master said to him at high table, in the spirit of genial scholarly reflection, "I've always found it rather pathetic that so much of Christianity is based on Judaism." That this was intended by an educated person as an opening for intelligent conversation in 1894—not, Schechter noted, in 1492, or even 1789, but 1894—was nearly as dismaying as reading Voltaire. Yet he also knew by now that some of these comments were meant not to condescend, but rather to explore terra incognita—part of the British thirst for venturing off to someplace exotic, where they could observe the natives in their natural habitats and then help themselves to the local treasures. The twins were adventurers, and Schechter was pleased to oblige them.

"Not nearly as extreme as what happens to these books and papers," he told them. "At first, they are stored in the genizah room in the synagogue. But eventually, they are buried in a cemetery, with a funeral. Like a person."

The twins looked at one another. Schechter could see that they were unsure whether to continue. They looked at him as if he had just told them that he sacrificed goats—as many people had innocently asked him, upon meeting him in Cambridge. When he gently explained to them that Jews had not sacrificed animals for nearly two thousand years, they were visibly disappointed.

"How often does this sort of funeral take place?" one of the sisters asked.

"Very rarely," Schechter answered. "Usually it would only be arranged if several scrolls of the Pentateuch needed to be disposed of, which would likely only happen if the synagogue had suffered a fire. Or if the genizah were completely full, I suppose. But many congregations never even bother to empty the genizah. Here in Britain the weather would degrade the documents eventually. But in a dry climate, papers and parchments could accumulate for centuries."

"So who would be responsible for maintaining such a storeroom?" one of the twins asked. "Not a librarian?"

"No, not a librarian," Schechter replied. "Usually it's just the custodian."

He watched as the sisters smiled.

▪ ▪ ▪

THIS IS WHAT JOSIE would like to forget.

When they reached the pit it was twilight: a summer mountain twilight, thick with the smell of wet wood and encroaching darkness, the twilight fragrance that children imagine to be possibility and adults know to be regret.

Future software titan Josephine Ashkenazi, thirteen years old, leaned against an enormous poplar tree, inhaling the twilight air along with compressed albuterol from a handheld pump. The mountain atmosphere was supposed to do her good, but hadn't. Earlier, closer to the campsite, she had had a full-on attack, sucking air out of a paper bag. Her sister Judith, one year older, stayed with her while the others kept walking, shaking Josie's inhaler with a practiced rattle of her wrist as she crouched on dead leaves and counted Josie's breaths.

"I'm so lucky you're here, Judith," Josie breathed, when her voice returned. She squinted through fogged glasses. "I couldn't do anything without you."

Judith twisted her own dark curly hair into a knot behind her head, letting out a soft snort. "Josie, don't be ridiculous. You could do all this yourself if you had to," she said. She passed Josie the inhaler, and stood. "Come on, I want to catch up."

"Can't we just sit here a little longer? They won't notice."

"They'll notice," Judith said.

The group of girls had been sent out to collect kindling for the fire, and had wandered very far from the campsite, intentionally. Everything girls her age did was intentional, Josie had noticed, a subtly calibrated collective thinking whose mysteries she could never penetrate, though Judith could. Judith ran ahead, and Josie sprinted behind her, laboring in the foreign mountain air. On the first night all the girls had compared their weights, and when asked, Josie had given hers in atomic mass units. There was no hope for her after that. She had hardened in the past year, building walls of facts around herself since her father's departure. But here she only had Judith, who was staring straight ahead as she hurried through the woods.

When they caught up with the other girls, Josie saw them standing with their backs to her, still and silenced. She slinked up behind them, craning her neck beside Judith, until she saw what they saw: the forest suddenly interrupted, giving way to a wide deep pit in the ground.

The pit was almost invisible until you were upon it, but then it opened up like a natural cellar in the earth, as deep and wide as an underground room. Its walls were sheer mud and rock. The sudden majesty of it hushed them, as though the earth had opened its mouth and breathed. The blue-gray air rattled with crickets as the girls stood at the pit's edge, their young bodies trembling against the futures within them. They circled the rim, wordlessly peering into the abyss, until Josie spoke.

"It's a sinkhole caused by glacial melt," Josie announced.

A girl huffed, exhaling contempt. "Yeah, 'cause it's freezing here." All the girls gleamed with sweat, balanced on the precipice.

"I mean during the Ice Age," Josie said. She felt it starting, the wave of information building to a crest within her, rising behind her diseased lungs and her slight suggestions of breasts, and she knew it would do nothing but hurt her more, but she couldn't help it, she never could help it. Like she couldn't help breathing. "The whole Berkshire mountain range was covered with glaciers for millions of years. When glacial ice melts, it forms crevices, and when gas that was trapped under the ice is released, sinkholes can form in certain kinds of—"

Someone shoved her.

"Look what I got," a girl called. She was fourteen, Judith's friend. Josie looked up and saw her inhaler, held high in the heat. "The glue sniffer!" The girls let out loud happy laughs, the silence splintered into whoops.

"I need it," Josie said. Her voice was hoarse. *Breathe in slow,* she thought. *Slow.* "Give it back."

A mistake, she saw immediately. She shouldn't have said anything, should have laughed herself. But it was too late now. The older girl was backing toward the pit, hoisting the inhaler higher into the haze behind her as the other girls laughed. Josie breathed in again, her eyes locked on the girl's hand.

She watched as the fingers on the hand slowly spread open. The inhaler fell.

The shivering silence returned. Josie wiggled through the wall of girls until she stood at the pit's rim, peering down into the abyss. Far below, a finger of bright red plastic lay lodged in dark dirt.

"Now you're on," the girl proclaimed, her eyes on Josie. "Who's got the rope?"

In seconds a bright stripe of fat white twine snaked out of a girl's pack, across girls' hands, between girls' legs, and slithered down into the pit.

Someone nudged her. She pulled away, until she felt her sister's warm fingers around her arm. "Just get it, Josie," Judith urged. "It's not that far down."

Josie looked at Judith. Judith's eyelids fluttered, and then she pushed Josie to her knees.

For an instant Josie clutched Judith's feet. The circle of girls tightened around them. She let go of Judith's sneakers, and felt the snapback as her sister pulled her feet away, kicking her aside. The casualness of that kick astounded her.

She glanced at Judith, but Judith had turned away, helping the others guide down the rope. Josie turned and lowered herself until she was sitting with her legs dangling into the abyss. Twenty feet below, the dark mud at the bottom of the pit was filigreed with a layer of trash. Her inhaler winked at her, red plastic glowing in twilight. The woods were darkening as wind breathed through thick leaves. Her hands clutched the edge of the pit as though it were the rim of a giant bowl, earth like thick clay molded between her fingers. She turned around, took hold of the rope, and began to slide.

She dropped below the surface and flailed her legs until she caught the rope between her knees. The world swung above her head, tree branches kaleidoscoping as she spun, knocking her head on the pit's wall while suspended between earth and sky. Above her, eleven girls circled the pit, their faces just visible above the edge, a ring of dark hair and grins. And Judith among them, imploring her. She looked down. The inhaler gleamed below, a perfect bottled version of what her father called the immanence of God.

The skin on her palms screamed and burned as she slipped down and crashed into the mud. Her body rolled on dirt, long black hair streaking dirt on her face and still-unfamiliar bra hooks digging into her spine as her back pressed against the earth. She heard animals scurrying through dead leaves, and laughter from above as she snatched her inhaler off the ground. She turned upward in utter triumph, and grinned at the ink-blue sky above the fractal branches of the trees. And then she heard the whoosh as the rope whizzed upward, the bright white snake retreating up the wall of mud and out of sight.

A joke, Josie knew. They wanted to enjoy hearing her beg. Thank God Judith was still above, watching her. How much humiliation would be required this time? It was like a game theory calculation. Josie was good at game theory calculations. She sighed, a deliberate theatrical sigh, and began the game.

"Come on, guys. Give it back."

They were still laughing above her. Someone spat, a white liquid hailstone that smacked Josie's sneaker with startling force.

"Maybe she can think her way out of that one," someone said.

The faces leaned around the edges of the circle, laughter pouring down into the pit. Josie scanned their eyes, steeling herself against them as she searched for Judith. Where was Judith?

"It's getting dark," a girl said. "How about we go back?"

Now the girl who had thrown the inhaler spoke, a wide grin on her face, perfect teeth paralleling the rim of the pit. "She's got her glue sniffer," she diagnosed. "It's not like she's gonna die."

"Give me the rope," Josie breathed. It was occurring to her, slowly, like creeping darkness, that this wasn't a joke, that this was real: the open throat of the earth, and the sky darkening above her. She breathed again, then called louder. "Please, give me the rope." She could feel the tears, prayed no one could see them. Where was Judith?

Miraculously, Judith appeared, a face along the edge above. She was running a hand through her hair, blinking. "Judith!" Josie shouted. "Judith, give me the rope!"

Judith's face turned, then dipped below the curve of the earth. Girls' feet and laughter thundered through the woods.

"JUDITH!" Josie screamed. "JUDITH!"

But she was alone. With her inhaler.

TWILIGHT LINGERED BELOW THE forest floor.

At first Josie tried to climb the walls, while the crickets laughed at her from the shadows. It would be a long time before the girls reached the campsite, Josie knew, and even longer before the counselors noticed she was missing. It was clear to her now that no one would tell them. By then it would be nightfall, and there was no trail. Already the sky above the pit was seeping deep blue ink between the branches overhead.

She climbed three or four feet up before crashing to the ground, this time bruising her ankle. It was difficult to stand up after that. Instead she crawled around the bottom of the pit, searching among the trash for useful objects. When she found an old tent pin, she tried and failed to use it as a foothold on the wall. She thought of tying her clothing together into a rope and throwing the end to the top, weighed down by a rock. But the rope wouldn't be long enough, and anything that would hold her weight at the top would be too heavy for her to throw that high. She tried digging out footholds with the tent pin, and managed to make three, but she could no longer put weight on her ankle. When she had exhausted all other options, she started screaming.

Nothing came of it except another attack, this one terrifying. Her paper bag was in her backpack at the top of the pit. She quickly pulled off a sock and gasped into it between albuterol puffs: she was drowning in air, hooking her inhaler into her mouth like a fish caught on a line. The sides of the pit rose up around her, merciless surfaces of mud and stone. For a long moment oxygen fled her brain, returning in a dizzying rush that flung her to the ground. She lay on her back looking up at the sky, feeling the frantic rise and fall of her chest as breath returned, but unable to fight the sudden fatigue that made the sky fade above her. As she drifted into dream, she saw something extraordinary: instead of dirt, there appeared, on the tall round walls of the pit, hundreds and hundreds of little doors.

The doors weren't quite large enough for a person to pass through, even crawling; they were like the doors of kitchen cabinets, and many were even smaller, stacked one above the other until they covered all the walls of the pit. They were made of bark, or clay, some even of acorns or leaves. Josie remembered—for one can remember, within delirium and dream—the children's discovery room at the natural history museum, which she still loved, where there was an entire wall full of drawers and cabinets just like these, each filled with a different treasure: a geode, a starfish, a glass-encased tarantula, a bone. She thought she might be able to climb out of the pit by standing on the doors, once they were opened. Near the bottom were what looked like drawers. She approached the nearest wall and tugged at a pinecone handle. The pinecone nearly came off in her hand, but then the drawer sprang open, bursting out of the wall until it banged against her waist.

In the drawer, she found Judith.

Not Judith now, as she had looked in the forest moments before, but Judith years earlier. In the drawer, a deep one, this Judith was perhaps seven years old, wearing her curly hair in two tight pigtails—which were the first things Josie saw of her, since Judith was lying on her stomach on the bottom of the drawer, propped up on her elbows on a sheaf of brown carpeting. In front of her was a yellow and red plastic game with a ticking timer and a tray full of indentations for plastic shapes. Judith was sorting bits of yellow plastic in her pudgy hands before dropping them into their places in the tray. Josie remembered the game, which she hadn't seen or thought of in seven years. It was called Perfection, and she always won it. The timer's bell rang, and the tray popped up and scattered plastic pieces across the bottom of the drawer. The Judith in the drawer jumped, alarmed, then scooted back until she was seated on her knees.

"I can never do it," Judith said, still laughing. It was a wonderful laugh, an unselfconscious cackle that Josie remembered from when the two of them used to play together, not so very long ago. Suddenly she understood that she hadn't heard Judith laugh like that in over a year. The sisters had entered an unmourned passage, the heartbreaking twilight of play. "How come you always win, Josie?" the Judith in the drawer asked.

Josie waited for Judith to look up at her, but she didn't. She was speaking to someone else, Josie understood, a Josie tucked into the wall of the drawer. A moment later, the Judith in the drawer lay back down on the drawer's carpet, reset the game, and lost it again. "I can never do it," she said again, and laughed again. "How come you always win, Josie?"

Josie closed the drawer. She was shaking now. She turned to the right, reached higher, and opened one of the cabinet doors.

Inside it, her father was seated on their living room couch at home, grading a high stack of problem sets on the coffee table in front of him. He had taken off his glasses to twirl them around a finger, his brown eyes squinting at someone across from him. From deep within the cabinet, Josie could smell food burning.

"Just consider this, Josephine," her father in the cabinet was saying. "Can God create a stone so large that even God can't lift it?" He sucked the end of his glasses, tapping a foot against the rug on the bottom of the cabinet. "It seems like a trap, but Rambam says, 'There are certain objects which the mind can in no way and by no means grasp: the gates of perception are locked against it.'" Her father's face, for reasons she remembered not understanding, was turning red. Before she knew it, he had said it all again. "Just consider this, Josephine . . . 'The gates of perception are locked against it!'"

Josie closed the door. She turned toward the other side of the pit, and pulled open a smaller drawer. Here she found herself, at the age of three, sprawled on her stomach in the bath. The bathtub filled the entire drawer, and the thirteen-year-old Josie dipped her finger into the water. It was warm, pleasant. She looked down at her own back, at her wet black hair smelling of baby shampoo. The girl in the bathtub drawer was examining a soap bubble. Suddenly Josie remembered that soap bubble, the one in which she had noticed her own reflection and wondered whether, if she popped it, she would disappear. Josie watched as the girl in the bathtub popped the bubble, then watched the very same bubble form again. She closed the drawer.

Josie looked up toward the upper edge of the pit, and at the hundreds of doors stretching between the floor and freedom, and at the fractal branches beyond. It would occur to her, years later, that there was a pit like this buried inside each person—fascinating, painful, and in the end so infinite that it was rendered useless. Why, she wondered? Who cared, in the end? What was the point of it, if you couldn't use it to climb out?

The most frustrating thing, Josie saw as she continued pulling doors open, almost manically, was that you never knew if you were going to find something priceless or something worthless, and the proportion of the worthless was overwhelming. Most of the smaller cabinets were filled with math problems in her handwriting, or jelly beans, or children who had bitten her in nursery school, or used condoms she had once found in the backyard. A larger one contained a chipped-toothed boy who had spent all of kindergarten calling her a dog; another held a teacher telling her to shut her mouth. She slammed doors in their faces. Of all of the cabinets and drawers, not one seemed to contain a flare, or a rope.

Couldn't they have been sorted? she suddenly thought. What if each door had been labeled, like an old library catalogue—by person, by date, by topic, by possibility? As it was, the drawers and doors circled her like the girls at the top of the pit, laughing at her. She had to escape. She tried mounting a foot on one of the drawer handles near the bottom of the pit, but it snapped off beneath her shoe. She kicked the drawer, enraged, and it bounced open.

Inside, her mother was seated in the pediatric emergency room, the tubing from Josie's inhaled drugs running across her lap to the other side of the drawer. Painted cartoon characters smiled on the drawer's walls. It could have been any one of a dozen emergency room visits. But it had to be the one in the winter of last year, because her mother was holding the nurse's pager—which, the nurse had complained, had been buzzing without end, making it impossible to respond. During her second inhalation treatment, Josie had fixed it.

"You're tough, Josie," her mother was saying in the drawer.

I'm not, Josie thought, the same words she had said then.

"You are," her mother answered. "The reason these things happen to you is because when they do, you use them to make other things better."

Josie pulled at the drawer, but it was a retractable one, and it snapped closed. When she pulled it again, she couldn't open it. She gave up, turned away, and opened one more door.

Behind that door, Judith was kneeling, holding out Josie's inhaler. The bottom of the cabinet was covered with pine needles and dead leaves; the walls inside were bark. "Josie, don't be ridiculous," the Judith behind the door told her. "You could do all this yourself if you had to."

Judith was right. She could. She looked up at the tall fading walls of the pit and saw that it was completely dark, the mud surfaces shrouded in starlight below the inked branches above. If the archive below the forest floor never existed, then someday she would invent it.

The Judith behind the door was passing her the inhaler. She took it, and put it back in her mouth. As she breathed in, she felt herself being lifted up, waking up, and then saw lights shining in her eyes, people kneeling beside her at the edge of the pit, a paramedic clutching a clear plastic mask over her nose and mouth.

And beyond them, Judith, holding the rope.

▪ ▪ ▪

JUDITH ALWAYS KNEW THAT Josie was brilliant. Every person who ever met her little sister had told her that. As an adult, Josie had become not merely attractive, but magnetic, drawing everything toward herself with an unconscious, irresistible pull: men, money, prizes, praise. But Judith seemed to attract only disappointments. After being fired from four different jobs in less than a year, she had gone to work in Josie's shining new office as if enslaved, bearing their shared surname like a brand on her back. To everyone at work, she was nothing more than Josie's sister. To everyone, at least, except for Itamar.

"Your sister is tough, isn't she?" Itamar asked.

They were in the sushi restaurant next door to the office, an excursion that was meant to be nothing more than a bite to eat before Judith went home, and before Itamar continued working. Itamar was always working. Josie had discovered Itamar on a business trip to Israel the previous year, and had imported him to run the company's operating systems. Itamar was a thin gangly beauty of a man, with nearly perfect English and a resistance to smiling. The first time Judith saw him, at a meeting whose language quickly devolved from English to pseudocode, she noticed how he pressed his lips together as though he were trying not to laugh. She had grinned at him until he suddenly started laughing, and Josie had barked them both out of the room. That evening the restaurant was dim and empty, more intimate than either of them had expected. The hostess seated them at a corner table lit by a paper lantern. Judith could hear the hush of his breath.

"Tough? Sure," said Judith—annoyed to hear Josie mentioned, but too enchanted to stay annoyed. His hands were on the table now, long thin fingers like a musician's. "When we were little, she was always tricking me," she added.

"Tricking you how?"

"Oh, stupid things," she said, unable to stop smiling. "I would write forged notes from our parents trying to get myself out of homework and tests, and she would sneak them out of my bag and show them to our mother."

"Then you were the tricky one," he said. "She was the informer."

"She's been an informer since birth," Judith laughed. "Josie was always working in intelligence."

She meant it as a joke, but Itamar frowned, distracted. "When I was in the army, I worked in intelligence," he said.

Behind him in the restaurant's shadows was a lacquered Japanese cabinet, its face formed from an elaborate series of doors. Itamar seemed that way to her too, then, a locked cabinet full of hidden compartments that could be opened only with the right keys. "What did you do?" she asked.

Itamar snorted. "Americans always think it sounds so important. You know what you do when you're nineteen years old in army intelligence? A tiny piece of something. That's it."

"What do you mean, a tiny piece of something?"

"Like you put a certain chip into a certain circuit board, five hundred times. Or you write the same piece of code, with some tiny variation, five hundred times. It's the most boring thing in the world. You have no idea what you're even making, because no one ever lets you see all of it. At the beginning you think that someday someone will promote you and tell you what you've been making all that time, but in the end it never happens. You just have to believe that you need to do your part exactly right, and accept that you may never know what it means."

Judith grinned. "That sounds like my life," she said.

Itamar laughed. Before they returned to the office, he kissed her on the lips.

Three months later, at a party celebrating the five millionth Genizah subscriber, Judith watched as Josie walked in the door—Josie, her long black hair shining down the back of her evening gown, with Itamar at her side, and a diamond ring on her finger.

"I know it's sudden," Josie told Judith a few minutes later, over the blaring of the band. "But Itamar's father is ill, and we didn't want to wait long. And getting him a green card would really help the company a lot. And life is short, isn't it?"

"At least in this world," Judith said.

Josie laughed as Itamar kissed her, and then she turned away, her long black hair swinging in Judith's face.

One cold morning seven years later, Judith read a message addressed to Josie, forwarded to both Judith and Josie by Josie's receptionist, from the board of trustees of the Library of Alexandria in Egypt—an institution that Judith seemed to remember learning about in a history class in fifth grade. She wondered if the message was a joke.

It wasn't. The library, it seemed, had been rebuilt by Arab philanthropists with grand ambitions. As its website proclaimed, "This library is no ancient dream, but a cutting-edge modern reality." The message to Josie, obsequiously written, invited her to come to Egypt for three weeks as a visiting consultant, to help develop the digital archiving systems for what the trustees hoped would someday become the world's largest library, for the second time in two thousand years. It was the sort of invitation Josie would barely have glanced at. But Judith looked at the swirling black arabesques of the library's logo on the screen and saw what might be possible.

"This consulting gig in Egypt looks like a great opportunity," Judith said when Josie walked into the office that morning. "It would be terrific publicity for the company, especially for overseas markets."

"You think?" Josie asked. She looked at the screen over Judith's shoulder, reading as she twirled her hair around her finger.

"Definitely," Judith answered. "And I bet it would be really interesting for you to go there. Isn't Genizah named after some Egyptian thing?"

"Of course, the Cairo Genizah," Josie said. "It was a huge stash of medieval manuscripts that were hidden in a room in a synagogue in Egypt. Not just books, but things like business receipts, letters, medical prescriptions, ordinary things like that. And nobody had even looked at them for a thousand years until—"

Judith was already tired of listening to Josie. "Right, I remember," she interrupted, though she didn't. "The point is, you'd have a great time. You could go look in dead people's filing cabinets or whatever. You love that kind of thing."

"That's true," Josie said, still twirling her hair. "But I'd be pretty worried about safety, wouldn't you? I mean, no one really knows what's going on over there now. After those riots at the embassy last year, and now with the new parliament—"

"Oh, come on, Josie. You think they'd let anything happen to you? This library is a world-class institution. They have Saudi Arabian billionaires financing the whole thing. They'd be watching you every minute," Judith said. "And they only need you on site for three weeks. I think you'd get amazing media coverage. Especially because everyone else is too chicken to go."

Josie was incapable of resisting fame. "Hmm," she murmured. "Actually, it would be nice to clear my head for a few weeks."

"Wouldn't it?" Judith prompted.

"I've had a lot to deal with lately, between work and Tali," Josie mused. "Maybe this would be a chance to take a deep breath."

The very existence of Josie's six-year-old daughter Tali, a black-haired beauty just like Josie, made Judith, still single, sick with envy. Judith's envy was a physical illness, a nauseous, aching, shivering longing whenever she saw that little girl. "You deserve a deep breath," Judith said.

Josie smiled. "Tell them yes," she said, and whirled away, her black hair flying behind her. When Josie left for Egypt three months later, Judith suddenly found herself, for the first time in years, able to breathe.

Judith barely thought of Josie after that, until Josie was taken hostage.

▪ ▪ ▪

THIS IS WHAT JUDITH would like to forget: a girl in a bathtub, her breath hovering over the face of the water.

In this memory Judith is four years old, and she is blowing bubbles, enraptured by how the soap-skinned bathwater bulges, by her breath alone, into a primal ooze. She raises her head to take another breath, her eyes level with the rounded end of the bathtub's faucet. And then she notices her reflection.

Her face appears on the faucet's shiny surface, her wide

gums and stumpy baby teeth sliding into focus. She moves closer, and her face flattens across chrome, distorted, until she backs away again. Now she can see the whole bathroom reflected in the faucet, curled into a perfect orb like a baby bird enfolded in an egg. In the miniature world contained within the faucet's circle, she can see her little sister Josie standing on a stepstool by the sink, and her mother brushing Josie's dark wet hair. If Judith tilts her head, Josie shrinks away, becomes insignificant, while her mother grows larger, her strong hands exaggerated against Josie's back. And now Judith watches, with absolute reverence, as her mother braids her sister's hair.

On the curved surface of the bathtub faucet, Judith sees her mother holding a new striped bathrobe and wrapping it around her sister. Three-year-old Josie's face is glowing above the bathrobe's colors, resplendent in the room's primordial light. Her mother bends down to Josie's little face. And then Judith hears her mother whisper to her sister, "Josie, I love you best of all."

This is the beginning, Judith's first memory, and nothing else matters. All of the worlds before that moment might as well never have existed.

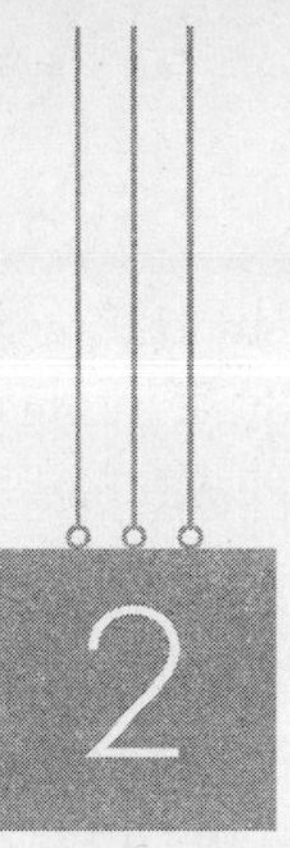

2

FOR YEARS, JOSIE had prepared for this possibility. *Someday when I'm in solitary confinement, I'll have the time to figure that out.* She had had this thought when she stopped playing chess, and again when she stopped teaching herself Japanese, and then again when she abandoned the remarkably ill-conceived master's program in statistics for the spectacularly ill-conceived doctorate in applied math. Later she saw that she wasn't indecisive, but what compelled her was a discipline that didn't yet have its own name: the study of patterns, of whether the past could be used to learn anything about the future—about whether patterns existed at all, or whether they existed only in the minds of people who sorted the information to conform to their own beliefs. She had created Genizah in part to test whether such patterns existed.

Instead she had learned that astonishing numbers of people cared mainly about their cats. And the problems she had long packed away to solve—whether dreams were mental garbage or a window to a world beyond what a waking person could perceive, whether nature or nurture mattered more, whether it was ever possible to throw something away—had all shriveled in her mind. They had seemed like discrete, captivating ideas once, long ago. But now they, along with every other thought or experience she had ever had, had become no more than tiny threads in a vast tapestry of obsession that occupied her entire being: the possibility of escape.

Her stupidity galled her, the memory of the mistake devouring her insides along with the terrible vomiting of those first few days. She had always taken a private car service from the library to the hotel. But that night she had been working later than usual, with Nasreen. Josie never understood Nasreen's position at the library. She was clearly several levels down from the men with authority, thin mustached figures with whom Josie had shared sugared tea and stilted conversation. Josie suspected that Nasreen had been given the job as her Soviet-style minder mainly because Nasreen had graduated from some sort of elite British school in Alexandria, spoke excellent English, and was a woman. The Egyptians had expected Josie to be a man.

When she got off the plane in Cairo and saw three men waiting outside of customs, one of whom was holding a sign with the library's logo on it that read "Mr. Ashkenazi," it hadn't even occurred to her that it was anything more than a spelling error. She walked right up to them, couldn't recall whether handshakes were appropriate, and gave a slight nod instead.

"Hello, I'm Josie Ashkenazi. It's a real pleasure to meet you."

"Good morning, madam. You are Mrs. Ashkenazi?" the oldest-looking man said. The younger two looked at each other, bemused.

Josie smiled, unaccustomed to the "Mrs."—which didn't even make sense, since Itamar's last name was Mizrahi. "Yes, I suppose I am."

"Very nice to meet you," the old man said. "Once your husband has finished with customs, we shall take you both to your hotel."

Josie opened her mouth, then closed it, then opened it again. "It's—it's just me," she stammered, suddenly feeling Itamar's absence beside her. She should have brought him, she realized. But she hadn't been willing to bring Tali too, and she had felt bad enough abandoning Tali for three weeks. And Itamar had told her that he hated Egypt. "I went there twice with my friends during high school, and both times I got sick," he had complained. "Both times! Twice I ended up vomiting in a hotel room. Listen, Yosefi, you don't need me there." Josie glanced down at her wedding ring and added, "He's at home."

Now the old man stared at her, confused.

"Excuse me," he said. "We are here for Mr. Joseph Ashkenazi. The computer executive. He is coming to work at our library. Pardon me, madam, but I believe this is—you are a mistake."

You are a mistake. The last time she had heard this about herself was from Judith when she was nine years old, when Judith had hurled it at her along with other insults. Judith claimed to be privy to certain conversations between their parents where they had supposedly discussed how Josie's conception had been a mistake, that if it hadn't been for Josie following so closely, fifteen months after Judith's birth, their mother might actually have finished her doctorate, gotten published, gotten hired, become a professor, lived a dream. Instead there was Josie, the mistake.

The mistake smiled. "Oh, no, that's me," she said, and took out a business card: "Genizah, Inc." "I'm Josephine Ashkenazi. At your service for all your memory-storage needs."

The man took the card in his hand, his fingernails more

carefully filed than Josie's. He held it close to his eyes, then at a distance, as though he couldn't make out the words. Josie's stomach sank. Someone had invited her; how could they not know who she was? Were these men just chauffeurs? It didn't seem so, and at any rate there were too many of them for that. Even if whoever had invited her was waiting in Alexandria, hadn't at least one of these well-groomed men looked her up? She clutched the plastic handle of her suitcase and watched as all three men edged away from her, backing off ever so slightly, turning their heads and glancing around the terminal, as though she had suddenly begun to smell.

"Ah," the man said, raising his glasses as he squinted at the card again. His mustache crinkled as he attempted a smile. Josie wished again that Itamar was with her, that anyone was with her. "Well, then, I believe we will take you to your hotel." For the rest of the ride, the men were silent. From that moment on she felt as though she were covered in filth.

During the first few days her hosts tried to awe her with the country's past. The pyramids and the other postcard sites impressed her, but what astonished her was the disarray of everything—not just the raging seas of cars and people in the streets, but the actual national treasures, the ancient remains that appeared to have been dumped into museums by earth-moving equipment. It reminded her of Genizah: at first, in beta testing, people had treated what they saved carefully, cataloguing their data like precious stones. But now no one even bothered to look at what they saved. There was no need. In the National Museum of Pharaonic Antiquities, Canopic jars and miniatures of the pharaohs' lives lay scattered in wide glass cases, sometimes covered in dust. It made sense, in a way, especially since the splendor of the pharaohs now only served to make the contemporary country seem pitiable by comparison. On a hot autumn morning two days after Josie arrived, the city was paralyzed by parades, those who had jobs released for the day, revelry in the streets. One of the mustached men explained to her that it was a national holiday, celebrating Egypt's victory over Israel in the war of 1973. The fact that Egypt had not actually won the 1973 war seemed in no way to dampen the festivities.

In between the places her guides brought her, Josie could sense an energy in the city, a live current of excitement just beyond her reach. A friend of hers who had spent a year in Egypt had told her that she needed to go to the concerts, to the bookstalls, to the outdoor fairs—to feel the country's vitality in the open air at night. But with the mustached men at her side it was impossible, as though an invisible gate stood between her and the people in the crowd. She had been advised by everyone not to go out alone. There was a shiny elite in Cairo: in the packed streets, expensively dressed young men, and even some expensively dressed young women, pushed their way through the crowds with cell phones welded to their hands, their eyes hidden behind sunglasses as they slammed taxi doors. But these seemed to Josie like a thin veneer, lipstick on the city's aged mouth. Most of the city seemed tired, wasted, reused: the sagging, peeling buildings, the diesel fuel from millions of battered cars, the recycled English-language T-shirts worn by poor men and boys stamped with phrases like "Jeff Lakes Day Camp" and "Lehman Brothers." Eye disease was so common that there were elderly people wandering the streets with no eyes to speak of, their hands thrust in front of them on canes as they walked like living mummies. Among the sunglasses, the blinded eyes, and the disappointed businessmen who dutifully escorted her from one floating Nile restaurant to another, only ogling men seemed to be looking at Josie, and then only at her breasts. Only later did she understand that she was being watched.

Alexandria was a slightly cleaner city than Cairo, slightly cooler, and, Josie was lulled into believing, slightly safer. The library itself felt to her like an empty shell, a giant, glassy, bossy modern complex of buildings as impressive as the pyramids and almost as vacant. The vast library didn't have nearly enough inside it, whether books or computers or, most of all, patrons. And what the library actually had was on the verge of becoming useless by disorganization alone, books lost forever simply by being incorrectly shelved, or software catalogues that rendered materials invisible by classifying them under the least relevant search terms. The extent of the task was debilitating, absurd. She felt abandoned, duped, until she met Nasreen.

Nasreen was a young woman, stylish but severe, with frameless glasses, fitted black pants, dark eyelashes, a pinched lower lip that made her look perpetually perplexed, and hair half-covered by a spangled headscarf that might as easily have been for fashion as for faith. The part of her hair that was visible was dyed an unlikely shade of orange. She invited Josie to dinner, and Josie assumed she would follow Nasreen back to her home when the day's work was done. But Nasreen had other ideas.

"Let's meet at half past ten," Nasreen said. "Nothing decent is open until then."

It was true. When Josie arrived at the waterfront restaurant whose address Nasreen had given her, she was amazed by the crowds. The city came alive after dark: by a quarter to midnight, thousands of children and adults were pouring into the streets, having dinner, shopping in stores that were closed during the heat of the day, eating ice cream beside the ink-dark sea. At the busy restaurant Nasreen had chosen, everyone was young and beautiful. Over grilled fish, Nasreen spoke about the library—the idea of reviving Alexandria's past, the donors from Saudi Arabia and Dubai, the awareness of untapped potential, the possibility of creating the greatest scholarly resource in the Arab world. It was a sales pitch, blather from a brochure. Only afterward, when Nasreen offered to take Josie out for ice cream by the water, did Nasreen ask, "Are you enjoying your stay here?"

They were walking under a row of palm trees on a promenade along the docks. Even here, among children clutching ice cream cones, the eyeless beggars were out in force. Josie ignored them, following Nasreen's lead.

Josie started to nod, but then gave up, sick of the show. "I have a six-year-old daughter at home," she said. It was an answer to Nasreen's question. She pulled out her phone, tapped it a few times, and showed a photo to Nasreen. On the screen, Tali was dressed as a fairy, vinyl wings tied to her back, her mouth hanging open. There was pink ice cream on her chin.

"She is beautiful," Nasreen said. A platitude. Her tone was controlled, courteous. "What is her name?"

Josie hesitated. It was a Hebrew name; would Nasreen notice? "Tali," she conceded.

"A lovely name," Nasreen said, neutrally, and licked her ice cream cone.

Nasreen must be single, Josie reasoned, and childless. No mother in the world would have been able to resist the temptation to pull out her own photos. Even a young childless married woman would have expressed some curiosity. And Nasreen was taking Josie out for ice cream, alone, at eleven o'clock at night. But perhaps there was some cultural expectation of escorting guests that Josie simply didn't appreciate?

She wanted to ask Nasreen about her family, but Nasreen's coolness held her back.

"I read that your company is very popular in America," Nasreen said, "not just for libraries and businesses, but for ordinary people."

Josie never stopped enjoying other people's admiration. "You could say that," she replied, pretending modesty. She couldn't help smiling.

But Nasreen did not smile. Her thin eyebrows were drawn together as she glanced at Josie. "I do not understand it. Why would ordinary people need a cataloguing system?"

Josie laughed. "You underestimate the average American's capacity for fascination with himself."

Nasreen didn't get the joke. "What do you mean?"

"You'd be surprised how many people want to keep records of what their cats ate for lunch over the past five years," Josie said. "The program automatically catalogues the individual's past, and then everything is stored on the network."

"But how could that happen automatically?"

Josie launched into her own pitch, just as Nasreen had. "Wherever you have a computer—whether it's a desktop or a tablet or a phone or pretty much any device—you probably have a recording component and a camera component," she recited. "Our software runs those, either continuously or at the user's request, then sorts the images and the voices with facial recognition and language processing. It also captures any text content you produce, like messages or tweets or whatever comments you post anywhere, and then archives everything based on your habits—or instincts, if you will." The term *instincts* was far from accurate, she knew, but she also knew that consumers seemed to like it. "Then two weeks later, when you want to remember where you put something or what you said to someone or what your cat ate for lunch, you can call up a record of exactly what happened."

"It sounds rather trivial," Nasreen said.

"Of course it is," Josie answered. "That's why I'm rich."

Nasreen did not smile, not even politely. It occurred to Josie that perhaps this sort of joke was less funny in a developing country. "There's more to it than that, of course," Josie said, trying to recover. "There's a social component too. You can choose to share whatever material you want with whomever you want, according to your preferences, or the software can learn those preferences from you. And there's also an augmented reality feature that compiles older materials and syncs them to wherever you are right now. On a mobile device, you can use it the way you use your eyes, but instead of seeing what's around you now, you can see what used to be there. Here, I'll show you."

Josie held up her phone, tapped the screen, and then turned it horizontally, facing the buildings behind them. Through the windowframe of the phone's screen, the city appeared, and then faded slightly. Over the ghosts of the dozen buildings in front of them, several structures appeared on the screen in black-and-white photos, lithographs and drawings, each labeled and dated with links to further information. As she moved the phone, other current buildings came into view, and occasionally another photo or drawing would appear superimposed on it. Most were labeled in Arabic, but five were labeled in English as well: *Royal Army Hospital, 1942*; *Villa of Sheikh Omar al-Hakam, 1857*; *Temple of Osiris, 4th century BCE; Temple of Apollo, 3rd century BCE; Neve Tzedek Synagogue, 1834.* Surprised, Josie tapped the screen on the last link. "The third-largest of sixteen synagogues in Alexandria prior to the Jewish community's expulsion after the 1952 revolution, Neve Tzedek was first constructed in . . ." But now Nasreen was leaning in, trying to see the pictures.

"It's like the City of the Dead in Cairo," Nasreen said. Her voice was melodic, unassuming, lovely. She ought to have no trouble meeting men, Josie thought. But was that even how things worked here? Josie guessed that Nasreen was in her late twenties, but she might have been anywhere between twenty and forty. Without the understood reference points of clothing, hair, makeup, posture, slang, inflection, it was impossible to know.

"You can do this with any city in the world," Josie heard herself say. "Actually this isn't a great example, because it's just pulling in what happens to be available online for this location. In New York or Cairo you'd see much more."

"All cities are really cities of the dead," Nasreen said.

The poetry of it surprised Josie. She looked around her, at the eyeless beggars and the children eating ice cream, and tried to imagine the Temple of Apollo, the Temple of Osiris. It was ridiculous; even the gods were dead.

Nasreen interrupted her thoughts. "What did you mean by 'instincts'?"

Josie bit her ice cream cone, feeling the crack of cookie and the wet sweet cream between her teeth. Suddenly it felt indulgent, almost obscene, to be enjoying this ice cream under these palm trees, in front of these beggars, on the ruins of the temples of dead gods. She retreated into script. "The software is designed to learn how you think, what your habits are, and even to learn the habits of people around you," she said. "When you've been using it for long enough, it actually predicts your future based on your current trajectory. Let's say the program notices that your usual habit is to drink one beer a day, for instance, but that lately you're having two or three. Or that you regularly send messages to men who don't reply to you three weeks after they first appear in your contact list. It tracks those sorts of things. That way, if you don't like where you're headed, you can see the pattern and make changes."

As soon as she'd said it, Josie realized that drinking and dating examples were perhaps not the best selling points in a Muslim-majority country. She racked her brain for something more appropriate. But Nasreen sucked the last of the ice cream out of her nibbled cone, and spoke.

"You have clearly been quite successful," Nasreen said, her voice level and thoughtful.

Josie absorbed the compliment, savoring its sweetness. They were standing by the railing at the water's edge. She looked out at the dark velvet sheath of the Mediterranean, gleaming under orange fluorescent lights. *All cities are cities of the dead,* she thought, imagining the remains of lost worlds buried beneath the water's darkness. It ought to have moved her, saddened her. But instead it intrigued her, as though it were a problem to be solved. She clutched her phone in her hand and resisted the impulse to drag its screen across the seascape, searching for dead maritime gods.

"But your idea is still rather foolish," Nasreen announced. "Most things that happen cannot be predicted, and are beyond our control."

Was it an insult, or just a badly translated thought? Nasreen was watching Josie, fixing her with her eyes to the railing above the sea.

"Well, of course you can't predict everything," Josie faltered. She gripped the iron rail, glancing down into the water below her. A white plastic bag hovered over the face of the water, a windblown ghost. "There are always going to be acts of God, as the insurance companies put it—earthquakes and all that. But even natural disasters are often at least slightly predictable. You'd be surprised." The wave of data and evidence rose within her, unstoppable, swelling like the black water below. "Before the tsunami in south Asia in 2004, flamingos in coastal areas flew off to forests on higher ground. There were probably similar migrations before the tsunami in Japan. Animals are very sensitive to environmental changes. They can hear sounds we can't hear, they notice temperature or pressure changes or magnetic fields, that kind of thing. There's probably a way to track animal behavior so as to evacuate humans prior to natural disasters. That's a great R & D opportunity, if you ask me."

Nasreen clicked her tongue, a dismissive snap. "That isn't what I mean," she said. "I mean ordinary events, between people. Those are also beyond our control."

"Some, sure," Josie conceded, to be polite. But there was an edge in Nasreen's voice.

"Not some. Nearly all," Nasreen said. "Perhaps everything."

Now Josie snorted, slipping her phone back into her bag. "That's just something people say when they've failed and don't want to take the blame."

She tried to make her voice light, but she had said it. The insult lay like litter on the ancient sea's edge.

Nasreen looked back at Josie, her eyes firm, then at the sea. Her nostrils were noble, her profile erect. She spoke, an incantation.

"There are innumerable ways for a person to be brought under the power of something or someone else."

Innumerable. The passive voice. The diction and syntax were oppressive. Was she just making conversation, or was she making a point?

"You mean like falling in love?" Josie asked. She thought of Itamar, alone with Tali at home. *Once your husband has finished with customs, we shall take you both to your hotel,* one of the mustached men announced in her head. She imagined Itamar here with her, leaning against the railing beside her, skipping pebbles on the dark water. And Tali among the six-year-olds out after midnight, Itamar showing her how to cast a stone into oblivion.

"Perhaps that is one way it could happen," Nasreen said. "But only one of many."

Just past the noise of the night, the water was nearly still. Josie heard children shouting behind them as the sea rocked gently, echoing with the hollow bump of boats tethered to the docks. Nasreen leaned against the railing, took the stump of her ice cream cone, and hurled it into the sea. By the time Josie turned around, Nasreen had already found her a taxi back to her hotel.

"YOSEFI! WHY ARE YOU calling now?" Itamar's voice blared through Josie's phone. She had tried and failed to get video feed to come through, cursing third-world bandwidth as Itamar's face disappeared. "Isn't it after midnight there?"

"It is, but I just got home," Josie said. She stared uselessly at the blank screen for several seconds before realizing that it wasn't worth waiting for the image to come back. The hotel air conditioning was making her head hurt. "Everyone here is up all night. It's too hot during the day."

"Did you get my message? Tali has an ear infection again," he told her, half in Hebrew. "Dr. Boodish says she needs to have tubes put in her ears. I arranged it for the week you get back, but if you don't like it you can cancel. How's Egypt? Are you still healthy?"

His words washed through her brain, their meaning dissolving. She felt her eyes beginning to close. "People here think they won the Yom Kippur War," Josie said in English. "And they don't have eyes."

She heard a yelp in the background, followed by a thump. "Here, I'll let Tali talk," Itamar said. "Tali, *Ima batelefon, dabri itah,*" she heard him coax. Tali whined in the background. "*Lo. Lo ahar kakh. Ein ahar kakh. Akhshav!*" Itamar said. His voice was harsher than Josie wanted to hear. "She doesn't listen to me," Itamar muttered under his breath. But Tali had already taken the phone.

"Mommy, you have to come home!" Tali cried. "Abba gave me medicine that tastes like poop!"

What time was it there? Was it a weekend? Josie had no idea. "Tali, I miss you," she said. "You have to take the medicine, okay? You have to do what Abba says." Josie glanced out her window at the carnival scene going on outside—an actual carnival behind the hotel, with rides on the backs of trucks, little children cavorting at one in the morning. Occasionally she heard one scream. She flopped back onto the hotel room bed, a teenage gesture. No one was calling for her.

Itamar's voice returned. "She went upstairs. She's really tired."

"That's okay," Josie yawned.

"Your sister wants to hire someone to handle the Canadian market," Itamar said. It was hard to hear him. Or maybe she just didn't want to hear anything involving Judith. "You can approve whoever she finds when you come back."

"They thought I was a man," Josie said.

"You told me that before, *metuka*. When are you going to get over this jet lag?"

"It isn't jet lag. People here really don't have eyes. It's like *Night of the Living Dead* or something. And you never told me that this is where T-shirts go to die."

"Yosefi, it's late there. Go to bed, okay? Your sister and I have everything under control. Sweet dreams," he said in English. Tali shouted something unintelligible as Josie hung up.

That night Josie dreamed of arriving at the waterfront restaurant, searching for Nasreen. When she spotted her, she found her seated at a table for four—with Itamar, Tali, and Judith. The four of them were all laughing together, and Josie wondered if they were laughing at her.

A WEEK LATER, AS the library's air conditioning made the hair on her arms stand on end, Josie was finishing a reboot of the library's image archive when Nasreen sat down beside her.

"I would like to study your program myself, to understand it," Nasreen said.

It was a relief to hear Nasreen's voice. The men who worked at the library barely spoke to Josie, acknowledging her as she demonstrated the software only with noncommittal nods and glances at her breasts.

"You don't study this software, actually," Josie replied. "It studies you. That's how I designed it. Here, I'll show you how it works."

This was the part that Josie loved: watching the awe on users' faces as buried aspects of their minds and lives were suddenly, stunningly revealed, in perfect order. It reminded Josie of showing her mother a teacher's glowing comments on her schoolwork, the gold star next to her name. She still aspired to gold stars. She crouched over the keyboard as Nasreen gently, almost unnoticeably, shrank to the side. Josie was used to that, too.

"Let's start with what's important to you. Family? Work? Personal interests?"

"Well, first of all things, the will of God," Nasreen said.

Josie's fingers hovered over the keys. She glanced at Nasreen's half-covered hair, her stylish pants. This was not what she had expected to hear. "I don't have a category sorter for that," Josie said.

"You should," Nasreen replied.

Her certainty irked Josie. A familiar feeling tugged at her gut: her father, before he abandoned them all for his newer, purer, more righteous life, arguing with her mother as he edited the kitchen pantry, tossing out whole boxes of cookies and cereal and replacing them with kosher brands. Now he was apparently a diamond dealer, happily supporting his five newer, better children—all sons, she once heard, and surely by now there were flocks of grandchildren—in a Hasidic neighborhood in Brooklyn, with a new and improved wife who was only seven years older than Josie. Josie hadn't heard from him since she was thirteen. Sometimes she wondered whether he ever looked her up online, and if he did, whether he was proud of her, or ashamed of her. Or ashamed of himself.

"The software only sorts things the user already knows," Josie said evenly. "We could create a category for 'religion' under 'hobbies and interests'—"

"Excuse me, are you a Christian?" Nasreen interrupted.

Josie grimaced. "Sure," she huffed. She had been advised before arriving, by nearly everyone, to tell people this—*just to make things easier*, as her friend who had spent the year in Egypt put it. She was surprised by how often it came up, and by how degrading it felt to lie—humiliating, like being a child again. Later it would take her captors less than half an hour to dig her documents out of the pouch under her shirt, notice the half-dozen Israeli stamps in her passport, and declare her an agent of the Mossad.

"Your Gospels tell you the will of God, don't they?" Nasreen asked. "Otherwise, what is their purpose?"

Josie bit her lip. She thought of the Hebrew words on an abstract painting that had hung on the wall in the house where she grew up: *What does God require of you? Only to do justice, and love kindness, and walk humbly with your God.* It had remained there after her father left, a rebuke. For a moment Josie entertained, purely as a programmer, the possibility of cataloguing the divine will. She could create three categories, for instance: one for doing justice, one for loving kindness, and a third for walking humbly with one's God. But the final category would override the prior two, she reasoned, since the very act of cataloguing one's deeds of justice or kindness would presumably disqualify a person from walking humbly with his God. It was like Benjamin Franklin's autobiography, which had unexpectedly captured her data-tracking imagination when she was forced to read it in school. Franklin had carefully documented his successes in pursuing the noblest of eighteenth-century virtues: temperance, industry, frugality, chastity, and of course, humility. That was the point where Franklin lost all credibility, in Josie's opinion. Ignoring Nasreen's question, Josie turned to the screen.

"The program has a setting for open topics, which allows information to be catalogued as it arrives in response to the query you set. You could create an open topic for questions about—about the will of God, for instance." This was absurd, Josie thought. But then what wasn't? At least it wasn't about a cat. "That would be more specific than having it sorted as a hobby, and it would allow the category to be included in other archives in the network."

"The will of God is not an open topic," Nasreen stated.

Josie glanced again at Nasreen, at her stylish pants. This

was not a conversation Josie wanted to have. "Let's focus on the software," she said.

Josie was relieved that Nasreen seemed to get the point. Nasreen gave a curt nod, pursing her lips.

"The idea isn't to teach the software about a subject," Josie continued, and heard the pedantry her sister hated seeping into her own voice. But now she felt Nasreen deserved it. "It's to teach the software the way you think, or how you would organize something—which in turn will reflect where you'd look to find it."

"Could it catalogue my dreams?" Nasreen asked. "I always write down my dreams when I wake up in the morning."

This was intriguing. Josie turned to Nasreen, noticing for the first time that Nasreen's eyes were green. "Really? What for?"

"In case there are any messages in them."

Josie looked back at the screen. Everything in Egypt was a disappointment. Even Nasreen, who had at first seemed so refreshingly normal, was turning out to be a crank. "Are we talking about, uh, messages from God?" she asked. She tried to suppress the sarcastic edge in her voice, but it sliced through the vowels nonetheless. "Because like I mentioned before, this software—"

To Josie's surprise, Nasreen shrugged. "Any sort of messages," she said. Her voice was lighter than it had been, and Josie heard something in it that she could barely identify at first: friendliness. "During the day we are occupied with things that are not very important. There is a blinding quality to the unimportant during the day, like bright light that doesn't allow us to see. Nighttime is our only chance to really be alive."

Poetry again. In Josie's mind, the bright refrigerated library around them faded, along with the past seven years, and she was in Ein Gedi at twilight, the oasis by the Dead Sea. Itamar had pulled the car up along the edge of the cliff and the two of them had climbed out, sitting down on a wide flat ledge along the precipice. Far below them, beyond their vision, a waterfall streamed down to the dark green gully at the bottom of the hundred-foot drop, the falling water a gentle, sibilant *shhh*, rocking the world to sleep. From the edge of the cliff, in the day's last light, they could see miles of desert beyond the oasis, tan and white and yellow-streaked mountains. The dark mirror of the Dead Sea lay at the mountains' feet. Stalagmites of salt floated like icebergs on its surface, an illusion of cold. The heat wrapped her bare arms even as the sky darkened. Before the light faded, she saw an ibex on the top of the cliff opposite—like a poem Itamar had once read to her, the animal's long face a violin, about to sing. Then night fell: a darkness so total that only Itamar's tongue against her skin reminded her that she was alive, clinging to the rim of the world.

"I dreamt last night that my mother and I were at my husband's funeral," Nasreen said.

This was more information about Nasreen than Josie had amassed in a week. Was Nasreen married? Widowed? She glanced at Nasreen's hands, searching for a wedding ring, but Nasreen had rings on several fingers, and it occurred to Josie that there was nothing universally symbolic about one's left fourth finger, that she had no idea what was normal here.

"It wasn't an ordinary funeral, in the dream. It was a pharaonic funeral, like the ones painted in the tombs." Nasreen lowered her voice as she continued, a rushed hush of words that hovered in the library's chilled air. "My husband's body was in a sarcophagus on a mourner's boat, and I was riding on it with hundreds of women I had never met before. They were all wailing and weeping, and I knew they were our slaves. But even though the boat was a pharaonic boat, the city on the riverbanks looked like Cairo or Alexandria now. There were dozens of houseboats and restaurant boats tied along the docks, not far from where the funeral boat was sailing. Then I saw my mother standing near the edge of the boat's deck. She was wearing a white robe and beaded necklaces, like the women in the tomb paintings. All around her were those wailing women, but she was standing there smiling. I never saw her so happy, and I was very relieved, because I thought it meant it was all a joke. She took my hand and pulled me to the side of the boat. She pointed at all the houseboats and floating restaurants and said, 'Now you can do it, *habeebti*. You know how to swim. Just jump.' I thought about it. I could even hear the music coming from those boats. But I didn't jump."

Josie exhaled, a long breath. *Cities of the dead,* she remembered Nasreen saying. It made sense now. She tried to think of something compassionate to say, but her mind went blank. *Your problem, Josie,* she heard Judith insulting her in her head, *is that you have no empathy. None. But I suppose when you're a genius, it doesn't matter if you think no one exists in the world but you.* She had to respond, if only to prove Judith wrong. But Nasreen spoke first.

"How would I create the catalogue for this dream?" Nasreen asked.

Josie was grateful for the chance to play along. "Well, if we were going to archive this, we'd try to sort everything by category," Josie said. "Let's create one category for 'mother,' another for 'husband,' another for 'funeral,' and then one for 'pharaonic period.'" She knew she sounded cold, clinical, heartless. But surely this was what Nasreen was looking for. She dragged a finger over the screen. "You want to create as many categories as you can think of. Maybe create one for 'boats,' and another for 'slaves.' And then you always need to add at least a few conceptual ones, like 'grief,' or 'antiquity.'" Josie typed quickly, more quickly than she spoke. "The conceptual ones are especially important. The idea is to see what reappears in other dreams. Then you can draw conclusions from the patterns. In the future, once the software learns what you care about, you won't have to do any more than enter a word or two."

"Of course," Nasreen said. With Josie showing her how, she classed the dream expertly. "I should also like to include a category for 'anachronisms,'" Nasreen added, in her British syntax.

Josie nodded. "Right, because the pharaonic funeral had modern people in it."

"And also because my mother could not be present at my husband's funeral. She died when I was nine years old."

Josie jolted, startled. Again empathy failed her. Perhaps Judith was right. "I'm—I'm so—I'm so sorry," she stammered.

But Nasreen was not interested in Josie's forced pity. She waved a hand. "If I have enough of these dreams, the program would begin to catalogue them for me. Is that correct?"

"Yes. And then you'd see a cloud emerge."

"A cloud," Nasreen repeated. There was a skeptical edge in her voice. Or was it just her accent?

"A cloud, like the ones we've been creating for the library catalogue system," Josie explained. She suppressed a snort. Had Nasreen heard a single word she had said in the past six days? It was like talking to Judith. Some people just didn't get anything the first time. "I don't mean offsite data storage. I mean a network of associated words or ideas, for search purposes. You'll have a statistical analysis of how often certain images come up. Once you start entering other dreams, you'll be able to see the prominence of certain themes. And then the variations on the themes will probably trend in specific directions."

"I have had this particular dream over a hundred times," Nasreen said.

"Well, that will make the archiving very simple," Josie replied curtly. She was done with Nasreen. She focused her eyes pointedly on the screen, aggressively closing programs, returning to the library catalogue. "Now you can see how this same program works for the—"

"What do you think my dream means?" Nasreen asked.

Josie turned to her. Was this an attempt at friendship, or a challenge? It was degrading not to know. "Are you testing my talent for psychoanalysis? Because I really just do software," Josie said.

"I am testing your talent for prophecy," Nasreen replied.

Was she joking? Being in Egypt was like being a child, unable to hear the words beneath the words, incapable of getting the jokes. She forced a laugh, hoping she had guessed correctly. But Nasreen did not smile.

"You are clearly a very intelligent woman," Nasreen said. "You are able to see patterns where others do not see them. So I would like to know what you think my dream means."

Josie drew in her breath, looking at Nasreen's shoes. Nasreen was wearing black ballet slippers, the kind that hip American women wore years earlier. But Nasreen's looked new.

"Well, without knowing you at all, I would say that you probably miss your husband very much, and your mother as well," Josie replied. It was the most innocuous thing she could think of.

"Why would it be necessary to know me in order to understand my dream?" Nasreen asked.

This was baffling. Was it not obvious? "To know what these people and ideas mean to you, of course," she said. The challenge of not condescending was immense.

"Why would it matter what they mean to me?" Nasreen asked. "The message ought to be clear on its own."

Josie considered this. In fact the dream did have a rather obvious interpretation, but it didn't seem like one Josie should share. "That would depend on if you think dreams are internal or external," she said. "I suppose the message ought to be clear to anyone if you believe that the dream's source is something outside of your own mind. But if the dream's source is in your own mind, then it should matter what these people meant to you."

"In the end it is not that different, is it?" Nasreen said, her dark lips set in a smug grin. "There is a message either way, just as I said."

For a moment Josie was silent, hovering on the edge of a respectful nod. But then she could no longer contain her irritation—with Nasreen, with the library, with the radiance of the past buried under the nonsense of the present, with the thick walls of illogic that had been closing in around her from that very first moment at the airport, when she had been sagely informed that she was a mistake. It was like being with Judith. Or like being Judith.

"It's actually extremely different," Josie said. She no longer held her exasperation under her breath. Her voice rose. "If the dream is some sort of supernatural message, or something reflecting the—the will of God, so to speak—then it should matter a lot, and you should care a lot about what it's trying to tell you. And if the dream is that kind of supernatural message, then presumably what it is trying to tell you is some sort of—prophecy, as you put it. Some kind of prediction or warning about the future that you couldn't otherwise know."

"Precisely," Nasreen said. Her boarding school accent was comically precise.

"But if the dream is actually an internal message, something from your own memory or imagination, then it can't be anything beyond that. Then it's just like—like a book the library owns but hasn't catalogued yet," Josie fumbled, unsure of the analogy. "It could be valuable, or it could be worthless. But if it's coming from your own mind, then it can't be a prophecy, because there's no external source of new information. It can only be like the archive, which is made up of things you already know, even if you've forgotten them. Then it isn't about the future, just the past."

"In the end," Nasreen said evenly, "they are the same."

This was becoming maddening. "They're not the same. They're opposites."

Nasreen smiled at her. "Josephine, I think that for you it is daytime all the time, even at night."

"What do you mean?"

Nasreen kept smiling. "For you every confusing thing on earth is a problem that can be solved."

"That's because every confusing thing on earth *is* a problem that can be solved."

For the first time since Josie had met her, Nasreen laughed. "The car you called should be waiting outside. I'll see you tomorrow."

"I HAVE ANOTHER DREAM for you," Nasreen said ten days later, after Josie had walked her through four different software options for sorting manuscript images. It was ridiculous even to be here, Josie thought. No one needed a CEO to do this. But Judith had been right: the trip had resulted in several news stories about the company's prescience and generosity in aiding the "emerging knowledge economy" in the

Arab world, for which Josie had been cheerfully quoted by phone. One reporter for a television network had even done an interview with her in the library's imposing glass lobby, followed by interviews with two of the mustached men. The publicity had been perfect; the stories had been reposted across the internet, and investment inquiries had been coming in at home.

But during her second week in Egypt, Josie had begun to understand that her Egyptian sponsors had their own goals. For them, her visit was their chance to set up a "joint venture," as the Egyptian businessmen liked to put it. It was going to be difficult to explain to them why that wasn't going to happen. There was no possibility of doing business here, Josie knew. Even the ancient tombs were often "closed for repairs" until the tour guides pressed cash into various people's hands. The most eager collectors of cash were the police. Was she being greedy? Or racist? Or merely smart? She was relieved that once she got home, she wouldn't have to think about it. Egypt would become a three-week pocket in her life, a brief and vaguely remembered dream. Two days before she was due to leave Alexandria, she was invited to a dinner at the Four Seasons Hotel where she was staying, with all sponsors present. By then she already knew how it would go: everything said by circumlocution, the words between words the only ones that mattered, and the brilliant prodigy Josie sitting at the table like a child, noticing with a sinking feeling that the adults were talking about her in her presence, and not in entirely flattering terms. That afternoon at the library, she was just starting to worry about what her inner businesswoman knew was coming: the "ask."

"In my new dream, I moved to America, and someone there buried me alive," Nasreen said. "What do you think it means?"

Josie grinned. "I think it means you're afraid of me."

Josie was going back to Cairo in three days, and back home two days after that. She was exhausted by Alexandria, by its insatiable library and the perpetually confounding Nasreen. She looked forward to freedom in Cairo, where she would be beyond Nasreen's orbit, shepherded only by the more pliable mustached men. She had plans to see the original genizah, the room in the nine-hundred-year-old Ben Ezra synagogue where hundreds of thousands of medieval Hebrew documents had been stored for centuries, because no one was allowed to throw away anything inscribed with the name of God, and because no one had bothered to throw away anything else. Her friend who had lived in Egypt had told her that a few Hebrew books still remained there, guarded by a Muslim man whose forehead was callused from years of daily prayers. All around her, centuries opened their doors, waiting for her to enter. Yet here in the library, the reincarnation of the great archive of the ancients, her world was reduced to Nasreen.

Nasreen smiled. She drew up a chair to Josie's computer and sat down beside her. "I have been meaning to ask you this," she said. "I have never been to America before, and I have often wondered: in America, what is the purpose of being alive?"

Poetry again. She couldn't possibly be serious, could she? "What do you mean?" Josie asked.

"I read once that it was the pursuit of happiness."

"After life and liberty," Josie retorted, in a jocular tone. But an unease hummed in her body, like a dull chronic pain.

"Doesn't happiness seem rather selfish, as a goal for one's life?"

A challenge. But Nasreen's voice was pleasant, almost upbeat. Josie considered it.

"There isn't any official purpose of life in America," Josie said. "The whole point of America is that the country leaves you alone to find your own purpose."

"What is your purpose, then?"

It was the same question Nasreen had asked the previous week, the one about the will of God. Perhaps this was a hobby for Nasreen, fishing for souls. Could she avoid taking the bait?

"To devote my life to helping other people," Josie answered. It was something her mother had often said, before early-onset dementia began devouring her brain: *Josie, you are the purpose of my life*. Josie imagined an adult's smile, a game-show buzzer ringing: her answer was correct. She turned back to the screen, hoping Nasreen would disappear.

"Is that what you are doing now?" Nasreen asked.

This was more than a challenge. Josie tapped the screen in front of her, swallowing sarcasm. "I'm helping to develop the greatest scholarly resource in the Arab world, aren't I?"

"But you are making money," Nasreen said quietly. "Quite a bit too."

Josie clenched her fingers over the keys. It was like sitting with the businessmen in the Four Seasons Hotel. Her wealth was her shadow, covering all of Egypt in its darkness. "Maybe you don't know this, but my company is doing this pro bono," she said, her lips tight.

"I do not mean now, I mean always," Nasreen replied. "You cannot claim that when you work for your own company you are devoting your life to others. You work for yourself."

Was this some sort of post-Communist nonsense? "Of course there's a profit motive," Josie said. "That's how you ensure quality. It doesn't mean the product isn't worth anything beyond the material. Your library wouldn't have invited me if they didn't think my systems were valuable for your future." Suddenly

Josie missed her mustached escorts, the elegant businessmen with their filed fingernails and their eternal disappointment. At least they hadn't questioned the premise.

Nasreen hesitated, then spoke, more loudly this time. "You create ways for people to gather tiny pieces of information, but you do not give them any way of knowing which information matters."

Josie uncrossed her legs, stamping, too loudly, against the refrigerated library floor. "That's not my job."

"You cultivate the trivial," Nasreen said.

Cruel! "What seems trivial now may become important later," Josie countered.

"You say it is not your job to tell anyone which information matters. But your program does try to predict what it will mean to each person. You interpret the information for them."

Josie felt the stone floor giving way beneath her feet. "The software just aggregates patterns. It isn't interpretive. It tracks the data. That's all it does."

Nasreen dismissed her. "You trust the trivial to dictate the future. You do not give any thought to what is truly important in life."

Now Josie was genuinely angry, anger she could taste in her mouth, her fury burning her in the refrigerated room. She was no longer arguing with Nasreen, but with Judith—and before Judith, with her father. She imagined holding up a mobile screen against this moment, seeing her father and Judith and her mother, *The Ashkenazi Family, Late 20th Century*. She refused to click on the link.

"You don't know anything about my life," Josie said. Her voice was cold, controlled, a cage containing a roar. "This is just my job." It wasn't even slightly true, of course. Itamar would have laughed. Even Judith would have laughed. But she needed to say it. "I have a husband and a daughter at home," she announced. "My life is devoted to them." The words sounded self-righteous, fake, even to her.

"You left them behind to come here. They are thousands of miles away."

Unfair, absurd! "I'm only here for three weeks."

"No woman here would have done that," Nasreen said.

"No woman here would have been invited," Josie snapped. 

She would have left the library, if she had known how. But she was at the mercy of the car service. Nasreen left instead. By nightfall Josie was alone, waiting for a car to pick her up.

"ITAMAR, YOU HAVE TO save me," she pleaded on the phone that night, in her frigid hotel room. The room's air conditioning was recalcitrant, refusing compromise, offering only frigidity or suffocating heat. She huddled under the bedspread at the Sahara's edge.

Itamar grunted, pecking at a keyboard on the other side of the world. "I can't talk, I'm at work. Can you text me instead?"

"I can't stand another minute here. This place is like living in an existentialist play."

"Yosefi, what are you talking about?"

"There's this woman here who keeps trying to lure me into some sort of existential crisis. I can't even explain it."

Itamar laughed. "An existential crisis? Please. If you were having a gastrointestinal crisis, then I might care."

"No, it's really upsetting, Itamar. I don't know how to describe it. This woman, she keeps belittling me—first it was subtle, but now it isn't anymore, it's like she's trying to make me justify my life. I don't even know what she means. She's dressed very modern, I don't think it's a religious thing, but it's—"

"It's four more days, *yekirati,*" he said in Hebrew. "Enjoy the fun parts. Be glad you aren't vomiting. Everyone likes the ice cream there. Go out and eat more ice cream."

That night Josie lay in bed, thinking of Tali, hoping to dream of her. Instead she dreamed that Nasreen took her out for ice cream. Just as Josie was about to lick the sweet white cream for the first time, Nasreen tore the cone from Josie's hand and threw it into the sea, grinning as she skipped it across the surface of the water. Josie woke up frozen in the air-conditioned room, unsure of whether it had been a dream.

THE NEXT DAY, her second-to-last in Alexandria, Nasreen barely looked at her. But they couldn't avoid each other; there was too much to be done. Nasreen took her through the library's storage rooms, making sure there were clear plans for each collection. Toward the end of the second floor, they walked through a room whose books were assembled in literal stacks, waist-high piles of peeling leather and yellowed paper. It was as though the paper had decided to reconstitute itself back into trees.

Josie paused in the windowless room under the dim overhead light. The air was warmer here, and shuddered against her breath. After so many days surrounded by smooth screens and pristine shelves, she stood motionless in this forest of words, suddenly aware of each buried book's life, long ago, in someone's warm hands. She breathed in the dark dry smell of cracked leather and rotting paper. Like inhaling a shadow.

"What do you keep in here?" she asked.

"Mostly rubbish," Nasreen said, lingering by the door. Her posture was proud, erect against the doorpost. "When we first started planning the library, we made a public call for materials. People sent us whatever they found in their grandmothers' closets, because there was a rumor that we would pay. They all think they've given us great treasures, of course. Hundreds of English books that we already own, for instance. And the same in French. The directors don't even want us to catalogue this room until we finish with everything else. It's really nothing but rubbish. I've looked."

Trivia, Josie thought. Nasreen's cell phone buzzed. Nasreen fished it out of her bag and began speaking in Arabic, her voice low, professional. Josie stepped toward the column of books by the door, and crouched slightly to read the spines. The bindings had flaked off many of them; most titles were illegible to her, even the ones in Roman letters. Josie picked up a decrepit volume from the top of the stack, the capital of a column of trivia. The book was small, but thick, its pages packed into a dense brick of paper. The binding flaked onto her hand as she looked at the cover. To her astonishment, it was in Hebrew.

"This is *Guide for the Perplexed*," she said aloud, almost unconsciously. She opened the book and read its title page, awed by how quickly the familiar letters resolved into meaning: *Moreh Nevukhim la-Rambam*, translated into Hebrew from the Judeo-Arabic by Shmuel ibn Tibbon in the year 4960—or, as Josie quickly calculated, 1200—and printed in Cairo in 1928. She flipped through its pages, smelling its dense blocks of print. She had never read it, and didn't want to. In her mental Genizah, she had entered her childhood living room. Her father, dressed in an undershirt, black socks, and ill-fitting pants, was hunched over an English translation of *Guide for the Perplexed*, delicately deboning the book with a four-color pen. He had already started growing out his beard, then. When she entered the room, he didn't look up.

"This book," he said, "should be required reading for being alive."

"Why?" Josie had asked.

"Because it explains why we think we know everything, when we actually don't know anything at all."

Her father was a mathematics professor at a no-name college twenty minutes from their home, and he spent his days convinced that he had been slighted by the universe. Josie and Judith and their mother were part of that slight—particularly their mother, who had often declared that her religious beliefs stopped at the idea of one god. She accepted that intuitively, she once told Josie, exempting it from knowledge, but anything beyond that—and of course, including that—was impossible to know. It occurred to Josie, based on her father's comment on *Guide for the Perplexed*, that perhaps her father and her mother actually agreed with each other.

"What is *Guide for the Perplexed*?" Nasreen asked. She had put her phone away now, and stepped toward Josie, looking over her shoulder.

"I—I don't know," Josie stammered. She regretted speaking. The last thing she wanted was to get involved in another conversation about the will of God.

"How did you even read the title?" Nasreen asked, pointing at the cover. "Do you read Hebrew?"

Josie panicked for a moment, mentally scrambling. *Trust me, it just makes everything easier*, her friend who had spent the year in Cairo repeated in her head. She flipped the book over, about to put it down, and then noticed the lettering on the book's back cover. "I read French," she said, which was true. *Le Guide des Égarés de Maïmonide,* the other side of the book said. *Édition bilingue.*

Nasreen sighed, bored. "It's quite ridiculous what people brought to this library. Some of the contributions weren't even proper books, just notebooks of someone's grandmother's recipes, or folders full of their grandfather's business receipts. A few people even brought stacks of old letters."

"That sort of thing could be very valuable in the future," Josie offered.

In the windowless room Nasreen was beautiful, her profile hard and statuesque under the bare incandescent bulb. Nasreen turned around, her back to Josie as she flicked off the light. The book was still in Josie's hands. Without thinking, Josie slipped it into her own bag as she followed Nasreen to the doorway.

As she closed the door behind them, Nasreen sniffed, a noble breath. "People will do anything for money," she said.

THAT NIGHT THE CAR scheduled to take Josie back to the hotel arrived fifteen minutes earlier than planned. She saw it idling outside the library windows as she finished her work. It was out of character for Alexandria. Usually, Josie was left waiting in the air-conditioned lobby for ages, as the prearranged time receded into the happy night air. Early was unheard of. But that night Josie was relieved and reprieved. Tomorrow would be the end. She hurried out to meet the car, jumping in and closing the door even after she saw that the driver was wearing a white T-shirt and jeans instead of the usual uniform and cap.

"Four Seasons, please," she announced.

"I stop for passenger first," the driver replied.

The driver's accent was light, pleasant. He smiled at her in the rearview mirror, as though he were eager to chat. What he said barely registered.

"What?"

The car had already moved around the corner, beyond the library's grounds. It pulled over near a gray apartment building, where a man in a black shirt and dark pants opened the door.

"He is passenger," the driver said.

Josie nodded, trying to seem unconcerned. She had been judging everyone and everything since she arrived in Egypt, but by now she had learned not to judge. "All right," she said. Her mistake.

The man climbed into the car, sliding into the seat beside her as the door closed. He had on sunglasses that covered most of his face. A moment later it occurred to Josie how odd it was that he was wearing sunglasses after nightfall. But by then he was smothering her with a rag that smelled of milk and poison, and her body sank into a dreamless sleep.

WHEN JOSIE AWOKE, SHE was convinced she was dreaming. She couldn't have been in the hotel room, because she was warm, her back slicked with sweat. For a fleeting instant she thought she was lying atop the cliff in Ein Gedi, feeling the warm desert air on her face and the bare rock beneath her. Then she returned to herself, rational, and knew the air conditioning must have broken. Something was wrong with the bed too; it was hard, like the ledge in Ein Gedi. She looked down at herself and saw that she was wearing the same skirt and blouse she had worn to the library that morning. She sat up suddenly and shook her head hard, fighting a thick and unexpected haze of dizziness. Then she saw that there was no bed.

She was lying on the floor of a small room, surrounded by four windowless walls. The walls were mottled, blotched with patches of cracked brownish plaster. An old room, unequipped for anything. Its only feature was a six-foot-long slab of stone about two and a half feet high, standing like a table parallel to one of the room's walls, with worn Arabic inscriptions on its surface. Aside from the stone, there was no furniture except a square yellow plastic bucket in one corner. Three electric lights hung from the ceiling, suspended from hooks, with black electrical wires running down along the walls and under a wide wooden door.

She tried to stand up. She lost her balance at first, then righted herself, more carefully this time, and stepped toward the door, trying the knob. It wouldn't move. She looked around again, at the lights and the walls and the door, feeling the hard stone beneath her feet. Then she looked down and saw that her feet were bare. She spun around, scanning the room and then her body for her bag, for her phone, for her watch, for her shoes, for the emergency pouch with her passport, credit cards, and cash that she kept under her shirt. Nothing. Her eyes widened in the room's bright lights. She fidgeted, rubbed her hands together, and noticed that her wedding ring was gone.

She was shaking now, breathing hard. She threw herself at the door, threw herself at the door again, screamed for help, screamed again, pounded, screamed, pounded, screamed, then wept, until she sank back down to the floor again, crawling to the back of the room, silent and defeated. Now she understood.

A loud clank jarred her out of a stupor of silence. The door opened, then closed, too quickly for her to rise from where she was leaning against the room's back wall.

A man entered. He was a short man, with short greased hair, a day's worth of stubble, and large black sunglasses that covered most of his face. The same man from the car, Josie thought. Or was he? He was wearing black pants and a black T-shirt with white English lettering on it. As he approached, the words printed on his shirt became clear: "Jon's Bar Mitzvah, April 28, 2007." Josie almost laughed. The man saw her smile, and to her surprise, smiled back, raising his thin eyebrows. For an instant it was as if they were friends.

"You had good dreams?" he asked.

His accent was dense, almost parodic. He was holding something long and dark behind his back, a stick of some sort. He squatted down, his face level with hers as she sat on the floor.

Josie was trembling again, her lips shaking hard. But now she sucked in her breath. Suddenly she knew that her only resources were her words and her brain. As always. All of life was like a game of chess. You just had to be the smartest person in the room. And for Josephine Ashkenazi, how hard was that?

"How much do they want for me?" Josie asked, controlling the quaver in her voice. "What are they asking for?" It was a knight's move, an indirect probe, one of the only moves available to her just then. The "they" was to belittle him, but also to find out who was involved. She needed to know one thing: was this some sort of fundamentalist insanity, or were these people just in it for the money? If it were merely money, she sensed, there was a possibility of remaining alive.

"Twenty million dollars," he said, with a proud smile.

Josie breathed out. Here, in the end, was the ask she had been expecting. If only the businessmen at the Four Seasons Hotel had been so blunt. "They could have at least been realistic," she said. She felt a flutter of pride, emboldened by her ability to respond without shaking. "Is this negotiable?"

The slap to her cheek astounded her, but not as much as the raised truncheon held before her eyes. As the black metal hovered beside her temple, her mind slipped into chess mode: she had just lost a knight, but other pieces remained in play. Surely she was worth more to them unharmed, wasn't she? She pushed away every human thought and held her breath.

"You are a very pretty girl," the man said, and smiled.

The smile horrified her much more than the truncheon, which was now resting on her damp cheek. She swallowed, trying very hard not to tremble. No one had called her a girl since she had given birth to her own. She already knew that he couldn't see her cry, that that would be the end: checkmate.

"A pretty girl. And a smart girl. We are making a movie of you, and we want you to be very pretty in our movie. No marks on your face." He tapped her cheek with the truncheon, then gave it a light smack. Her hand flew to her face, but by then the metal club had suddenly flipped downward, cracking against her shin. She crumpled, doubled over on the floor. "Your leg is not in this movie," the man said as she groaned. "Just your face."

From the floor she saw the man looming above her, the irrational words "Jon's Bar Mitzvah" wavering on the periphery of her vision. In her delirium she imagined Jon's bar mitzvah, Jon himself a prepubescent pimpled boy in an ill-fitting suit beneath an enormous prayer shawl, his voice cracking over an ancient scroll as the man in the sunglasses stood beside him, one hand on his shoulder, controlling, guiding, proud.

When Josie stopped groaning—was it five minutes later? five hours? five days?—the man was holding up a cell phone, its screen in front of his sunglasses.

"Read this," he said.

She thought he meant the phone, but then he threw a ball of paper at her, still suspending the phone in the air as the paper landed behind her.

Josie made a point of standing up to get the piece of paper

instead of crawling across the room. Her leg howled. She unwrinkled the page and scanned the handwritten words, printed with a ballpoint pen in curled block letters that looked almost Russian. She sank back to the floor, gulping at the air until she could speak without moaning.

"This doesn't even make sense," she finally said.

The man held up the truncheon. "Your other leg is also not in this movie. Read."

He meant read aloud, she understood. She balanced herself as she knelt, the humiliation total. If he had told her to lick the floor she would have done it. The paper shook in her hands. "Hello, I am Ashkenazi and I am held against a will," she read aloud. These people were amateurs, she thought. That probably made things worse. She tried to smile at the camera, imagining Itamar and Tali behind it, until the man raised the truncheon again. "I dream to come back to you," she recited. "I have the human condition. Please make a wish to put me in a safe."

The man fiddled with the phone before leaving the room. An instant later the door opened again, and someone's arm reached in to deposit a plate full of pita bread and a large plastic pitcher of water in the room before slamming the door shut. Before Josie could haul herself up, she heard the clanking sound of locks. Alone, Josie pulled up her skirt and examined her leg. Below the knee it was swollen, bright red and purple. She crawled to the water and the bread. She had the presence of mind to pour some water on her hands before eating the bread, avoiding drinking. Instead she chewed on the sawdust pita and stared at the slab of stone, trying to find clues as to where she might be.

The stone was too high to be a bench, and too low to be a table. She tried sitting on it, but found it too painful for her injured leg to dangle several inches from the floor. As she eased herself off, she looked at it more closely, running her fingers across the carved Arabic lettering on its surface. In many places the letters had been worn away. One end of it protruded slightly higher than the rest, as if the slab had once been a bed with a headboard. As she inched herself toward the stone's raised end, she saw that it really had been a headboard once; a jagged edge marked where some large part of it had been broken off. Not a headboard: a headstone. She stepped back as she realized that the stone was a sarcophagus.

It was the City of the Dead, she understood now. This must be one of the thousands of half-abandoned tombs, the ones built in the Middle Ages with rooms for visiting mourners to sleep with their dead relatives—rooms now occupied by the living. She remembered it from online guides she had read before coming to Egypt. Was there a necropolis like that in Alexandria too? Josie didn't think so, though she couldn't be sure. More likely she was back in Cairo, in the enormous cemetery that had become an endless slum for squatters, so engorged with the destitute and the criminal that no stranger who entered could find his way out. No one would ever find her.

As the air in the room began choking her, she at last surrendered to the mute wail of the jug of water her captors had placed beside the sarcophagus. There was no cup. She poured the water directly down her throat. It wasn't long before she began vomiting.

The next hours and days passed as though she were crawling through a dark tunnel of dirt and filth. She burrowed deep into the ground, filling the plastic bucket again and again as she draped herself across the stone floor, twisted in delirium. If the man came in to empty the bucket, he did so only when she was asleep. Sleeping and waking blended together into one long night, her body a tight clay jar containing the dark thick agony of her gut. When she dreamed she dreamed of snow, long winter mornings, waking up to hear that school had been canceled, the world dipped in white, receding into cloud. Awake, she imagined moaning into her lost phone to Itamar, to Judith, to her demented mother, to Tali. *If you were having a gastrointestinal crisis, then I might care,* she heard Itamar laughing. *I have the human condition,* she begged him. *Please put me in a safe.* As she woke from a dream that was nothing more than snow, she found herself lying beside the sarcophagus, her sweat- and vomit-drenched body pressed against the stone house of the dead. She turned her head to see a new figure standing above her in the room.

It was a woman, wearing a black sheath that covered her entire body but her eyes, like the Saudi wives she had seen on the Nile waterfront in Cairo walking several paces behind their husbands. The woman's eyes, like the man's, were hidden behind opaque sunglasses. She was holding a large white plastic bag.

The woman took a dark pile of clothing out of the bag. "Take off your clothes, and put these on," the woman said. Her English was much better than the man's. She placed the clothing on the floor, a shapeless brown shirt and shapeless brown pants.

Josie remained curled against the sarcophagus, too weak and too terrified to move.

"It is only because your own clothes are covered with filth," the woman said. "I will stay with you until you change."

So she wouldn't be raped after all, Josie thought, astounded. She clung to the thought like a piece of driftwood in a shipwreck, its truth irrelevant. *They can't possibly hurt me if this woman is here.* She was still too weak to stand up alone. She allowed the woman to ease her out of her blouse and skirt, sliding on the baggy pants and a shirt that was more robe than shirt, reaching to her knees. A uniform. She was a prisoner now, stripped. The woman put Josie's stained clothing in the white plastic bag.

"Drink this water," the woman said, holding out a plastic bottle. "And take this pill. It will help your stomach."

The woman was sitting on the floor beside her. Josie tried to twist the cap off the bottle, but she couldn't, plastic sliding in her weakened hands. The woman took it back from her, snapping the cap off effortlessly and holding it up to Josie's mouth. Josie sucked the liquid like a baby, opening her mouth obediently as the woman placed a tablet on her tongue, a coin for the underworld. She glanced down at the woman's feet and noticed her shoes, black ballet slippers.

"Nasreen?"

The woman leaned back, or Josie imagined that she did. Had the woman's voice sounded like Nasreen's? Only slightly, but perhaps slightly was enough. Josie looked back at where the black sheath rose around the woman's nose, then looked again at the shoe. It was an extremely common type of shoe, she admitted to herself, surely irrelevant. But it couldn't be irrelevant, she thought desperately. If it were irrelevant, then everything was irrelevant, being alive was irrelevant. Josie squinted, searching for features beneath the veil, behind the plastic sunglass lenses. She could see nothing, but that hardly mattered.

"Nasreen! You have to help me!" Josie wailed. She gagged, choking on water and remnants of vomit in her throat. The woman turned from her acrid breath. "Are we in the City of the Dead?"

The woman said nothing.

"It's the City of the Dead. It has to be," Josie cried, and

pressed a hand against the sarcophagus. "There's a dead person in this room with me." She barely knew what it meant anymore. She swallowed acid.

"You do not know where you are," the woman said. "You do not even know if it is day or night. Finish the water."

If this woman was Nasreen, Josie reasoned, it must be nighttime. Otherwise she would be at the library, wouldn't she? *Nighttime is our only chance to really be alive.*

"Nasreen, you—you—but I don't understand it. We were eating ice cream together."

"Finish the water," the woman repeated.

Josie saw what was happening. Strategy was necessary. She tried another move, a desperate one. "Nasreen, I know that there is nothing more important to you than the will of God. You can't possibly—"

Now the woman answered. "You know nothing about the will of God," she said.

"Why would you help that man?"

The woman leaned toward Josie, and Josie could feel the expression on the woman's face, through the sheath of black cloth. The woman's presence made Josie shrink, until she was very, very small, cowering in the corner of the small stone room. "Because he is my husband," she said.

"But—but your husband is dead," Josie ventured. A dare. She felt a wave of strength as cold water flooded her gut.

The woman laughed. "In my dreams."

Josie gagged. Was it just an expression, or did the woman mean it literally? To Josie at that moment it didn't matter. "Nasreen, please, you have to save me. Nasreen, I have a daughter at home. You saw her picture. Please, don't let them kill me. Nasreen, please, you have to tell them—"

The woman bent toward her again. Then she lowered her

face to Josie's, crouching on the floor beside her. "Do not be ridiculous. No one is going to kill you. Your company is going to pay the ransom, and everything will be over."

Josie looked down at her new brown shirt. "The company can't pay twenty million dollars for me," she said softly.

"Why not?" the woman intoned.

"We—we—I know there's a lot of hype, but we're not profitable yet. We don't have twenty million to pay—not in liquid, not in anything. It would take ages to pull that together, if it could be done at all. Is this—is this negotiable?" As she said it, she felt the slap against her face again.

The woman clicked her tongue, a sound that rattled against the walls of the room. "You are supposed to be smart, but you must be very stupid," she said. Josie listened to the voice, the tone, the dismissive snap, and was sure it was Nasreen. But her own mind was unreliable now, a wasteland. "The money comes from insurance," the woman was saying. "They only take foreigners from overseas companies, because they know the insurance will pay."

The woman hadn't touched her, but the words were a blow to Josie's gut. She was remembering Itamar sitting with her in her bare apartment, the size of this room—the bed a couch, the table a desk, the window a square of shadowed concrete overlooking a parking lot—right after she incorporated the company, working through strategies, still dizzy from sudden success. "'Comprehensive K & R coverage,'" she had read aloud to him from an insurance company's brochure, laughing. "That's kidnap and ransom insurance, of course. I love how there's even an abbreviation for it."

But Itamar's face had turned pale. "Don't buy it, Yosefi," he had told her, his voice in English carefully controlled. "That's what makes it possible. Did you know that Lufthansa used to pay the PLO not to hijack their planes?" His earnestness surprised her; the *did you know* sounding strangely teenaged even through his accent, reeking of a weird and shameful urgency. This was before she met his father, before she heard how he had been taken prisoner in 1973 in Egypt, in the war Egypt hadn't won.

Josie looked at the floor, at the streaked vomit at her feet, and breathed in filth. "There's no insurance," she heard herself say. Aloud.

In that terrible instant she understood what she had done. A mistake, a catastrophic mistake, a mistake that dwarfed the correctable error of not getting out of the car: a mistake so enormous that it swallowed her alive. She had put herself in check. Her nausea returned, a thick wool blanket stuffed into her mouth. The sarcophagus slid into her line of vision, bearing her own body to the underworld. She would die in this room.

The woman paused, a black statue. Then, very quickly, she stood. "Goodbye, Miss Ashkenazi," she said.

Josie tried to rise from the floor, but she was still too weak. Instead she rose only to her knees. She fell on her hands and began groveling, begging like the blind.

"Don't tell him, Nasreen. Please, please don't tell him." Was it Nasreen? Or was she delusional? "You can't tell him. Nasreen, please—"

"Goodbye," the woman repeated.

Josie tried again to stand as the woman opened the door, but even sitting up was a struggle. As the woman walked away, she turned in the doorway, pure darkness behind her. She reached into the white plastic sack and pulled something out, which she cast on the ground.

"This was in your bag," the woman said. And then she closed the door.

Alone, Josie crawled across the floor to retrieve it. It was a crumbling book, otherworldly, like something from a half-forgotten life. It smelled of vomit from her clothes. On its cover were words in French, *Le Guide des Égarés*. She flipped it to the other side, reading the Hebrew letters: *Moreh Nevukhim. Guide for the Perplexed*. She lay down, prone on the floor. She pulled herself to the bucket in the corner, and vomited again before collapsing into dream.

When she woke, the man in the bar mitzvah shirt had returned to the room. She tried to pull herself up, managing to struggle to her knees.

"Something very bad has happened," the man said. "Very, very bad." He slid the truncheon casually along the surface of the stone coffin. "But you can make it better again."

Now Josie was shaking again, not from the illness but from fear. She saw the sheathed woman standing behind him, a dark shadow beside the closed door.

"You are going to be in another movie," the man announced. "But in this movie, you are going to be very, very ugly." He pointed the truncheon at her, and then held up his cell phone in his other hand.

"We have decided that we do not want your money. What we want is you."

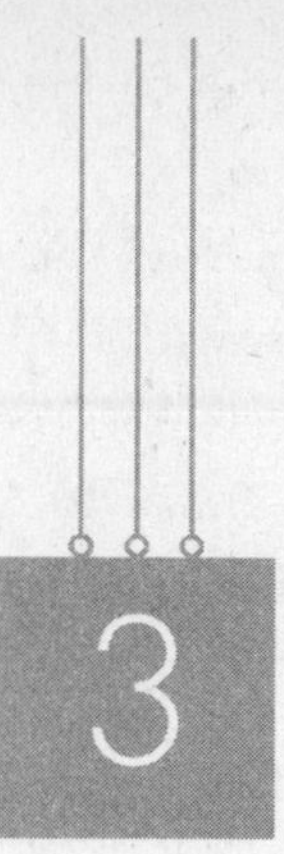

JUDITH HAD COME TO treasure the feeling of opening the door of Josie's house—which she now simply thought of as *the house*, the way she once thought of the apartment where she and Josie had grown up: not quite hers, technically, but nonetheless, if you had to describe it, home. *The house*. It was a feeling of peace.

It happened slowly. The software might have tracked it, the program constantly running in the background, beeping to alert her to dangerously high levels of smugness. But the first thing Judith did when she came to the house was to shut down the software. For the present, there would be no past.

The seven days of mourning had ended almost four weeks earlier, but Itamar still had barely gone back to work. In the first two weeks, predatory camera crews made it impossible for him to leave the house, and once a reporter somehow got hold of his cell phone number, he couldn't answer his phone either. The kidnappers' first video, eighteen precious seconds of Josie in her own clothing reading from a crumpled page, had been sent to Itamar. Despite the kidnappers' warnings, he had contacted the CIA. He had even called a friend of his father's who had retired from the Mossad. He was convinced that this was the mistake that led to the silent and somewhat blurry video that went viral on the internet four days later, in which his wife was hanged from a ceiling pipe in an otherwise featureless room.

He wallowed in the details: how her arms and legs were bound with packing tape over strange brown clothes that weren't hers (he could not stop imagining her stripping off her own clothes; he could not stop his nausea when he imagined who else might have stripped her), the dark brown pipe where they had tied the rope (was it clay, or rusted metal?), the shadows against the mottled brown walls (was there some kind of stone bench in the room, or maybe a countertop? from some angles it seemed so), and most of all, the single lucid close-up image of her face before the black plastic bag was pulled over her head. He would pause the video there, though the pause would make her face distort slightly. Her right cheek was colored by an enormous purple bruise, and dark blood crusted on her upper lip. Her long black hair was wet (was it water, or sweat, or something else? sweat, he decided on the tenth viewing), and pasted in clumps across her forehead. But what horrified him were her eyes. Her eyes had always entranced him, because unlike the eyes of nearly everyone he had known in his life, hers never seemed to be serious. She would tell him about a program virus, or about a company loss, or about her father's abandonment, or about her mother's decline into premature dementia, but regardless of how solemn she was or tried to be, her eyes invariably gleamed as though anticipating the punchline of a hilarious joke. When he first met her he found it unnerving. "Can't you be serious about anything?" he would demand. "I *am* serious," she would insist. "*Deadly* serious!" And there it was in her eyes: the joke. Later he understood that she was sincere. She simply saw everything as though it were happening in a room she hadn't entered; for her, even personal catastrophes were merely opportunities, challenging puzzles to solve. Soon he himself became one of her happy puzzles, eager for the vindication in her open eyes as they made love: the punchline, the solution. In the video, the lighting in the room made the pupils of her eyes into two dark round mirrors, showing twin miniature silhouettes of the cell phone camera recording her. She was sexless, lifeless, already dead. He wished he could unsee it, wished unseeing were possible. While attempting to unsee it, he watched it four thousand times.

For Judith, once was enough. It was she who told him to stop watching, and to change his phone number. She was astounded to discover that he listened to her. And then Judith understood what she could do.

SHE SAW IT FIRST during the shiva, the rather arbitrary seven days of mourning which took place not after any funeral, but after various news outlets had acknowledged the execution video and announced to the world that Josephine Ashkenazi, software genius and female digital business pioneer ("the first woman . . ." they always said, as though she were Eve), was officially dead. Judith had known very little, before then, about Itamar; she hadn't known that he and Josie had lived out parallel childhoods on opposite sides of the world, that they were so oddly, extraordinarily the same.

"Itamar, he is a chess winner," Itamar's father told Judith during those seven days, in his stilted English. "In the city of Be'er Sheva, Itamar is champion!"

"Was," Itamar muttered. He was slouched on an armchair

whose cushions had been removed, his feet in sweat socks. "In 1995. Who cares?" Judith noticed how he winced.

"1995!" his father bellowed. His father's accent was heavy, endearing, with a refreshing disregard for the past tense. Judith had begun to like him. "In Be'er Sheva, half the people are already from Russia in 1995. To beat Soviet people in chess is only for a genius!"

"Josie used to win chess championships too," Judith said, hoping to smooth the cringe from Itamar's face. "She was only eight the first time she won." For the first time, she was amazed to discover, she felt proud of her sister—as though her sister's death had freed her to regard her without envy. It was unexpected, liberating.

"In high school, before the army even, Itamar uncovered a blood glue," Itamar's father proclaimed, with proud irrelevance. "He has patents, only seventeen years old!"

"'Discovered,' not 'uncovered,'" Itamar muttered.

"What's 'blood glue'?" Judith asked.

Itamar's father laughed. "Glue made of blood!"

Judith wished she knew Hebrew; it occurred to her that if she did, she would have liked this man even more. "Huh?"

"He means a biocoagulant," Itamar sighed. "For sutures. It was just an improvement on an existing product. It really wasn't such a big deal."

Judith sat back in her seat. After years of studied boredom at Josie's many discoveries, she was awash with a beautiful feeling: genuine awe, astonishment at the sheer power that trembled in certain human minds.

"I never think Itamar can find another genius," his father continued. "I always think for a woman to be a genius like him is impossible. I don't even believe she is a woman when I meet her. I say, 'Itamar, you idiot, you bring home a man wearing a dress!'"

"Abba, maspik," Itamar pleaded. His voice was weak, tired.

"I know the Egyptians will kill her," his father said. "Only a pharaoh can stop them from killing her. They want to kill me in '73, but they still have Sadat then. With their pharaoh, they cannot kill people except with special arrangements. But now they have no more pharaoh, so how can they not kill her?"

"Abba, maspik," Itamar snapped. Even Judith understood him: *Enough.*

Later, after his father had fallen asleep elsewhere in the house, Itamar spoke to Judith as if speaking through her—rambling blindly, his voice spilling like water over the edge of a cliff.

"When she first came to our office I thought she was Israeli," he said. It was dark by then, the horrifying early darkness of a late autumn afternoon. The other visitors had already left; Tali had been sequestered with a babysitter in her bedroom, coloring. In the living room Itamar and Judith were alone, remembering Judith's sister.

"She shook my hand and told me her name was Josephine," Itamar recalled, "and then she immediately demanded to see what we could do, how our programs worked, why they were better than hers. I thought it had to be a nickname, that her real name must have been Yosefa or Yaara or Yael, because there was no way any American could speak Hebrew like that, or dress like that, or act like that, like a platoon commander." Judith marveled: everything she had loathed about her sister was exactly what had made her sister's husband fall in love.

Their first date, he told Judith, was at the ruins of Caesarea, the archeological site north of Tel Aviv, where ancient rabbis had been tortured and executed by the Romans nineteen centuries earlier in a giant stone stadium on the beach. He had been there on school trips; it had not occurred to him that it could be romantic. He had laughed when she suggested it. When they stood in the middle of the ruins of the hippodrome, he made a joke of it, intoning lines from the story's traditional retelling in his fifth-grade teacher's imperious voice: "'The Romans tried the rabbis for their ancestors' crime of selling Joseph into Egypt, and sentenced them all to death. They wrapped Rabbi Hananya ben Tradyon in a Torah scroll and burned him alive. As the scroll burned around him, Rabbi Hananya called out, 'The parchment is burning, but the letters are flying free!'

"We all had to repeat that part," he had said to Josie, as they stood in the cool breeze from the water. "'The letters are flying free.' I hated that! I just thought, the guy died, it was terrible, so why are we repeating it again and again? Why can't we just let him be dead?" And then Josie had surprised him.

"Because the letters are still here, in the air," she said.

At first he thought he hadn't understood her, or that she hadn't understood him, that perhaps her Hebrew wasn't as good as he'd assumed. But then she told him: "Everything that happened here still exists—what happened with the rabbis, what happened with your fifth-grade class, what happened this morning. All of it is still here. If it were made of stone, we could dig up the remains, like the hippodrome. Just because it isn't made of stone doesn't mean it isn't still here."

He laughed. "I didn't know you were a poet."

She smiled, then answered in English. "It isn't poetry, it's physics. There is such a thing as time dilation. My mother wrote half a dissertation about it. We don't have the maps or tools to access it, but that doesn't mean the past doesn't still exist."

He laughed again, still unsure of whether she was joking. "So draw me a map," he said.

He was being sarcastic. He was shaken when she squatted down, her white skirt billowing around her like an ancient woman giving birth. She took a coin and began using it to trace curves in the sand. "I'm talking about a traversable wormhole," she said. "Or actually multiple traversable wormholes in configuration. It's called a Roman Ring." (Later that night, he dug out his English dictionary and looked up the words, perplexed, awestruck.) She drew various shapes, interlocking ovoids and spirals, erasing and re-erasing, mumbling under her breath, unable to get it right. He watched the intensity of her face, the otherworldly beauty of her black hair and white skirt inside the enormous Roman ring. He shuddered when she looked up at him, daring him to join her, to step into a hole in time.

"Nothing ever really disappears," she said, "even when you want it to."

A rush of wind thrummed off the waves, blowing her diagrams to dust as both of them laughed. Underneath the aqueduct, she kissed him.

Judith listened to all this and was surprised to find herself weeping. These were all the things she had hated—Josie's arrogance, Josie's certainty, Josie's conviction that the laws of the universe did not apply to her—all the things she had hated for decades, the things she had built her life around hating. But now she saw what it was like to be someone who didn't hate this demanding, insistent, driven woman—someone who instead knew who she was. It occurred to her that she had never known her sister, that she never could have. The gates of her own perception had been locked against it.

"There were so many days when everything was so perfect, I just wanted to put those days in bottles and store them in the basement, like wines," he said. "At the arboretum last spring there were thirty-five thousand daffodils in bloom. We were walking with Tali there before Passover, rolling her around in the flowers and watching them bounce back up around her. I remember thinking, this can't be right, it can't be possible to be this happy, something has to change. It's almost like I expected this."

It had never seemed right to Judith either—Josie's stunning brilliance, her joy after joy, her wealth, her fame, her handsome husband, her beautiful little girl, while Judith wallowed in mediocrity, losing one job or boyfriend after another, perpetually aimless, perpetually alone. But now that it was gone, it all seemed wonderfully right, all of it deserved. And she was ashamed.

"How can I ever show Tali what her mother is like?" Itamar asked. "She's only six. She'll never know."

Judith considered it. Should she say something comforting, or something true? She thought of Josie's great discovery, her gift to the world, her gift to her child. "It's all in the software," Judith told him. "You can look up any of it forever."

Itamar slowly, slowly shook his head. "The strange thing is," he said, "I don't want to."

Later that night, after the evening visitors had come and gone, Judith was getting ready to leave and wandered around the house, looking for Itamar. She almost gave up when she thought to look in Tali's room. There she found him, huddled with his little girl in her bed.

Judith stood still in the doorway, watching both of them sleep. Tali's dark hair was spread around the pillow like an inkspill as her father's arms encircled her shoulders. One of her little hands clutched his, and held it to her lips. The air trembled in the darkness with the duet of their breaths. In the doorway,

Judith remembered something she had long forgotten: how one night after her father left, long ago, she had lain in bed crying silently, wishing for endless sleep, wishing for oblivion, wishing sixty years would pass in the blink of an eye, wishing she were an old, old woman for whom all of this was a dead and buried memory. In the darkness of that long black night, she was startled out of the abyss by a hand on her shoulder, mooring her to the edge of a cliff. Her little sister had climbed into her bed and held her, wrapped her arms around her, took her older sister's hand in hers and rested it gently against her lips. Judith looked now at her sister's little girl. What she thought was gone, destroyed and regretted forever, now lay stunningly alive before her, breathing beauty held tight in this man's arms. Josie had always had grand ambitions, plans to change the world, vast and complicated dreams. But what Judith wanted was so simple, and now she knew where to find it.

ONE COLD NIGHT, JUDITH came to the house claiming she needed to look through her mother's insurance records—something she had done many times during those weeks since Josie's death, as the house sank into winter darkness. When Itamar opened the door for her, his tall thin body stood framed like a portrait in the glowing light of the hallway behind him. He pressed his back against the open door, effacing himself as the light and warmth of the house spilled before her. She reached to hug him, the casually meaningless clutch-and-kiss of in-laws, but then she saw that his head was pressed into his shoulder, with his phone tucked against his jaw. She was a minor character in his life, she knew, an inconvenience. "But you don't have to look at it that way," he said to someone who wasn't her. "The whole situation could change in a matter of weeks." She hung up her coat and made herself at home.

Snow had begun falling outside when she emerged from the basement filing cabinets and sat down on the L-shaped couch in her dead sister's living room. She had long felt uncomfortable in this room: she remembered sitting on this same couch many times as Josie and Itamar cuddled each other across from her, smiling at her, flaunting an almost vulgar happiness. But now the slight draft in the room was refreshing, an airing of bones. Judith contemplated the stacks of detritus on the coffee table: catalogues and magazines that no one had bothered to throw away, along with piles of first-grade papers, words beginning with the letter A repeated endlessly in red crayon.

"Sorry, I couldn't hang up," Itamar said as he finally entered the room. "Idiot client. This person actually thought that 'cloud computing' meant that his data is stored in the air above his head. Like I'm God, managing the storehouses of snow. He asks me, 'But isn't it in some kind of radio wave or satellite feed?' No one knows how the world works anymore. It really isn't that hard to understand. People just don't bother to find out."

His arrogance was familiar: Josie's old pride. But from a man it was intriguing, sexy. Itamar sat down without looking at her, skidding a finger across the screen of his phone. He was still wearing his wedding ring, she noticed. She wondered how much time would have to pass before he would remove it.

"It must be hard getting back to work, with everyone relying on you," she said when Itamar slid his phone into his pocket. This was her ploy, of course: empathetic flattery. But perhaps Itamar would not notice. He noticed little. Even now he was glancing around the room, searching for someone more worthy of his attention, itching to retrieve his phone from his pocket again. He patted the rectangular tumor on his thigh. In her mind Judith saw a door closing, and shifted her foot to prop it open. "What are you going to do about Tali?" she asked. "You aren't going to have time for her."

"You're wrong about that," Itamar said. An electronic bell tolled in the next room. He rose as if summoned. Judith assumed some company gadget had lured him away, but to her surprise he returned quickly with two mugs of tea, handing one carefully to her. She preserved the image in her mind of him hovering gently above her, his thin gray sweater covering his tall frame, his dark-haired hands passing her a hot mug with a delicacy bordering on love. "I haven't told anyone yet," he said, "but I'm thinking of selling the company, so I can just be with Tali."

Judith had raised the mug to her lips, but now she put it down on the table at her knee. She forced a laugh. "You can't be serious."

Itamar didn't smile. "I could use the life insurance payout, but it makes more sense to sell, especially now," he said. He seated himself, talking to himself.

"Sell the company," Judith repeated.

"Yes, to be with Tali," he said. "I should probably take her to Israel. My father would like me to. There isn't much reason for us to stay here anymore."

She detected something officious in his voice. He was testing her. He drank, eyeing her, and put the mug down on the crayoned pages, planting his hands on his knees. "It's the right thing to do," he said weakly. Inside the words was a question mark, intended for her alone. In that moment, in his pleading face, Judith sensed her own untapped power.

"Josie would kill you if you sold her company," she announced. "She would return from the other world and strangle you in your sleep."

It was bold, but it worked—far better than she expected. Josie's name was like an electric shock. Itamar shuddered, stricken. Then he covered his face with his hands. He looked beautiful that way, vulnerable. And such beautiful hands.

She admired his hands, and the top of his dark-haired head against the pane of the window behind him. Snow turned her own reflection into a grainy film, a clip from a documentary: the present moment after it became the past, trapped within this room. At last he raised his head. "I know that, Judith. Do you want to make me sick about it?"

"No, I want to help you," she said. She put out a hand, a dare. She knew he wouldn't take it, but the possibility fluttered between them, a breath in her open palm. "You need to go back to work and start running the company, the way she ran it." She avoided Josie's name this time, yet still she saw him cringe. "What I can do is take over at home."

He squinted at her. He used to wear contact lenses, but he hadn't bothered with them in weeks. His glasses were wire-rimmed, high style from ten years earlier. Judith had never seen him wearing glasses before Josie's death. The lenses were intimate, the way they enlarged his brown eyes, softening them. It occurred to her that Josie had seen him this way every day, before bed perhaps, or early in the morning, or in the middle of the night, whenever their little girl was hungry or sick or had woken from a bad dream—all the endless, ordinary, unrecorded hours when the two of them, roused from the dead of night, formed a miraculous presence that became a life. "What do you mean?" he asked.

"My department doesn't need me in the office all day long," she said. "Josie was just doing me a favor by giving me this job. You of all people know that." She watched as Itamar winced again at Josie's name. There was something pleasant about his flinching, Judith noticed, a warmth in seeing him crumple. It flowed through her like a wave of hot water in a bath. "I could come here to be with Tali after school. It wouldn't be a big deal." She shrugged, as if this were an afterthought, rather than the creation of a world.

"Ridiculous," Itamar snapped. He was working hard to keep his voice level; the result was a low sneer. "We always took turns coming home in the evening to be with her, but it isn't like we don't have help," he said. The "we" still sounded natural to him, it seemed, or rather he needed it to. Oh, what he needed, Judith thought. "You know that Tali has a babysitter," Itamar said. "Tali loves Joy."

"Yes, Tali loves Joy, because Joy lets her watch cartoons all afternoon. That isn't what she needs."

Itamar's voice tightened. "How do you know what she needs? I'm her father. You've never even had a child."

This hurt her, the way Josie's name hurt him. She thought of defending herself, but she knew she would lose. Instead she flattered, sympathized, groveled. "It's just that I know how much Josie loved you both," she said. The name lingered in the lighted room. "And I know that Tali needs as many people to love her as possible."

It almost worked. Itamar rubbed at his knees, humbled, until he thought of a reply. "But you don't know Tali."

"Of course I do," Judith said. Judith had spent much of the seven days of mourning with Tali, playing a game that Tali had invented—something involving estimating the number of jelly beans that could fit inside a doll's decapitated head, filling the head with the beans, and then reattaching the head and concealing the doll in an enormous pile of dead leaves outside the house, for elaborate reasons concerning explosives and elves. Judith had dug the doll out just before it rained.

"You don't know how she is when she's just with us," Itamar insisted. "Tali is—she's not a typical six-year-old. You really don't know." 

Snow danced in the windowpane behind Itamar's head. A door opened in Judith's memory: she and Josie hiding under the covers of her bed while a snowstorm raged outside, six-year-old Josie laughing maniacally as Judith shined a flashlight through the sheets. Then Josie had opened the window to test the storm's wind velocity, and had drenched Judith's sheets in snow and ice. Josie had found this very funny, as she returned to her own dry bed. Yes, Judith really knew. And she knew what she wanted.

"It was different when there were two of you," she said. He was lovely, she thought. There was an almost erotic tilt to his neck as he hunched his elbows on his knees. She wished she could run her hand along that neck, slip her fingers beneath the warm wool of his sweater, feel for the hardness of bone. "One of you always went home to be with her in the evenings, even when the other was overwhelmed. But you're always going to be overwhelmed now, Itamar, unless you do something about it."

A vein in his neck bulged. "You're telling me to fire Joy and hire you to empty my dishwasher, now that my wife is dead."

"No, I'm telling you to keep the babysitter, let her do more of the housework, and have me come to help."

"Help with what?"

"With life, Itamar. With showing a little girl how to be alive. The way her mother would have done it." Or should have done it, Judith thought. Judith was no longer ashamed of cruel thoughts.

Itamar was looking at his hands now. His beautiful hands.

The air shivered between them before he spoke. "Last night before Tali went to bed, I let her watch TV while I used the phone," he said. His accent was heavier than it usually was. He and Josie had mostly spoken to each other in Hebrew, Judith knew, or perhaps that was only when someone else was listening. Judith barely remembered the little Hebrew she had been taught; Josie, of course, had mainly taught herself. "When I finished my phone call, I found Tali sitting on the floor, with a cracked egg on the rug in front of her," Itamar said. "She was acting like a baby, playing with food. I yelled at her, and she said she was sorry. But when I took her up to bed, I saw that there was another cracked egg on the stairs. I said, 'Taluli, did you crack that egg too?' Then she told me that in school they had been learning about healthy foods, and that everyone was telling her that we need to be strong, so she wanted to be sure we had enough protein. She said it in Hebrew: *helbon*. I don't even know how she knew that word. From my father, maybe? I don't know. But in Hebrew it's also the word for something inside an egg—the clear part, not the yellow. I can't remember the English word."

Itamar was always exacting, Judith thought—demanding, flawless, like his wife. Without her he was slipping. "Eggwhite," Judith assisted.

Itamar squinted at her, skeptical. "Eggwhite?"

There was a more scientific term, but she couldn't remember what it was. Josie would have remembered in an instant. Judith shrugged. "That's what it's called," she said.

Itamar sighed, and continued. "Tali had taken out all twelve eggs, all of them. A full box of eggs."

"Carton," Judith corrected, though it was unlike her to correct him. Josie would have corrected him.

Itamar nodded. He liked being corrected, Judith noted. "A full carton of eggs. She had cracked a different egg in each room of the house."

Judith imagined the little girl, her black hair just like her mother's, rubbing eggwhite into the carpet. The thought thrilled her. Tali, she sensed, had what her mother had never had: a thirst for vengeance.

"What did you do?" Judith asked.

Itamar sucked in his breath. "I hit her." He looked at the floor. "Not hard. Well, a little hard. She has a—a bruise."

A *bruise*? Judith thought, astounded to find herself suddenly sickened. She had to stop herself from repeating it aloud. Instead she looked at Itamar's arms, which bristled with dark hair at the edges of his sweater's woolen sleeves. He was like a wounded animal, caught in a merciless trap.

He buried his face in his hands. "I can't do this," he said. "I can't believe I hit my daughter. My own daughter. I don't—I don't know what I was thinking. If I was thinking. I wasn't thinking. There was no thinking." His whole body heaved as he breathed. "I can't do this."

"Itamar, all I want is to help you," Judith said softly. At that moment she believed it was true.

He raised his head. His mouth was hanging open, a silent howl. She thought he wouldn't respond. When he spoke, his voice was small and still.

"Joy told me she can't come tomorrow," he said. "She has a family emergency."

Judith snorted as Itamar clicked his tongue, the Hebrew

equivalent of a snort. Their transatlantic disgust met in the air between them, snapping like static. For the first time in weeks, both of them laughed.

"Can you—can you take Tali home from school tomorrow afternoon?" he asked.

"With pleasure," Judith said. She meant it.

TALI WAS AS BEAUTIFUL as she was strange, an alien girl dropped from the far reaches of outer space onto a new and terrifying planet. People would claim that this was because she had lost her mother, the poor thing: her mother's newsworthy demise had earned her a permanent pass on life. But the truth was that she had been strange long before Josie left for Egypt. Tali didn't have friends in school, but this did not seem to bother her. Her world was populated by a series of imaginary friends whose presence in her life was vivid enough that her parents at first thought they were her real classmates, even though she had given them names like Svorgolet and Blangey. For weeks her parents believed that these were the names of Indian children in their daughter's class. Nor was Tali's oddity confined to imaginary friends. Each day brought a different madness. Once for an entire month she declared that she was a gavial—a thin-snouted South Asian crocodilian, as she pedantically explained—and attempted to bite anyone who dared to suggest that she was actually a girl. She dressed her toy dinosaurs in sexy Barbie clothes. Of course, she dressed herself exclusively in orange. She sniffed markers, imagining that they smelled like their colors even when they didn't, and walked around all day with her nostrils dyed dark green and blue. All of this had been adorable and endearing in preschool and even in kindergarten, but none of it was even slightly acceptable in first grade. At the urging of the kindergarten teacher she had once been examined by a neurologist, who tested her for various disorders before deciding that Tali was simply weird. What was perhaps even stranger was that despite her parents' illustrious careers, Tali did not seem to be particularly smart. She could not read more than a few short words, could not write more than her name, could not retell a story she had just been told, could not count past thirty-nine, confused cause and effect. Worst of all, she seemed completely uninterested in listening to anything the teacher said at school, or in learning anything new. School testing revealed no developmental delays; it was concluded that Tali was simply not very bright—or, at best, perhaps her lack of engagement was due entirely to her own choice. Her parents pretended these things did not matter to them, but they did. The first-grade teacher hated her. It was not surprising that Joy preferred to park her in front of the TV.

Judith arrived early at the school to meet Tali, asking parents and babysitters where the first-graders would be dismissed. At the appropriate door, women gathered in clumps, staring into their phones, stamping their feet against the cold. Since moving back to Massachusetts to be closer to her demented mother—a move she resented so deeply that she had rejoiced when Josie moved her fledgling company to Cambridge for the same reason—Judith had viewed these half-working mothers with a deep, delicious envy, which she disguised as contempt. But now Judith qualified as one of them, at least for the afternoon. She moved closer to two women who weren't looking at their phones, hoping to insert herself into their conversation. She knew how to insert herself, she thought.

"At first I had no idea what he had in his mouth," the woman in high-heeled boots was saying. "Later when I called poison control, they told me that if you're going to eat feces, you should eat the feces of a herbivore, because at least it doesn't have any parasites."

For reasons Judith could not understand, this made the second woman laugh. Judith failed to come up with anything to add. Fortunately the school doors surged open at that moment like a breaking dam, releasing scores of children onto the sidewalk. It didn't take long to find Tali. The girl barreled toward Judith, her nose glowing with bright green and purple streaks. She had been smelling markers again.

"JOOO-dith!" Tali cried. "I remembered you were coming to get me today. I thought I would forget, but I remembered!" Her breath hung in a mist in front of her little face. She beamed, as if she had just won a prize.

"Yes, here I am," Judith said. She inhaled cold air, invigorated. She could not remember the last time someone had been so happy to see her. Her mother, now in assisted living, was convinced that she was Josie. When Judith visited, her mother confided in this imagined Josie, complimenting Josie's genius and devotion while Judith cut up her pills. When Judith once dared to tell her that Josie had been murdered, her mother had laughed. "That is so unlike you," she said.

Judith was afraid that Tali's smile might vanish, but she was armed. She had brought Tali a new toy, a craft project in a box, and wanted to present it right away. "Here I am," she reaffirmed. "And I have something for you—"

But Tali had her own material to share. "You have to see what's inside my backpack!"

The little girl threw her bag down on the sidewalk beside a

heap of old snow. Children and adults were still crowding the entrance. To make room, Judith shuffled into the snow pile by the school's brick wall. The sound of cracking ice beneath her feet comforted her.

"I invented a goodness medicine," Tali was saying.

"A what?"

"A goodness medicine," Tali repeated, with genuine impatience. Her long black hair, unbrushed, was draped over her face like a theater curtain as she crouched beside her bright pink backpack. Her hair was a tapestry of clumps and knots. Presumably Joy was the one who usually brushed it, or Josie; Itamar had surely never spent a fraction of a second thinking about his little girl's hair. Judith reached over to rake away the knots, then thought better of it. A bodily memory shuddered through her: Josie at five years old, fresh from the bath, and their mother gently, carefully, lovingly combing Josie's long black hair.

"Abba said I was being bad and not listening," Tali said when she raised her head again. Judith had once found it unnatural, pretentious even, that Tali used the Hebrew *abba* instead of *daddy*, but now she was grateful. It felt less possessive, less real. *Abba said I was being bad.* Like an imaginary friend. She thought to look for the bruise, but the girl was bundled, mummified in orange vinyl. "I invented this medicine to make me better," Tali continued. "When I drink the medicine, it makes me really really good! Wanna see?"

"Uh, sure," Judith replied.

Tali pulled a paper cup out of her backpack. Inside it was an acorn, a crumpled tissue, and a penny. Judith looked into the cup and wondered, as she had often wondered since Josie had been taken, if she were dreaming all of this, or, if she were awake, if she had crossed into some sort of parallel world whose rules she didn't understand. Josie would have grasped the rules immediately, interpreted the dream. For Josie everything was always clear. Even the publicized version of her death made sense: she was a martyr for the grand cause of information technology, for the high holy values of knowledge and cultural exchange. Despite the deep illogic within this story's veins, it worked. Josie herself would have liked it. As for Judith, she was up to her knees in dirty snow, staring into a paper cup stuffed with trash.

"See the goodness medicine?" Tali asked. "I made it myself. And now I get to drink it." She raised the cup to her lips.

"Whoa, don't actually swallow that stuff," Judith said, and made a grab for the cup.

Tali snatched the cup away from Judith's hand. She flattened her mouth into a deprecating frown and pointed into the cup, looking straight at Judith. "You are so silly, Judith! This stuff is NOT the medicine."

Judith glanced at the other children. Their parents and babysitters were talking on cell phones, dragging them by their hands as the children called to each other, laughing. Judith's stomach hurt. It really was a parallel world, she understood. These other women managed by ignoring it. For the first time, she doubted she could do this. *I don't know what I was thinking,* she heard Itamar say. "You just told me it was medicine," she said weakly.

"No, no, no! The medicine is INVISIBLE!" Tali screeched. "The acorn and the tissue and the penny are the stuff that MAKES the medicine. They are *ingredients.*" Her voice was shrill now, pedantic, as though she were the adult and Judith the child. The little girl's tone rattled around in Judith's head.

Suddenly she was seven years old again, assigned to walk her younger sister home: bracing herself against a lecture about how the earth formed, about how germs died, about how feeble her own mind was and always would be.

"Because an acorn and a tissue and a penny all together doesn't make sense at all," Tali pointed out, with an irrepressible delight in the rightness of her logic. "Listen, here's a joke I just thought of now! What's the same about an acorn, a tissue, and a penny?"

Judith tried to think of a correct answer. This, she recognized, was part of the slow slide into madness. "None of them know how to ride bicycles," she said. It was a joke her father once liked to make. She still loved her father, despite having heard barely a word from him in twenty years. She looked him up online on occasion, even sent him messages sometimes. Josie never forgave her for that.

Tali wouldn't either, it seemed. "Wrong!" she shouted. "Try again: what's the same about an acorn, a tissue, and a penny?"

Judith suppressed a sigh. "I don't know. Tell me."

"NOTHING!" Tali announced, jubilant. "See? The ingredients don't make sense! Only the INVISIBLE part makes sense!" She let out a loud, cackling laugh.

Like a mad scientist, Judith thought. Or just a miniature of her mother.

"Now I'm going to drink the invisible part, and turn good. Wanna watch?"

"Okay," Judith mumbled. She was compliant now, cowed. Her feet sank deeper into the snow.

Tali mimed drinking from the cup, then looked up at Judith. Her expression was suddenly fixed in an odd smile, like a doll's. "Hello, Judith, you are my new mommy," she recited in a monotone. "I will listen to you forever. Wherever you go, I will go. Your people shall be my people, and your God shall be my God."

One of the books on Tali's shelf at home was a comic book of children's Bible stories. Tali was obsessed with it, Judith later learned, and had convinced her babysitter Joy to read it to her multiple times a day. Joy, a devout Filipina Catholic, had happily complied. "See how the medicine works?" Tali asked. "Do you like it?"

Judith breathed in, a long, slow breath. She was deep in the pile of snow now, sunken down to the dead frozen leaves from the previous season, before Josie left for Egypt, when none of this would have been possible. Beneath her feet were a season's worth of days, lived and bloomed and thrived and blazed with color before falling, floating down, finished, in a heap at her feet. Somewhere underneath the snow and leaves there was a deep pit, with another girl abandoned in it. Judith kicked at the snow until she couldn't see the bottom anymore.

"I love it," she said.

Tali looked up at her, and her eyes were full of an unbridled and unexpected joy. This, Judith understood, was what that parallel world of children was like: the surprises were often happy ones. Maybe it wasn't frightening at all, Judith considered. Maybe her deep terror was merely a side effect of wonder.

"Maybe you can have some too!" Tali exclaimed.

Judith smiled. "What would it do to me?" she asked.

"It would turn you into Mommy!"

The sky spun over Judith's head. She sank down, squatting in the snow. "That's something I've been looking for my entire life," she said.

Tali considered her, squinting one eye: skeptical, like her father. Judith noticed now that she had blue marker streaks on the backs of her little hands, as though she had tried to trace her own veins. "Really?" she asked.

The question was real. And Judith was ready. "Yes," she said.

Tali smiled, a slow, proud smile, as though all were once again right with the world, and all because of her. She tugged Judith's sleeve until Judith leaned in to listen. "Don't tell Abba," she stage-whispered in Judith's face. Her dark eyes were wide, urgent. "If we don't tell him, then maybe he'll think you're Mommy too! And then it will really work! But you have to promise not to tell him. Okay?"

Nothing about this was okay. But Judith reverted, backing into a child's aptitude for happiness. "I won't," Judith said. "I promise."

"Here it is," Tali intoned. Her voice was deep and grave. She held the cup out to Judith, an offering to a foreign god. "Don't forget, only drink the invisible part."

"How could I forget?" Judith asked. She lifted the cup to her lips and drank.

TWO WEEKS LATER, EARLY on a Sunday morning, Itamar summoned Judith to the house, his voice on the phone rich with reluctance. He had to go into the office for a bit to deal with a hardware problem, and could she possibly stop by to stay with Tali?

Judith came over immediately, and stayed in the house until a flustered Itamar returned home, just before noon. She and Tali had been building a forest out of blocks, in which unlucky princess figurines were meeting their demise at the hands of meat-eating theropods. But then Tali had abruptly lost interest, complaining that she was tired. Judith laid her down on the couch in the living room and noticed something familiar in the little black-haired body, in the way that little body shivered. When her father returned, she told him.

"I was about to call you," she said. "Tali is breathing really fast."

Itamar hung up his coat and came into the living room, glancing at Tali on the couch. "Little kids always breathe fast," he said. He bent down and kissed the top of Tali's head. "Hello, *hamuda*," he said to her. Tali didn't acknowledge him. He stepped away, patting his thigh, the pocket with his phone in it.

"Little kids don't breathe *that* fast," Judith said, pointing at Tali. "That's forty-five breaths per minute. That's not okay."

"Mmm," Itamar replied noncommittally.

Judith looked at the small body on the couch. Tali had rolled over now, turning away from them. "You need to take her to the doctor," Judith said softly. "I think the pediatrician has weekend hours, but they probably close early. You should take her right away if you don't want to get stuck going to the emergency room."

"That seems unnecessary," Itamar huffed. "She looks fine to me, just tired. And how would you know how fast she's supposed to breathe? Maybe that's just the way she breathes."

Judith dug her fingernails into her palms. "I spent years doing this with Josie," she said, her voice calm and controlled. She knew the name would wound him. Itamar trembled, though he tried to hide it, running a hand through his hair. "At this age they're supposed to breathe at twenty-five breaths per minute when they're resting, or even less than that," Judith continued. "Not forty-five. She needs an inhaler. Do you have one in the house? Josie outgrew all that years ago, but I'd bet she'd still have kept an expired one—"

Itamar blew a puff of contempt. "Tali doesn't have asthma.

She has a cold. You just don't know what it's like with kids. You have no idea how often kids get sick. *Shtuyot*." *Nonsense*: the worst non-obscene Israeli insult, after the word for *sucker*. "It's nothing. You don't know."

"I know," Judith breathed.

Itamar stepped back to the couch where Tali was lying on her stomach, her head turned away from the rest of the room. He sat beside her and ran his fingers through her hair. Judith saw how hard he was trying, how desperate he had become. "You're okay, aren't you, *metuka*?" Itamar asked.

Tali turned briefly to face him. Her eyes gleamed like round wet glass. "Don't wanna talk," she groaned, and turned away.

"She's tired," Itamar said. "Of course she's tired. And okay, yes, she's probably coming down with something." His desperation was naked now, shameful. "I'll give her some aspirin."

"You have to take her to the doctor," Judith seethed.

Itamar looked at his watch. There was an unbearable tension in the way he turned his wrist. The wrist itself was virile, dark hair accenting the strong ropes of veins beneath the skin. "I have a conference call in three minutes."

"Today is Sunday," Judith said. She laced her voice with acid.

Itamar noticed, though he pretended not to. "The call is with a vendor in Tel Aviv. It's a weekday for them there. They're staying late for me to call in."

"Fine, then I'm taking her."

Something shook through Itamar's body, a live wire of rage. "She's my daughter, Judith. My daughter, and no one else's!" His voice cracked. He tried to hide it, rubbing his hands along his own arms, lowering his voice. "If someone takes her to the doctor, it's me."

"Abba," Tali whispered. Judith was sure he would sit down beside her again, but he didn't.

"Then take her now," Judith said.

"I'll take her, once I finish this call. Nothing's going to happen to her in the next twenty minutes." Itamar left the room. His body was still shaking, but he walked with his back erect, an affront.

Judith whispered to Tali. "We're going now. Okay?"

"Okay," Tali said. She coughed, and then vomited.

When the doctor saw Tali, he put her in an ambulance. The hospital didn't discharge her for another three days.

"I WISH I KNEW how to thank you," Itamar said.

He had brought Tali home from the pediatric ward late that afternoon. Judith had explained to him how to use the nebulizer machine that had come home with her. Judith also administered the medication at home for the first time, propping Tali on her bed and fixing the mask over her face and reading picture books aloud to her as the machine grumbled, spewing compressed air through a tube and forcing it through a plastic vial of albuterol aimed at Tali's nose and mouth. Then Judith and Itamar both put an exhausted Tali to bed. As Itamar hugged her, Judith sat on the bed beside him, her arm around both Tali and her father. They became one body, a circle enclosed around their little girl. The naturalness of it shocked Judith. Itamar too, it seemed. Judith felt his arm tremble. She left the room quickly and hurried downstairs. When he came down to say goodbye to her, she was already wearing her winter coat, standing by the front door of the house. He came down the stairs hanging his head, until he was standing before her.

"I can never thank you enough," he said. His voice was quiet, humbled. "Her oxygen level was really low. If she had gotten there any later—"

"You know how to work the nebulizer now, right?" Judith interrupted. She kept her words cold, managed. "You have to treat her every four hours around the clock for the rest of the week. Don't forget. Set your alarm."

"I don't have the right kind of brain for this sort of thing," Itamar said.

There was an ache in his voice, a pleading. Judith blew a puff of air, trying to dispel it. "People much dumber than you have dealt with this," she told him. "You can handle anything." It was what everyone had always told her sister.

"No, I can't," he said. "If I had been alone with her, my daughter would be dead."

She looked at his shoes. "I have to go," Judith muttered pointlessly. "Don't forget to set your clock."

She leaned in to kiss him goodbye, reaching for the casual in-law embrace, pecking his cheek. He held her shoulders for a long moment, and rested his head beside hers. And then he took her in his arms and pressed his tongue between her lips.

It was a mistake, surely it was a mistake, she thought as he opened her coat, then opened her shirt, and she did not stop him. Cool air blew across her breasts. He slid his hands under her bra, then leaned her back against the door. His hands flowed over her body like warm water on her skin. She slipped her hands around his back, beneath his sweater, under his belt, under his pants, beneath his shorts, around his hips, dislodging the phone in his pocket. He opened her bra and bowed before her, tracing her skin with his tongue; he took her breast in his mouth and lapped her up as though she flowed with milk. But now he wept openly, crying as she had never before heard a man cry. His head shivered on her shoulder as he pressed her against the door, his hands still clutching her breasts. He sobbed into her neck, a long low howl. He was trapped, and starving.

"She would forgive me, wouldn't she?" Itamar wept, and poured his hands between her legs, at the door of the world. "Do you think she would forgive me?"

"I forgive you," Judith whispered.

He wept and wept until Judith wept with him, gasping, sobbing, pressed against the house's locked front door.

TALI HAS JUST NOTICED her reflection in the faucet of the bathtub. Judith is rubbing soap on her neck, feeling the wet down of the girl's back, the little points of her shoulderblades angled like wings lifting her skin from her rippled spine, long black hair pasted against her skin like spilled black paint. Her back curves beneath Judith's knobbed hand, her body curling like a baby bird enfolded in an egg. Her eyes appear in the chrome surface of the faucet, and Tali pauses to stare at herself, captive in that instant, unsure, in her six-year-old mind, which one of her is real.

"Mommy," she says, "There's the other me!"

The word *mommy* shudders through Judith, wind blowing through her throat. She doesn't correct her.

"Yes, there's the other you," she agrees. She glances at the reflection, and in that moment she imagines looking out at Tali through the chrome surface like a lens, seeing the girl distorted and unchanging in the center, and then seeing her entire future compacted in that circle. She sees Tali growing older, her curiosity hardening into intelligence and then arrogance, careless pride pushing out from beneath her skin like the insistent wings of shoulderblades on her back. She sees the boys who will love her, the ones whose hearts she will shatter without even hearing the crash; she sees the woman the girl will become, beautiful and proud, every marvel she creates almost an accident. Judith even sees the girl's own daughter, a dark-haired beauty at her mother's feet, drinking in her words. And Judith sees what lies before her: the possibility of changing the past forever.

At bedtime she kisses her little girl good night.

"Stay with me," the little girl begs. "Stay with me until I fall asleep."

"I will," Judith promises, and stays, stroking the silk sheath of the girl's brushed black hair as the girl drifts into undeciphered dreams.

Judith stays for a long, long time, wondering who will forgive her.

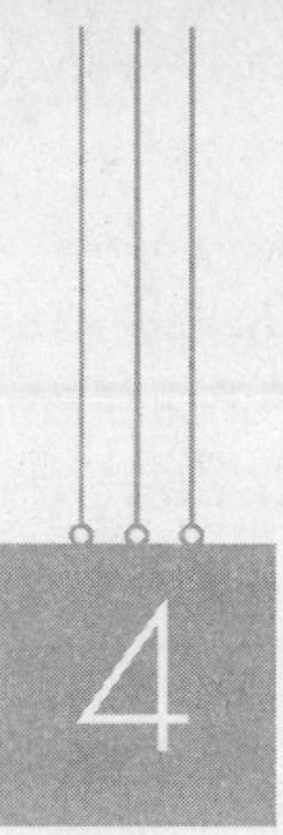

4

IN A WINDOWLESS ROOM in Cairo, Solomon Schechter struggled to breathe.

He remembered the first time it had happened to him, the terrifying sensation of the world encircling his throat and tightening its grip. He was nine years old, in Romania, bringing medicine home from the pharmacist for his brother. The road was old, a route pounded by barbarians crossing the Carpathians centuries before, and wound its way past the ruins of a fortress. But now it was neglected and overgrown with roots and weeds. He walked with awe through the tunnel of naked branches above his head. He loved to climb trees, but that day he felt the grip of the earth on his feet. His twin brother was burning with a fever that refused to break. He heard a rumble of thunder above the trees and decided to hurry. He started running, and soon he felt his breath speeding, thumping, pounding as if his brother's fever raged within him. He slowed to a stop, and as he stood beneath the branches and the darkening sky, he felt his *neshamah*—his soul, his breath—being released from his body, gusting out of his mouth while his body stood still. He gasped, stabbed by a sharp, sudden, alien pain, and tried to reel his soul back in, but it refused to return. As the world whirled around him, he steadied himself with Hebrew verses engraved on his memory: *Everything that breathes will praise God. The breath of all that live will bless Your name*. His eyes followed his breath up into the air and saw the letters of the words flying free. When he awoke he was lying in bed beside his sick twin brother, with a saline pipe from the pharmacist in his mouth. It happened to him often after that, the flight of breath and life—whenever he entered an unfamiliar place, until he found a way to conquer it.

Egypt was like England, Schechter had immediately noticed: full of stone ruins that no one understood, and full of people who never said what they meant. He was prepared for heat, and for poverty, and there he was pleasantly surprised—when he arrived in December the weather was warm, but far more bearable than a humid Romanian summer, and the tourist districts of Cairo were full of opera houses and French dancing classes and elegant cafés, the eyeless beggars confining themselves to the archeological sites. What he was unprepared for was the absolute ruin of the country itself, the completely unrestored splendor of the ancients poking through the city's modern skin like the bones of a dying man. Beggars had set up camp in warrens of ancient tombs, the famous pyramids were piles of rubble stripped of their alabaster, and enormous ancient obelisks lay on their sides, their inscriptions ground to dust. The poor holed themselves up in the shade of ruins, constructing shantytowns out of broken slabs of frescoed stone, while Europeans in pith helmets presided over sweating workers who dug up the ancient dead for German and British museums. It was like watching birds pecking at a giant's corpse.

Schechter was equally unprepared for the endless misdirection, the fundamental assumption that what anyone said was only the tiniest fraction of what was implied. His dragoman in Alexandria had told him that the Metropole Hotel in Cairo, which the spectral twins had recommended, was completely booked, but that the Royal Hotel, in a "more simple" location, was available at half the price. Mindful of money that wasn't his—his expenses were being paid by Professor Charles Taylor, Master of St. John's College—Schechter told the agent to book the Royal. The agent had then consulted several letters in his breast pocket, peering at them meaningfully through a monocle before informing Schechter that in fact the Metropole *might* be available, that a room *might* be arranged, except that it was so very difficult to make the arrangements so very quickly, of course, when telegrams were so very expensive. Schechter failed to understand that the agent was asking for a tip. He found himself in a dump on a street full of brothels. His Englishness and his wealth were his shadows—even though in England no one thought he was English, and not a penny of the money was his. He couldn't leave his filthy hotel room without leaving a trail of Professor Taylor's money behind him, a slick of slime like the trail of a slug.

He had come to Cairo armed. The university had supplied him with a letter of introduction to the Grand Rabbi of Cairo, which Schechter himself had written in biblical Hebrew and which the registrar had insisted on wax-sealing with the university crest, as well as binding with a red silk ribbon. Schechter had almost removed the ribbon; it seemed so ridiculous. But when he collected his letter of introduction from the Chief Rabbi of the British Empire, he noticed that the Chief Rabbi's secretary had bound his letter with a silk ribbon as well. When Schechter finally met Rabbi Aharon Raphael ben Shimon, Grand Rabbi of Cairo, he understood the ribbons.

The rabbi was sitting behind a tea table in a sunny stone

courtyard full of potted palms in a modest house in Ismailiya, one of the city's most expensive European neighborhoods. Even though a servant had ushered him in, Schechter saw the man seated in the courtyard and thought that there had been a mistake, that he had accidentally been brought to an audience with a Coptic priest. The rabbi was wearing a floor-length black robe with an elaborately brocaded collar, embroidered entirely of gold and silver thread in a delicate pattern that continued down from his neckline to the floor. Several golden medallions were suspended from his neck, like the heavy gold crosses he had seen Copts wearing around Cairo. The man had dark skin, a thick curly gray-black beard, stylish spectacles, and a surprisingly young-looking face. On top of his head was an elaborate dark turban-like hat with a shining golden band around it, the crown of an ancient king. In his mouth was a cigarette.

Schechter stood before him paralyzed, suddenly short of breath. Then he noticed the two letters of introduction sitting on the table—their red silk ribbons, Schechter saw, now casually wound around the man's tall thin glass of bright-smelling coffee.

"Blessed be he who comes," the rabbi announced in Hebrew, and stood, stubbing out his half-smoked cigarette. "The esteemed scholar and righteous man in Israel, Rabbi Shneur Zalman ben Yitzhak, may he go from strength to strength."

Schechter leaned back, feeling naked in the bright sun. He had not been addressed in conversation by his Hebrew name for almost thirty years. The rabbi's accent was all wrong, of course, the Hebrew words a stretch of long dry vowels and gutturals, as though the language itself had desiccated in the desert air. But the words were the words of Schechter's father, addressing him by the name that God would call him in the next world. Schechter bowed his head, noticing the gold embroidery along the hem of the rabbi's robe grazing the stone floor. The clothes were absurd, Schechter thought. He withheld a smirk as he removed his own pith helmet.

"Rabbi Aharon Raphael ben Shimon, I am honored to have the merit of living in your generation," Schechter said. He spoke in Hebrew—which was a bit like speaking in Latin, since no one he knew of had spoken it in conversation for the past nineteen centuries. His years in England made him reflexively offer his hand. He lowered it quickly, and bowed his head.

"May the merit of our ancestors intercede on our behalf," the rabbi answered. He motioned for Schechter to sit on a wooden stool as he lowered himself back into his own cushioned chair.

Schechter had met men like the rabbi before, holy men who spoke primarily in verses and aphorisms. The last he had known was the second son of the Skvirer rebbe, who, not being the first son of the Skvirer rebbe, had been forced out of his father's court to run a yeshiva Schechter once attended. The man was deeply bitter, and expressed it by speaking only in quotes. He and Schechter had had entire conversations by exchanging biblical verses, mainly from Ecclesiastes. According to the son of the Skvirer rebbe, all was vanity. The sun was shining in Schechter's eyes as a servant poured him coffee in his own tall glass. He squinted, put a hand to his hair to check that his yarmulke was in place, and placed his pith helmet carefully beside his feet, wishing he was still wearing it.

"I see you have read the notices from the academy abroad, as well as from our esteemed teacher Rabbi Hermann Adler, Chief Rabbi of the British Empire," Schechter said, "may his wisdom expand to the ends of the earth."

"Amen," the Cairo rabbi replied. Beneath his crown, the rabbi appeared, for a moment, bored.

Schechter breathed, steadying himself. He knew already

that the next step was not pleasantries about the weather, as it would have been in England, but gifts, the prettier the better. He reached into his satchel and took out his first attempt.

"As you have heard, I am a scholar of Torah, though only the humblest of scholars. I would like to present you with one of my books—an annotation of the *Avot d'Rabbi Natan*, the only scholarly edition of that much-neglected chapter of the Talmud." He removed the book from his bag and passed it to the man across the table.

The rabbi took it, opened the first few pages, then examined its leather binding. "Of the making of books there is no end," the rabbi quoted.

Ecclesiastes, Schechter knew, was never a good sign. The rabbi yawned, and sipped his coffee.

Schechter stiffened, and tried another tactic. He reached into his bag and extracted an open box of French cigarettes, which he had bought in Marseille the week before. He held it out to the rabbi. "Perhaps your eminence would enjoy these as well," he said.

The rabbi examined the box and helped himself to one. "Please, take them all," Schechter said, placing the box on the table beside the book. This time the rabbi looked up at him and smiled, a genuine smile. As the rabbi struck a match, Schechter leaned forward.

"I have heard that last winter you merited to make the acquaintance of our esteemed teacher the Chief Rabbi's brother, the illustrious scholar of laws Elkan Adler, may his strength increase," Schechter tried.

The rabbi raised his dark eyebrows and exhaled smoke. "May his wisdom be heard in distant isles," he said. It didn't sound like a compliment.

Schechter hesitated before forging ahead. "Rabbi Elkan"—

this wasn't the right title, Schechter knew, but how else in ancient Hebrew would one describe a British lawyer?—"informed me that he was able to enter the storage room in one of your ancient houses of assembly. He brought back many written works to our distant isle, but none of great worth."

In fact Elkan Adler, to hear him tell it, had been escorted to a medieval synagogue, led through a hole in the wall above the women's gallery, and allowed to enter a room full of ancient papers, where he was left alone for three hours—a privilege he had obtained from the Grand Rabbi in exchange for a large donation to the synagogue. In three hours he had managed to bring home only a few illegible documents and a chronic cough. The librarians at the Bodleian at Oxford thought he was a fool.

The rabbi frowned. "The stone that has been rejected shall become the cornerstone," he quoted.

"In my country it has also lately been noted that certain works unknown in the West have appeared from merchants in Cairo," Schechter continued. "Works of great Torah scholarship, never before seen in the holy tongue, that merchants in Cairo have sold to visitors from overseas."

"Whoever honors the Torah will be honored by all mankind," the rabbi quoted, and yawned through his nose.

Schechter could almost see the wall rising between them, but he pressed ahead. "I have also corresponded with the illustrious Rabbi Shlomo Aharon Wertheimer of Jerusalem, the book merchant, who has procured many holy works from Cairo and has sold them to the libraries of many nations."

"May all nations take on the yoke of His sovereignty," the rabbi quoted, and blew smoke.

"The difficulty is that the Jerusalemite's prices are high, and fees for shipping manuscripts are high as well," Schechter said. He tried to maintain a delicate tone, without complete success.

"And one never knows what one is getting, without seeing the works in advance. It is nearly impossible for the libraries in the West to know whether the works are worthy."

"Torah is the greatest merchandise," the rabbi quoted, his expression still utterly blank.

Now Schechter was getting angry. No, he thought fiercely, it would not end here. His three-thousand-mile quest would not terminate with this stone-faced Oriental blowing smoke in his face. He gritted his teeth. "I have corresponded with the rabbi in Jerusalem," Schechter said, "and inquired about the source of the manuscripts he has sold to our library in England. He insisted that these holy works came from a genizah in Cairo, but he professed not to know precisely where the genizah was located. He told me that all of the writings he has acquired from Cairo came to him through a Yemenite agent, and the Yemenite refused to divulge his source, except to say that a beadle of a Cairo synagogue was involved."

"Never trust a Yemenite," the rabbi said.

It wasn't a quote. Schechter put down his coffee and saw that the rabbi was examining him, eyeing his face, his red beard, his blue eyes, his linen suit, the pith helmet Schechter had placed at his feet.

"So you are yet another Ashkenazi who has come for the genizah," the rabbi said, and leaned back in his chair. "Like the English and the Germans digging up the dead pharaohs. It astounds me. So many people come from around the world just to collect our garbage."

Schechter's mouth opened, about to explain everything that this man in his ridiculous turban could not possibly understand. He imagined picking up his pith helmet and storming out the door. But at that moment he felt his breath quickening, the panic of a nine-year-old boy, the world encircling him, strangling him. *Breathe in,* he told himself. *The breath of all that live will bless Your name.* His breath returned as he understood what he needed to say.

"I—that is, the royal kingdom whose munificence has brought me on my journey," Schechter declared, "am prepared to expand on the price Rabbi Wertheimer of Jerusalem has received for the works he has purchased from your beadle. In fact, I can say that I am prepared to extend my kingdom's unprecedented generosity. For," he quoted, in what he hoped would come across as a humble voice, "the study of Torah supersedes all."

The rabbi drew his dark eyebrows together, squinting in the sunlight. "There are those who pretend to be rich, but have nothing," he quoted.

It was from the book of Proverbs. Without thinking, Schechter completed the verse: "And those who pretend to be poor, but have great wealth."

The rabbi leaned forward, and smiled. Schechter had found the key.

"What you are looking for isn't here in modern Cairo," the rabbi said. "You will have to go to Fustat, the medieval fortress, to the Palestinian synagogue."

The door was opening—just barely, but light was seeping through. "Palestinian?"

"Yes, the one built by the Palestinian Jews, the ones who came here from the Holy Land after the Fatimid conquest, one thousand years ago. It is older than the synagogues in this part of the city. The synagogues here were built by the Jews who came here from Babylonia only nine hundred years ago. The genizah you are looking for is in the Palestinian synagogue in Fustat."

Schechter waited silently as the rabbi inhaled cigarette smoke, letting it flow out of his nostrils. Had he made it in?

"But I cannot advise it," the rabbi said. "It has been said that a serpent guards the door to the room, a descendant of the serpent who provoked our ancestors in Paradise."

Schechter stared at the rabbi, hoping that this was a joke. A *serpent*? It was like something out of one of his children's books, the one about the girl who fell down a rabbit hole. But the rabbi's face was deadpan, earnest—or at least the sort of earnestness that one pretends for children.

"The serpent in Paradise offered mankind the fruits of the Tree of Knowledge," Schechter replied, in careful biblical Hebrew. He felt idiotic, as if he were talking to a book. "Your serpent does the opposite."

"Ibn Ezra hints that the serpent in Paradise transformed himself into the revolving sword that guards the Tree of Life," the rabbi intoned.

Where? Schechter thought. His mind reproduced the Hebrew page of the Pentateuch, locating in his mind's eye the margin of the page with the medieval scholar Ibn Ezra's commentary on the text. There was no such hint, of course. The rabbi knew it. They had graduated to fake quotes. He glanced at Schechter, his eyebrows raised, waiting to see if Schechter would call his bluff. Schechter drew in his breath.

"Rabbenu Tam suggests that the snake in Genesis becomes the snake in Exodus that transformed from the staff of Moses before the Egyptian king, to show the snake's repentance," Schechter replied. This, naturally, was also horseshit. Schechter could compete on horseshit. "Surely your snake would be willing to repent as well."

The rabbi smirked. "The snakes in the pit where Joseph was

thrown by his brothers before they sold him into Egypt showed no remorse. As Rabban Gamliel said, 'A stranger sent to Egypt will suffer the serpent's tooth, as Joseph did in the pit.'"

The quoting game was much more fun when one wasn't limited to actual quotes. Schechter parried with nonsense of his own. "But when Joseph's brothers sold him into Egypt, they didn't know that they were saving themselves from the famine that would come years later, after Joseph interpreted the king's dreams and showed him how to save the country from starvation. Rabbi Tarfon said in the name of Rabbi Elazar ben Azariah, 'Strangers who come to Egypt shall enrich the land through dreams.'"

The rabbi smirked. He was no longer wary of this pith-helmeted foreigner, Schechter saw. He was having fun. "But Joseph's brothers' arrival in Egypt led the people into centuries of slavery," he said, clearly enjoying himself. "Saadia Gaon said, 'Beware all those who venture to Egypt,' and Rav Amram Gaon said, 'In foreign lands one must be on guard against misunderstood dreams.'"

"Indeed," Schechter nodded, with mock seriousness. "And it is also said that after the exodus, Jews should never live in Egypt, as it is written in Deuteronomy: 'Do not cause the people to return to Egypt . . . because God has said to you, Never again return on that road.'"

This was a real quote. The rabbi's smirk disappeared. Now the leader of the two-thousand-year-old Egyptian Jewish community leaned toward the redheaded foreigner, and stared in silence. A long moment passed before the rabbi spoke again.

"The synagogue in Fustat is in the old part of the city, where Rambam once lived," the rabbi said. "The building is over a thousand years old. But Fustat's fortunes have changed in recent times. The Nile altered its course by a thousand cubits.

Fustat had been a wealthy place, important for business. When the river moved, those living in Fustat were left destitute. It was a great tragedy for the Jews of Fustat."

Schechter raised his glass and sipped his coffee, summoning sympathy. "How unfortunate," he said. "And this was in recent times?"

The rabbi nodded. "Seven hundred years ago."

Schechter managed to keep his coffee in his mouth.

"It was a great tragedy. Few Jews live there anymore," the rabbi said. "We have reconstructed the exterior of the building, but we have not been able to complete the repairs to the interior. The costs have been prohibitive, and because the congregation there is slight, there are few in the community who are willing to support it. If only some wise visitor would truly appreciate its worth! But alas," he quoted, "when there is no flour, there is no Torah." The rabbi let out a loud sigh.

Schechter swallowed. This, of course, had been Elkan Adler's mistake, the same mistake Schechter had made with the agent in Alexandria. He had paid, but not enough.

"How fortunate for you that I have arrived at precisely your time of need," Schechter grandly announced. He thought of Professor Taylor, of Professor Taylor's scholarship, of Professor Taylor's money, of Professor Taylor slapping him on the back, wishing him well. The cavalier attitude toward money, common among people who never actually had to earn it, felt forever foreign to Schechter. He spoke like an actor in a play, as though he were wearing a costume, dressed in royal robes. "I would be pleased to make a generous donation toward the costs of the synagogue's repair."

The rabbi smiled, but said nothing. Instead he drank more coffee, then lit another cigarette.

Schechter was puzzled. Had he done something wrong?

It reminded him of when he had first arrived in Vienna from Romania, of seeing adults in strange clothes doing outlandish things: intelligent men walking about with their backs straight and their heads high in the air like arrogant fools, sophisticated men shaking each other's hands like children, rational men eating their meals without washing their hands first, elite men and women walking arm-in-arm on the boulevards without a whiff of scandal. Everything seems absurd until one learns the code. What was the rabbi getting at? Schechter was wracking his mind for an appropriate way to ask when the rabbi spoke again.

"I have never seen the tombs of the ancient kings," the rabbi said.

This seemed to be a complete non sequitur. Was it a quote? If it was, Schechter couldn't place it. He had never before heard a Hebrew quote he couldn't place. His breath caught in his throat.

The rabbi continued. "They are not distant from here, but alas, the day is short and the price of the journey is high. Woe betide me, that I may go to my reward in the world to come without having seen the wonders of our own."

Schechter gave up. "What tombs?"

"The graves in which the ancient pharaohs were entombed, though thieves have long since removed the bodies of the idolaters and their idols as well, may the one true God be praised."

So the rabbi was indeed acquainted with reality, Schechter noted. Now he wondered which tombs the man meant. He could be referring to any one of dozens of excavation sites. For the past few weeks Schechter had been keeping up with the latest archeological research in the journals at the university library, preparing for his trip. "Do you mean the discoveries at Tanis?" he asked. "They do sound impressive." He took a sip of coffee, which had become unpleasantly lukewarm.

"Not at Tanis. At Giza."

This time Schechter choked. "The *pyramids*?"

The rabbi watched him calmly, smiling at him as he coughed, breathed. Finally Schechter stammered, returning to Hebrew, "But—but you've lived here all your life!"

The rabbi nodded. "Many in our holy congregation do not venture to the tombs, for we do not wish to be seen paying respects to the graves of the pharaohs who once enslaved our people."

Schechter considered this. "But the pyramids were built at least a thousand years before the ancient Israelites are even mentioned in any source," he said. He heard the pedantry in his own voice poisoned with helplessness, an overtone of protest. It was slowly occurring to him that facts were irrelevant.

The rabbi leaned back, heaving another dramatic sigh. "I have long wished to journey to Giza, to fulfill my dream of spitting on the pharaohs' graves," he said wistfully.

"Giza can't be more than an hour's ride from here," Schechter pointed out.

"*Halevai*," the rabbi replied, in a plaintive voice that seemed oddly childlike coming from a man in gold and silver brocade. He sighed again. "Would that I had the means to make the journey, in a fashion worthy of a man of my station!"

Schechter had resisted the obvious, but now there was no longer any point. "I would be pleased to take you to Giza," Schechter announced. "In a hired coach." He tried to make his voice grand, munificent with Professor Taylor's money. Schechter had considered asking the university for a grant, but Taylor knew that if Schechter told the university of his plans, word would be out, and the likes of Adolf Neubauer or David Margoliouth at Oxford might well have beaten him to Cairo—to the great embarrassment of the entire university, and of Taylor himself. Surely Taylor wouldn't begrudge the rabbi an excursion to the pyramids, Schechter thought, if that was what it took to open the door. "We can go tomorrow if you like."

The rabbi smiled again and sipped his coffee, but once more said nothing. Schechter felt his own irritation welling up, the pique that, he knew, could turn into fury in minutes. But he could not destroy everything now. He swallowed his rage as the rabbi spoke again.

"My brother, may he prosper, is a scholar and teacher, a righteous man," the rabbi said. "He instructs learned visitors in the Arabic tongue, so that they may better comport themselves in our great city. But woe betide him, his students have become few in number, so that his family barely survives. My esteemed Rabbi Shneur Zalman, may your family never know such misfortune."

This seemed implausible at best. Schechter had counted three servants so far in the rabbi's courtyard alone. He thought of his own years of traveling in fourth-class train cars, to save a bit more of his pathetic salary to send home to help his family. But by now Schechter fully understood. Like British weather conditions, the rabbi's hypothetically starving brother was well beside the point.

"Without sufficient students, my dear brother eats the bread of idleness, a sin against the Holy Name," the rabbi was saying. "Would that there were more learned visitors in need of his services!" The rabbi sighed once more.

Schechter suppressed a growl, and spread his lips in an enormous grin. "How fortunate that you should mention it!" he exclaimed, with an enthusiasm worthy of his four-year-old daughter. "I have always dreamed of studying the Arabic tongue with a private tutor. Surely no instructor in England could compare."

The rabbi smiled once more. Schechter thought of his own twin brother, and then of his five other brothers and his elder sister. He offered a silent prayer that the rabbi didn't have more siblings—and then another prayer that he wouldn't invent any.

Schechter was contemplating the rabbi's coffee-stained teeth, wondering if he would be obliged to remit payment for dentistry as well, when the rabbi finally spoke again.

"I collect royal seals," the rabbi said.

"Pardon?"

"Royal seals. Emblems that kingdoms issue to their citizens, so they may send letters to distant lands," he said.

"Stamps?" Schechter asked in English.

The rabbi didn't understand, or chose to ignore him. "I own many seals of this type, having acquired them from visitors to my father's court since I was a boy. It is a cherished dream of mine to have British royal seals. Of course I already have those seals used by British emissaries in North Africa. The ones I still seek are those issued by the Queen for use within her borders, those adorned with the most recent images of the Queen. But alas, like that of a virtuous woman, the Queen's price is far beyond rubies."

The rabbi sighed once more—a magnificent, theatrical sigh. The sheer virtuosity of his performance made Schechter want to applaud.

Stamp collecting, Schechter marveled. He could manage that. "I can obtain the royal seals for you," he answered, matching the rabbi's stilted Hebrew. "Consider it my gift, if you will set me as a seal upon your heart." Song of Songs, of course.

At last the rabbi smiled. "My esteemed colleague," he exclaimed, "you have found favor in my sight!" He picked up Schechter's book from the table and kissed it three times. Then he stood, and Schechter stood up with him. An instant later the rabbi was embracing him—and then, to Schechter's alarm, kissed him on the mouth.

Schechter resisted the urge to wipe his lips on his sleeve. When the rabbi handed him his pith helmet, Schechter knew he had arrived.

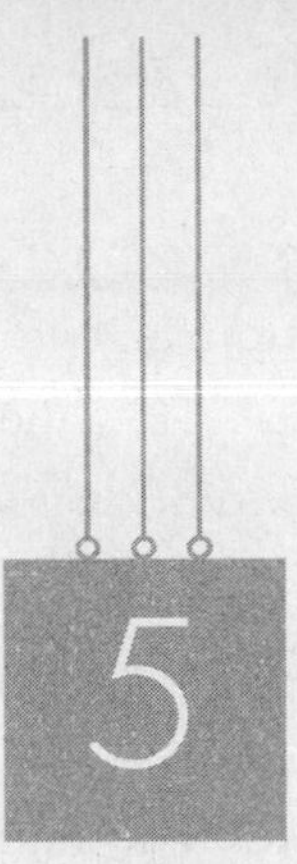

In the name of God, Lord of the Universe:

To my honored pupil Joseph (may the Rock protect you), son of Judah (may his repose be in Paradise),

Ever since you resolved to come to me, from a distant country, to study under my direction, I thought highly of your thirst for knowledge. This was the case ever since your letters and compositions in rhymed prose came to me from Alexandria, before your grasp was put to the test . . . When I commenced by way of hints, I noticed that you desired additional explanation, urging me to expound on some metaphysical problems. I perceived that you had acquired some knowledge in those matters from others, and that you were perplexed and bewildered; yet you sought to find a solution to your difficulty . . . When, by the will of God, we parted, and you went on your way, our discussions aroused in me a resolution which had long been dormant. Your absence has prompted me to compose this treatise for you and for those who are like you, however few they may be. Farewell!

At night, Josephine Ashkenazi had begun studying the Hebrew and French edition of *Guide for the Perplexed.* In the realm of fantasy, in a ten-by-ten-foot room, she became convinced that Maimonides had addressed his treatise specifically to her.

The cell phone video of her execution had been surprisingly easy to create. At first she had had a reflexive dignity, refusing to cooperate. The man wearing the "Jon's Bar Mitzvah" T-shirt (at first they never seemed to change their clothes; she sometimes imagined that they too were prisoners, that this prison was much larger than the room) had nodded, and had then invited in two other men, shorter and seemingly younger than he was—the first wearing a T-shirt that said "Bear Stearns" and the second wearing one that said "Doctors Without Borders"—who held her against the sarcophagus and whacked her with truncheons until she complied. Mostly they had beaten her legs, presumably to protect her precious brain from injury, but that had not stopped Doctors Without Borders from occasionally slamming her in the head. Her captors had a surprising sense of propriety: the woman who may or may not have been Nasreen had come in again, once Josie was gagged, to thread the rope into a harness beneath her arms under her shirt before binding her arms and legs with packing tape. During the hanging itself she was terrified, convinced that the harness under her arms wouldn't work, that she actually would die. When they cut her down, she was unconscious. When she awoke, her battered ankle was attached by an iron shackle to a three-foot-long chain which ended in a bucket-sized block of poured concrete in the corner of the room. The sarcophagus was no longer within her reach.

It occurred to her, after her hanging, that no one would ever look for her again, that Itamar and everyone else she knew were probably certain she was dead. Which made it abundantly clear that ransom and release were no longer options, and that her captors' ultimate intent was to murder her for real. When would they do it? Surely not for a while; otherwise the faked execution would have been unnecessary. But then what was their purpose in keeping her alive? She considered the obvious possibilities, but beyond the beatings, none of them had ever touched her, except for the woman who might or might not have been Nasreen. Yet it had been impossible for her to walk down the street in Cairo or Alexandria without men eyeballing her; more than once, on crowded sidewalks, she had even felt strangers' hands along her legs. Soon she couldn't think about it anymore, couldn't think anymore at all. Instead, she stared at the sarcophagus and fell into a long and demented sleep.

When the man returned she was slouched in the corner of the room between the concrete block and the wall, dreaming of Tali—odd dreams, sick dreams, dreams where she coated Tali with cake frosting and licked it off her daughter's arms. She could feel it beginning to happen: the descent from earth to underground, the abandonment of logic, the sinking into inarticulable thoughts, the transformation from woman into animal. She awoke with the clank of the lock. Seeing the man enter the room with a thin steel bat in one hand made her shake violently, uncontrollably. Her chained leg rattled against the stone wall as warm urine trickled between her legs. But when he spoke, his words nudged her back to what once was real.

"You are a famous lady," he said. "You make famous computers." He smiled, and waited for her to reply.

Suddenly that person existed again: Josephine Ashkenazi,

inventor, executive, winner of prizes, interpreter of dreams. It was likely a trick of some kind, this odd flattery, but she seized it.

"Yes," she said. Her voice shook. She sat up and spread her long and shapeless brown shirt across her lap, hoping he would not notice the puddle on the floor. She imagined herself crossing a long and narrow bridge, controlling the fear. "I'm a software developer." *I determine outcomes,* she reminded herself. *I decide what happens next.* She felt a flutter in her chest, as though she were at a job interview. If she didn't get this job, she would die.

The man seated himself on the sarcophagus, hopping up onto it as though he were jumping onto the back of a pickup truck. He bumped his heels casually against the block of stone. "You write codes," he said, stroking the stubble on his chin. He was wearing a different shirt, she noticed. His new shirt was solid black, with a collar and buttons. Perhaps this was a special occasion? She made a point of noticing his shirt, of checking the breast pocket for a brand (there wasn't one), of clinging to anything that suggested a reality beyond the room, beyond her own body, holding tight to the rim of the world. He stared at her through dark sunglasses, his lips pursed. "Machine code," he said, as if clarifying. "You write machine code."

"Machine code?" Josie asked. It had been years since she had attempted machine code. "I don't—" But now a switch clicked in her brain: the crucial importance of not saying no, of not making another mistake. The answer, from now on, had to be *yes, yes, yes*—yes to everything, yes to the impossible. She needed to impress, to amaze, to exhibit at every opportunity her right to exist. "Do you mean programming languages? Like C? Or C-Sharp, or objective-C? Sure, I know those. Others too," she said. The truth was that there were only one or two languages that she could really think in. Ten years ago she had come to understand that all the others were more or less the same, but with slightly different syntax, like dialects of a spoken language—and from then on she could learn a new one within a few days. Of course what really mattered now weren't languages, but frameworks, not that she could even begin to explain that to this man—and of course these days she never had her hands in the weeds anymore. Coding was for her employees. But she thought of the beating, the hanging, the disemboweling mistake of telling the truth. She glanced at the sarcophagus and reaffirmed. "I know a lot about code." But why on earth would he care about code?

"What is objective-C?" the man asked.

The cell had become a college computer lab. She looked at his scruffy sunglassed face and imagined him as a student, a twenty-year-old innocent who just wanted to know how things worked. It was surprisingly easy, as long as she didn't look down at her bludgeoned, shackled leg. "Objective-C is a superset of C, but object-oriented instead of procedure-oriented," she said. Her words in this room were surreal, although coding was the opposite of surreal: man-made, controlled, entirely unmysterious to anyone who bothered to learn it, its supposed mysteries nothing more than revelations of one's own inadequacy. That was what she had always loved about it—its intolerance for nonsense. "It's used for mobile applications on Apple devices. C-Sharp is for all platforms except for Apple." This was beyond irrelevant, she knew. But she sensed the possibility of awing him with irrelevance. It occurred to her that he had probably never even heard of C. The only way to avoid sneering was to imagine she was speaking to Tali. She pictured Tali, Tali's smile, Tali's sneer. But then she saw Tali once more with cake frosting on her arms and cheeks—the tug of the irrational, pulling her down, down, down below the surface of reality. She blinked her eyes. "They're all just different ways of writing applications," she heard herself say.

The man leaned back, another smile spreading on his face. He was clearly confused, and impressed. Josie almost felt proud. "The machine code," he nodded.

"It isn't machine code," Josie said. The wave of accuracy surged within her, unstoppable, like nausea. Since childhood she had suffered from it. "Machine code is the internal binary programming that's used in the physical processor. That's not what C and the other languages do. They—"

He held up his thin steel bat, the sort Josie remembered using in gym class, centuries ago, on another planet. She fell silent.

"There is the police station of Cairo," he said, almost thoughtfully. "The headquarters. Like in *CSI*." As if he and Josie were friends, reminiscing about old TV shows, good times. This must be Cairo and not Alexandria, Josie reaffirmed to herself, pretending that it mattered. "You will help us. You will be our little helper." He smiled at her. He liked to smile.

Us, Josie heard. Did that mean the woman who might or might not be Nasreen? Or Bear Stearns, or Doctors Without Borders? Or was there some larger group of captors just beyond the door? He waited for her to reply, or to acknowledge him. But she was baffled, and terrified. She stared at the bat. A police station? Were they going to remove her from the room? She ran his words through her mind as though they were programming commands, translated into sense on the screen of her brain. She would be dragged into an Egyptian police station at gunpoint, and then used as a hostage for some impossible demand. They might as well prop her up in front of a firing squad. *Our little helper,* she heard again. She had become his slave. But what he said next shocked her.

"The police use your computer program," the man said, with a sick grimace on his face. "GEH-NEE-ZAH."

The name floated in the stale air like an unpleasant smell. The days since her capture had been the longest amount of time she had spent since childhood without looking at a screen. Now her own program was summoned before her like a lover, the cool glow of its smooth, dirtless, entirely logical screens a pure fantasy, empathetic magic. She thought of the interface she had created for it, not "files" like most applications, but instead an infinitely expanding number of doors: doors of varying sizes and shapes, wooden doors, steel doors, cabinet doors, cellar doors, French doors, painted doors, revolving doors, locked doors, doors that led to tunnels and hallways and staircases and spiral staircases that led to other doors, doors that would spring open on screen to reveal whatever a person had forgotten to remember. She opened a door in her mind and saw Itamar's face when she had told him—in the dark hollow of the night when they first kissed, during a conversation that felt like burrowing into a deep underground cavern leading to the promised land—how embarrassed she always felt by her success. The shame seeped out from reasons buried deep within her: because of the resentment she felt from every person around her like subtle vibrations in the air, because of her sense that the resentment was deserved, because of her arrogance that she had never been able to shed. And also because of something more, a sense that shook the ground beneath her feet—that she was trying to cross the boundary of human limitations, that she was trying to stop time, that everything she had ever done in her life was exactly the opposite of walking humbly with one's God. She had never admitted it to anyone before, how ashamed she was. But with Itamar that night, for the first time in her life, the air around her stood still. "You shouldn't be, Yosefi," he had said to her. And then, in Hebrew, the words she needed to hear: "You have given a gift to the world."

"Egyptian police, they are bastards," the man said, his mouth still pinched in a grimace. "They were bastards before the revolution. Everyone thinks it is different now, but now it is only worse. Now it is army and police, but the same. I saw GEH-NEE-ZAH there, when they arrest me. Your computers are helping bastards."

Bastards, Josie thought—as distinguished from the people who held her captive and bludgeoned her with metal bats. If she weren't in so much pain she might have laughed.

"I only make the software," she said, aware of how pathetic she sounded, of how pathetic she was. But his words gave her hope. If the Egyptian police were sophisticated enough to be running her systems, perhaps there was a chance that someone there could still find her? She shifted her hips, then winced, struggling not to moan. Her leg was hurting her again.

"Bastards," the man repeated, and then made a noise Josie didn't recognize at first. A cough, perhaps, or a hiccup. He made the noise again, a cry strangled by a gasp. Then he said, "They killed my son."

Josie held her breath. Was the man even old enough to have a son? She had imagined him to be younger than she was, irretrievably immature. Perhaps he was; perhaps he had had a child as a teenager. Or perhaps his child was young, Tali's age. Would police kill a child Tali's age? She looked again at his oiled hair, his bristling jaw, his thick hands around the bat. Had the bat belonged to his son?

"They have records of everyone," the man continued. "Everything. Pictures, messages, places. They remember everyone. All with your computer program. Before the revolution was bad, but now with the army it is the same, sometimes worse. If they want someone they cannot find, they take the family, kill the family. They follow everyone. They find my son by his cell phone. He is thirteen years old. Now they follow my daughter."

Josie looked down at the shackle around her leg, the thick iron ring that dug into her skin. *You have given a gift to the world,* Itamar said in her mind. A thousand arguments rose in her throat, flavored like bile. She would have no pity for this man, she decided. She allowed herself to sink into the waves of residual pain from her legs, from her ankles, from the soles of her bare feet, from her hard swollen cheek. *Your problem, Josie,* Judith said in her mind, *is that you have no empathy. None.* If only it were true.

"Some machine codes can destroy computers," the man said now, in a philosophic tone. "Like a plague."

She realized only after a pause that he had asked her a question.

"You mean malware?"

He cocked his head at her.

"Like a virus?" she clarified, though technically viruses were only a subset of malware, and not even the relevant subset. She swallowed her corrections, silencing the pedant within her.

The man smiled again. "Yes, the virus. You will make the virus, and destroy the police records," he said, and slapped his hands together, a gesture that was less a clap than an imaginary door slammed shut. "Can you do this?"

Never in her life had she attempted malware; never, in all her endless building, had she ever tried to destroy anything at all. The inconceivably vast mental effort of programming—the colossal, evolutionarily unlikely process of creating something from nothing, the almost obscene control over individual electrons, the act of telling nature how to move, the harnessing of a nearly divine power to direct outcomes, to determine fate—all to make something *not* work?

But now she watched the man beginning to sneer as she hesitated, and recalled the only thing left in the world she could do: say yes.

"Of course I can," she announced.

The man furrowed his brow, suspicious. "How?"

Did he doubt her, or was he testing her? She had to make it sound obvious, she realized, easy. People who knew nothing about programming always assumed that for people like her, it was easy. She would embody the myth.

"I could certainly damage machines that are using my own applications," she said. "No one knows the product better than I do." That hadn't been true for ages, of course. It had been a very long time since she had done any direct coding for the product at all. But if it were an old enough version of her software, there was some small chance that she had herself designed it. A small chance, her only chance.

"Very good," the man said. He was testing her, she saw. Josephine Ashkenazi was good at taking tests.

"There are always bugs to exploit," she said. "Even the newest version has bugs. It's just that we haven't found them all yet."

"Bugs," the man repeated.

She ignored him, absorbing the risk. "The question is how old their version might be, and whether they bothered getting the patches for it. They're probably running one of the older versions. We haven't even marketed the newer ones overseas, outside of Europe and Israel."

"You sell computer programs in Israel?"

She sucked in her breath, steeled herself. "Yes," she said. And then, after a split-second calculation weighing dignity and risk, she added, "Of course."

"Why?"

"Why wouldn't we?" The "we" brought her comfort, more than she hoped. It was like holding Itamar's hand.

"You sell right away to Israel but not to Egypt? In Egypt we have millions more people. Millions more customers!"

Pointing out the vast differences between the two countries seemed like a poor idea. Was he that dumb, or was he provoking her? It was impossible to tell. She thought of Nasreen, of how she never could understand what Nasreen said, how she was unable to tell the difference between what Nasreen said and what Nasreen meant. Was the woman who had hanged her Nasreen? "A lot of our software developers are Israeli," she said. "If we didn't sell it there, someone there would come up with something better before we did. They're our competition."

"Egyptian police are using Israeli computers?"

"My company is American." As though that were better.

"But programs are made by Israelis."

"And lots of other people."

"Egyptian police are using Israeli computers," he repeated.

"Practically every computer system in the world has Israeli components. Pentium chips were invented in Israel." Don't be insane, she begged herself. She tried to push back the data surging within her, tried channeling it to safety. "But the machine code is in binary, and the numerals are Arabic," she offered lamely. "So Arabs invented the digits every computer is made of, if we're going to start parsing where everything is from." Restricting the flow of data was impossible, she saw; it surged, it overflowed. In minutes she would bleed again.

"Machine code," he said. This seemed to please him.

Josie closed her eyes, briefly, to prevent herself from rolling them. But the relief of evading another beating brought unspeakable joy.

"You will make the virus," he commanded.

"Yes," she said. As if it were a choice.

The man grinned, a wide, warm grin. "I will bring you a computer," he said, beaming. "Do you need special kinds?" It was as if she were his daughter, deciding what she wanted for her birthday.

She thought carefully, seizing her chance. "I would need a new or at least a recent machine, with a recent operating system," she said. "Not a Mac, unless they use Macs. I'm sure they don't use Macs." She thought of the sparkling new machines in the Alexandria library, the glowing marble edifices of the library complex beyond the crowds of paupers in the streets of the city. Which was real, and which was the dream? "I'd also need whatever version of the product they're using, so I could test it, and the developer tools from our internal website," she added. "And network access."

"Network access?" he asked.

"An internet connection," she replied. She said this as casually as she could, as if it were a mere accessory, rather than a rope thrown into a pit to save her life.

The man understood instantly. "No," he growled. "No internet. No."

"I can't transmit a virus without network access," she lied.

"Then you are not necessary," he said. "We do not need you anymore."

He had called her bluff. To her surprise she was impressed, and humbled. How could she have expected to outlie a criminal—especially one who had spent enough time in police headquarters to know what software they used?

"I could do it without network access if you download the developer tools for me, and if you give me a USB drive once it's finished," she said quickly. "You would have to send someone physically into the police headquarters to infect their machines with it, but it would work. Even better, because then I wouldn't have to guess where the bugs are in their firewall."

"Better," he repeated, and smiled. He took a small notepad out of his back pocket, along with a little stump of a pencil, and flipped through its pages. She looked at the Arabic script on the pages as they fluttered by, and the obvious joke formed in her mind: "*To do: 1. Kidnap software executive. 2. Pick up dry cleaning.*" For an instant she fantasized about sharing the joke with Itamar, the two of them laughing about it over dinner, adding more items to the list: "*3. Order Girl Scout cookies. 4. Record execution video. 5. Change shirt.*"

To her astonishment, as she sat chained to a concrete block in an ancient sealed room, her mind allowed her, in the instant of that mental joke, to actually *be* in her kitchen in Massachusetts with Itamar, just as vividly as she was sitting in her cell. She could hear his cartoonish laugh (the laugh that had embarrassed her, years ago, when they first met), feel his thin fingers on hers on the warm wooden table. She could even smell steamed broccoli, which she sometimes ate with dinner because she felt that she should, even though she didn't like it. In her kitchen in that mental moment, the steamed broccoli smell gave her pause. She didn't like broccoli, but she particularly loathed its smell. The smell suggested that her momentary escape wasn't a fantasy at all. It was something else, though she could not yet understand what.

"USB," the man said. His voice snapped her back into the prison room. She watched him struggle with the letters as he recorded it on the little notepad.

"I can write it all down for you," she offered. She thought of Joy, Tali's babysitter, of how every day in her house had once begun with her going over things with Joy, carefully inscribing grocery lists for Joy, delineating what brand of fish sticks Joy needed to prepare for Tali. A door slammed in her mind, eliminating a world. The man passed her the notepad, and held the bat above her head.

"You write," he said. "I bring. And then you will make the code."

AS A CHILD SHE had read a picture-book version of *One Thousand and One Nights*. She knew now what would happen: when the code was finished, they would kill her. The solution, of course, was never to finish. She would become a software Scheherazade.

During the days—she knew now when it was daytime; the clock at the corner of the screen was an oracle (if the time it displayed was even correct)—she wrote code. Most mornings, one of the guards—for that was who Bear Stearns and Doctors Without Borders were, teenage guards who even seemed to be employed on a schedule (were they paid? or were they the man's other sons?)—would bring in pita bread, an open can of unheated vegetables or beans, a plastic bottle of water, and a surprisingly decent laptop (had they stolen it from somewhere?), which he would plug into an extension cord that ran beneath the room's thick wooden door. He would then put the machine on the pail-shaped block of poured concrete, awkwardly balanced beside the chain, and wait for its screen to illuminate. He would open the program, watching with her as the English words "Genizah" floated up from the center to the corner of the screen. Then he would leave. And Josie, after running a fruitless daily search for nearby Wi-Fi, would crouch over the machine and enter another world.

Josie proved herself to be an excellent slave. Terrified of what might happen if she had nothing to show at the end of each day, she worked harder than she ever had. She had not coded in several years, but it was like riding a bike again, or speaking a native language after living for too long in another country. She started out, tried, wobbled, stuttered, wavered, was convinced she had forever forgotten how to do it. And then, within a week, it was as if time had never passed. The developer tools—many newly created in the time since she had last written code herself—were dazzling to her, thrilling. It was like attending a school reunion, meeting old acquaintances and their new spouses and children, the intervening years rendering them far more fascinating than they had ever been before. In this dungeon, the tools were the closest thing she had to friends.

The work focused her, saving her from the wrenching despair that overtook her each night, as well as each day when the laptop failed to appear. (Was someone else using it for work? For school? She never found any other files on it, but still she wondered.) It occurred to her—it pressed on her, the possibility lowered like a weight on her gut—that there were things she could insert into the program, indicators of her presence, cries for rescue; it occurred to her that this might be her only opportunity to evade her own murder. But what could she say? Even if she could be certain that she was in the City of the Dead, the cemetery encompassed hundreds of thousands of buildings; it was a neighborhood larger than many of the world's cities. The thought lingered in her body, gathering strength as her body healed.

In the meantime the malware slowly, painfully slowly, took

shape. Each morning when the machine arrived—after the maddening wait to discover whether today was a day with no computer, a day of emptiness—she waited impatiently to attain the mental state called flow, when writing code no longer felt artificial, but became normal, fluent, emerging like a first language, a casual conversation with an electron. Flow arrived more and more quickly, an antidote to pain. The architecture of the program was immersive, overarching, like constructing a city, suspending the earth on a void. She envisioned it as a photographic negative of Genizah, a program that eliminated memories instead of preserving them. But to see if the program worked, she would need something to erase. And so she began to build a Genizah of Tali.

Josie and Itamar had created an elaborate electronic archive of their daughter—the kind that many parents maintained for their children, now that Josie's software had made it nearly effortless. It was a database of tens of thousands of photographs, video clips, medical records, report cards, art projects, all the detritus of a child's life, preserved in digital form. But that was at home, on another planet. Josie had nothing now except what she remembered—and she discovered that her own creation had hobbled her. It had been years since she had needed to remember anything: her software had turned all memory into history, stories replaced by collections of evidence. But after many nights of staring at a sarcophagus, of pounding the walls, of feeling herself slipping into oblivion, she sensed the ancient human power stirring within her. And during the days she began, in the barest of notes, to write things down, concealing each note behind a miniature electronic door.

Tali home from the hospital, screaming nine hours a day, she wrote, and stored it behind a tiny door that turned a faint pink when the program classed it under "baby girl," even though Tali had never been the sweet sort of baby girl who evoked the color pink. Behind a circus tent flap that labeled itself "entertainment"—though that wasn't quite accurate either—she stored the words *Tali riding the train around the zoo, convinced at the end of the ride that she was getting off at a different zoo from the one where she'd gotten on.* Josie had thought of it as a pleasant, funny memory, but now that she closed the cheerily wrinkled tent flap over it, she recalled that it wasn't: when she had tried to explain to Tali that the zoo hadn't changed, Tali had become hysterical, fanatically insisting that her version of the world was real. On a shelf in a virtual closet labeled "games"—the software had not yet learned her instincts—the program filed away the words *Tali playing checkers with Itamar, winning, and gloating.* Through an aircraft door labeled "travel," she wrote, *Tali on a flight to Israel, shouting in Hebrew at the* minyan *near the bulkhead that they were blocking the emergency exit.* As she wrote it down, she remembered the minyan, the quorum of ten religious men praying together in the aisle of the plane, and Tali's fierce English whisper after Josie had tried to silence her Hebrew rant. "*Safety,* Mommy!" Tali had screeched in her bright orange T-shirt. "They aren't being *safe*!" Tali's fervor had surprised Josie, springing as it seemed from no experience of Tali's at all; she wondered whose arguments were braided into her daughter's genes. Behind a white painted door on the screen that the software labeled "playtime," Josie wrote, *Tali talking to her toys when she thinks she is alone.* Behind rows of smaller doors, labeled only with paltry cryptic words like "childhood" and "emotion"—how Josie felt the aching absence of photographs and videos now, the pathetic poverty of words!—the program automatically deposited more of Josie's memories as she typed them in: *Tali insisting that she will grow up to be a man. Tali insisting that she has been permanently transformed into a peacock. Tali's face when she gets angry. Tali's face when she falls asleep.*

As she closed each door on the screen, Josie could not deny

her growing impression that the Tali in this Genizah was very different from the Tali in the archive at home. The Tali in the photographs and video clips that Josie and Itamar had preserved was adorable, bright, a delightful child who made adults smile. But this newly remembered Tali was fierce, demanding, anything but cute. To Josie's aching dismay, she couldn't tell which Tali was more real.

Josie revised the software in her head again and again until it wasn't software at all, but a pathway to dreams. She opened its doors, wandered through them, descended spiral staircases until she found herself in a subterranean garage, climbing into the driver's seat of her own car. She glanced up at the rearview mirror and saw her daughter in the backseat, black hair hanging in ragged unbrushed ropes around her little face.

"How do we know that dinosaurs are real?" Josie heard Tali ask. "Maybe somebody just made fake bones and put them in the ground!"

It was a real memory, this question of Tali's, though Josie couldn't recall when or where it had taken place. What she did remember was that the question had occasioned a discussion about carbon dating, geologic time, the book of Genesis, and Piltdown Man, all of which weirdly captivated six-year-old Tali. Tali's obsessive interest in whatever interested her mother was creepy, Josie had often thought, as if Tali were not an actual person but rather a projection of Josie's own fantasies. Josie tried her best to date the memory, to recall the exact situation when Tali had asked about dinosaurs being real. She really had seen Tali in the rearview mirror, she remembered, Tali wearing her puffy orange vinyl coat—which dated the conversation to last March or earlier, because in October when Josie had left for Egypt, it hadn't yet been cold enough for Tali to wear that coat. (That coat would hardly fit her by now, Josie realized. Had Itamar bought Tali a new coat yet? She wondered, briefly, before forcing the thought from her mind.) But perhaps Josie was only inventing these details now, to console herself. It was certainly possible, wasn't it? As a test, she tried "remembering" the incident another way—imagining that the conversation had taken place with Tali in the bathtub, or on a playground swing.

The playground swing was implausible; Tali had never stayed on a swing long enough to talk. But soon Josie had reconstructed the memory during Tali's bath, and it was wonderfully vivid, better even than the apparently actual memory of the conversation in the car. The bathtub memory wasn't merely of the conversation, but of Josie's feeling of the conversation's falseness: her sense that Tali was asking her precisely the questions Josie had hoped she would ask, reveling in her mother's pedantic explanations as few people ever had before, precisely as though Tali were nothing more than one of her mother's dreams—which the Tali in Josie's memory actually was. The new memory was not merely visual, but also filled with odors, with textures, with the fragile humidity in the room. In the new memory Josie was running her hand along Tali's black-fuzzed back, rubbing soap into her slick skin. Little shoulderblades rose beneath Josie's fingers like wings. The warm bathroom air in Josie's nostrils was heavy with whining pediatric smells: urine, toothpaste, artificial fruit. She smoothed her palm against Tali's spine as though she were sculpting a warm and breathing child, molding her flesh, fashioning her from clay. Tali's too-loud voice echoed against the bathroom tiles:

"How do we know that dinosaurs are real? Maybe somebody just made fake bones and put them in the ground!"

Josie searched her mind for evidence and found none. Itamar might remember the original conversation, the real event, she thought desperately. But he hadn't been there, and even if she had told him about it, it wasn't the sort of thing he would remember. As the software had proliferated, he had begun remembering things best when he could verify them on a screen. Josie slowly realized that her mourning for her family was layered with a shameful mourning for her phone—for her own Genizah within it, for the chance to climb through the window of the little screen in the palm of her hand and back into all the perfectly catalogued memories of Itamar and Tali, to pass through that window into the life she had once lived—and then she wondered if her phone still existed in one of her captors' pockets, maybe just a few feet away, the tunnel to the past concealed right behind the large locked door of her cell. Deprived of the trove of material that she had digitally preserved, she had no way of knowing whether or not any of her memories were true ones—no method of carbon-dating them, no means of distinguishing her actual daughter from a Piltdown Man made of her own discarded bones. Without the software, none of it was real.

The pit of oblivion lay just beyond the computer screen, a gaping void beneath the scrim of the false world she had created, a fall into nothingness. At the bottom of that pit, Josie knew, was the death that awaited her—and not merely death, but abandonment, the knowledge that her body would be dumped in an ancient river, that she would be swallowed by the earth and no one would ever know. It was comforting to think that Itamar and Tali already believed she was dead, that no further adjustment would be necessary. When the guards took away the computer each night, Josie closed her eyes and pretended the machine was still before her, a thin screen of memory shielding her from the abyss. With her eyes closed she could feel herself falling, and she clutched tight at every flimsy detail she could remember or imagine: the names of Tali's teachers, the first time Tali had laughed as a baby, the kind of toothpaste Itamar used every morning, the smell of his hair, the weight of his hand in hers, the shape of the lenses of his glasses as he squinted his eyes behind them when they kissed. She understood now why everyone wanted to save these things, the endless logs of what their pets ate and what their lovers wore and what their children said. They were ropes thrown down into the pit.

At night, when the guards took the computer away, she began to read *Guide for the Perplexed.*

ACCORDING TO THE VOLUME'S introduction, Rabbi Moses, son of Maimon—Rambam, as he was called in the book's Hebrew half, or Maimonides on the book's French side—had died in the year 1204 in Cairo, where he had been chief physician and surgeon to the sultan Saladin. As Josie gleaned from a cursory flipping through the book, the surgeon spent most of the first several hundred pages explaining why God had no emotions and no qualities, and why anyone who read the Hebrew Bible in a literal fashion was an idiot. Not needing several hundred pages to be convinced of this, Josie had almost given up reading when a page toward the end of the book fell open before her.

There are five theories concerning divine providence, she read.

Divine providence?

Providence, a pious French footnote clarified, *concerns not only divine protection (providing of necessities, etc.), but also divine omniscience and foresight, which is directly related to divine protection through the Holy One's understanding and anticipation of mankind's needs.*

Josie looked around her cell, at the sarcophagus encasing

a forgotten corpse, and almost laughed. The man in the "Jon's Bar Mitzvah" T-shirt was her providence now, she thought. Or whichever guard was bringing the food, or deciding when she would die. But she kept reading.

First theory. There is no providence at all for anything in the universe; all parts of the universe, the heavens and what they contain, owe their origin to accident and chance.

Chance would explain a lot, Josie thought. But she had to admit that it was contrary to evidence. The arrangement of protons and electrons in the world, she had had occasion to notice, was not only not random, but was even somewhat adjustable by the likes of herself. She had gotten into that car of her own accord on her last night of freedom, with no one forcing her. No one had made her come to Egypt either; she had simply fallen for Judith's flattery. The only chance involved in her captivity, as far as she could see, was that Judith was her sister—that Judith had hated her, that Judith had preyed on her vanity and enticed her into going on this absurd and arrogant mission to deliver intelligence to the developing world like a god from on high—and that Josie, solely because of the random fact of sisterhood, had taken her seriously. But that didn't count as chance either, unless Josie thought of Judith as a kind of virus, a morally meaningless opportunistic infection that ate her alive. That, too, was contrary to evidence.

Second theory. While one part of the universe owes its existence to providence, and is under the control of a ruler and governor, another part is abandoned and left to chance. . . . Providence sends forth sufficient influence to secure the immortality and constancy of the species, without securing at the same time permanence for the individual beings of the species.

Interesting, Josie thought, and slightly more palatable. But what mechanism governed what was chance and what wasn't?

This is the view of Aristotle, the text clarified: *Everything which does not come to an end and does not change its properties (such as the heavenly spheres, and everything which continues according to a certain rule), is the result of providential management. But that which is not constant, and does not follow a certain rule, such as instances in the existence of the individuals of each species, is due to chance and not to management. For instance, when a storm or gale blows, it undoubtedly causes some leaves of a tree to drop, breaks off some branches of another tree, and stirs up the sea so that a ship goes down with a whole or part of its contents. Aristotle sees no difference between the falling of a leaf and the death of the good and noble people on the ship.*

This struck Josie as rather circular, to say that things that didn't change were under "management" (for what further management would be required?) while things that weren't, weren't. The example of men drowning in a shipwreck puzzled her even more; she sensed that that was the real question here, the question of catastrophic accidents. It was her own question, too—but only if she considered what had happened to her an accident. At what point did securing immortality for the species stop and securing immortality for individuals begin? Were the dinosaurs extinct due to the will of God, while a single baby stegosaurus's fate was left to chance? More relevant, was she herself only fair game for chance now, since Tali had already been born to perpetuate her genes and continue the species on her behalf? The logical absurdities that followed from this idea were worse than the first.

Third theory. According to this theory, there is nothing in the whole universe, neither a class nor an individual being, that is due to chance; everything is due to will, intention, and rule . . . Each leaf falls according to the divine decree.

This, Josie thought, was plausible—particularly if one violently neutered the idea of "divine decree" into something less debatable and equally immutable, like "laws of nature." She thought of the many brilliant and proud people she had worked with over the years, and their almost universal, gleeful disdain for the possibility of the unknowable. Her career had been spent surrounded by the outspoken atheism of nerds. It had always struck her as an immense arrogance. Pretending to agree with them was something that still shamed her, even after her success. But the idea of everything following the divine decree was too depressing to consider, leaving everything pointless while claiming to do the opposite. If no one could explain or predict divine or even natural decrees, then this idea was no different in practice from theory number one.

Fourth theory. Man has free will, and therefore has the ability to act meaningfully in obedience or disobedience to divine law. . . . All acts of God are due to wisdom; no injustice is found in him, and he does not afflict the good.

Josie looked at the shackle around her leg, at her beaten body chained in a dungeon, and remembered the thought that had haunted her since she first awoke in this abandoned tomb: that she had earned this, that her arrogance alone had driven her into this pit. She still suspected it was true. Perhaps Nasreen was right, and her life had been a cultivation of the trivial; perhaps she had added little good to the universe. Josie had lived her life in an aggressively rational world, but this unacknowledged belief in the ultimate justice of the universe lingered within her like a ghost.

To her surprise, the author demolished this theory in a paragraph, just as he had demolished the other three. He mentioned birth defects, and she wondered what illnesses he must have encountered as a doctor eight hundred years ago. But the main problem, he claimed, was the impossibility of free will existing alongside an omniscient God—or, Josie apologized to an imagined audience of atheist nerds, alongside the laws of physics and genetics as their own form of fate. Then the book provided its Fifth Theory, one of "absolute free will."

Fifth theory. It is due to the eternal divine will that all living beings should move freely. Another fundamental principle is that all evils and afflictions as well as all kinds of happiness of man, whether they concern one individual person or a community, are distributed according to justice. We are only ignorant of the workings of that judgment.

This seemed to Josie to be merely a slightly worse version of the fourth theory, until the author clarified it in a way that stunned her.

My opinion of this principle of divine providence I will now explain to you.

It may be mere chance that a ship goes down with her contents and drowns those within it, or the roof of a house falls upon those within; but it is not due to chance, according to our view, that in the one instance the men went into the ship, or remained in the house in the other instance . . . Divine influence reaches mankind through the human intellect, and divine providence is in proportion to each person's intellectual development.

Josie struggled through the footnote in old-fashioned French:

As a physician, Maimonides knew of the human capacity to ease or even eliminate sufferings that were supposed by many to be ordained by God. This passage considers intellectual capacity to be the element of the divine image granted to humans (cf. Part 1, Section 1). Divine protection of humanity, in this view, is not effected by direct divine intervention in human affairs, but rather by the divinely bestowed gift of intellect, which affords men the opportunity to alleviate or prevent misfortunes.

The idea was heartless and beautiful, humming in the dungeon room like a classical fugue, an intricate harmonics of faith and reason: utterly and cruelly logical, intolerant of nonsense—

and, Josie imagined, infused with possibility. All Josie needed to do, to fulfill both divine and free will and her husband's and daughter's dreams, was to think her way out of this room. But what if she failed?

As she fell asleep that night, she thought of her mother.

Not her mother now, lost to a disease no human was yet smart enough to cure, but her mother in days long past: when Josie was a child, and her mother was a prophet.

"Don't be too good, Josie," her mother had once warned her.

Josie now remembered that she had been in the car then, in the front passenger seat next to her mother, on her way to an evening violin lesson. Her father had moved out weeks earlier, and Josie had noticed her mother's brittleness. Josie had tried to distract her. She spoke, her voice too fast as she tried to fill the silence, about how she had been unable to play a certain concerto with any degree of quality, no matter how much she practiced. Her teacher, a bitter Russian Jewish immigrant who had once been a principal in a regional orchestra but who now worked as a supermarket cashier, had told her in his heavy accent that perfection was attainable, that not attaining it was failure. Her father liked him.

"Don't be too good," her mother repeated, staring through the windshield. "You will be punished for being too good. And if that happens, don't be surprised or think it's unfair, because it will be your fault."

At thirteen, Josie read the Bible of adult words literally. "I don't think Mr. Vedemyapin is going to punish me for improving my Liszt."

The car stopped at a light. Josie's mother turned to look at her, rubbing mascara off her face. She had recently found work at a doctor's office, her notes and drafts for her unfinished dissertation on string theory dumped into boxes in a closet, behind a locked door. She frowned.

"You're a lot like your father, you know," her mother said, in a voice that glanced off Josie like a tangent, a perfect Platonic line directed elsewhere. "You remind me of him."

Beneath the words, Josie heard what her mother meant: *Don't remind me.*

FIFTY DAYS AFTER SHE had first been captured (for she knew the date now; it loomed before her at the bottom of the computer screen, a slow burn at the root of her soul), Josie was writing code, toggling back and forth between the code and Genizah on her screen, when the voice of her captor jarred her back into her cell.

"What is this?"

It was a moment of what programmers called dump shock—the world-shaking instant of being forcibly removed from the flow of codewriting and thrown back onto the alien planet called Earth. She hadn't even heard the door to the cell opening; the man appeared as if created from nothing, a talking ghost. She jolted, staggered on her knees from her crouch on the floor, jerked out of a happy dream. It had begun to feel normal to her to work while kneeling on the floor, in chains. After fifty days, she knew who she was now.

"I give you blank program," he said. He was bending above her, squinting at the laptop. She glanced back at it and saw that Genizah was open, her mock Genizah, her fabricated memories on the screen. "You are writing English. Not machine code." She could hear the fury in his voice.

She tried to control her hands as they trembled. It was as

though he had ripped off her clothes. "It's—it's just to test the software," she stammered. She was surprised that her voice was hoarse. She clutched the keyboard as though covering her naked body.

He tore it away, stripping her.

"First day of school," he read aloud, rounding the vowels. He pronounced "school" as "shul." "Tali says her best friend is named Sor—Svor—" He looked at her. She watched as his face deepened, choking back an almost animal rage. "You are sending secret messages."

"I was testing the malware," she begged. "I can't test it unless there's some content in the—"

A vein in his neck bulged. "We are not stupid. You think we are afraid to kill you?"

Josie clutched at her chain, her fingers tapping its links compulsively, like keys. "You can erase it all," she pleaded. Her voice was shaking now. "It's nothing. Look, I'll erase everything." She pulled herself up to stand, nearly fell, bowed before him to reach the keyboard, and quickly deleted all the text behind the door, purging her child as the man watched. *It's nothing,* she thought. Beneath the vanished text was a glowing, lurid void. "I can show you all the doors, the whole archive, and erase absolutely everything. The malware was going to erase it anyway. That's what I was testing."

"Erase it now."

"But the malware—" she corrected herself, or de-corrected herself—"the virus isn't finished yet. When it is, you can just stick in the flash drive and it ought to erase everything immediately."

"No. Now." He put the laptop back down on the concrete block. "I will see if you are lying. Erase it now."

The steel cuff scraped Josie's ankle as she sank back to the floor, rearranging her legs. She began opening doors on the screen, trying not to read what she was deleting. She worked quickly as she listened to the man's hard breathing behind her, emptying imaginary closets and rooms behind imaginary doors. But then she opened a door she hadn't remembered making. She clicked it open.

Tali told me and Itamar that the rabbi at the nursery school had taught her about God. I asked her what she had learned, and she told us, "God is one." We nodded, like proud idiots. Then she said, "But I'm bigger, because I'm already three."

That night in bed, Itamar told me that whenever he hears people argue about whether God exists or whether the world is fair, he feels like the argument is not just silly but dirty, and he had never understood why until now. "Because when people talk about that," he told me, "I imagine that from God's point of view, it's as if we're arguing about whether God is three years old." I hadn't known how much he believed.

The software had labeled the door with the words *Tali's soul.*

Josie stared at the screen, transported to her bedroom on the other end of the world. Tali's comment was the kind of thing that she would have saved in the software at home. She probably had; she usually ran the recording components when Tali was around, and it was a cute joke, the kind of adorably funny mistake that cute children make, and that was what Genizah was designed to save. But it now occurred to her that she never would have thought to record what Itamar had said.

The voice jarred her back: "Erase now."

She babbled absently, still in that room. "I will, I am, I just—"

The man grabbed her by the neck. She turned around and stared at his dark glasses until he released her, her elbow knocking against the concrete block. When she saw him raise his hand again, she spoke.

"At home I use Genizah to keep records of my daughter—

pictures, movies, school projects, things she says, everything," she said, almost in a whisper. To her astonishment the man did not interrupt her. "Genizah arranges everything intuitively. I don't have any photos or anything now, so I just wrote down what I could remember." It was a lie, she knew. She remembered nothing. The man remained silent. "The software sorts everything so you can always find it," she continued. Her words came almost automatically, as if she were speaking to the businessmen at the Four Seasons Hotel. "It can time-lapse your photos so you can see a person growing, or locate where the pictures were taken, or cross-catalogue with other people's archives, or match handwriting or a voice to a particular time period. Things like that. When you have enough material to work with, you can almost build an entire person out of this. It's like bringing someone back to life."

She swallowed, rubbing her face. She felt unspeakably tired. What purpose did it serve, after all? They would kill her at some point no matter what, and everything would be forgotten. And Tali was too little, Tali wouldn't remember her, Tali would know only what she and Itamar had stored in the software—how she had once been an adorable, silly child, with brilliant parents who had no souls. Josie would become no more than an electronic mother, illuminated waves and particles on a screen. Most likely she already was.

"I'll erase it now," she said.

The man stood before her, his hands at his sides, and spoke. "Can you make a Genizah of my son?"

FUSTAT, SCHECHTER SAW out of the rabbi's carriage windows, had indeed seen better days. Its narrow streets were like open sewers, their cobblestones covered with a thick sheen of urine and filth. Schechter had spent his first three weeks in Egypt in imperial Cairo, among the opera houses and cafés and wide boulevards of what could easily have been mistaken for a European city if it weren't for the hansom cab drivers dressed in ankle-length robes. But now he was traveling through a neighborhood that appeared to have only deteriorated since the death of Maimonides in the year 1204. Schechter had grown up in poverty, but he had never seen anything like this. Thick rivers of brown sewage flowed along the open gutters at the center of each tiny stone street. The calls to prayer from the minarets which he had heard from his hotel room were here amplified by church bells and by the cackles of injured chickens, who wandered the alleys as though ownerless. Children dressed in rags crowded their coach, banging on the glass windows and pointing to their mouths until the turbaned driver threatened them with his whip. The worst was the tannery, an alleyway crammed with enormous clay vats full of red and orange dyes and shaded by drying skins that hung suspended on ropes between the buildings. The odor transcended the normal experience of smell to become aural, visual. It was like being inside a dead horse.

In the previous three weeks Schechter had labored mightily to get here. Besides his trip to Giza with the rabbi, his Arabic lessons with the rabbi's insufferable brother, and his telegrams back to Cambridge to ensure the shipment of large quantities of stamps, there had been other elaborately dressed men to convince of his worthiness, more people to bribe. Among the Jews of Cairo he had also discovered one asset, a wealthy man named Moise Cattaoui who even had a street named after him in the city, and who happily invited Schechter over for eminently edible meals. Most important, Cattaoui had gotten Schechter a room at the Metropole. But now Schechter was closing in on the prize: the Palestinian synagogue in Fustat.

"I have heard that our holy congregations in Europe preserve only those documents that are inscribed with the name of God," the rabbi said. "But it has been our community's custom, for these many centuries, to retain all documents written in the letters of the holy tongue, regardless of their contents. As you can imagine, we have preserved vast quantities of garbage." The carriage lurched over a loose stone, just missing the carcass of a donkey that had been abandoned to rot in the street. Schechter watched the flies crawling across the dead beast's moist open eyes. "The exterior of the synagogue was renovated several years ago, as I mentioned," the rabbi continued. "At that time the contents of the genizah were removed and placed in the courtyard for several months during the repairs to the roof, and they were only recently redeposited. So you may find that the older materials are on the top rather than the bottom, or in general the contents may be in some disarray. It has been years since I have seen it myself."

Schechter thought of the rug salesman, the twins' Mr. Maimoun. There must have been endless opportunities for such people to help themselves. *Disarray,* he thought. He watched as they drove past a pile of severed sheep's heads.

When they arrived at the synagogue, Schechter was relieved to see that it was surrounded by a thick stone wall with an iron gate, which succeeded in keeping out most of the chickens. The building itself, a solid stone rectangle with a crenellated roof like a castle, was much larger and more imposing than he had expected—larger than any synagogue he had known in Romania, and more beautifully painted in greens and blues. The rabbi led him to the building's enormous embossed metal door, and pushed it open.

Inside was a synagogue-tomb, a cool, dark space that looked as though it had last been renovated in the late Middle Ages. The room was large, with a two-story ceiling accommodating a women's gallery on the second floor. The only light came from the open door and a few narrow windows above the women's gallery. Large chunks of plaster had fallen from the walls. The stone floor was worn down in so many places that the tiles spread before Schechter's feet like the swells of a rough sea at dusk. The ceiling was wood and stone, in an intricate painted geometric pattern like the ones Schechter had seen everywhere in Cairo, except here the colors were obscured by soot. The benches along the sides of the room were dark wood, and three were so badly broken that they were actually lying on the floor, sleeping under thick blankets of dust. In the otherwise empty center of the room was a wide stone lectern whose decorative carvings were nearly worn away. The ark at the front of the room, where the Torah scrolls were kept, was a ten-foot-high wooden cabinet whose paint had peeled so badly that the colors were indistinguishable. Above the ark, carved in plaster, were words in Hebrew that were so chipped and covered with grime that Schechter could read them only because he already knew what they said: *Know Before Whom You Stand.*

"This is our custodian, Bechor Maimoun," the rabbi announced. While Schechter was studying the ruins, another man had materialized at his side—a thin man, ageless, in an ankle-length gray robe and a large black skullcap, with a thick brush of a beard, and hands so delicate that Schechter wondered whether he filed his nails. The man smiled, offering Schechter a slight bow. Schechter remembered the twins in Cambridge. *Yes,* he thought as he watched the man slide his hands into the sleeves of his robe, *I would very much like to buy a rug.*

The rabbi turned to the custodian and muttered something in Arabic, which Schechter's three weeks' worth of lessons with the rabbi's obsequious brother failed to render intelligible. Soon the man hurried away. "He will meet us on the other side with a ladder," the rabbi said.

Schechter coughed, inhaled dust, coughed more. "Why a ladder?"

The rabbi glanced at him. "You are here for the genizah, aren't you?"

Schechter saw that asking questions was pointless. The rabbi turned, and Schechter followed him, surprised to see that they were going out the main door again. Schechter swallowed his curiosity and let the rabbi lead him around the building to another smaller door, which opened onto a narrow stone staircase. It was becoming harder and harder to believe that anything worthwhile would be waiting for him beyond it, but Schechter stayed silent as they climbed the stairs and then passed through a closet full of buckets and brooms. "We are so busy with repairs," the rabbi announced, apparently to explain why they were walking through a broom closet—though the building seemed to Schechter to be in the greatest possible state of disrepair, and also empty, save for Mr. Maimoun. At the end of the broom closet the rabbi pushed open another door. To Schechter's surprise they were now standing in the women's balcony, just above where they had entered. Bechor Maimoun was waiting for them, having once more emerged out of nowhere. He leaned a rotting wooden ladder against a high, decrepit wall made of a patchwork of plaster and brick. The ladder hit the wall just beneath a large rectangle of dark filth, sending chunks of plaster raining down to the floor.

The two men looked at Schechter for a long moment in silence. Schechter waited for either of them to speak. The two kept staring at him until the rabbi waved a hand at the ladder. "Are you going up?" he asked.

The ladder clearly led nowhere. Was this some sort of trick? "Up where?"

"Inside!"

Now Schechter looked up again, to where the ladder touched the wall. As the sun moved into a window across the gallery, he could see that the dark rectangle at the top, which he had thought was just a patch of soot-covered plaster, was actually a small wooden door.

"What you are looking for is there," the rabbi said, pointing to the top. "Climb!"

The custodian offered him a lantern, which he lit with a match from his pocket. Still skeptical, Schechter took the lamp and began to climb, with the rabbi and the custodian holding the ladder. At last he reached the door.

The door was about half the size of a normal door, like a cupboard. It had a wide, filthy threshold, which Schechter used to rest the lantern on as he manipulated the door's small iron latch. Then, with one firm push, he pressed the door inward and lifted his body off the ladder until he was sitting on the threshold, with his legs swinging into the room. To his surprise, there was no floor. His legs were dangling in dark space. Then his foot brushed against something, something that made a loud crunching sound. An enormous cloud of dust blew into his face. Schechter coughed, a long and painful series of coughs that echoed through the room in front of him. He stopped coughing as the dust still hung in the air, and held up the lamp in front of him.

When the clouds cleared, he saw below him a sea of paper.

He had pictured a room full of shelves or cabinets or drawers, a kind of morgue for dead books. But this was an ocean—or, considering the narrow dimensions of the room, more like a well. Papers filled the entire narrow room up to the height of the building's gallery, rising up in a heap like the swell of a wave near the threshold of the door, where the most recent corpses had presumably been dumped. In places he could make out whole books bound in leather, and at several points the wooden handles of Torah scrolls poked through the ocean's surface. But most of it, the bulk of that thick and heavy sea, was loose paper.

Some of it was printed, typed, woodcut, but as Schechter looked more closely, he saw that much of it was not. Hebrew letters stared up at him, drowning him in a vast sea of thought. He leaned in, lowering himself down until he was actually standing in the papers, supported by parchments several feet below him and still well above the level of the floor outside. He was immersed in paper up to his waist. And, perching the lantern on the threshold of the door, hardly thinking about fire or dust or rot or anything else, he began to read.

The first paper he saw, near his right sleeve, was a marriage contract. He picked it up and read the first lines, the lines that were the same but for the particulars as the marriage contract he had with his own wife. This contract's first lines announced that the wedding ceremony between David the son of Abraham and Miriam the daughter of Joseph had taken place in Fustat on a Tuesday, on the fifteenth of the month of Av, nine hundred fifty-seven years before. He lifted it out of the pile and imagined this young couple, suddenly feeling their presence in the room. On the back of the parchment he found another paper, stuck to the first. It was a bill of divorce for David the son of Abraham and Miriam the daughter of Joseph—whose marriage had apparently been dissolved in Fustat on a Wednesday, the eighth of the month of Elul, ten years later.

Schechter shuddered, breathing in more dust. Near his other arm he saw a dark paper with large Hebrew letters. As he lifted it, he saw that the letters were written in repeated rows, in an awkward hand, the letters *kaf* and *lamed* scrawled again and again, looping absurdly in and out of the dark ridges that someone had scored into the parchment. Some little child hundreds of years ago had been learning how to write. Stuck to the child's page was a page written in much smaller adult letters, a passage so disintegrated that Schechter could only make out a few of the Hebrew words: *and if anyone believes in the existence of demons, that person has sinned against the Holy One and shall be forgotten for all eternity, for those idolatrous thoughts are the source* and here the page was torn. Schechter reached to adjust the lamp, broadening the light. As he moved, he noticed a parchment near the doorway with letters arranged in careful squares, as though for a puzzle, or an amulet. He picked it up and read the neat, emphatic words beneath the boxed letters: *May this spell destroy the demons who have possessed Miss Yair, so that she may love me for all eternity.*

Schechter looked around at the fathomless pit of paper. The air in the room was alive, trembling with the thoughts of the thousands of people whose names were inscribed in the parchments below. He sifted the papers before him, lifting them like sand and letting them slide between his fingers. He turned, heard a crunching noise, mourned whatever document must have been ground to dust beneath his feet, and spotted a piece of parchment with carefully written verses inscribed on it, dark ink on dark vellum, like the scraps the twins had shown him a lifetime ago in Cambridge. He seized it, unable to believe what he had in his hands. The words, he saw immediately, were from Ben Sirah:

There are some that have left a name,
so that men declare their praise.
And there are some who have no name,
who have perished as though they had not lived.

In some dark closet of his mind Schechter heard a voice, a voice so distant and irrelevant that it took him several seconds to realize it was the rabbi's. The shout echoed toward him from beyond the well:

"Is this the garbage you want?"

Schechter placed the poem aside—but there was no "aside," it was all a well, a deep and bottomless well of lives, the lives of everyone who had left a name, and everyone who had perished as though they had not lived.

Schechter tried to speak, coughed, choked, tried again. "Yes, yes!" he shouted.

"Then perhaps we can come to an agreement," the rabbi called back.

The words jarred Schechter back to the world outside the

room. This time he understood immediately. He stared at the papers below him, thought of what Professor Taylor had given him, calculated what he had left, calculated what he might still need. Suddenly money seemed irrelevant. He was dipping his feet into eternity. But the rabbi below wanted an answer. And he was the one holding the ladder.

"I can offer you three hundred pounds sterling for it," Schechter blurted.

Three hundred pounds sterling! It was more than four years' worth of rent on his house in Cambridge. But what else was Taylor's money for, if not for this?

Somewhere outside the hole in the wall, Schechter heard a sudden gasp, and then loud laughter. When the laughter finally faded, he heard the rabbi call out, in a bright tone, "Take whatever you like!"

As a matter of fact, Schechter liked it all. The next day he returned with canvas bags.

WITHIN DAYS THE PREVIOUSLY empty synagogue was full of people. Each day Schechter would take a carriage from the Metropole to the synagogue in Fustat, and each day he was met by a phalanx of men and women whom the rabbi had sent to assist him. Schechter quickly discovered that they preferred to be compensated for their efforts not through the lowly method of per diem payment, but rather through baksheesh, which had the added benefit of being payable for services not rendered. Such services ran the gamut from carrying large bags full of documents down the ladder to considering doing so, and included such niceties as offering condolences when he was overtaken by coughing fits and wishing him the best when he sneezed.

Bechor Maimoun, the twins' supplier, was the worst of them. When the number of sacks of manuscripts rose to eighteen, Schechter returned to the genizah one morning to find two sacks missing. The beadle insisted that Schechter had counted wrong, and Schechter had no choice but to believe him. Two weeks later, Maimoun indicated that he had a number of manuscripts for sale that had been discovered in a different genizah, in the graveyard outside of town. When he showed them to Schechter, they included pages of books that Schechter had already bagged.

"If these holy writings have found favor in your sight," Maimoun said in his stilted Hebrew, "I would be pleased to offer them to you, at the price of only fifty shillings."

Schechter was overwhelmed by a coughing fit. "Damn," he gagged in English. "Damn, damn, damn. I'm a fool."

Maimoun smiled, and inquired in Hebrew, "What is 'damn'?"

"We have in our language a little word of one syllable which is full of theological meaning, and is used as a sort of charm against people who annoy us," Schechter told him, and pulled out his wallet.

But it didn't matter. None of it mattered, the living didn't matter, because Schechter was too deeply immersed with the dead. For that is how he saw the books and papers he collected now: as dead people, buried in the genizah the way that bodies are buried in a cemetery, until, miraculously, the act of reading brought them back to life. He mourned each time he found a paper he could not read, and had to fight the urge to read every paper he touched. It was like watching dry bones come back to life, the reanimation of a world. He felt, as he worked, an all-powerful arrogance, a sudden and stupendous triumph over time and death. But after two weeks it became clear that reading was hopeless, like stepping into quicksand, being sucked down into the depths of days until he could no longer breathe. Already he was choking. Matilda would do something for him, bring him something to ease his sickened lungs, he thought. The fact that Matilda was several thousand miles away seemed irrelevant to Schechter as he gagged. But he had to keep working. His only goal, now, was to bag as much material as he could before he ran out of money for baksheesh. He carefully peeled a piece of vellum off the filthy gray brick wall.

At first glance he assumed it was yet another leaf from a Bible, or some sort of compilation; every other phrase was a quote from Isaiah, Genesis, Samuel, Kings. By this time he barely looked at the parchments, but whenever he came across a biblical compilation, he was careful to give it two seconds' more time before tossing it into the sack. He held the vellum up to the light from the hole in the wall. But its words (twelfth- or thirteenth-century, it appeared, based on the handwriting) soon resolved into a personal letter, written in a kind of biblical composite, as nearly every personal letter in the room had been—like listening to the Grand Rabbi, words laden with too many ribbons and pearls.

He was about to drop it into the canvas sack when he began to cough, the same cough that had plagued him every day since he had begun his work in the darkened room. He stared at the letter as his lungs calmed, checking whether the lack of oxygen had affected his senses. Worn down, drowning in a sea of words, he cleared a space amid the piles of papers and dirt and crouched on printed litter, holding the letter in the air above him as his vision resolved. Yes, he could still read; the words on the scrap in front of him were eminently clear. He tested himself on a few lines in the center of the page.

Suddenly he became someone else, a man opening his mail

eight hundred years before. The letter spoke in an almost human voice:

> *The worst disaster that struck me recently, worse than anything I had ever experienced from the time I was born until this day, was the demise of my brother, that upright man (may the memory of the righteous be a blessing), who drowned in the Indian Ocean while in possession of much wealth belonging to me, to him and to others, leaving a young daughter and his widow in my care.*
>
> *From then until this day, that is, about eight years, I have been in a state of disconsolate mourning. How can I be consoled? For he was like my son; he grew up upon my knees; he was my brother, my pupil. It was he who did business in the marketplace, earning a livelihood, while I dwelled in security.*
>
> *My only joy was to see him. The sun has set on all joy. For he has gone on to eternal life, leaving me dismayed in a foreign land. Whenever I see his handwriting or one of his books, my heart is churned inside me and my sorrow is rekindled. In short, I will go down in mourning to my son in Sheol. And were it not for the Torah, which is my delight, and for scientific matters, which let me forget my sorrow, I would have perished in my affliction . . .*

The page trembled like a living thing in Schechter's hand. He sensed the man who had written it fuming over his shoulder, angered and ashamed, as though Schechter had come across him in the very moment when he was weakened and stripped, grieving in a windowless room over a catastrophe that no one could possibly understand. He wanted to turn to that nameless man—the grammar indicated that it was a man—and reassure him that everything would be all right. He wanted to be the one to tell that lie. But the man didn't seem like the sort who would believe him. "I will go down in mourning to my son in Sheol," the man had written—the words of Jacob in the Bible, when his sons deceived him into thinking that his favorite son Joseph had died.

That verse had made Schechter shudder since he was a child. He remembered his father as he had last seen him, through the window of the train that he took to Vienna when he was seventeen years old, after he had told his parents that he could no longer remain in their house, in their town, in their world. His father had blessed him before he boarded the train, covering his son's head with the thick hands he used to slaughter bulls in his butcher's abattoir. Schechter felt like a mute calf as he saw his father's face. As the train pulled away, he shouted out the window about visiting for the new year, but he knew they would never see each other again. His grief had filled the railway car until he was unable to breathe.

The weeping man who had written the letter was surely in Sheol now, Schechter thought. He recalled a description he had once read of Sheol, the only hint in the entire Hebrew Bible of any afterlife at all: a netherworld deep beneath the earth, enclosed with locked gates, a dark buried room that was the fate of every person who ever lived, no matter their good or evil deeds—a place, he recalled, of unrelenting silence. No one after biblical times ever spoke of Sheol. It had been replaced by cheerier visions: divine judgment, the resurrection of the dead, underground caverns through which the revived would crawl to Jerusalem at the end of days, the righteous feasting on the flesh of the leviathan, the justice and mercy of the world to come. But Sheol, the dark room of oblivion, was what haunted him. It was what haunted everyone.

He looked around the dark room, at the heaps of unread

words entombed in earth, and knew. This is what becomes of all of us.

The words of the letter grew dimmer in the fading light. As he turned over the piece of vellum in his hand, he noticed the signature at the end of its long lament: Mosheh ben Maimon.

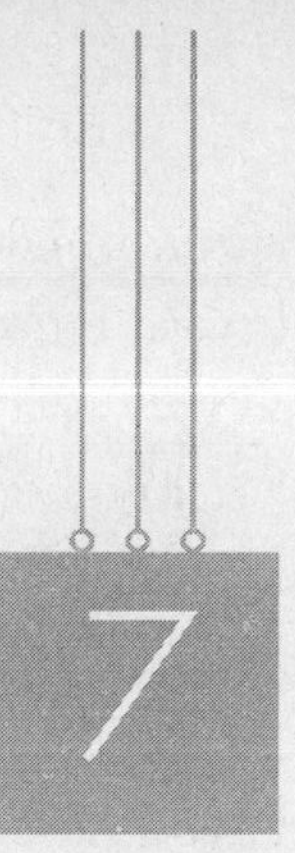

The impossible has a stable nature, one whose stability is constant and is not made by a maker; it is impossible to change it in any way. Consequently we do not ascribe to God the power of doing what is impossible. While philosophers say that it is impossible to produce a square with a diagonal equal to one of the sides, it is thought possible by some persons who are ignorant of mathematics. I wonder whether this gate of research is open, so that all may freely enter, and while one person imagines a thing and considers it possible, another is at liberty to assert that such a thing is impossible by its very nature; or whether the gate is closed and guarded by certain rules, so that we are able to decide with certainty whether a thing is physically impossible. . . . We have now shown that there are things which are impossible, and whose creation is excluded from the power of God. It is now clear that a difference of opinion exists only as to the question to which of the two classes a thing belongs; whether to the class of the impossible, or to the class of the possible.

Musa loved puzzles. He was fanatical about them. The other boys in the neighborhood were fanatical about soccer, but for Musa it was puzzles. When he was a toddler he was captivated by the cardboard kind that his mother bought cheap on the street; he mastered those quickly, putting together forty-eight pieces in minutes. As he grew older, he started creating puzzles of his own. He would break plates in order to reassemble them, fold and cut paper to build geodesic shapes in three dimensions. When the family worshiped in the mosque, he would train his eyes on the patterns of the medieval tiles on the walls. At nine years old, he pointed out to his parents how the tile patterns were regular, all sequences of pentagons and decagons interspersed with rhombuses with endless minor variations, but that they nonetheless never once replicated, despite being spread out over enormous surfaces—potentially infinite surfaces, in fact. The pattern would imitate itself, always following its own rules of symmetry in ten directions. But it would never, ever, ever repeat.

His parents didn't believe him at first. The mosque had been built eight hundred years before. Its architects could not have been using infinite patterns; they could not have understood that sort of math; even his parents, reasonably educated people, did not understand it. Musa proved it to them, demonstrating at home with paper and scissors. It was true: the secret code of a divinely generated universe, an infinity that never repeated but nonetheless always conformed to simple rules, endless generations of infinitely varied cells, plants, moments, arguments, love stories whose infinite variations were relentlessly confined within rigorous laws as generous as birth and light, and as unforgiving as gravity and death—all of it had been discerned by their ancestors, grouted onto the walls in front of them. Only Musa had noticed it.

Josie had begun recording this one evening when her captor arrived in her cell and sat down beside her, bat in hand, forcing her to type his words into the program as he spoke endlessly about his son. She recorded it all in simple English, explaining how one could use an online translation system (she listed a few free ones) to bring it into clumsy Arabic, filing it away in the software behind the appropriate doors. It sickened her, but she did it, replacing the thoughts and descriptions and memories of Tali that she had accumulated in the program's labyrinth of rooms—proud Tali, weird Tali, friendless Tali, crocodile-obsessed Tali, the Tali who was barely more than a shadow of whatever adult she might become—with this new dead boy. The malware project had been suspended for now, it seemed. She shouldn't have cared about this, but she did, feeling the old ache from years of coding, the wrenching frustration of all of her work gone to waste—a strange feeling, considering that her only real goal ought to have been to prolong the project forever, to never finish it at all. But now there was something new to accomplish, another impossible goal. "Keep that agile mentality," she had once repeated regularly to every person who ever worked for her. "Deliver greatest business value first." Greatest business value in this dungeon, she reminded herself, was whatever kept her alive. And what was keeping her alive, now, was the digital revival of Musa, the dead Egyptian boy.

What sickened her most was that she was jealous of Musa. Or, more accurately, jealous of Musa's parents, despite the horror they had endured and despite the horror they were now inflicting on her. For their child was the sort of child she had hoped to have, a child with an obviously discernible intellectual talent, a child who taught his parents things they had never known about the world. But it was a childish thing to hope for, she saw now, childish in every sense of the term—to hope one's child would be a superior version of oneself. As Musa had known, the world was rigorously patterned, but the pattern would never repeat.

"You will put these photos inside the machine," Musa's father said.

He had come in that evening for the second time, after her hummus-and-pita dinner, and Josie braced herself for the physical nausea he still aroused in her, avoiding the humiliation of eye contact. But when she glanced up at him, feeling his eyes boring through her behind his sunglasses, she stared in surprise. In his right hand was an object that took her many long moments to identify, something that made the stinking air shudder with what the ancients once described as magic, holiness, access to the firmament, a route to communion with the divine. It was a phone.

The phone was a first-generation smartphone, a four-year-old knockoff that Josie, in her former life at the pinnacle of human creation, hadn't seen in a very long time. But to see a phone of any kind in this tomb now was jolting, electrifying. She thought of the passages she had read the night before in *Guide for the Perplexed*, on the difference of opinion over what was possible. She had the odd sensation that an impossibility had just occurred—as if he had just drawn a square with a diagonal the same length as its sides, or as if Tali, with blood pulsing through her body and a smile on her lips, had just walked through the door. Josie did not even recognize the feeling it aroused in her: hope.

"Nice phone," she murmured, to say something. The words were filthy in her mouth, thick with ash and dust. It occurred to her that there couldn't possibly be any connectivity in this dungeon. Or could there be? She noticed that he was holding his bat. She felt her legs beginning to shake. It was a reflex now, whenever she saw him. She was his dog, his slave.

"My wife buy for me," he told her with a grin. She wondered if it were true, then mentally kicked herself, reminded herself that surely it wasn't. Nothing this man said was true. Maybe he had never even had a son. Or more likely, he had created the particular son he had been forcing Josie to record in the software, sculpting him out of distorted and false memories and then trying, ridiculously, to use Josie's program to breathe him into life. Josie knew what he was doing; she had done it herself. The Tali she had created, in the program and in her mind, was just as false, like everything human beings create—a lifeless lump of clay, inspired by no more than vanity.

He sat down beside her with his shoulder against hers as he tapped the screen of his miraculous phone. It was the first time anyone had touched her since the hanging, months earlier. Josie blinked her eyes and imagined that it was Itamar resting against her, remembering the first time she had rubbed against his warm, beautiful body. They had been sitting next to each other at a lab in the computer science department at Bar Ilan University north of Tel Aviv, while they waited through a break in a conference where they both were speaking. They had both migrated to the lab to check their messages—a visit that would soon feel as outdated as stopping by a telegraph office, but not then, not yet. She had asked him where he was from, and he had shown her on screen with a program that was still in beta testing, giving her a satellite view of the limestone apartment bloc in the crowded neighborhood where he had grown up. She felt it now in this dungeon, as though she were there in that air-conditioned lab from years ago: the tingle of his surprisingly soft shoulder against her sleeve as she slid her chair next to his, the jolting and unexpected thrill of feeling his arm pressed against hers as he took her into outer space to show her his past. She hadn't known, until that moment, that she liked him. It had left her shaken, bereft of her steadying arrogance, stumbling for words.

"You were expecting a palace?" he had asked. He had felt the shift of her sleeve against his, and had thought it was because of the squalor on the screen. "My father came from the *melah* in Marrakesh. For him this is a palace."

Salt, the word meant. She was confused, but pretended not to be. Suddenly, for reasons she could not completely explain, it had become important to understand this man, or to make him think she understood him. Later she looked it up: it referred to the Jewish ghettos in North African cities. They had apparently persisted, for the poor at least, until the 1950s, when boycotts and pogroms left Arab Jews with few choices but to flee. She hadn't known. "No, it's—" She had stuttered, searching, suddenly forgetting her most basic Hebrew, falling back on English. "It's just that it isn't very different from where I grew up." She tapped the keyboard and showed him the apartment building where she and her mother and sister had moved after her father left, where her mother still lived.

"Right by the train tracks," he noticed.

She laughed. "I never needed an alarm clock," she said, then hesitated. But the warm shudder of his arm against hers made her speak. "My mother still lives there. She won't let me move her."

Unlike everyone she knew, he didn't ask her why, didn't force her to lie to avoid saying what she knew to be true: that her mother was punishing herself, living the life she felt she had earned with her mistakes, the life she felt she deserved. Instead, he nodded.

"Some people only want what they make for themselves," Itamar said. "If they didn't create it, they think it isn't theirs." She breathed, haunted. It was precisely true. His words lingered in her mind like a sweet, aching smell.

Her captor's voice jarred her back into the present. "Look, here is Musa with his puzzles," he said.

She kept her eyes closed for another instant, living in the fantasy, feeling the man's sleeve against hers. Then she admitted defeat, and returned to the darkness of the room's electric light.

"See this one he built? It is with playing cards, but cut up, so when he moves them the numbers are changed. I cannot explain."

Josie looked. The boy in the picture was skinny, with a slightly crooked nose—not nearly as handsome as his father had described him. But there was something about him that startled her, a familiar quality in the engrossed delight on his face as he flourished a thin hand in an awkward showman's gesture, displaying what even Josie had to admit was an impressive origami-like house of cards. It had been so long since she had seen a child, since she had seen someone who wasn't evil, since she had seen someone who was happy. She swallowed, refusing to cry.

The man was smiling under his mirrored sunglasses, a new kind of smile that she hadn't seen before. "Can you put the pictures on the computer?" His tone was innocent, vulnerable.

"Sure," she said brightly, as though Itamar had just asked her to pass the salt. She heard her own cheerful tone and felt like spitting on herself. *Don't forget,* she reminded herself. But why not forget? Why not help this man, give him comfort? There was so little she could do, good or bad, from inside this tomb; why not use the one power she had to give another person some happiness, to give him the gift of these precious moments with his dead son? This was madness, of course, madness disguised as kindness. But she could no longer distinguish between the two. Wouldn't she want someone to do the same for her—indeed, wouldn't she submit to any torture just to see a photograph of Tali again? Wasn't she aching, dying, to send a single message with the oracle of that phone?

"I have the USB cable, but I cannot do it," he said, taking a wire from his pocket and connecting the phone to the laptop. "You take." And then he handed her the phone.

I wonder if this gate is open, Josie thought, in the words she had read the night before, *or closed and guarded by certain rules, so that one could decide with certainty whether a thing is physically impossible.* For it was physically impossible that she was now holding her captor's phone in her hand. Were the rules suspended? Was the impossible suddenly possible?

The man saw her pause, saw her staring at the phone. If he recognized that the laws of the universe had been altered at that moment, he gave no notice. He pointed at the laptop's screen. "Put the pictures in," he said.

His tone was still gentle, urging only slightly, as though he had made a polite request. He seemed not to remember the bat he had placed on the floor. Josie opened the program, clicked a few times, followed some prompts on the phone's screen. She was alarmed by how familiar it all felt, her hands moving quickly, automatically, like swimming after stepping down into a deep cold pool. For a long time he watched over her shoulder as she began uploading the photos, peering at the screen with a hard, tight smile across his jaw. But as the photos became redundant—the man, it seemed, was the type who liked to snap pictures of anything, multiple shots of the same occasion from different angles, unedited—the computer began to slow down, taking its time.

"Can you make it faster?" he asked her.

"Sorry, you have a lot of pictures in here," she said, shaken again by her own casualness, by how normal it felt to be treated as though she were the tech support guy from down the hall. "This software is a few years old, and images are a lot of data. It's going to take awhile."

She was surprised that he didn't seem to show any interest in learning how to do it himself. It was repetitive, relatively simple; she could have taught him what to do in minutes, but apparently he had grown accustomed to having a slave. He stood up, still hovering for a time, as though hoping to see the next picture of his son appear on the screen again. Then he turned away, looked at his watch, and wandered over to the opposite corner of her cell, taking a small booklet and pencil out from his back pocket. She watched him from the corner of her eye as she waited for an image to load. He opened the booklet, stared at it, and drew his dark eyebrows together over his sunglasses before scribbling something in it with his pencil. Then he sank down to the floor, seating himself against the wall and engrossing himself in the little book. As he adjusted his position, she saw the booklet's cover: Sudoku. He wasn't so different from his son, she realized. In another life, on another planet, she and he might have become friends.

Blood thrummed in her weakened body. In an instant she understood what was suddenly, shockingly, possible.

She glanced at the man again, now fully absorbed in his book of number puzzles, and ran what she was about to do through her head as though it were a program, checking for bugs. If he were simply to sit up, if he were to give the slightest glance at the phone in her hands, he would kill her. It wasn't a question. The only question was whether he would strangle her immediately or torture her first. *But if I do nothing, he will still kill me,* she reminded herself. She thought of the hanging, of the rope around her shoulders, of the dark plastic bag over her head, of the tight choking jerk of the harness around her neck. It would happen again, she knew, no matter what. *I am already dead. I am already dead.*

With stumbling fingers, she shifted the phone out of its photo mode and hurriedly typed in Itamar's cell phone number, astonished and invigorated that she remembered it. For a fleeting second it was as though she were at home, or at the office, sending him a quick text or replying to his, reminding each other to tell the sitter to pick up Tali at three instead of four because Girl Scouts was rescheduled (again), to make Tali an appointment for a flu shot, to sign up for Tali's parent–teacher conference and would 8 am on the 24th work for you? Josie had spent years resenting those moments, all the minuscule mindless tasks that take up every available second of every day of raising a child. But now, as she held her captor's phone in her hand in her private dungeon, the thought of doing even a single one of them was miraculous, saturated with gleaming, blinding beauty. Itamar's number glowed in the light in her hand.

Weeks of programming for fourteen hours a day had regrooved her brain, plowed and sowed it with the habit of anticipating incompatibilities. For fear that the message wouldn't go through, she added Judith's number. Then, in absolute terror, in letters that stuttered like the child she had become in the past months, she wrote the first and only thing she could think of:

im still here dont tell anyone come get me love josie

She hit send, and then approved, shaking in terror, when the phone told her that it could only send the message when a signal was available. This, of course, was the most horrifying part—that the message would be sent only when the man emerged from the dungeon, and wouldn't he surely see it then? Wouldn't it most likely register only as a failure, without ever being sent at all? Even if it did go through, wouldn't an international text consume whatever money he had in his account, or wind up prominently on his bill? Wouldn't it linger in his phone, sitting in his sent mail, blindingly obvious in its English words, conspicuous in every possible way, signed with her own name? It would, it would. But it didn't matter, she reminded herself. *I am already dead.* She had become like her demented mother, alone in a room, inaccessible to the living, drowned in the past, drowned by the past. *I am already dead.* And suddenly, as she toggled back to the photos of the dead boy, she was already free.

The man looked up. "Is it finished?" he asked.

"Sorry, I—it was going slow," she stammered, still shaking. "Almost done. I'm up to these ones of him with this girl." She tilted the screen toward him, angling it so that he could see what she had seen: a picture of the skinny boy with an equally skinny girl, a short girl with pigtails and dark bangs, a girl who couldn't have been more than six years old. The girl, Josie now noticed with unease, was wearing fairy wings.

He sat down beside her again, looked at the screen. "Yes, his sister. They were best friends." He cleared his throat, adjusted his sunglasses. "I did not know that a girl could be like him. She is starting too, with the puzzles," he said, with a small grin. "But she is only a girl."

Josie wondered what he meant by "only"—that she was young, or that she was female? She thought of asking him, before remembering where she was, who she was, why she was. She remained silent, burning with what she had done. The pictures loaded slowly into the program, and when it was finished Josie showed him how the facial recognition tool would sort them, how it would adjust which doors it put his son behind based on the setting of the photograph, which other people were in it, the expression on his son's face. Eventually the man nodded, smiled. For what seemed like an endless amount of time, he sat at the computer beside her, traveling through the software's many rooms, opening doors. Sometimes he let out gasps of happy surprise, other times he bit his lip, suppressing a smile. Josie watched him as he moved through the palace she had built for his son. He laughed, shuddered, sometimes even spoke—happy Arabic exclamations with his finger pointed at the screen, directed at the person she had buried within the code. By the time he reached the last unexplored door, he was grinning so hard that he had to tilt his head toward the ceiling, exhilarated. She could see that he didn't want to stand up, didn't want to leave. He was alive in the house of the dead.

"I have also movies of him," he said, when he finally turned to Josie. Joy still lingered at the corners of his mouth. "In a camera at my brother's house. Can you put movies in?"

"If they're in a digital format," Josie said. She looked down at the shackle around her filthy leg. The guards only brought her a bucket of water and a rag to bathe with every few days, if that, and only rarely threw her a bar of soap. Her bare feet were encrusted in dirt. Did Itamar and Tali do this, she suddenly wondered—were they at home now plowing through the software, laughing at her jokes from years ago, pretending that she was still alive? She was surprised by how much the thought unnerved her, by how hard she hoped that they never did. "You'd have to put them on a flash drive."

The man clapped his hands, like a child at a birthday party—or, more accurately, like Musa at his own birthday party, the photos of which she had just loaded into the machine. "I will make it on drives," he said.

She thought he would leave her alone then, with the computer. Usually she was expected to continue coding until long after what passed for dinner—several exhausting hours during which one of the guards would periodically check that she was working on the code, before removing the computer for the night. The malware was nearly done, as the man knew well from the demonstrations she had made for him every few days, often with a truncheon pressed into her back. Twice he had even brought a gun, which he had held against her jaw, laughing, as she typed. He enjoyed watching her tremble. But the man didn't seem to care about the malware now. Astonishingly, he didn't even ask to see it. Instead he shut down the laptop, picked it up, and began to leave the room. He jumped the few steps to the bolted door, almost dancing.

"You will do more tomorrow," he told her as he opened the door, with the bat wedged under his giddily shaking arm. Before he left, he turned back toward her. And then he said, "Thank you."

THAT NIGHT JOSIE HAD an argument with the dead author of *Guide for the Perplexed*. Her objection concerned the omniscience of God.

She had followed him through his argument on the nature of evil—an argument which made more sense to her, even in the depths of her dungeon, than any other idea she had ever heard. *Men frequently think that the evils in the world are more numerous than the good things,* he had written, *that a good thing is found only exceptionally, while evil things are numerous and lasting. Not only common people make this mistake, but even many who think they are wise.* The words gave her strength. She thought of the many miracles outside—air, light, leaves, water, every healthy person she had ever known—and of those that swirled around her even now: the astounding, nearly impossible fact that she hadn't been raped, that she had barely been beaten, that she was weirdly and horribly and undeniably alive. Despite all the visits from the man and his guards, she hadn't even been groped—which in Egypt was beyond miraculous. She looked at her fingers as they held the book and was overwhelmed by the network of veins that she could see through her translucent skin, the delicacy of muscle and bone. She imagined holding Tali in the delivery room, the tight grip of her newborn girl's fingers around her own—the power in those fingers, how they clutched her thumb as if speaking, saying: *Mommy, never leave.*

The evils that befall men are of three kinds, Rambam patiently explained, and Josie read along, wondering into which category her own agony fell.

1. *The first kind of evil is that which is caused by the circumstance that man possesses a body, and is subject to genesis and destruction . . . Aside from the necessary degeneration of the body, you will nevertheless find that evils of this type are rare: there are thousands of men in perfect health, and deformed individuals are a strange and exceptional occurrence, not even one-thousandth of those who are perfectly normal.*

This was true, Josie thought—unjust, ungracious, and uncompassionate, turning people into numbers as any scientist would, but still utterly, undeniably true.

2. *The second class of evils are those that people cause to each other . . . These evils are more numerous than those of the first kind, and their causes originate in ourselves. This kind of evil is nevertheless also not widespread. It is rare that a man plans to kill his neighbor or to rob him in the night.*

> *Many persons are afflicted with this kind of evil in great wars, but these are not frequent, if the whole inhabited earth is taken into consideration.*

This was also true, she knew—even though now the author was being unjust, ungracious, and uncompassionate to her. She appreciated his honesty, and was impressed that he seemed to express no interest in explaining her statistically meaningless place in the universe. The idea that her suffering was demographically insignificant, that it did not reflect poorly on mankind, was a strange and unexpected comfort.

> 3. *The third class of evils are those that everyone causes to himself by his own actions. This is the largest class. It is especially of these evils that all men complain . . . The soul, when accustomed to superfluous things, acquires a strong habit of desiring things that are not necessary . . . Men as a rule expose themselves to great dangers, for instance by sea voyages, or the service of kings, and all this for the purpose of obtaining that which is superfluous.*

This gave Josie pause. Twenty million dollars' worth of ransom surely qualified as superfluous. But her entire trip to Egypt had been superfluous too. *Sea voyages,* she thought, *and the service of kings*—the arrogance of a different millennium, but still the same. She, it was true, had always thirsted for more. Judith had known her thirst for acclaim, and had goaded her, tested her—for that was what all this was, wasn't it? A test? For if it wasn't a test, or a punishment or trial of some kind, then that would mean she was merely a statistical irrelevance—and could that be true? Rambam himself must have been the sort who lived a life of enviable moderation, never tempted to demand more, she thought with petty disdain. But now she had more questions: Was the desire to remember a dead son superfluous? Was the desire to see a living daughter?

It was then that she reached the book's most puzzling part, its impossible part. Even to think through the concept, she found, was nearly impossible. Yet she read it eagerly, as a riddle that she had no choice but to solve:

> *The fact that God knows things while they are in a state of possibility, when their existence belongs to the future, does not change the nature of the possible in any way. That nature remains unchanged; and the knowledge of the realization of one of several possibilities does not yet effect that realization. . . . The fact that laws were given to man, both affirmative and negative, supports the principle that God's knowledge of future and possible events does not change their character. . . . According to the teaching of our Torah, God's knowledge of one of two eventualities does not determine it, however certain that knowledge may be concerning the future occurrence of the one eventuality.*

Josie considered this as she lay in her cell, living through the various eventualities that her message had set into motion. If the future was already known by God, then how could alternatives be possible? They weren't. That much was clear to her, and should have been clear to anyone as obsessed with reason as the author was. Because wouldn't that imply that some things were unknown to God? That God had chosen to remove himself from human affairs, to limit his own power, just to make room for human freedom? Who needed a God of that sort? Or—and this was the argument that frightened her—was it merely ignorance, the humbling admission of all one could not know, that made human freedom possible?

A footnote on the French side elaborated:

> *One can imagine people walking through a valley, with an observer perched at the top of a mountain overlooking the valley below. The observer sees where the people are headed, knows when they will turn back due to an obstructed trail, knows which route will lead them to the valley's end. But the people in the valley, choosing their route without knowing what lies ahead, experience free will. All the possible paths through the valley exist, and the observer above sees where each of them lead. But this does not mean that the people in the valley do not choose their paths. Their ignorance of the eventualities ahead is the source of their free will.*

She remembered a conversation she had had with her mother, years ago. The conversation had been about string theory, about the possibility of a universe that existed in a comprehensive predetermined design. "It's probably good that I stopped being a physicist," her mother had said.

They were in the emergency room, Josie remembered, as they often were then. Her father, who already spent most nights away from home, had declined to join them. Eleven-year-old Josie, finished with her math homework and immobilized by the oxygen tank that tethered her to the wall, had asked her mother about what she had studied, long ago. She hadn't known, before then, that her mother had lived another life, that there was a path out of the valley that had long ago been blocked. Many years passed before she understood that she was the one who had blocked it—that it was her birth, fifteen months after

Judith's, that had been the final insurmountable obstacle which made her mother's career impossible. Her mother explained to her what she once had learned about the woven, singing fabric of the universe. "If I had continued," her mother said, "I would have reached a point where I would have had to stop believing."

"Stop believing in God?" Josie had asked.

"No, stop believing in people," her mother said. "Physicists like to tell you that the data leave no room for a God who controls the universe. That's absolutely true. But what they don't like to tell you is that the data also don't leave any room for people to have free will. I used to like that, then."

At that moment the nurse came in to check Josie's oxygen levels, and Josie had forgotten to ask her mother why she had liked it.

Which of the eventualities would come to pass? Would they come to kill her in the morning, after her captor discovered the message she had tried to send, or was there some obscure reason to hope? If the end was already known to God, how could any of it be within her power at all? Was the route through the valley up to her?

When she fell asleep at last, she dreamed of Judith.

In her dungeon she dreamed often of Judith, had dreamed of her many times. In her dreams she imagined alternatives, eventualities that with absolute certainty hadn't happened—and, with equal certainty, could have. In one dream Josie was playing chess with a nine-year-old Judith again and again, and Judith won every time. In another dream she imagined her mother standing behind Judith at the bathroom mirror, ignoring Josie as she braided Judith's hair. She dreamed of walking to school with a twelve-year-old Judith, of twelve-year-old Judith teasing her with problems and riddles that she tried to solve but couldn't, while Judith laughed and laughed. The frustration of it shocked her, yet now it felt familiar: the impotence, the stunting infantilizing rage, like being trapped in a tiny room. In another dream, she saw Judith owning the company, married to Itamar, raising Tali. She saw her husband in bed with her sister, saw her daughter laughing and hugging her sister, while she herself burned in envy. The fire of her fury woke her in the night. She jolted awake to find her mouth pressed against the filthy stone floor—terrified by her own anger, and wanting nothing more than to hold Judith, to tell her that she understood her now, to ask for her forgiveness. But all of these dreams were impossible nonsense, Josie knew, like the diagonal of a square being shorter than its sides.

THE DOOR CLANKED OPEN, rousing Josie from a deep and demented sleep. It was the two teenage guards.

Usually only one of them would wake her in the morning, heaving the door open and throwing her food to the floor. Sometimes whoever had thrown the food would talk to her. More often he would laugh at her, or taunt her by placing the food just past where her chain could reach, waiting for her to beg. But this time there were two of them, both smiling as they entered the room and closed the door behind them. Their smiles confused her. She thought of the previous night, of how overjoyed the man had been. She sat up quickly, suddenly expecting them to be bearing good news, happy surprises.

One of them reached into his pocket and withdrew a phone, the same phone she had held in her hand the day before. He turned its screen toward her. She strained at the shackle to see what he was showing her, but she already knew what it was:

her message. Had it been sent? She struggled to her feet, pulling the chain tight to see the details. But by the time she stood up, he had already slipped the phone back into his pocket. The two of them watched her now, still smiling. And then they descended.

It was like that: a descent, like a wave crashing on top of her, enveloping her and crushing her in a brutal churn of water and salt and sand. At first she tried to dodge the metal rings they wore as they punched, the boots they kicked with, the steel bars they slammed into her legs, her buttocks, her feet, her knees. But once the wave had crashed over her it quickly became indistinguishable, the pain no longer affecting something as trivial as a body part, but rather all-encompassing, world-consuming. Salt burned her, blinded her. She was inside a molten scream that had replaced the entire world. With her mouth full of boiling lava, she recognized that burning incandescent space. At Tali's birth her labor had progressed quickly, so quickly that the doctors had not had time to give her the anesthesia she had always planned to have. While it was happening she had imagined that she was being tortured, drilled through with power tools. Now, as the waves of blows crested and fell, she bit her bleeding lips and rallied. She imagined herself giving birth to Tali again, pretended that the pain had a purpose, convinced herself that on the other side of this room of infinitely dense agony there was a narrow door, and if she could only drag her body to that door, her body itself would open and she would give birth on the floor of an ancient forest and see the face of her daughter again. Until she lost consciousness.

They left her alone after that. For hours, for days. For a long time she assumed she had been left to die. When she awoke she groaned for hours, unable to move, unable even to bend her neck to see the ruin of her own body. When she found the strength to move an arm, she pulled at the ends of her hair, which by now had grown down to her waist. She was amazed at how heavy it felt, as though the strands of hair had thickened into coarse brittle ropes. Only when she stretched a clump around to her face did she see that the ends of her hair were saturated with blood. She looked down and saw her blood-soaked clothes stuck to her bruised, razed skin. Her bare feet were lacerated, bulging, unrecognizable, her left ankle so engorged with bruises that the shackle dug into her skin. But to her astonishment, her hands and arms were almost normal—stained red from her hair and clothes, yes, but not broken, not bleeding. Her head, too, seemed barely bruised. Later she would understand that this was intentional, that they had decided in advance which parts of her body were disposable. Now she stared at her beautiful palms, at her reddened hands, as if she had been finger-painting with her own blood. She looked at her stained pristine hands and imagined that they were Tali's, that Tali had been painting, that Tali needed a bath. *Yes,* she thought, tracing her own fingerprints, *you need a bath. Don't worry, I'll get you cleaned up real soon. Even those red marker stains under your nose. It won't hurt, I promise.*

Trying to sit up took hours, and finally was impossible. After what might have been years, she let herself scream, hoping that the screams would evoke someone's mercy, or someone's frustration, or at least a human voice answering hers, if only to tell her to shut up. She kept screaming until she couldn't scream anymore. Some time later she began hearing screams, and it occurred to her that perhaps she wasn't alone, that perhaps there were other prisoners around her, somewhere beyond the tomb. It took much longer to realize that she was only hearing her own voice. She had fallen down into the pit.

WHEN SHE AWOKE TO the clank of the lock, she found herself delirious, expecting to see Itamar, Tali, Rambam. Instead, it was Musa's father.

For a moment Josie was lost, uncertain whether she was dead or alive. Then, in a drumming rush of pain as she tried to rise from the floor, she remembered everything—the message, the beating, the journey to the underworld, the mangled flesh that had replaced her body, the void that had replaced her soul. She remembered these things as though she were traveling through the software, opening doors and wondering what beautiful image might await her behind each one—because when she opened the doors in the software at home, there was never anything but beautiful images, the ugly and unpleasant ones buried beneath a carefully curated past. She crawled through the events of the past days as though burrowing through long dark tunnels. She no longer knew what was real and what was dream.

He stood against the door, his arms folded against his chest. His smile was hard and bare. She wondered what was behind his sunglasses; if perhaps there might be nothing behind them.

"You practiced dying again," he said.

How had he known, she wondered. For a moment she marveled at his control over her, how nothing at all remained of her own will. He was omnipotent, omniscient, aware of all possible outcomes. Was he what Rambam had meant by the omniscience of God? Then she looked down at her battered legs and understood that he had meant nothing more than the beating, that it was all physical, all past and present in this tiny room, that he had no special power over the fate of her soul. She told herself this. It was astoundingly difficult to believe.

"It is good to practice, because soon we will kill you."

Good, Josie thought. The thought comforted her. At last.

"But my wife says you must finish the programs first," he said. "She is the only reason you are not dead yet."

Programs? The word was uncanny, like something from a dream that had appeared in real life. She tried translating it in her head, wondering if it was a word in Hebrew, Arabic, French. What did it mean?

"She wants the virus done. And she wants—she wants Musa."

Now Josie remembered. She had invented something, long ago, something that made people think that the past still existed, that it was still part of the world they lived in, that it was something that could be visited, preserved in perpetuity, like the mummified pharaohs in their tombs. But the tombs had been for the underworld. Her swollen eyes glanced at the sarcophagus in the room, in the city built for the dead, and she remembered the ancient ruins she had visited lifetimes ago, before her capture, the pharaohs whose servants had stored everything they would need after their deaths. These people, her customers, her masters—for her customers were her masters, even at home—they were much worse than that. They believed that the dead ought to live in *this* world, and her work had fed that belief. It had never occurred to her, until now, that the act of reliving the past could consume the future, that regret regularly ate people alive. She had never known how wrong she was, that it was possible for her to be so horribly wrong, that she had always been wrong. Suddenly she knew.

"You will finish the Genizah of Musa," the man told her. "My wife wants all the pictures in it. And the movies. And she has more things to tell you, things to keep inside the doors. You will put him there. He will live in your program, so we can have him there forever."

Josie clenched her teeth. She closed her eyes and remembered one of the tombs she had visited with her mustached hosts when she had first arrived in Egypt, with its painted butlers and bakers marching across the room's frescoed walls: slaves like her, forced to serve the dead. She thought of the real men and women who corresponded to the paintings and wondered how many times they had been beaten, how many times they had dreamed of the impossible. She looked down at her hands, her stained uninjured hands, the hands her masters had ensured were perfect—so that she could continue to record the mythology of this dead child, so that the mythology could replace this dead child. She felt a rush of air through her chest, stretching her beaten ribs. Suddenly she remembered what she had known thousands of years ago, when she had held the man's phone in her hand: that she was already free.

"No," she said.

The man breathed in. Josie looked up at him, and expected him to pounce. Instead he was tilting his head toward her, his eyes still hidden behind his mirrored sunglasses. But his mouth hung open. To her surprise he didn't speak. And to her shock she heard herself speak again.

"No," she repeated. "Your son is dead. And my daughter—my daughter is still alive. You can kill me, but you can't kill her."

She watched his fists tightening. She was sure now that he would pummel her into the ground. Her body cringed, independent of her mind. Then she saw him tremble, a strange vibration that moved from his hands through his arms to his stubble-covered jaw. He shuddered, shaking until he began to make strange noises, strangled noises, coming from his throat. He turned, and leaned against the door. Then he pounded it with his fists, over and over again. The throttled noises kept coming as he lowered his head, pressing his forehead against the doorframe. She watched with a sick, sad satisfaction. She had beaten him more brutally than he could ever beat her.

He opened the door, and lingered in the doorway. She had never seen the door open so wide before. It was usually opened and closed quickly, and usually while she was sleeping; she had never before had a chance to stretch herself into a position to catch a glimpse of the slightest shadow of what went on behind it. Now she was so swollen and bruised that she could barely sit up, let alone stretch the chain. But she raised herself, with incredible agony, to see what lay beyond him outside the door. To her astonishment she saw daylight. Not direct sunlight, but daylight nonetheless, a long parallelogram of golden light lying across a stone floor. Was she above ground all this time, up beyond the underworld, among the living?

One of the guards then appeared in the doorway, with the laptop and the extension cord. He didn't look at her, and she wondered if he was ashamed, if he was capable of shame. He hurriedly set it on the floor and booted it up, casting the extension cord into her cell. She had once thought of it as a rope, leading to her escape. But now she knew that it was nothing more than a fishing line, and that she had been the fool who had taken the bait. Outside the open doorway, she was shocked to hear a child laughing. Were they in someone's house? But now the door was closing, the gate sliding shut.

"Finish the programs," she heard Musa's father call as he left. "And then you will die."

When the door was closed, she turned the computer off.

THEY BEGAN WITHHOLDING FOOD. At first Josie wondered if this was a logistical problem, some glitch among the guards that had nothing to do with her. She was no longer used to mattering, baffled by the possibility that her behavior could have consequences. When she understood what she had done, power stirred within her.

Without food she became lighter, freer. The pain was still too great for her to stand up, but she made an effort to sit, to move, to use her perfect arms to drag herself as far as her chain would stretch. The sensation of fasting felt familiar to her. It was as though she were praying, rising above her own body. She found herself preparing for death, reciting the Hebrew confessional, the memorably alphabetical list of personal sins. She was amazed anew by how subtle they were, by how they mainly weren't about things like physical theft or violence, but instead captured the tiny decisions that led to the diminishment of lives. *For the sin that we have sinned before you unwillingly or willingly; and for the sin we have sinned before you by hardening our hearts . . . For the sin that we have sinned before you by being arrogant . . . For the sin we have sinned before you with haughty eyes, and for the sin we have sinned before you by impudence . . .* The words ran through her mind like music; sometimes she sang them aloud. It was while she was singing that the door creaked open—slowly, without the angry clang that she still heard constantly in her mind. She was surprised to find that she didn't tremble, that she was no longer even slightly afraid. When she raised her head she saw the woman, sheathed in black from head to toe, standing in the room with her.

The woman's black ballet slippers startled her, jolting her into another world, one she couldn't identify at first. She felt it first as a chill—a memory of a sensation she hadn't felt in months, cold artificial air against the back of her neck. The chill was imaginary, but arresting, blowing her back to something she had long forgotten. Then she remembered it: standing in the refrigerated Library of Alexandria, freezing, and talking—with arrogance, with impudence, with haughty eyes, with a hardened heart—to a woman named Nasreen.

"He is not here now," the woman said. "I will bring you food."

Josie looked at her, not bothering to shrug. Food seemed irrelevant. Surely this was some new game, some attempt to manipulate her. Perhaps the man was even outside now, waiting with his pictures, his truncheon, his teenage goons. She no longer cared.

The woman approached her cautiously. Under the veil, Josie saw her flinch. It occurred to Josie that the look and smell of her own body must be appalling, that she hadn't seen herself in months, that she was still swollen, still bruised, still covered with dirt. The woman hesitated for a moment, then sat down beside her. She carefully took Josie's hand in hers. Josie twitched, unthinkingly, and felt a flush of pride as she pushed the woman's hand away. But the touch had been exquisite. She breathed, and inhaled the sweet thick fragrance of the woman's shampoo. The smell lingered in her mouth like food.

"I think many people in Egypt will like your—your computer program," the woman said. "Please help me to remember: what is it called?"

For a long time Josie hesitated, unwilling to speak. But the woman was leaning toward her. Her breath smelled like toothpaste. Josie could taste it in her own mouth. "Genizah," Josie answered.

The woman leaned back, satisfied. "Yes. This Genizah," she said. Her veil fluttered before her breathing mouth. "You do not even know how good it would be, to have this program here for everyone. In this country everyone has lost someone. In every house someone is dead."

Josie looked up, reminded, suddenly, of a verse from the

book of Exodus—that after the Egyptians suffered the tenth plague, the death of Egypt's firstborn, "there was not a single house without one dead." She traced her own teeth with her tongue, did not speak.

"We would like you to make this Genizah for us," she said. Josie remembered the woman's voice now, from that day or night, somewhere on the other end of a valley of days and nights, when the woman had brought her water, medicine, clothes that weren't drenched in filth. She remembered how startled she had been that the woman's English was better than the man's. "For everyone," the woman was saying. "An open program, one that the whole country can use. But many Egyptians do not have computers. They use computers only in internet cafés, or on a phone. It will need to be open for everyone."

Josie shifted her body, inching away from the woman. Her legs ached. This was merely more madness, she recognized now, nothing but another corner of the same dark pit. "The consumer editions of Genizah are all accessible online," Josie said wearily, as if playing a recording of her own voice. "There are mobile applications that anyone can download. Everything is password-protected. People just have to buy a subscription, or pay for the download."

The woman shook her head. "This is impossible for Egyptians," she said. Josie understood what the woman meant, what she wanted. "It would be a gift to the people of Egypt."

For a moment, Josie entertained the idea, thinking like a programmer again—considering how to hack the paywall, remembering, vaguely, that it was one of the last things she had coded herself. It would be easy for her, she realized. But then she stopped thinking, and remembered all that had happened. She was finished, she reminded herself.

Josie looked at the woman, or at the black cloth that covered her, for a long time. It was like a shroud. Did the woman wear it all the time, or was it merely a disguise, like the man's sunglasses? Somewhere beneath it, Josie forced herself to think, was a person with a mind, with interests, commitments. A life. But what kind of life?

"I heard a child outside," Josie said. "A girl. Is she—is she yours?"

The woman was silent. But the smell of shampoo and toothpaste invigorated Josie. "I saw a photo of her, with her brother," Josie said. "She reminds me of my daughter." Josie waited, unsure of whether to dare. "Does your daughter know that I'm here? Does she know why I'm here?"

The woman remained silent. Josie listened to her breathe. When she spoke, she did not answer Josie's question. Instead she answered the question behind it.

"Your program will not bring back my son. That is true," she said. She spoke with her head erect, her voice low. "I know. I am not asking you to bring him back." Josie listened for a crack in her voice. But the woman refused to indulge her. "I am only telling you that this country is built out of tombs. We are very good at building tombs." She paused, leaned forward. "On the computer you could build a new city of the dead, for people now. And then everyone would see how big that city is."

Josie tried to snort, to dismiss the woman's words. But her breath caught in her throat.

"You do not know it, but I have protected you," the woman said.

Another impossibility, Josie thought. Then she remembered what the man had told her: *She is the only reason you are not dead.*

"The hitting, I could not help," the woman continued. "But I would not let them touch you. I told them that if they did I would smell it, I would see it in their faces, and I would tell someone, I would tell everyone. I know they never touched you."

Josie shifted against the wall, ignoring the pain.

The woman breathed out, a long, hard breath. The veil fluttered like a moving shadow across her face.

"If you could do this for us, all of Egypt would thank you. And if you did, then I—I—" the woman stammered.

Josie sighed, glancing with contempt at the laptop in the corner, where she had pushed it out of her own reach. Everything seemed useless, laughable. The power in the machine, the one in which she had invested more than half her life, was no power at all.

Then the woman finished: "I would bring you out of this room."

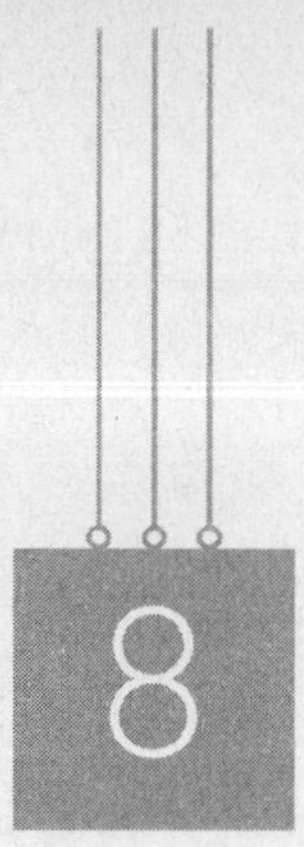

OFTEN, WHEN SHE was with Tali, Judith returned, in her mind, to the pit.

The pit was much too deep, she remembered. She hadn't known how deep it really was until she saw her little sister at the bottom of it—smaller than she had ever seen her, so far away that Judith could barely see the breathing, beating beauty that had always terrified her. All she could see, then, was a tiny dark-haired creature crying out her name. The power she had felt at that moment had been overwhelming, intoxicating. She had never before known what it was like to matter. She thought of it often now, whenever Tali asked her for the inhaler. She held the plastic cylinder against the girl's pleading face, watching her cough, counting her breaths, and understood what once might have been.

"I'm so lucky you're here, Judith," Tali said one afternoon after her breathing had calmed. "I couldn't do anything without you."

"Don't be ridiculous," Judith said. "You could do all this

yourself if you had to." After she said it, she remembered saying the same words to another girl, in a darkening poplar forest, before she discovered just how true it was. But this time Judith smiled, because this time she knew it was a lie. The new little girl smiled back, and Judith kissed her.

Judith was home now, finally—living in what she now thought of, without hesitation, as her own house. She hadn't yet given up her apartment, but it had been weeks since she had returned to it. Everything she needed was here. She spent each night in her dead sister's bed, sleeping by Itamar's side. For the first month it was like performing in a play, trying to guess what her sister might have said, what her sister might have done, what would make him happy. But as days and nights passed undocumented, dropping one by one into oblivion, she slowly stopped pretending and started living. She was aware of the gossip at the company and among everyone they knew, but to her own surprise she didn't care. It was as though she were floating above the world, flying in a dream. Eventually she and Itamar even spoke of new problems, new developments, things that were apparently unrelated to the horror that had made this new life possible. But everything was related to it. Like the fact that the company, for the first time ever, was beginning to falter, the number of subscriptions holding steady instead of growing for the first time in years. It distressed Itamar to the core—not because of the money, but because of Josie.

"I feel like I'm killing her again," he confided one night in bed. Judith had suggested selling advertising in the software—the obvious option, one that their closest competition had chosen years ago. But Itamar corrected her. "No, we can never do that," he told her. His voice at night was different than it was during the daytime, Judith noticed: softer, warmer. He laced his arms around her neck, running his fingers through her hair. "She never wanted Genizah to be one of these things where you can't touch anything without someone trying to sell you something, where everything you do is pillaged for new ways to get your attention, or your money."

Judith used to cringe when Itamar talked about Josie in bed, but she didn't anymore. His hands were wandering between her shoulderblades, caressing the stunted points where she might have grown wings. She listened, entranced. "Every time we open our eyes now, we're surrounded by people who want to use us, and we're expected to think there's nothing wrong with that," he said. "Genizah was meant to be different, with nothing in it except what mattered to that person. It was supposed to be a—a sacred space."

"A sacred space," Judith repeated, as her sister never would have. To her joy, Itamar did not flinch. She had just begun to see into Itamar, to discover the hidden vault within him. At first she had known only what he needed her to be, and she had obliged him. From him she had learned, without words, what he and her sister had done, how they had danced, and she had allowed him to lead her. It was safer to pretend that she already knew him. But in recent weeks there had been a subtle shift between them, as if Judith had at last nudged her sister out of the bed they shared.

"Yes, something that no one else can touch, unless you invite them," he said that night. "Like your body."

She assumed he was speaking generally, a reference to the body of any person on earth. He had always closed his eyes when they were in bed together. But now he looked at her face. No one had ever looked at her like that before, except for Josie, reaching up from the pit.

"You are beautiful, Judith," he whispered, and took her breath away.

After they made love she had lain in bed for hours, amazed, unable to sleep as his chest rose and fell in gentle rhythms beside her. She gazed at the glowing blank canvas of the ceiling and relished a fresh and unexpected feeling that she had never before experienced, one that her dead sister had once lived with nearly every day: not merely love, but certainty. Judith was now the happiest she had ever been in her life. And that was when, in the most silent hour of the night, she heard the buzzing of a message landing in her phone.

She rolled in the darkness and looked at the dim glow of the phone's screen as it vibrated on the night table, wondering what calamity awaited her. Something about her mother, she guessed. She picked up the phone, glancing again at Itamar's long thin body, that narrow oasis of joy in the vast wastes of her life. She read the words on the screen, then sat up in shock:

im still here dont tell anyone come get me love josie

It was impossible, she knew as she stared at the screen. Absolutely impossible. At that moment, Judith decided that it would remain impossible.

Her first impulse was to erase it, as she had erased everything else. But as she sat in her sister's bed, something pulled at her, some double-helixed string stretching across the universe, and she could not quite summon the unbridled brazenness she would have needed to cut herself completely free. She tapped at the phone until the message was saved—something the software would have done automatically, if she hadn't disabled it. If she had been a different person, she might never have slept again.

Instead she rolled over and draped an arm across the beautiful man who lay beside her, glanced at the clock and thought of the little girl who would wake her at dawn, pulled up her sister's striped multicolored comforter, and tumbled blissfully down into a deep pit of unremembered dreams. She slept well, reveling in sweet oblivion, until Tali kissed her into the new day.

A FEW WEEKS EARLIER, she and Itamar had attended Tali's parent–teacher conference together. Josie had often mentioned that Tali wasn't reading, that Tali wasn't even interested in reading. Josie had said this with a kind of perverse pride, Judith remembered, as though she were inverting the usual maternal guilt: instead of trying to live her life through her child, Josie was so satisfied with her own success that she pretended not to mind if her daughter was raised by wolves. But now Judith saw how maddening it must have been for her sister, how profoundly disappointing, and all the worse for the shame that the disappointment bore as its shadow. Tali was only in first grade, and one could never be publicly disappointed about one's child being average. Josie had bragged about how Tali couldn't read, Judith now understood, because she had tried and failed to teach her.

Judith thought of this as she settled into the child-sized chair next to Itamar's in a classroom decorated with posters of anthropomorphic animals. She could feel the warmth of his body beside hers as the teacher regarded both of them with a sympathy that bordered on a thrill. The teacher then spent the first seven of the allotted ten minutes bemoaning the family tragedy and excusing everything Tali had done since then—it seemed that Tali had hardly completed any classwork, had failed three different assessment tests, and had shredded "about four or five" paperback picture books with her teeth—by saying how of course after everything that had happened, Tali couldn't be expected to be at her best. Toward the end, the teacher mentioned, almost in passing, that while Tali had "tremendous potential," the little girl had adamantly refused even to attempt to learn to read.

Itamar had driven them both to work afterward in a huff. "You can see how much that woman is enjoying this," he grumbled in the driver's seat. "This is probably the most exciting thing that's ever happened to her. We're her entertainment. I can't even look at her without thinking of that interview she did on that stupid local TV show after it happened. Cry, cry, cry. How do you say it in English—a princess?"

"Drama queen," Judith said. She was still surprised by how much she enjoyed correcting him, teaching him. It was an unfamiliar delight to her, knowing what someone else didn't know.

"Drama queen," Itamar repeated. "Exactly." This seemed to please him. In the cold car, the slight smile on his face warmed Judith's bones. But what the teacher had said bothered Judith, tormented her. At last she decided to speak.

"I didn't think she was so awful," she ventured carefully. "At least she's paying attention to Tali now. Josie was always complaining that this teacher barely remembered Tali's name."

Itamar fiddled with the radio, looking for a traffic report. Judith could feel him shutting a door in her face, and tried to prop it open.

"Do you think we should do something about Tali?" Judith asked.

"Do something?" Itamar asked. "Like what?"

Judith was thinking of a psychiatrist, someone to whom they could outsource the girl's apparent rage and despair. But as she watched Itamar fidget in the driver's seat, she knew that the very idea would set his nerves aflame. Instead she decided to broach the smaller subject: the relatively trivial question of Tali's mind.

"I don't know, maybe find her a tutor?" she tried.

Itamar clicked his tongue. The noise used to irritate Judith, but now she considered it a kind of secret code, part of the language she was learning. "A tutor? She's in first grade."

"But she's not even trying to learn how to read."

Itamar grinned, a gesture that flooded Judith with relief. "You saw the books in that room. Would you want to read them? 'I lost my puppy.' 'I'm a whining, self-absorbed pigeon.' 'I'm a pig whose parents indulge all my whims.' I was more concerned that they're barely teaching any math. What did that drama queen say, that subtraction was 'not age-appropriate'? Maybe it's time to change schools."

Or maybe, Judith thought, it was time to change Tali.

THAT DAY AFTER SCHOOL, when Tali asked Judith to read her a story while she was eating her snack, Judith told her, "No. Today I want you to learn to read to me instead."

With her mouth full of cookie, Tali frowned, a superior frown. Judith recognized that frown. "I don't like reading," Tali announced.

"Why not? You like stories, don't you?"

Tali slowly broke her cookie into pieces, eating each piece until the entire cookie had disappeared into her mouth. Her movements were deliberate, annoying. As she sat down at her sister's kitchen table, Judith was suddenly jolted by an odd memory: sitting at her family's kitchen table at Tali's age, and marveling as she watched her impossibly tall, impossibly thin father piling astounding amounts of food into his mouth—oblivious to calories, oblivious to the laws of conservation of mass that he had tried to teach her, oblivious to the world. He had remained oblivious. After Josie's death, he had sent Judith a message online, wanting to be her "friend." He had seen the news reports, he wrote, and had wept for days. Where did Judith live now? Could he come to the shiva? His wife and children, he wrote, sent their condolences too: "May God comfort you among the mourners of Zion and Jerusalem. Blessed be the True Judge." It was the first time Judith had heard from him in twenty years. In honor of her dead sister, Judith ignored him.

"Can I have another one?" Tali asked with her mouth full.

Judith had already learned a few things about dealing with Tali. If Judith showed the slightest hint of frustration, she would have already lost. She took out the box that she had already put away and pulled out another cookie, which Tali immediately snatched. "Tali, I asked you something," Judith said patiently. "Don't you like books?"

"Sometimes," Tali said, spewing crumbs. "But I hate reading. Because the letters are big liars."

"What are you talking about?"

This time Tali stopped eating. "They lie," she said. "You try to read them, and you think you're right, but then it turns out you're wrong, because they lied. They have an E in them, or a G or an H or a W or a K, and then when you try to read them, it turns out those letters are just faking and they actually make a different noise from their real one, or they don't even make any noise at all. There are supposed to be rules about how they sound, but that's a lie too, because the letters hardly ever follow them. It's all just a big lie."

Judith held her breath as Tali took another bite. Then, aware of the risks, she said, "You're right. Most of the letters are liars."

Tali, who was breaking off another piece of cookie, paused. She stared at Judith. It seemed that she and Judith had something in common: it was so rare that anyone heard what they were saying that when someone did listen, they were both, despite themselves, stunned. Tali held the cookie halfway between the table and her mouth, its chocolate chips and her long tangled hair dark and striking against her bright orange shirt. She did not speak.

Judith saw her chance, and seized it. "But the good part is that some letters have superpowers," she announced. "They can do things that are supposed to be impossible."

Tali continued staring. Judith leaned back. No one had ever looked at her that way before. "Like what?" the little girl asked.

Judith breathed in, profoundly aware of the likelihood of failure. "Like E," she said. "If an E is hiding at the *end* of the word, then he's almost always a secret agent E. He doesn't make any noise, like you said. That way everyone thinks he doesn't matter at all. But even though he seems like he's not important, his superpowers let him change the way the rest of the word sounds."

"Huh?" Tali asked. To Judith's surprise, it wasn't a dismissive sound, but an intrigued one. The girl was sitting up in her chair, leaning forward, listening. She had put the cookie down.

Judith stood up quickly, knowing that the window of wonder was about to close. She grabbed a piece of paper and a pencil from the kitchen counter behind her, and brought them to the table. Tali was still staring.

"Look. If I write H–A–T—" she began, and turned the paper toward herself, writing the letters as large and clearly as she could. It was odd how familiar it felt, this gesture of turning around a page with giant letters on it while sitting at a kitchen table, across from a dark-haired girl who took the paper from her hand. She shuddered as she recognized the moment: sitting at a table long ago with Josie, as Josie wrote simple words in patronizingly large letters—four-year-old prodigy Josie, teaching her older sister how to read. Josie had given up quickly, then. But Judith wouldn't. "See, H–A–T. That's—you can read that, right?"

Tali struggled, quietly. In the girl's silent refusal to ask for help, Judith recognized her mother. "Hat," she said finally. It took her far too long.

"That's right," Judith said simply. She knew by now not to overpraise; Tali found it insulting. "But if I put an E on the end, what is it?" Judith asked, drawing the E's thick perpendicular bars on the end of the word.

Tali stared at the paper again, working. "Hatty," she finally said, defeated.

"That's what it should be. Except that this is a superhero E, so he used his superpowers to change the word!"

Tali groaned. "See? I told you. Liars."

"No, see, the superhero E makes the other letters *stop* lying. He tells the other big sound in the word"—Judith deepened her voice, and made an exaggerated frown—" 'Tell me your real name.' " A rush of pleasure flowed through Judith's body as Tali laughed. "And then the other vowel in the word—that's the letter that makes the big sound, like 'ah' or 'oh'—has to say his real name. So now the A in the word isn't allowed to sound like 'ah' or 'a,' like in 'hat,' because he got caught by the superhero E. Now he has to stand up and say, 'I'm an A,' and sound like his name. So it really spells—"

Tali was staring at the word now, tracing the A with her finger. She looked up at Judith in wonder. "Hate?"

Judith nodded.

"I read it myself?"

"Yes, you did."

"I HATE reading," Tali announced, exactly as she did

nearly every day. This time she was grinning. "But I like this game. Are there other secret superhero letters?"

Judith smiled. "Sure, lots."

"Can you tell me about some more?" Tali asked.

"Only if you promise to listen," Judith said.

WITHIN WEEKS, TALI HAD begun reading back to Judith. Judith selected Tali's reading list carefully, going to the library and the bookstore on her own to eliminate Tali's interference. She avoided books involving characters who were mothers, though in the realm of children's picture books this was next to impossible, leaving her only with books about inane animals and their friends. Even the inane animals often had mothers. It worked better with longer chapter books, which she had begun to read aloud to Tali before putting her to bed. To Judith's amazement, these books nearly always featured a main character who was an orphan. Invariably this orphan character was neglected and abused in a manner worthy of Dickens, until some sort of larger-than-life supernatural figure—whether an actual giant, or merely a teacher or another adult endowed with superhuman powers of empathy and love—came along to rescue the child and unlock the child's secret magical powers. These were Judith's kind of stories. And Tali, as Judith gently taught her, slowly began to recognize the words.

Itamar couldn't believe it. As far as Judith could tell, Itamar had long resigned himself to the possibility that his daughter was stupid, and had decided to love her for reasons other than her mind. Tali herself was the one who wanted to surprise him. One night when she knew he would be home in time for dinner, she wrote him a letter, leaving it at his place at the dinner table. The letter was short, but it made Itamar's jaw drop when he saw the orange construction paper on his plate. The paper was empty except for four penciled words that had taken Tali a full ten minutes to write: *Abba I love you.*

"Did you—did you write this yourself, Tali?" Itamar asked. Judith could hear how he tried to make his voice sound casual, cushioning himself against hope, masking his shock.

Tali nodded, her head bobbing endlessly as she began to babble. "See, 'love' has a superhero E, but it's a superhero who the bad guys tried to catch. So the 'o' sounds like 'uh' instead of 'oh,' because he's a superhero who can't use all his superpowers."

Itamar barely heard her. He was clutching the paper, staring at the letters, running his finger underneath them, as though he were the one learning to read. As he finally bent down to embrace his daughter, Judith saw tears forming in his eyes. That night after Tali had gone to bed, Itamar lay with Judith for a long time, clasping her tightly in his arms, refusing to let her go. As she fell asleep, he whispered in her ear: "Thank you."

ONE EVENING, WHEN TALI'S sitter had gone home—Judith had reduced the sitter's hours, preferring to run the house without a shadow—Tali lay on her stomach on the couch off the kitchen, using Judith's phone while Judith cooked. Judith had downloaded various animated games onto her phone just for Tali, including the ever-enduring one involving birds blowing up pigs. From Tali's unbridled enthusiasm, Judith was fairly certain that Josie had never let Tali play with her phone. Which made the moment even more beautiful. She chopped tomatoes happily, waiting for Itamar to come home.

"I pressed something wrong and the birds went away,"

Tali called from the couch, wiggling in her orange pajamas. "Fix-it-please."

"In a minute," Judith said.

It was late, close to Tali's bedtime. Tali had already eaten, but Judith was fixing dinner now for Itamar, dicing tomatoes and cucumbers into what he called a salad. Learning a person was like learning a new language, discovering superpowers. Juice spurted from the tomatoes and slicked her hands with thick fertile acid. She licked a finger, wetting her lips with her tongue as she imagined Itamar licking the back of her neck.

"It's all words on the screen now," Tali was saying. "I tried to go back to the birds a few times, but it just keeps showing more and more words." Tali was tapping the screen repeatedly, dragging her finger in endless circles across the glass. "Instead of birds, there's words. Words, birds, words, birds," Tali sang "The birds are words, the words are birds. Birds are curds, words are turds."

"Don't talk about turds, it's rude," Judith informed her.

"Why, what's turds?"

Judith snorted, smiling. "I'll get the birds back for you in a minute," she said. "Just let me finish with the tomatoes. My hands are covered with seeds."

"Wait, look," Tali said. "I can *read* the birds! I mean the words. It's easy!"

"That's wonderful," Judith smiled. "Soon you'll be able to read whole books. And then you can read any story you like. I knew you could do it." Encouragement meant everything, she had learned. She had been reading parenting books lately, memorizing their mottos. There was a lightness to her fascination, a bright and brilliant wonder. She mattered now.

"I can *already* read all of these words," Tali called. She

was sitting up with exuberance, holding the phone in the air. "Except for one that's long. An, an-yuh, an-yuh-oh-nee. Oh, wait, it's another superhero E! An-yuh-ohn."

"Anyone," Judith said. "That one really is a liar."

"Okay, NOW I can read all of it! Listen! 'I'm still here, don't tell ANYONE, come get me, love, Jos—Josai—Josie'?" Tali flopped down on the couch. "Hey, that's Mommy! I didn't know she was allowed to text. Can people text when they're dead?"

Judith dropped the knife. It skidded through pulp, falling into the sink as ice cracked through her veins.

Tali kept talking, marveling at the handheld screen. "Why do you think she says 'come get me'?" Tali asked brightly. "Maybe she doesn't like being dead. We should definitely go get her if—"

Judith's breath came back in a thick, heavy gasp as she looked up at the little girl. She stepped over to the couch, her shoes filled with molten lead.

"Give me that," she rasped.

"I want to play the bird game," Tali whined.

Judith wrenched the phone from Tali's hand.

"Hey!" Tali shrieked.

"We're going to play something else," Judith announced loudly.

She strode back to the sink and put the phone facedown on the kitchen counter, well out of Tali's reach. Tali scrambled off the couch and began following her, slipping across the floor in her socks.

"Hey! No fair!" Tali screeched as she skidded toward the phone. "You promised I could—"

Just then the door opened, blowing Itamar in.

"Abba, guess what?" Tali roared.

"Tali, you need to go to bed," Judith said loudly—her voice

firm, put-upon, a message to Itamar. *It's been a rough day with her,* she imagined telling him later. *You wouldn't believe.*

But Tali had been growing in the past few weeks, and her reach now exceeded Judith's expectations. As Judith glanced up at Itamar, the little girl stretched herself on tiptoes and snatched Judith's phone off the counter, knocking the air once more from Judith's lungs. Then she ran at her father, slamming him against the wall as she threw her arms around his legs, the phone with its tomato juice clutched in her hand.

"Whoa, *hamuda,* slow down," he smiled, and brushed her hair from her face.

"Guess what?" Tali panted as she looked up at him. "Remember how you told me that people who are dead aren't allowed to talk to alive people?"

Itamar sighed. Judith struggled to speak, but she could no longer breathe. "Except in your imagination, or in dreams," he said. "That happens sometimes." He stooped down to kiss the top of his daughter's head.

"But you were WRONG!" Tali proclaimed. "Guess what, Mommy texted us and I even read it myself!" And then she pushed Judith's phone into her father's face.

Itamar was still trying to smile when Judith saw his face turn pale. For a long time he stood still, his body a pillar of salt pressed against the wall. Then he moved his hand toward Tali's, as if in a trance. Tali put the phone in his palm, dropping her own arms obediently to her sides. He straightened against the wall again and held it high in front of his face, oblivious to the tomato seeds dripping onto his fingers. Judith flinched as he squinted, moving the phone closer to his own eyes.

"What is this," he murmured.

It wasn't a question. He looked down at Tali. His skin was

ashen. "Tali," he said, his voice low, *"at katavt et zeh, nakhon, metuka? Nu, yofi, ani ge'eh she-at yoda'at likhtov, aval likhtov mashehu kazeh al Ima? Zeh be'emet lo matzhik."*

A wave of nausea rose in Judith's throat as she wished she understood. It ached in her that Tali knew more of him than she did. But then she saw Tali glancing at her, aware. And Tali, with a poise that would have been unthinkable for her only weeks before, answered both her father's question and Judith's.

"I did NOT write it. I don't make things up about Mommy. How could I write that anyway? I couldn't even read the big word."

Itamar stuttered, switched to English, as if suddenly aware of Judith's presence in the room. "You—you—you must have written it. You had to. You—"

"I'M NOT LYING. I DIDN'T WRITE IT!" Now Tali was screaming, her little body wrenching into a bright orange flame. "You don't believe me! You NEVER believe me!"

Tali ran up to her room, engulfed in loud, gagging sobs. Itamar glanced at the phone again. Judith was sure he would stare at it forever. But instead he raced up the stairs behind his daughter, calling her name, without even looking at the phone in his hand. Judith was astounded: it was something the Itamar she knew just a few months ago would never have done.

He stayed in Tali's room for a very long time. Judith thought of following them, but knew that she couldn't. Instead she went to sit down on her dead sister's living room couch, next to the framed photograph of Tali on the end table. *I invented a goodness medicine,* she heard Tali say in her head. *I'm going to drink the invisible part, and turn good. Maybe you can have some too!*

Someone must have been moving things around in the

house, because when Judith reached the couch, she saw that the picture wasn't of Tali. It was of Josie at six years old, her beautiful black hair identical to her daughter's.

Judith inhaled a long breath of invisible air, a breath that drew in everything she had done in the past weeks and months. As she waited for Itamar to return, she looked at her little sister's face and saw what now hovered before her: the possibility of redemption.

"TALI DIDN'T WRITE THAT," she said when Itamar at last entered the room.

"I know," he said, and lowered himself onto the couch beside her. The intimacy of it startled her, frightened her. She still did not know what to expect. "It's from an overseas number."

Judith cleared her throat, deciding what to say. "It's actually a Cairo number. I remember that area code from when I had to send around her information before her trip." She avoided using Josie's name.

Her stomach swayed as Itamar held up her phone again, wiping the tomato seeds from its sides. He stared at the screen, bit his lip as he read the number again, read the words again. *I'm still here. Don't tell anyone. Come get me. Love, Josie.* It was unfair, unreal.

"It's impossible," Itamar declared.

"Not impossible," Judith said. "Improbable, maybe, but—"

"It must be a joke."

"Well, if it is, it's not very funny."

"Not a joke," Itamar corrected himself, irritated. "I mean a trick. A trick, that's what it is."

"How could it be a trick?"

"Of course it's a trick. It's someone who knows about her,

knows what happened, but still wants something from us. Probably some bastard who knows the guy who took her and thinks he can still get some money. Maybe he thinks we might pay him for some kind of remains. Or not even that. Maybe it's just some asshole who thinks he can get something out of us. It could be anyone. Tricks like that happen all the time."

"Tricks like that would only make sense before someone's been dead for four months," Judith said.

"A message like that would also only make sense before someone's been dead for four months," Itamar answered.

"Why would she say not to tell anyone?" Judith asked.

"There is no 'she' here," Itamar muttered, then raised his voice again. "Because that way whoever wrote it can keep getting things out of us, of course."

"You can't tell me that you don't want this to be real," she heard herself say.

There was the slightest hint of a taunt in her voice. The teasing tone had been completely unintentional, unexpected—and one of the few true things she had ever said to him. She immediately regretted it, hoped he hadn't heard it. But Itamar heard it.

"Why are you torturing me?" he pleaded. His voice was high, almost childlike. Then his eyes changed, hardening suddenly from begging to glaring. She could feel the energy in his body focusing, tightening, the way it did in bed. "Fine, torture me," he spat. "I've been tortured before. I can take it." In his familiar pride, she thought she heard her sister. Judith tried to object, to explain. But Itamar held up a hand to silence her, and kept talking.

"Let's pretend this is real, just like you say," he announced. He spoke loudly now, clearly, like a television anchor. "My wife is alive, the Messiah has come, the dead are rising from their graves and sending text messages to the living. Good. I accept.

If it's really her, if it's really true, then why would she write to you and not to me?"

"Because I made you change your phone number," Judith said.

Itamar was silent. In the void left by his silence, Judith stared into the dark hole of what she had done, and dared.

"I think we need to go there," Judith said quietly. "What if she's still alive and sending this was dangerous for her? What if she needs us?"

Itamar frowned, pursing his lips. "Don't be absurd. If that were true she would be dead already, or at least she would be by the time we got there." He shook his head hard, then harder, as if trying to detach his head from his body. Judith looked down at her feet again, into the depths of the pit. "She *is* dead already," he said. "I can't believe I'm even talking about this. All of this is absurd."

"But would it kill us to go there, just to find out?"

Itamar laughed, a hard cold laugh. "Yes, Judith. Yes, it would. You think I can go there now, with a Hebrew name, with an Israeli passport, to track down some criminal trying to lure me into a trap? Great idea."

"Well, then get the CIA involved. Someone needs to look for her."

"Stop it, Judith! This is not her. Don't you understand? It's not her!"

"Abba?"

Tali was standing in the doorway. She had dressed herself in winter pajamas, with a summer nightgown layered on top, because she "couldn't decide" what to wear—a Tali absurdity, one that Judith didn't usually allow. The little girl's lips were trembling.

Itamar turned and saw her. Judith watched as his eyes softened, as he became someone else. "Go back to bed, *metuka,*" Itamar said gently.

"Abba? You said that Mommy was alive."

"Go back to bed. You're having a dream."

Tali clung to the doorpost behind her, pressing her body against it as if nailed to it fast. "I wasn't dreaming," she said. "I wasn't even sleeping."

"Maybe you were asleep but didn't know you were asleep." Itamar smiled at her.

"I know I wasn't asleep. I was sitting on the top of the stairs listening to you."

Judith swallowed. Itamar turned red.

"Mommy texted us," Tali said. "I thought she sent it while she was dead, but now I heard you say she's alive."

"Tali," Itamar whispered.

"You said it yourself. You said, 'My wife is alive.' That's Mommy."

Judith watched as Itamar rose from the couch. He approached his little girl as though she were a dangerous animal, whom sudden movements might surprise into an attack. "Tali, it isn't what you think," he said, bending down in front of her by the doorpost of the room. "I wish it was, but it's not." He tried to take her hand, but she clutched the doorpost, unwilling to let go.

"Who texted us, if it isn't Mommy?"

"Probably some mean person who wants to trick us," Itamar said.

"Why would a mean person want to trick us?"

"The same reason a mean person wanted to hurt Mommy," he said. "No reason. Or because they want to feel important by hurting someone else."

"Why would that make them feel important?"

Itamar paused as Judith cringed. "I am so glad you don't understand that," he finally said. He took his daughter in his arms. At last she let go of the doorpost, and clung to her father. "Tali," he said quietly, "can you please go back to bed?"

Tali was tired, Judith could see: the deep exhaustion of a child for whom a single day passes like a lifetime. "I don't want to," she said.

"Come with me," Itamar said to her softly, and took her by the hand. Another lifetime passed as Itamar brought her back to her room. At last he returned to Judith.

"This is a dream," he told her as he settled back onto the couch. "That's all it is. Don't be fooled by these people." He put her phone down on the couch beside his leg and slid closer to her, until his knee was touching hers.

She had steeled herself to face him, but with his touch her resolve gave way in an instant, as if it had never been. Relief blew through Judith's lungs like a gust of wind.

"You really think so?" she asked. She made her voice timid, childlike. It still burned in her, her eternal envy of the little dark-haired girl.

"I'm sure of it," he said, and caressed her knee. "Anyway, there are all kinds of bastards looking to make money off of her. This is nothing new."

Judith sighed, astounded by happiness, like a prisoner inexplicably set free. She fell against his chest as he stroked her hair.

"The most recent nonsense is that someone has been pirating the software overseas," he was saying. "A guy in sales told me about it today. Apparently it's available now in the Arab world as a free download. Someone must have hacked it. We never even marketed it to them, did we?"

Still drinking in fresh air, Judith hesitated. "We did, actually," she answered. "That's the whole reason she went to Egypt, remember?"

Itamar looked at her. In his look she imagined that she saw a rebuke: *The whole reason she went to Egypt was because of you.* She swallowed as she tried to recover. "But we only sold them the institutional edition," she said, speaking quickly. "The newer consumer versions aren't there."

"I thought she was working on expanding the overseas consumer market."

"In East Asia, yes. Not in—"

Itamar clicked his tongue. "Thieves. They're just thieves. They think everything needs to be free, and they don't even know what that means."

"Who's 'they'? You mean people in Egypt?"

"I mean people everywhere. Every idiot with a computer. They think Facebook and Google and all that are free, and they don't even know all the ways they're paying for them. Nothing is ever free."

Suddenly his eyes narrowed.

He sat up straight until she shifted, raising her head as he withdrew his embrace. "You knew about this," he said.

"What?"

He straightened further and picked up her phone again. This time he did not stare at it. Instead he began tapping the screen, dragging his finger across the glass, tapping, tapping again. Judith shivered, shaken by a deep awareness that something had gone horrifically wrong. She was about to grab the phone from his hand when he spoke.

"The date on this message is from almost a month ago," Itamar said. "When did you see it?"

Judith shifted on the couch. Twilit nights kaleidoscoped at

her feet until she looked down at the floor and saw the pit, her sister deep within it, calling her name. She had run away, then. She was only fourteen, she told herself. But fourteen had been old enough.

"I don't know," she lied. "Earlier." But she knew it was already too late.

"Earlier when?"

Judith did not speak.

"Why didn't you tell me?"

She thought of lying more. She had lied to him before, many times—lies of omission, lies of intention, outright lies. It had become normal for her with him, natural even. Plausible lies began to swirl in her head: she had been swamped with messages that day and hadn't seen it; her phone had been acting up; it had been filtered out as spam; she had seen the unfamiliar number and assumed it was junk. She almost used the most plausible lie of all: *I didn't think it was real.* Instead she settled on a lie that had turned out to be the truth.

"I didn't think you'd believe it," she said.

Itamar breathed. He tapped at the screen again. An otherworldly silence descended upon him, as if he were surrounded by a halo of held breath. Judith watched him as a strange fear overtook her.

"But *you* believe it," he said at last. "You believe it, and still you never told me."

"I don't know if I believe it," she tried. "I—"

Itamar's body began to tremble, a terrifying shudder, like a volcano about to erupt. When he spoke, his intonation was dark and cold. "You believe it. And that is exactly why you never told me." His lips shook. "You monster."

Judith held up her hands, surrendering. "Itamar—"

He had already risen from the couch, clutching her phone

in his tight red fist. "Josie never liked you," he said. His voice had become unearthly, as though she were hearing frequencies beyond the human range, a physically impossible sound. "I thought she was being silly, or unfair. I never understood why." His fury rattled within his towering frame, like a wild animal caught in a cage. Tiny drops of white spittle formed at the corners of his mouth. And then he growled: "Get out of my house."

It was unfathomable, impossible. Judith choked, strangled. "Itamar—" she began, when she could finally speak. But she could think of nothing more to say. It did not matter. He was screaming now, his body transformed into a column of fire.

"Get the fuck out of my house," he roared. "Get away from my daughter. Get out of my house!"

Judith tried to speak, but Itamar's fire consumed the room's air. The house was in flames. She fled for the door. As she ran out and down the house's front walk, she paused only to pick up the phone that Itamar had thrown after her, grabbing it from the ground after its screen shattered on stone.

THE NEXT MORNING JUDITH awoke alone in her old apartment. She had fallen asleep long past midnight, collapsing in her clothes. Dawn was glowing outside her window. She wished she could go back to sleep, tried closing her eyes, tried erasing everything. But something kept urging her awake, a subtle shudder in the room. Many moments passed before she realized that her phone was vibrating on the table beside her bed. She groped for it, eager to shut it off. Under the screen's shattered glass, a message emerged. It was from Itamar.

At first she was too frightened to read it. Instead she put the phone back down and let fantasies play through her mind. Itamar never woke up before he absolutely had to, she remembered; a message from him at this hour must mean that he had been up all night. She allowed hope to lead her as she picked up the phone once more. But she soon discovered that Itamar was still asleep, because the message was from someone else.

der judith i mis you plese brig mommy bak love tali

That day Judith did not go to work. Instead she bought a last-minute ticket to Cairo, and boarded the plane that night.

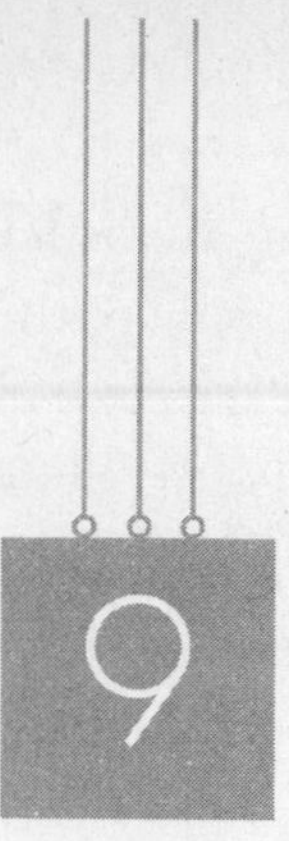

IT WAS IMPOSSIBLE. Not because such things never happened—in fact, they happened often, very often. To ordinary people. That such a thing would happen to David was inconceivable. David, Mosheh's younger brother, was an extraordinary man, the kind of person who lived his life in such an exquisite balance of business and scholarship, commandment and commitment, that the idea that something this horrifying would ever happen to him belonged only in the realm of the impossible. The idea that Mosheh had caused it was more unfathomable still. Yet as of the previous week, or in point of fact, the previous several months, this was reality. The world that God had created had changed colors, buried in thick gray ash. And it was Mosheh's fault.

Mosheh ben Maimon contemplated these things as he made his daily trip by mule between the center of Cairo and his home in Fustat, during those ashen months in the year 4931—or as the Muslims called it, 549; or as the Christians called it, 1171. At home it was impossible to think about it. He was confronted from the moment he walked in the door each evening with an endless stream of patients, rich and poor and everything in between, as though every Jew from Ashkelon to Ethiopia had been invited to Mosheh's home in order to describe his rheumatism in excruciating detail. Often these evening consultations went on for so long that Mosheh had to lie down during them, out of sheer fatigue. After dinner the scholars would arrive, each waiting his turn to expound on (it seemed) whatever aspect of Mosheh's commentary on the Mishnah currently interested Mosheh the least. They would then inevitably ask for Mosheh's authoritative opinion, which would necessitate further hours of discussion and disputation when he and they inevitably disagreed. Late at night, he would often devote several hours to working on a new condensation of the Talmud that, he hoped, would make it possible for future scholars to avoid spending their entire lives on the Talmud alone. On worse nights, he would spend the time on correspondence with physicians or scholars abroad, preparing himself for whatever demands the vizier might make the following morning. After that, he would at last collapse in his bed, grateful to God that the day had been too grueling for him to ever think of himself. But then, long past midnight, David's little girl would somehow avoid the sleeping servants and her own sleeping mother and sneak into Mosheh's chamber, staring at him with her father's eyes until he awakened in the night. She had had a bad dream, a bad omen, she would explain in a whisper—and in the depths of a dark and silent room, she had mistaken him for her father. He invariably sent her back to bed. Then he would remain awake until dawn, banging his head against the invisible walls of the world. So it was only on his daily journey to and from Cairo that he ever thought about what had happened, or why.

It had begun—Mosheh remembered again and again and again, in a merciless spiral of memory that burrowed down into the earth—with a breath.

Mosheh was a personal physician of al-Qadi al-Fadil, grand vizier of Cairo. Ever since Mosheh's training at the royal court in Fez, where he had determined the cause of a prince's death by investigating the appropriate dosages of the Great Theriac antidote, he had never doubted his own ability. And since his arrival in Egypt three years earlier, preceded by piles of laudatory letters from doctors and nobles all over the Maghrib, the grand vizier al-Qadi al-Fadil—a hunchbacked poet-prince who was impressed not only by Mosheh's scientific mind but also by his unexpected talent for rhymed prose—had never doubted him either.

But in the months before the calamity, Mosheh had begun to feel inadequate to the task, and he had wondered if al-Fadil sensed it. The vizier had recently hired an additional Jewish doctor, Hibatallah ibn Jumay, who had rapidly risen to stardom in the royal court. Ibn Jumay had achieved this fame by mere luck. The doctor had been attending a noble's funeral when he noticed that the dead man's feet, protruding from the funeral cloth on the bier, were standing erect rather than lying flat—indicating that the man was actually alive. The royal court, including al-Fadil, was now convinced that ibn Jumay was gifted with supernatural powers, a messianic soul imbued with the miraculous ability to resurrect the dead. And ibn Jumay had shrewdly never denied that he could work magic. Just seeing the man's smug face made choleric bile rise in Mosheh's throat.

But much else had changed in Cairo in that frightening

year—most notably, a new dynasty that was considerably worse than the last, shutting down libraries and demanding that people like Mosheh and ibn Jumay mark their clothing with a yellow badge. The vizier had wisely shifted his allegiance toward the new dynasty's sultan, Saladin, vanquisher of infidels. It was this new sultan who, at critical moments, could not breathe.

The vizier had mentioned this to Mosheh during one of their regular consultations, eager for his opinion. "Sometimes," the vizier confided to him in a hushed tone as the two of them strolled through the gardens together, "His Majesty tends to crumple in violent coughing fits, very unbecoming." He paused on the sandstone walk, breathing in jasmine as he lowered his voice. "I have heard from his courtiers that he has even been known to vomit phlegm, in public. On other occasions, I am told, His Majesty breathes so rapidly that it becomes necessary for him to take to his bed. What do you make of it?"

Mosheh saw how the vizier drew his eyebrows together as he spoke. It was unlike the vizier to worry: he was a careful man, but a happy one, a man who understood that happiness was its own powerful medicine. Mosheh often thought he stood straighter when he smiled, despite the hump on his back. But the vizier had been a protégé of the previous sultan, scion of the Fatimid regime—the remnants of which the new sultan was in the process of rooting out. He saw, now, that the vizier was afraid.

"Such things are usually the result of poor diet," Mosheh offered, keeping his voice clipped, professional. "Another potential cause is mental agitation. Is that likely in His Majesty's case?"

The vizier laughed, a sound that harmonized with the trickling of the fountain behind him. "Well," he said with a grin, "if I were faced with the Assassins plotting against me in the Sinai, an Isma'ili insurgency in Cairo, and the Crusaders at my door in Gaza, I might describe myself as mentally agitated, yes."

Mosheh smiled, grateful that the vizier seemed at last to be at ease, and ventured a comment of his own. "And I might have trouble breathing in that situation as well," he said, aware of the risk, "especially if I had noticed that taking to my bed was the most sensible way to avoid the problems at hand."

The vizier stopped smiling, his brows furrowing again as he hunched below Mosheh's height. This time he glanced around the garden, ensuring that they were alone.

"I think you might feel differently if you were to examine him," he said, lowering his voice once more.

"Examine the sultan?" This was bizarre, unreal. Mosheh tried his best to hide his alarm, coughing into his sleeve. "I would hardly be qualified to—"

"Observe him, I mean," the vizier clarified. "I am required to appear at court tomorrow, and I would like you to join me. My back has been bothering me, as you know." Mosheh heard this and stood still. "I would ask ibn Jumay to come as well," the vizier added, "but he is ill with a fever, and isn't likely to recover by tomorrow." The name made Mosheh swallow, but he was still amazed. Luck, pure luck!—or, he corrected himself, evidence of divine providence at work. "If one of my own doctors were to help the sultan, then none of us would have anything to fear. Just observe him, please. At a distance, of course." The vizier was pleading now, his voice surprisingly meek. Mosheh nodded. "And then tell me if you can provide any medical advice."

Mosheh went home that day as though floating, trembling as a driven leaf. A strange excitement seemed to buoy him above the fear that had haunted him in the past few months, ever since his brother's wife had sewn the yellow badge onto his robe. He suspected that the sultan's illness was nothing more than an elaborate ruse, and he looked forward to spotting the symptoms of a royal performance. Even to confirm such a thing to the vizier would surely anchor his place in the vizier's court, perhaps even above the despicable ibn Jumay. That night he poured his distraction into a letter he had been writing to Jewish scholars in France, who had inquired about the reliability of astrology in predicting the future. It took some effort to dismiss their concerns without being rude. But as he wrote now, he found himself imagining his own future in the royal court.

Three disagreements exist in matters of predestination and free will, he wrote to the rabbis of Provence. *Imagine this situation. Here is Judah, a poor tanner whose children have died in his own lifetime. And here is Joseph, a rich perfumer whose children stand before him.* The situation was somewhat extreme, of course, as hypotheticals always were. In the back of his mind he could not help but envision a much pettier scenario: *Here is Mosheh, a rational, responsible, and realistic physician who can barely dream of serving the sultan. And here is Hibatallah ibn Jumay, a complete charlatan, who will surely rise to ever greater fame.* He sighed, focused, and continued writing.

1. *Philosophers maintain that this is due to chance. It is possible that Judah could become a rich perfumer and have children; and Joseph could become an impoverished tanner and witness his children's deaths.*
2. *Astrologers, whose follies are widespread, maintain that it is impossible that a given thing should change. Never will Judah be anything but a poor childless tanner, nor will Joseph be anything but a rich perfumer with children, for it was fixed at the time of their births.*

Both of these positions are falsehoods. For what then would be the purpose of the commandments? In that event, no one could do anything he set his mind to, since something else draws him—against his will—to be this and not that.

3. *The true way we walk is this. We say, regarding Judah and Joseph, that nothing draws one to become a rich perfumer and the other to become a poor tanner. The situation could be reversed. But we maintain that this depends on the will of God, that all this is just. We do not know the end of the Holy One's wisdom. We must believe that if Joseph sins, he will become impoverished and his children will die, and if Judah repents, he will grow rich and succeed. If someone says, "But look, many have done so and still have not succeeded," that is no proof. Our minds cannot grasp how divine decrees work in this world and the world to come. What is clear is that astrology is considered falsehood by all men of science.*

As he concluded the thought, Mosheh wondered if he were being too harsh—if, perhaps, the scholar who had written to him might not be a tanner himself, or a man who had lost a child before his time, a man like the biblical Job. But this seemed irrelevant in the face of the rational truth. As he dropped off to sleep, he thought only of reward and punishment, of how everyone, in a manner obscure to even the brightest of men, must get what they deserve.

The following morning, as if it had been planned by a benevolent God, Mosheh witnessed the sultan's suffering.

FOLLOWING A FEW STEPS behind the vizier, Mosheh could not control a slight shudder as he entered the throne room for the first time in his life. He hadn't approached the palace since the Fatimids were overthrown, and even then he had only been to the harem, tending to sick concubines—girls who had been captured overseas, girls who sometimes barely spoke a word of Arabic, girls who were often so young that they had never even bled before being forced to bear some courtier's child. It was a part of his work he never spoke of in Fustat. Entering the harem and watching the girls cringe before him was painful enough that he would usually just dispense the relevant potions and antidotes to the oldest-looking maidservant, hoping against all logic that she would be able to read the prescriptions he wrote indicating the dosages needed by some poor girl who had been stricken with the nameless infection—an infection whose potentially fatal quality he never mentioned to the women in the room. Surely they all knew it.

But now, in the enormous throne room with its endless mathematical tiles expanding in all directions toward infinity, Mosheh watched in wonder as the vizier and everyone else present dropped to their knees before a small man seated on an enormous dais in the front of the hall. The vizier respected Mosheh's religious refusal to bow before mortals, but the sultan surely wouldn't. Just that week, Mosheh had completed the section of his new codification of the Talmud on idolatry, on when and whether it was ever permissible to bow before an idol. Weighing the commandment forbidding idolatry against the law to preserve life at nearly any cost—but not at the cost of idolatry, adultery, or murder—Mosheh saw in an instant that he was the only man standing in the room. He considered the possibility of execution, and dropped to his knees. As he pressed his face into the plush rug on the throne room floor, feeling cool silk on his forehead at precisely the spot where his Muslim neighbors' brows were callused from years of daily prayers, he told himself that he was merely dissimulating, pretending to bow before man while he was really prostrating himself before the king of kings. When he rose from the ground, he shivered as if shaking off filth before finally peering over the vizier's shoulder at the newly crowned king.

The sultan was much shorter than Mosheh had expected. He was a small, ugly man, with a thick beard and a slight figure that nearly drowned in his brocaded robes as he rose from his throne. He looked almost comically harmless. But when the sultan opened his mouth to speak, Mosheh was astounded. Saladin's voice was cavernous, booming, bursting with pitch and fury—a commanding, explosive sound that slammed the room into stunned silence. As he harangued some visiting diplomat for what was apparently a catastrophic error in a message sent to the Crusaders at Gaza, the dozens of nobles and servants around him moved back, as if edging away from an encroaching fire.

"Do you think it's acceptable to have the Franks knocking at the gates of Cairo?" the sultan shouted. The short, narrow-chested king pushed aside several servants to step closer to the now cowering diplomat. His royal mouth frothed, spewing hot, fast breath. "Is that why we overthrew the Fatimids? To rid Egypt of heretics, only to see it conquered by infidels?"

"Your Majesty, I merely requested their aid against the Assassins," the diplomat whimpered. "The Assassins have already broached the gates of the city, Your Majesty, and after the previous attempts on your life—"

"You deserve to be impaled."

The sultan reddened as he thrust his face at the cringing diplomat, and then he began to pant. Mosheh almost expected him to draw his dagger and disembowel the poor visitor himself. Instead Saladin leaned back, his breathing growing faster by the second as his face burned. Then he gasped and fell to his knees, still panting, on the marble floor.

The term was *asthma,* just as Hippocrates and Galen had described it. Mosheh watched as the sultan's royal body convulsed, wracked by uncontrollable coughs, gasping for air like a fish caught on a line—clear evidence of the bronchial spasms that Hippocrates and Galen had illustrated, and which they had described as a form of epilepsy affecting the lungs. Despite the shocked paralysis of everyone in the room, Mosheh jumped.

Remembering a similar episode among the servants at the royal court in Fez, he dashed to the coffee tray beside the throne. Then he knelt at the sultan's side and, to the bewilderment of all present, offered him coffee. When the sultan momentarily regained his breath, he drank, and calmed. As the sultan's breathing eased, Mosheh backed away from him and returned to his place behind the vizier, hoping to render himself invisible. But everyone in the room was watching him.

The following day, when he returned with the vizier to the sultan's court, the sultan shocked him by addressing him, face-to-face.

"Musa ibn Maimoun al-Yahudi," he boomed. "Al-Qadi al-Fadil has mentioned to me that you are a talented physician. And my courtiers all witnessed your intervention yesterday during my suffering."

Mosheh hesitated, unsure whether it was proper to speak. With a nod from the vizier, he opened his mouth. "It was a privilege to assist Your Majesty," he said.

"I was curious as to your professional opinion, ibn Maimoun," the sultan continued. His voice was softer now, inviting. Mosheh still trembled. "Would you recommend coffee as a cure for my predicament?"

Mosheh hesitated. Should he say yes, to impress the king? The man was surely hoping for a cure. Ibn Jumay would have provided him with the best nonsense money could buy. But Mosheh's rational brain would not allow him to speak less than the truth.

"Your Majesty, I unfortunately cannot prescribe coffee as a consistently effective treatment," he admitted. "There are substances in coffee that dilate the bronchial tubes of the lungs, and the moist vapor from the coffee's heat may have been helpful as well. Those facts, and the probability that the convulsions were just then coming to a natural end, might explain its apparent effectiveness during your—during the incident yesterday. But for patients suffering from Your Majesty's ailment, I would rather recommend moderation in all things. I very much regret to say that coffee is hardly a cure for Your Majesty's condition."

To Mosheh's surprise, the sultan smiled.

"You are certainly not stupid, ibn Maimoun," he declared. "Obviously coffee is no cure. If it were, I would never have developed this trouble. I already drink coffee several times a day." Mosheh drew in his own breath as he realized that the sultan's initial question had been a test. The sultan gestured to a servant, who brought him a glass full of steaming coffee. Mosheh watched as the servant sipped from the glass, paused, and then passed it to the sultan. "A safe and healthy drink, even if not a miracle," Saladin said, grinning as he raised it to his lips. It took another long moment before Mosheh understood that the servant had been checking for poison. "What, then, would you recommend?"

Mosheh hesitated, gathering his thoughts. "Your Majesty, the most effective treatment for asthma involves a regulation of physical functions, returning the body to an appropriate balance of humors, as Hippocrates describes," he said patiently.

"The ancient physicians explain that this can be done through changes to the diet, moderation in physical exertion, ample rest, altering the quality of the air in your chambers through fumigations, particularly during the damper months, and"—here Mosheh hesitated as he often did in the vizier's court, where the nobles' private reality frequently conflicted with common sense—"I would also add to these recommendations a moderation in one's relations with the fairer sex, for while the ancients do not mention it, this realm too would undoubtedly affect—"

The sultan cut him off. Mosheh knew why. "Ibn Maimoun, you are boring me," he loudly announced. The courtiers around him checked the royal face for a smile, and then allowed themselves to laugh.

Mosheh bowed his head, waiting for the laughter to pass. He reminded himself of his other life in Fustat, where people waited for hours merely to stand in his presence, where his was the only opinion that mattered, where no one would dream of laughing at him, much less the servants of a king. In Fustat—and not merely in Fustat, but everywhere among Jews across the planet, from France to Yemen—he was Rabbi Mosheh ben Maimon, the Great Master in Israel, the human embodiment of Torah, the personification of the divine scholarship required by the covenant with God. It was only here, he forced himself to remember, that he was Musa ibn Maimoun al-Yahudi, the nobles' slave. He remained silent.

"Do I have time to learn everything the ancient physicians had to say?" the sultan laughed. "No. That is your responsibility, and you needn't share it with me. And to return the favor, I promise never to ask you for advice on how to defeat the Franks." The sultan smirked, and drank more coffee. "All I need from you, ibn Maimoun, is a cure. Not a 'moderation of the humors.' Not an 'adjustment to the royal chambers.' Not your medical advice on which of my wives or concubines should be brought to me this evening." The courtiers tittered again, after the sultan blessed them with a smile. "No, ibn Maimoun. I want a *cure*. Do you understand?"

Mosheh cleared his throat, suddenly afraid he might fall into a coughing fit of his own. "Your Majesty, I must advise that a chronic condition—"

The sultan stood as Mosheh cowered. A servant adjusted Saladin's robes for him as he began moving toward a door behind his throne. "Enough," he announced, waving a hand. "I haven't time for this. One of the ladies in the harem is ill. Go treat her. And then go back to your synagogue and find me a cure."

That evening in Fustat, Mosheh could think of little else.

"SOMETHING IS TROUBLING YOU, Mosheh," his brother David said.

The brothers were dining together, as had become their habit during the two years since their father's death. A servant had already cleared away the dishes, removing the remains of a date and apricot stew, and the two had just finished reciting the blessings after the meal. But Mosheh, reluctant to meet the petitioners who he knew awaited him in the courtyard, had lingered at the table, drumming his fingers as he hummed the final words of praise. David had noticed. "What is it?" David asked.

Mosheh disliked sharing his concerns with his younger brother. It struck him as a sign of weakness, against the natural order. But since their father's death, Mosheh had felt the enormous burden of authority, of knowing that there was no longer anyone in the world in whom he was entitled to confide, or to whom he could express any form of doubt. David was right: he was preoccupied. No study of Torah would be possible this evening, he told himself, if he remained this way. That alone was justification enough to do something as petty as telling David his thoughts. He breathed, and spoke.

"I have a patient who is suffering from asthma," Mosheh said. The sultan wasn't his patient, of course, or at least not in any sense but the aspirational. But to Mosheh, this slight distortion seemed harmless, then. "The only treatments I know of are moderations to the diet and so forth. But the patient absolutely insists on a cure."

"An important patient, I imagine?"

Mosheh frowned. "All patients are important."

David stroked his beard. Mosheh still thought of David as a boy, but he was a man now, and a more worldly man at that. They had traveled together involuntarily since childhood, fleeing one country after another—Spain, Morocco, the Holy Land—but David as an adult had become constitutionally incapable of remaining in one place, and had become a traveling merchant. At twenty-four, David had already traversed the world, from Córdoba to Bombay. Mosheh would never admit it, but he admired him.

"I have often been surprised by how physicians elsewhere treat illnesses," David offered. "Often their approach is quite different from ours."

"What do you mean?"

"In India, for instance," David said. "On my last voyage there three years ago, the captain of the merchant ship on which I was a passenger fell ill with a horrific catarrh. All the passengers were talking about it, particularly since we had already buried the first mate at sea. Everyone was frightened. With what little I've gleaned from listening to you speak about your studies, I would have simply recommended complete rest."

"That's certainly the standard treatment for catarrh. Along with hot liquids for relief of inflammation."

"Under the circumstances, complete rest was impossible. The sea was quite rough, and none of us had slept in days. I never expected him to live," David said. "But there was an Indian physician who had boarded our vessel in Cochin, and the Indian administered a certain potion to him. The captain recovered within a week. I was astounded."

"What sort of potion?"

David laughed. "If you had been there, you of course would have asked all the intelligent questions. All I know is that it was something created by God, a plant or herb of some sort, dissolved into a kind of tea. It was my impression that it was a plant which only grows in that climate. It occurred to me that there must be many plants of which you and I know nothing, and which God saw fit to scatter throughout the world without providing every nation with the same ones. Perhaps it was the divine hope that men might trade and share the various blessings they have been given, and thus complete the sacred work of creation."

It sounded harmless enough, but Mosheh heard the faintest echo of idolatry in his brother's words. He grimaced. "If God is perfect and unchanging, and omniscient as well, how can he be said to hope?" he said. "One can only hope for a particular outcome if one is ignorant of the future."

David reddened, and Mosheh regretted what he had said. It was true, of course, but he had humiliated his brother. The tradeoff was one that eternally disturbed him.

But this time David surprised him. He had been surprising Mosheh more and more since their father's death, challenging him in ways previously unheard of. "Is it really impossible to suggest that God might wish for something particular from us?" David asked. The meekness in his voice struck Mosheh as pretense, a younger brother feigning innocence in the rivalry between them. "The divine commandments require as much."

"The divine commandments require free will," Mosheh corrected. "That doesn't mean that God isn't aware of all the eventualities resulting from that free will. The Mishnah tells us that 'everything is foreseen, yet freedom of choice is granted.'"

"That's always baffled me, I'll admit," David said. His candor, Mosheh noted with relief, had returned.

"The fact that outcomes are already known by God doesn't preclude free will," Mosheh said. "It enhances it. Think of the story of Joseph in the Torah. His brothers sell him into slavery in Egypt, but then his ability to see the future allows him to save the nation from famine. When his brothers arrive in Egypt to buy food from him, he could have refused them completely. He had the freedom to do that, even with his advance knowledge of how the famine would progress. What shows his free will isn't how he controls the future, but how he controls the past. He doesn't tell his brothers how cruel they've been; he doesn't punish them. Instead he tells them—"

David provided the quote, like the obedient student he had always been. "Do not be sad or angry at yourselves for selling me here," he recited, and then Mosheh joined him: "'because it was to save life that God sent me ahead of you.'"

The biblical Joseph appeared to Mosheh in his mind—brilliant in his insight, blessed with profound intelligence, unconquerable by his fellow men, able to foresee the future, glorious in his service to the Egyptian king. The man felt familiar to Mosheh: not like a friend, but rather like a possibility.

"That troubles me too," David was saying. "If Joseph's brothers committed this horrible crime, then how can Joseph claim that their crime was actually a benevolent act of God?"

"It's a form of forgiveness," Mosheh replied. "The sages taught that forgiveness is one of the seven things that was created before the world itself. That's only an allegory, but I think it's an allegory for this very problem. Forgiveness has to exist before the world is created, before anyone makes any choices that would need to be forgiven. That's what I mean when I say that forgiveness is only possible when one is able to control the past."

David raised an eyebrow. "But we can't control the past."

"That's true, but also irrelevant," Mosheh said. "I mean that we control the way we remember the past, and that's what matters in the present. We choose what is worthy of our memory. We should probably be grateful that we can't remember everything as God does, because if we did, we would find it impossible to forgive anyone. The limit of human memory encourages humility."

"Most of us don't have to work so hard at remaining humble," David said with a smirk. "Just being your brother is more than sufficient to remind me that I am but dust and ashes."

Mosheh coughed. After two years, he still felt his father's absence—or rather, his presence, the odd eternal presence of the dead. Mosheh imagined how their father might have answered David, surely by saying something comforting and deeply true, perhaps reminding David that each person must always know that the world was created for his sake. But Mosheh was not their father, could not be their father, did not know how to dispel the shadow of his brother's envy. Shaking off his father's ghost, Mosheh changed the subject.

"Did you try to purchase any of that miraculous plant, while you were in India?" he asked.

David was clearly relieved that the conversation had returned to earth. "The plant? No, I'm sorry to say. I was only dealing in rubies and diamonds, as always. Foolishness. Rocks as money! Can you imagine if we were to use plants as money instead—plants that aren't merely beautiful, as gems are, but actually useful as food or medicine? What a wonder it might have been if I had been just a bit more far-sighted, don't you think? Of course, that is why you are the scientist, not I. And that is why al-Qadi al-Fadil has never invited me to his court."

That night, Mosheh found himself awake near dawn, despite the deep exhaustion that always haunted him. It was one of the only times of day when he could be alone. Normally he would have studied Torah, focused his thoughts on the divine presence, prayed. But as he held up a lamp to the few shelves that constituted his private library, he found himself taking down not a commentary on the Pentateuch, but a medical codex that he had barely opened before. For most medical questions he went straight to Galen—or rather, to the Galen in his mind, for from the age of twenty he had committed the texts of both Galen and Hippocrates to memory, and since then he had added Avicenna's *Canon of Medicine* to his mental storeroom. But what David said about plants had haunted him. He knew now what he wanted to read.

Several weeks earlier, a visiting physician from Constantinople had presented a beautiful book to him—written by an ancient native of a town near their beloved city—as a gift. The gift was in honor of a letter Mosheh had written to the Jewish community there, which had both enlightened them in a matter of Torah and, it would appear, completely cured the ailing son of the head of the community, a boy who had been on the brink of death. Mosheh privately doubted that his letter had had any effect at all on the child's health. In his letter he had barely given passing comment to the case, except to recommend an herb or two which he hardly expected to help. People do recover spontaneously, he knew—perhaps even the captain of David's ship was one of their number—and he had accepted the Constantinople community's gift to him with a degree of shame. It was a fine gift, too: a new translation into Arabic of a medical work that had previously only been available in Latin. Even the Arabic translation was only available in Baghdad; the community leader in Constantinople had come across it through a traveling merchant selling medicines. Mosheh intended to donate the volume to the library in the synagogue so the whole community could use it, and so that he could avoid seeing it every day. Every time he noticed it on his shelf, he remembered the boy in Constantinople and felt ashamed again. For this reason he had barely opened it. He grimaced as he pulled the book down. The book was a translation of *On Medical Substances,* by the ancient doctor Pedanius Dioscorides. It was a lexicon of herbs.

Dioscorides, Mosheh learned from the book's introduction, had been a physician traveling with Nero's army, and in the course of his journeys across the world he had done precisely what David regretted not doing: gathered and recorded samples of every useful medical plant known to man, or at least known to him. The volume itself was utterly astonishing. It not only listed hundreds of herbs, but also provided detailed illustrations, descriptions of uses, recommendations for dosages, and warnings of possible side effects for each one. And in something that even a rationalist like Mosheh could not help considering a human form of divine grace, Dioscorides had been intelligent enough to organize his work not by the names of the herbs, but rather by their therapeutic uses, with chapters devoted to Warming, Drying, Soothing, Binding, Relaxing and so forth. It was as if the volume had been written with precisely Mosheh's predicament in mind. And so it had been, since his was the predicament of every physician for millennia: how to heal the most intractable cases, to transform the impossible into the possible. Mosheh read, his hopes giving way to mere curiosity, until the first light appeared at his window. As his eyes began to close over the folio, he saw what he was searching for.

According to Dioscorides, a plant known as *ephedra sinica* had been used in China to treat asthma for two thousand years—or, as Mosheh quickly calculated, three thousand years before the present day. For those afflicted with asthma, the ancient pharmacist wrote,

> *Orientals are known to boil the stems of this plant, at dosages of five siliqua per quartarius of heated liquid. The patient then ingests the resultant liquid while inhaling its fumes, for rapid restoration of calming breath. Ancillary effects include temporarily increased agitation and palpation of the humors, though these effects are balanced by the efficiency with which the substance is known to regulate the respiratory tract. Common in western China,* ephedra sinica *is also known in India, where it is used in a similar fashion. Indian dosages differ, however, resulting in the ancillary effect of prophetic dreams.*

Mosheh replaced the book on the shelf and returned to his bed, dreaming what he believed to be prophetic dreams.

"ARE YOU PLANNING ANOTHER trip to India this year?" Mosheh asked when he and his brother had finished their meal the following night.

"Not exactly planning. Thinking about it, yes," David said. He was smiling, contented with food and family. Mosheh envied his brother's talent for happiness. "I was just now beginning to gather capital and materials to trade. I hadn't yet settled on a date of departure. Of course I would want to time my visit so as to benefit from the monsoon winds in the summer. The journey on the Nile and then overland to the port on the Gulf of Aden will take me eight weeks at least. Realistically I would have to leave nine months from now to make the most of the winds. Or I could also leave right now, I suppose, though that would be rather ambitious. As I said, I'm only beginning to think about it."

Mosheh spoke. "If you were to go as soon as possible, I would be honored to assist in financing the journey. I would like to entrust this to you." He passed David a silk sack.

David leaned forward, opening the bag with his large steady hands. As he peered inside, his puzzled expression turned into one of astonishment.

"It's three hundred dinars," Mosheh said, when David remained silent. "You may count it if you'd like."

David breathed. He was no longer smiling. "I don't need to count your money. However much it is, it's too much. This entire house only cost us two hundred."

"I'm quite aware of that," Mosheh said.

"Well, then, what on earth is this for?" He tried to grin again, though Mosheh could see he didn't mean it. "Would you like me to build you a palace in Malabar? I don't think the climate would suit you."

"Ephedra sinica," Mosheh said.

"What?"

"The miracle plant. The one that cured the captain on your last voyage. I've identified it. It grows in India and China. Doctors there have been using it to treat asthma for thousands of years."

David laughed out loud.

Mosheh ignored his laughter, just as he had ignored the sultan's. "I would like you to come home with as much of it as you can manage to acquire," Mosheh said. "Of course I cannot even guess how much such an item would cost, but—"

David interrupted. "Don't you think your important patient could provide the funds himself?"

Mosheh frowned. His eagerness to serve the sultan was shameful, he knew. He would say nothing. "For this patient, it would be a question of trust."

"Why? Would he think I was running off to India with his money?"

"Understandably so," Mosheh replied.

"If he is so important, surely he can take steps to protect himself."

Mosheh could see that David assumed the patient in question was the vizier. He winced as he thought again of ibn Jumay, the man who told a lie simply by never telling the truth. "This patient has endured attempts on his life in the past, some involving poison," Mosheh said delicately. "He is not a trusting man. I am convinced that asking him to finance the trip in any way would be a mistake in many respects. But I expect we could recover the costs quite easily. The patient will surely be eager to purchase the remedy upon its arrival."

"After he's given it to one of his servants first," David grinned. "Or to you."

Mosheh remembered Saladin's servant sipping coffee, and carefully continued. "David, I don't think you appreciate the possibilities that would arise from this, for both of us," he said slowly. "This patient is hardly the only one in the kingdom who suffers from this illness. Can you imagine if all of Egypt had access to this medicine, just as India and China do? And it wouldn't merely be doctors in Egypt who would suddenly be able to treat this ailment. It could benefit the entire Maghrib, from here to Fez. Perhaps even farther. Just think how we would be spreading the divine miracles of creation."

"And just think how much money we would make."

"David," Mosheh said, in their father's voice.

David looked down, humbled, but Mosheh knew he was admonishing himself. Mosheh was already imagining himself as Joseph, the far-sighted servant of an Egyptian king. He noticed that his brother was still grinning.

"You know, it's possible I wouldn't even need to travel all the way to India for this," David said. "At the port at 'Aydhab near the Horn of Africa, there are often Indian goods for sale. I'll admit that I never searched for this particular item before."

"But if it weren't available there—" Mosheh began, testing him.

"Then I would continue on to India," David finished. "I'll arrange the trip immediately." He rose from the table with Mosheh's sack, then bowed to kiss his elder brother's hands. "For the honor of God's creation."

"May your free will be the will of God," Mosheh said as the brothers embraced.

David smiled. *"Insha'allah."*

THE NILE PORT AT Fustat was a terrible place. The docks were mobbed by crushes of people and animals as each ship unloaded its goods—glass, pottery, spices, dyes, paper, silks, and every other material that made Egypt the crossroads of the world. For most people, especially people like David who lived on trade, the port at Fustat was a marvel. But what made it terrible were the other commodities being unloaded at the same time as the spices and dyes: rows upon rows of bound slaves, pulled onto the pier by ropes and occasionally prodded by whips. Most of these slaves, Mosheh and everyone else knew, hadn't been purchased at proper slave markets but instead had been taken captive in other cities, or even pirated from other ships. He could hear them speaking and knew they were educated men and women. The previous year he had personally handled the ransoming of thirty captured Jews in Alexandria, including, other than the women and children, five doctors, seven merchants, and a scribe.

The cargo he saw being unloaded now, as he and David maneuvered through the crowds, consisted of what appeared to be a family of six, including two small and angry-looking boys, two pretty teenage daughters with their hair hanging loose and bare like harlots after someone had clearly stolen their veils, and an older couple fat enough to have once been rich. Each member of the family was fastened to a common rope by a thick metal ring locked around his or her neck, while a sailor pulled the rope along the pier. The daughters, Mosheh saw, seemed to know what awaited them. They were crying silently with their eyes pinched closed, unable to wipe at their tears with their wrists bound behind them. It was difficult for Mosheh to avoid thinking of the harem, of the young girls whom he had repeatedly tried and failed to treat, incapable of preventing not only their humiliation but their ultimate meaningless deaths. The captives' father—stripped to the waist, with a dark beard and curly dark hair on his pale thick chest—shouted at one of the sailors in an almost literary Arabic, cursing him in something approximating rhyme. This prompted another sailor to use an iron rod to knock him to the ground, which in turn caused the whole family to trip, jerked by the rings around their necks, into a moaning heap on the father's bleeding back as the sailors laughed. Anyone on any long journey could wind up just like this, Mosheh thought, stripped of everything, bound at the wrists and neck and paraded down a pier in a foreign city like an animal. He glanced at his brother and saw him averting his eyes.

Oar-driven galleys crowded the port, and it took some time to find the one on which David had booked passage, bound for Qus, the city adjacent to the ruins of Luxor—a three-week journey upstream. As David's baggage was loaded onboard, Mosheh could hear the rower slaves in the lower decks as they beat drums, singing in a language Mosheh could not understand.

David, fidgeting as he watched the dockworkers hauling his bags onto the ship's deck, was tapping his feet to the rhythm, beating out time. He had apparently heard the song before. When the last bag had been loaded, he bowed his head before his older brother. Mosheh thought of their father, who had seen David off on his last journey, and placed his hands on his brother's head, offering him the ancient words: "May God bless you and protect you; may God shine the light of his face on you and be gracious to you; may God lift his face to you and give you peace," as David responded to each phrase with "Yes, may it be his will." At the last moment, as Mosheh lowered his hands from David's head and David recited the verse from Isaiah to begin his journey—"When you pass through water, I shall be with you; through rivers, they shall not overwhelm you"—Mosheh felt his brother's hand slipping out of his as a dockworker shouted for passengers to board at once.

"Don't worry about me. Don't even pray. Please," David said as his hand fell from his brother's.

"I'll worry about you every day," Mosheh said. He had meant to say something comforting, but the truth was irrepressible.

"Worry about your patients. For them your worry is useful," David insisted. Dockworkers were coming between them now, pushing Mosheh aside as they began to loosen the ropes that tied the ship to dry land. "As for me, I'll be in the hands of God."

"Not literally, of course," Mosheh said reflexively. He and his brother had had endless conversations on the incorporeality of God. Correction always came to Mosheh unbidden, like breathing.

"Of course not." His brother smiled, and turned away.

In the instant that David turned his face from his brother and bounded up the plank, Mosheh saw—as if viewing layers of stone in the face of a cleft rock—the briefest glimpse of the many moments that lay below this one in this place, in the port at Fustat. His brother's face turned, and suddenly Mosheh saw their dead father standing next to him, as he had been when they had seen David off three years ago, his father's brow already haggard as he shouted some blessing to his son walking up the plank. Beneath that moment, Mosheh saw himself and his brother and father disembarking from another ship when they first arrived in Fustat after fleeing the Crusaders in the Holy Land, their legs unsteady as they stepped slowly onto the solid stone pier for the first time, knowing, from years of studying the divine commandments, that they were sinning against God as they returned to the land of their ancient enslavement. In that layer Mosheh could still feel the pulsating sensations, alternating like the twin drums of a heartbeat in time to the drums of the slaves below deck, of revulsion and relief. Underneath that moment, Mosheh could see, in a flash of unwanted poetic vision, thousands of slaves like the ones he had just spotted on the docks, centuries of tortured people being unloaded in Fustat. And buried beneath centuries, in what could only be imagination or prophecy, he saw the original Mosheh, a baby yet unnamed, as his enslaved mother set him in his little woven basket into the Nile, pushing him away from her. The riverbank sank with the weight of permanent farewells. But nostalgia was the religion of fools.

Mosheh shook off these visions, disturbed by the denseness of their illogic. As he strained to hear something that David was just then shouting to him, he thought, strangely and irrationally, of his father's hand on his deathbed—of how that old sallow hand had clutched his in the midst of extreme agony and then, despite Mosheh's fiercest grip, slipped out from between Mosheh's fingers as his father turned his face to the wall, exhaling his soul. Mosheh fought the memory, mentally drowning it in the Nile as he watched David disappear into the crowds on the ship's deck. He thought again of the infant prophet's mother casting him into the waters, could not erase her image from his mind. But Mosheh did not believe in omens.

IN THE MONTHS THAT followed, Mosheh suffered more anxiety than he had ever thought possible for a rational man. He immersed himself in science during the day and in Torah study during the night, but around the edges of this fortress of knowledge, marauders inevitably invaded, stealing his peace. The vizier would ask him a question, and he would see the man's lips moving without understanding the words. At the market he rode through on his way home each day, the fruits all appeared to rot before his eyes, the customers bargaining for foods that would poison them. A door closing would make him jump.

David had made an almost identical trip three years earlier, Mosheh reminded himself. At that time Mosheh had been nervous too, but also preoccupied with his new position with the vizier—and, he realized, their father had been alive to do the worrying for him. He remembered now how his father had spent the weeks and months between David's letters in a strange cold daze, writing excessively long legal opinions and seldom speaking to visitors. If Mosheh spoke to him or asked him a question, he would invariably reply with some fatalistic aphorism about the inscrutable will of God. It was maddening, he remembered. David's own little family had changed as well. During David's last voyage, his little girl had been no more than a baby. Now Mosheh often overheard her assaulting her mother with questions. "Is Abba going to China? To Jerusalem? To Alexandria? To Fez?" Her questions made Mosheh uneasy. All were treacherous journeys, he knew, the imagined ones no more than the real. Misunderstanding her father's promise to return in the new year, she became irrational as only a child could be, ridiculous.

"Maybe Abba is going away to visit all the days from last year," Mosheh overheard her saying to her mother one evening. "Are the years that already happened in a place a person can go?"

"No, my love," David's wife had told her.

"Because we don't have a map?" she asked.

"Because days that have passed belong to God," her mother answered.

"Where does God keep them?" the girl asked.

Mosheh had wondered, then, if he should interrupt and answer her question. But the answer David's wife gave surprised him, and silenced him.

"In a genizah," she said softly. "But only God has the key."

MANY MONTHS PASSED BEFORE the letter arrived. When it did, it was so worn and filthy that Mosheh could barely read it. But he laid it down on his writing desk, shaking out the sand between its pages, and before long he had memorized its every word.

To my beloved brother Mosheh, the Great Master in Israel, may God bless him, protect him, and carry him from strength to strength:

I write this letter from 'Aydhab on the Gulf of Aden, hoping to reassure you that I am well, may God be praised, though I am distraught to think of how anxious you must be. I have been wandering the marketplace here aimlessly, without knowing where I am going or even why I went out at all, as I imagine how you must be worrying. I must offer my thanks to the master of the world that I may write you these words and soothe your troubled mind.

I write to tell you that if God wills it, I shall continue on to India. The market here in 'Aydhab has been disappointing; no new imports have arrived in weeks due to unfavorable winds. Do not misunderstand what 'Aydhab is. If it weren't for the port, no one would ever have heard of the place. There isn't a single structure here that isn't made of dung. Nothing at all grows here, and the tribesmen who live here survive only on imported food, and by fleecing travelers and merchants like me. After all that I have endured, the sea voyage to India, God willing, should be a blessing.

The journey to this point has been an ordeal. The voyage up the Nile was, may God be praised, without incident, and we arrived at Qus just before Passover. The holy community at Qus welcomed us for the holiday, which we celebrated with great joy. After Passover, my travel companion Ma'ani and I joined a caravan bound for Bir al-Bayda, where we planned to hire camels and purchase necessities for the trip to 'Aydhab. It was there that Ma'ani suggested that it would be safer to travel on our own overland to the port of 'Aydhab rather than with the larger caravan that was then departing from Qus. He had some idea in his mind about a pair of travelers being less appealing to bandits than an entire caravan of traders—that, and of course, some nonsense about what his favorite astrologer had read in the stars. I trusted him, which is the greatest evidence yet that I am nothing more than a fool.

I began to regret our choice to travel on our own at precisely the moment when it was too late. The terrain the camels had to cross was treacherous, and several of the oases where we hoped to rest along the way had dried up and disappeared. At one point Ma'ani fell ill. He was so weak by the time we reached the next oasis that I had to carry him to the well. By that time I was weak myself, and I feared that if we were to perish, God forbid, there would be no way for anyone to know what had become of us. The thought of the agony you would suffer as a result was more distressing than the thought of my own demise. With gratitude to the master of the world, I can report that I am now in the best of health, and that the scars of our journey linger only in my mind.

The judgments of the Lord are true and righteous altogether. When we arrived at 'Aydhab, the caravan that Ma'ani had refused to join arrived at the city gates just behind us—and as Ma'ani had predicted, they had indeed been attacked by marauders during their journey. Not only their valuables but also much of their water was taken, and several of them had died of thirst. Atallah ibn al-Rashidi, whom you will remember as our friend al-Rashidi's eldest, was among those robbed, though he survived. I hope you have received this letter before receiving any word from him; I was sure that you would recall how I was traveling with his party, and that when you heard of how their caravan was attacked you would panic. Please assure al-Rashidi's family that he is alive, praise God. He intends to continue on to India despite his immense losses.

Ma'ani regards the attack on the larger caravan as evidence of the truth of astrology—and as a result I cannot abide Ma'ani's company any longer. He has now attached himself to another party, and he and I will continue on to India on different ships. When I return to Fustat I will indulge myself by telling you all the details of the ordeal I suffered on the trip with him from Qus. I cannot but regard my survival as a miracle of divine providence, of God protecting me not merely from marauders, but from the consequences of my companion's foolishness. It was nothing less than divine providence that preserved my life as we crossed the desert with no additional travelers to ensure our safety. I have now replaced Ma'ani with Mansur; you know the man and his discourse. Ma'ani has since boarded another ship bound for India. I plan to stay in 'Aydhab to wait for better winds, because other ships that have left this week have foundered. I have already heard how our dear friend ibn Atiyyah lost all of his baggage with the exception of his money when his ship went down, and ibn al-Maqdisi suffered the same. Please inform their families that they survived.

Do not worry about me as I continue the journey, for he who saved me from the desert and its terrors will surely save me from the sea. Please also calm the heart of the little one, my dear wife, and her sister, without alarming them or making them despair. And most of all, please do not pray for me—

because by the time you read this letter, nothing you can say to the master of the world will matter, and if a man cries out over what is past, his prayers are in vain. I embark on this voyage entirely on your behalf. Be steadfast, and God will compensate you and rejoin me with you.

By the time you read this I expect that I will already be in India, but it is God's plan that will be accomplished. The ship will likely leave in the middle of Ramadan. I am writing this letter now on the 22nd of Iyyar, and the express caravan back to Qus is about to depart, so I must hurry to send it to you in time. Please remember that God is watching us, and knows what our future holds. I pray that God will see fit for us to embrace each other again.

David

Mosheh kept this letter in his pocket during the days that followed, touching its worn leather surface whenever he concealed his hand from the vizier. Feeling it against his fingers was like passing his hand through a flame.

With the vizier, there was nothing to discuss. The sultan had gone off on a campaign in Syria and likely wouldn't return for another six months. In his absence, al-Qadi al-Fadil seemed to breathe a sigh of relief, and was only puzzled that his trusted physician appeared not to do the same. Ibn Jumay graced the court daily now, offering the vizier endless potions to soothe his ailing back. But the vizier noticed Mosheh's silence, and at last asked him, on a private walk in the palace gardens, what was troubling him.

"The cure," Mosheh admitted. "For the sultan. Such a thing does exist, it seems. My brother went to India to fetch it. Please don't mention it to anyone."

The vizier could not hide his joy. "His Majesty will be thrilled. You and I shall be protected forever, if God wills it." He grinned, and stood taller.

Mosheh repeated, "If God wills it."

The vizier noticed that Mosheh did not smile. "You are like the sultan in the *Thousand and One Nights,* while you wait for your brother to return," he said, still grinning.

Mosheh could not hide his puzzlement. He had mastered the Arabic sciences, the anatomies, the words of the great philosophers. But no one had ever taught him stories—or as he thought of them, nonsense.

"The sultan who marries Scheherazade," the vizier prompted. "The lady whom the sultan keeps alive night after night, to discover the endings of her stories. I think you are like the sultan, waiting for the conclusion, unable to sleep. The first story she tells the sultan is even about a merchant."

Nonsense tired Mosheh, put his nerves on edge. But he had to indulge the vizier. "What sort of merchant?"

"One like your brother, who travels to faraway lands," the vizier said. His delight was palpable, like a refreshing breeze. The vizier loved literature, reveled in pointless beauty. Mosheh respected him, and pretended to care. "In Scheherazade's first story the merchant stops to rest along his journey, and as he eats dates, he throws the pits at the ground," the vizier explained. "Then a demon pops out of the earth, claiming that one of the date pits killed his son. He demands the merchant's blood in recompense, like an old heathen before the appearance of the Prophet, peace be upon him. But the merchant is a pious man, and he says"—and here the vizier recited from memory—"'To God we belong and to God we return. There is no power and strength save in God, the Almighty, the Magnificent. If I killed your son, I did so by mistake. Please forgive me.' But the demon doesn't accept the Prophet's teachings. Instead he insists, 'By God, I must kill you, as you killed my son.'" The vizier paused.

"Does he kill him?" Mosheh asked, despite himself. *To God we belong and to God we return,* he thought. It was fatalistic, and in its twisted way, false. For if the man really had killed the demon's son by accident, Mosheh thought, surely he was still responsible in some way, even if not to the point of a capital crime; at the very least, the man shouldn't be able to get away with offering a perfunctory apology while actually blaming fate. He thought of the tractate of the Talmud he was condensing at home in Fustat, in which endless arguments raged about the degree of responsibility incurred when a person dug a pit into which another person fell. There was always some degree of responsibility, he understood. If something were to happen to David, he and David were both responsible, he most of all. Otherwise, what was the purpose of being alive?

The vizier laughed. "You'd have to read it, I suppose. It spins into more and more stories, until you feel like you're being drawn into a kind of vortex. The sensation of reading it resembles drowning. It's meant to show how the young lady keeps herself alive by repeating these tales, but in the process the sultan really does drown in them. He loses himself completely. There are limits to what a man's mind can hold."

Mosheh frowned, and decided not to reply. If there was a moral to this story, it escaped him.

He was amazed by how often he felt the urge to pray—specifically, to utter precisely the vain prayer that he himself had just identified in his current codex as apostasy. *One who supplicates about a past event utters a vain prayer,* he had written in his notes, quoting the Mishnah: *If a man's wife is pregnant and he says, "God grant that my wife bear a male child," this is a vain prayer. If he is coming home from a journey and he hears cries of distress in the town and says, "God grant that this is not from my house," this is a vain prayer.* One did not pray for rain in the summertime; one did not pray for the impossible. David was surely already in India by now, Mosheh reminded himself, day after day. He read his brother's letter again and again, knowing with perfect faith that there was nothing further to discuss with God.

ONE NIGHT IN FUSTAT, many weeks after David's letter had arrived, a man appeared at Mosheh's door, a man Mosheh did not recognize. The man waited silently in the courtyard behind dozens of petitioners, until he was the last visitor of the night.

The moon had already risen, thick and round, illuminating the courtyard in the darkness. Mosheh glanced up at it and noted that four months had passed now since David's departure. It brought him comfort, each night, to look up at the moon and know that David in India was watching the same glowing celestial face. But now the silver light was shining on the stranger's face: a man David's age. When Mosheh invited him in, he seated him on a couch while he laid himself down on the couch opposite, too exhausted to stand or even sit as he waited for the man to describe his ailments.

"How may I help you?" he asked, perfunctorily. He was already counting time in his mind, waiting for sleep, waiting for peace, waiting for David's return. He modified his question, hoping to get to the point: "Where does it hurt?"

"Great Master in Israel," the man addressed him humbly. "I am sorry to meet you under such circumstances."

"Under what circumstances?" Mosheh asked, unable to drain the languidness from his voice. He assumed the man was referring to his own travails, some vague medical problem that Mosheh would be expected, as always, to cure. He examined the man from his couch, noticing the man's thin frame, his untrimmed beard, his sallow skin. The man was ill, no question. He was looking down now, avoiding eye contact as he straightened the yellow patch on his robe.

"Great Master in Israel," the man said, "I am Rashid ibn Abdullah, the brother of Mansur ibn Abdullah."

"Mansur ibn Abdullah," Mosheh repeated absently. The name sounded familiar, but in the haze of fatigue he could not think of how he knew it. It was then that the man withdrew a parchment from his robe. Of course the man wanted a prescription, a dosage, a blessing—any sort of nonsense to cure his aching body. Everyone in the world was seeking a cure.

"Mansur ibn Abdullah, who was traveling with your brother from 'Aydhab to Malabar," the man said. "They boarded the ship to India together."

Now Mosheh sat up. He stared at the man, puzzled, as the man passed him the parchment. Mosheh took it in his hand, glancing at the opening lines. They were filled with the usual formulas of respect and wonderment for addressing an older brother. Mosheh didn't bother to read them through. Instead his eye skipped to the end of the greeting, where he saw the words *Nothing can describe what I survived on my voyage, thanks be to the Holy One, may his name be praised.* Survived, Mosheh thought. So all is well. He sighed, once again feeling his own fatigue, and looked back at the man.

"Please read the letter, Great Master," the man said.

The man's voice was quaking. A symptom of some sort, Mosheh reasoned. He was ready to conclude the evening, exhausted. "I cannot read it now," he said curtly. "Tell me what is ailing you."

The man leaned back in his chair, pausing for breath. Finally he spoke. "The ship to Malabar was caught in a storm," he said.

The slowness of the man's voice caught Mosheh's attention. Mosheh was listening now, avidly listening. He found himself suddenly praying, begging God with the vain prayer: *God grant that this is not from my house.*

"My brother managed to preserve his own life by clutching a plank that God's providence carried away from the squall," the man continued. "He witnessed how your brother, may his memory be a blessing—"

The man continued speaking after that, for hours, for days. But Mosheh did not hear him. Instead he scanned the words on the page, unable to recognize the letters. He had forgotten how to read, how to think, how to breathe. Only the letter's final line resolved itself into meaning before his uncomprehending eyes: *Blessed be the True Judge.*

EIGHT DAYS LATER, WHEN Mosheh rose from the week of mourning—a physical rising, unaccompanied by any elevation of the mind—he wandered into the Palestinian synagogue with a pile of useless papers under his arm. Friends and colleagues, students and patients had mobbed his house relentlessly since the news had spread; this was the first time in a week that he had been allowed to be alone. He had walked through the neighborhoods by way of minor streets and alleys, avoiding people he knew, strolling carefully in the gutters as the new dynasty's laws prescribed. At the synagogue, services had long concluded. No one was there but the custodian, who was sweeping the floor. Mosheh usually prayed at a study hall near his home, and usually came to the synagogue only on holidays, when petitioners would crowd him so horribly that he could barely move in the room. The thought of his own fame sickened him. It was his own arrogance that had caused this horror—the ridiculous quest to conquer the world, to invite death in the service of a cure. He would never do it again, he privately vowed, would never even encourage others to take those arrogant risks, not even for the sake of his patients. Mosheh had written his compendium of the laws of repentance years before, and knew that the only way to seek absolution for sins against the dead was to gather ten men by the grave of the deceased. His brother's body lay at the bottom of the sea. No one could forgive him.

He stepped quietly into the synagogue. The custodian, whom Mosheh diagnosed at a glance with a congenital mental deficiency, did not recognize him. Mosheh was grateful. The simple man shouted a greeting, invoking God's blessings. Mosheh did not reply.

Instead he stood in the back of the room for a very long time, near the stairs to the women's gallery. There was a small door to the storage room on the main floor, he knew. But no one had been able to open that door in fifty years, because of all the parchments pressing against it from within. The synagogue officers had since cut out a little door high in the wall on the second level, from which they dumped whatever papers no longer mattered down into the well below.

When the custodian left, Mosheh ascended to the women's section, where he found the ladder that was kept alongside the wall that held the little door. He righted it, and climbed up until he reached the tiny doorway. With more force than he thought he had, he thrust it open. Far below him lay a shallow sea of parchments, codexes, and scrolls—two hundred years' worth, all inscribed with the name of God, as was his brother's letter.

He discarded his other papers first: notes from his study of the Mishnah, drafts of letters he had already mailed abroad, error-riddled copies of books he had already published, until only one document remained in his hand. He read his brother's letter one more time, lingering over the ink of his brother's name. And then he cast it down into the papers below, dropping it into eternity.

WHEN THE SULTAN SALADIN returned from Damascus the following year, he appointed Musa ibn Maimoun al-Yahudi as royal physician, despite ibn Maimoun's failure to provide him with anything more than a treatise he had written on the treatment and prevention of asthma. The treatise, several hundred pages long, described a strict and carefully moderated regimen of diet, exercise, sleep, and sexual function that would best control the patient's symptoms.

It never mentioned a cure.

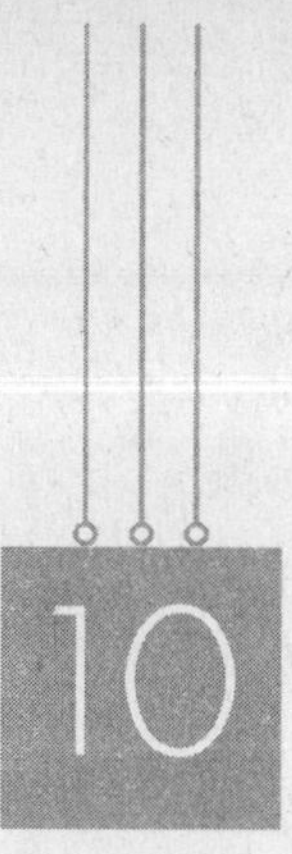

10

EGYPT WAS UNLIKE anything Judith had expected. She wasn't sure quite what she had been expecting—pyramids? sand? men in flowing robes?—but what she hadn't expected was the vast diesel-fueled parking lot called Cairo, unnavigably thick with cars, smog, and stray cats. The noise was deafening, even before dawn, as she attempted to sleep off the agony of the flight, the agony of the previous day, the agony of her entire life: amplified calls to prayer blended with the endless honking and groaning of trucks. Her hotel in Cairo was empty except for journalists, all of whom seemed to be accompanied by bodyguards. But Judith had no interest in Cairo. Her unease blurred into exhaustion as she took a private car service to Alexandria—or as her driver called it, "Alex"—where she had an appointment at what was once the largest library in the world. As she woke up in the car to the fresh smell of the sea, in a city that looked like a slightly cleaner version of the one she had just left, she remembered the email message she had received from the library director:

My dear Miss Ashkenazi,

I am terribly sorry upon the loss of your sister, who was very generous to our Library in her last days. Our entire Library mourns her passing.

Unfortunately I will be in London during the week you mention. If it is important for you to speak with someone when you arrive on Thursday, then I regret to say that the only person available would be our archival media director, Nasreen Jumay. Miss Jumay worked extensively with your sister, peace be upon her, and could perhaps answer some of your questions before I return the following week. Please inform us if this is inadequate for your needs.

With great sympathy,

Marwan Seladin

Judith already knew that it would be inadequate for her needs. Irritated by the "my dear Miss Ashkenazi" (she couldn't recall ever being addressed as "Miss" in the previous ten years), she suspected that she was being pawned off on the only woman in the building. But after dumping her suitcase at a deserted waterfront hotel, she proceeded by taxi to the library and was stunned by what she saw.

The library rose up from the waterfront like an ancient fortress surrounded by a moat, enormous pyramids and spheres and sloping glass ceilings emerging from water and surrounded by a barricade of palms. The complex spread for acres in every direction, and it took Judith some time, walking across the huge unshaded stone plaza in the surprisingly mild sunshine, to find the colossal multistory wedge of granite, inscribed with house-sized hieroglyphics, under which was the building's main entrance. Once inside, she was immediately immersed in frigid air, as if she had jumped into an ice bath. The lobby was endless, blond flooring and skylights stretching in every direction like a desert of wood and glass.

She was twenty minutes early. She took the time to wander up the stairs to a balcony over the vast reading room, which buzzed with headscarfed women and neatly dressed men clicking at computer keyboards that rested on what appeared to be miles of study carrels in every imaginable configuration. On the balconies above their heads, illuminated glass display cases glowed with Arabic manuscripts and ancient statues made of ivory and gold. The idea that this library was in the same country as the cat-strewn city she had driven from that morning—or even the cat-strewn streets a few blocks away—was bizarre, as though aliens had created a private landing pad for themselves in the middle of the diesel-drenched country. Glancing at her watch, and avoiding eye contact with the young men and women hurrying down the halls beside her, she returned to the frigid lobby, still stunned. There a smiling man with perfect fingernails met her, and quietly escorted her up a wide staircase and down a hall to a spotless office, where he abruptly said goodbye and vanished down another corridor. Inside the office, Judith met the woman who may have been the last noncriminal to see her sister alive: Nasreen Jumay.

NASREEN, AS THE LIBRARIAN insisted on being called when Judith greeted her as "Ms. Jumay," was much younger than Judith had expected—perhaps in her late twenties, though it was difficult for Judith to guess. Nasreen was wearing stylish tapered pants, a shimmering silk blouse, and a headscarf that barely covered her gleaming hair, which was dyed a peculiar shade of orange. Her face was carefully made up, accenting her subtle beauty. Her thick, dark eyeliner made Judith think of ancient Egyptian princesses, though Judith immediately dismissed the thought, assuming she was indulging in some oblique form of racism. Nasreen's accent was British, vowels and consonants polished to perfection. Judith wondered if her sister had felt the envy she felt now, standing before such a striking, poised, and apparently accomplished woman. Then she remembered: if she were Josie, she would never have envied anyone. She wouldn't have known the meaning of the word.

"Welcome," the woman said, rising and sweeping herself around a neat blond wood desk to stand before Judith and take her hand. When she spoke, her voice was brusque, businesslike, beautiful. She reminded Judith of Josie. The shock of recognition alarmed her. Compounding Judith's surprise, the woman not only grasped her hand, but raised it until she had touched it to her lips. It felt intrusive, invasive, as though Judith were being stripped.

"I am so, so sorry for your loss," Nasreen said. "We were all stunned by this unthinkable tragedy. My colleagues and I wish you and your family much comfort during this terrible time." Judith wondered if the words had been rehearsed. But the librarian's voice was earnest, drained of pretense. "I was so grateful for the time your sister spent with us, may peace be upon her."

Judith marveled at the idea of her sister resting in peace. It was implausible. She had never seen her sister sit still. Would a woman like Josie even want to rest in peace, after she died? Judith eyed the Egyptian woman again.

"My supervisor, Mr. Seladin, informed me that you wished to learn more about your sister's visit here," the woman said. "Please, have a seat."

"I suppose that's right," Judith replied. She perched on the edge of a chair opposite Nasreen's desk, glancing at the books along the shelves of Nasreen's office. Most were in Arabic, though there were at least two shelves of English and one of French. Another brilliant woman, Judith thought, and felt the paper burning in her purse.

"I will tell you that your sister's work was absolutely instrumental in bringing our systems to their maximum potential," Nasreen said. "She is—she was very professional. Eminently professional. As you know, our library aims to be the greatest scholarly institution in the Arab world, and the Egyptian people recognize this. During the demonstrations leading up to the revolution, there was a great deal of looting elsewhere. But here, the young people of the city joined hands with each other and stood in a protective ring around the library. This is how important the maintaining of knowledge is to the Egyptian people. It has been true since ancient times." Judith noticed how little this had to do with Josie. She tried to interrupt, but failed. "We have an entire school of information sciences here, and the highest-capacity digital archives in the country. Your sister's systems were a perfect match for our digital needs. She came with a data implementation plan, and then she trained our staff in how to—"

"Actually, I'm much more interested in how she was kidnapped," Judith blurted.

Nasreen drew in her breath. "There is a police report," she said. "She was last seen getting into a car outside the main lobby. The police determined that—"

"I know. I read the translation of the police report months ago," Judith said. "I didn't come here to hear it again."

Nasreen stared at her, clearly insulted. But Judith could not wait any longer. Josie never would have. She took the piece of paper out of her bag and pressed it onto Nasreen's desk, turning it around to face her. "Do you recognize this number?"

The woman bent her head down over the paper Judith had given her. She looked at the number for a very long time. For an instant Judith felt the dread she had felt when Itamar first glanced at the screen with Josie's message, the stomach-sinking horror of a world coming to an end.

"No," the woman said.

The finality of that syllable was a door slammed in Judith's face. For a half hour more, Judith tried asking further questions, pulling possibilities out of the air. But it soon became clear that the woman knew nothing, and Judith gave up.

"Mr. Seladin will be back on Monday," the librarian offered politely as she escorted Judith to the lobby. "I'm sure he will be able to tell you more about the investigation. In the meantime, please feel free to come back if you think of anything else you would like to know. We are indebted to your family." She kissed Judith's hand again and retreated back up the stairs, leaving Judith in the vast open space just before the metal detectors at the building's front door.

Judith considered leaving immediately, but she had nowhere else to be. Instead she wandered into the reference area and watched people tapping away at dozens of new computers. The piece of paper where she had copied out the phone number was still in her hand. She had already tried calling it, of course, and had gotten nothing but a recording in Arabic. The man at her hotel's front desk in Cairo had translated it for her; the number was disconnected. She wasn't surprised. Everything in Egypt seemed to be a dead end. But now something obvious occurred to her: *I'm in a library!*

She stepped up to one of the reference computers and began

poking at its menus, searching for a way to begin. But the English-language screens were hard to navigate, and frustration consumed Judith quickly. She hurried to the reference desk, toward the headscarfed woman behind it.

"Excuse me," she said delicately, and placed the paper on the desk. "I'm trying to identify this phone number. Could you look it up for me?"

The woman regarded her with a smile. "English reference, one level up," she recited.

"I don't need a reference in English," Judith said, trying to mask her irritation. "I just need—"

"English, one level up," the woman repeated, and waved a hand at the stairs.

Judith followed the wide staircase back up to the next floor. She was about to wonder where to go when she found herself returning to Nasreen Jumay's open office door. She tapped on the doorpost.

"Nasreen?" she asked. "May I come in?"

Nasreen looked up from her computer, startled. "Did you forget something?"

"I'm—I'm sorry to interrupt you again," she stammered. She stumbled into the room and pressed the piece of paper onto Nasreen's desk again. "I was going to ask at the English reference desk but—well, could you just look this number up for me?"

Nasreen took the paper again, holding it as though it were slightly dirty. "It's not a landline, is it," she said, not quite making it a question.

"No," Judith said. "Someone sent me a text from it."

Nasreen frowned, and handed the paper back to Judith. "We don't have a database for mobile numbers. You'll have to contact the telephone company."

"But—but this is a library. The finest research facility in the Arab world and all of that," Judith said. She was descending into sarcasm now, desperate. She put the paper on Nasreen's desk again, turning it toward her. "You're using my sister's systems here. Can't you just run a search and see?"

Nasreen looked at her for too long. "You sound just like your sister," she said quietly. "If I closed my eyes, I would think she was here in this room."

Judith slid into the chair opposite Nasreen, surprised to find herself fighting back tears.

Nasreen blinked, and finally smiled. She took the paper and entered the number into the computer on her desk. A moment later her face turned ashen, her eyes fixed on the screen. For a long time she was silent.

"Did you find anything?" Judith asked.

Nasreen turned to Judith. "Not in any of our databases, no. Only in my personal database. My Genizah," she said.

"What?"

"Your sister made a private Genizah for me, while she was here," Nasreen said. Her voice trembled slightly. "I was laughing at her about it, about how useless it was. People saving all their personal details forever—it was so ridiculous to me. But after she died I started using it a bit. Not for anything private, of course, just as a way of maintaining my own records and contacts at the office. I—I don't believe this." Nasreen paused, her eyes still fixed on the screen as Judith stared at her.

"Nothing came up when I searched the library's archives," she continued. "But it automatically searched this computer too. And now I've found it." She held up Judith's piece of paper. "This phone number belonged to my sister's husband."

My sister's husband. The words confused Judith at first, as though she stood accused. But then she began thinking again, and felt the slam of shock. "What?"

"My sister's husband. He—they live in Cairo, in the City of the Dead."

"What's that?" Judith asked.

Nasreen sighed, a curt, steep sigh. "It's a city of tombs, in the southeast of Cairo. Muslims in Cairo used to build tombs with bedrooms, places for mourners to sleep with their dead relatives. It's a custom left over from the days of the pharaohs. The City of the Dead is an enormous cemetery made of these tombs. In the last fifty years the tombs have been taken over by beggars. Hundreds of thousands of people live there now, perhaps even millions. Most of them don't have running water or electricity. It is—what is the word? A slum. A slum for the living and the dead."

Nasreen paused, as if she were uncertain whether to reveal more. But Judith remained silent, riveted to every word. "My brother-in-law is the richest man in this cemetery," Nasreen said. "His house has electricity, because he steals it from one of the mosques nearby. He built a pipe for water to come to his house from the well outside. He also took over the houses of his neighbors. The neighbors even collect his garbage for him now. He is like a pharaoh there. The king of the city of the dead."

Judith thought of the library she was sitting in, the vast treasure chest of books and brains, an enormous fortress of marble and glass. Then she looked again at Nasreen, at her pretty clothes, at the silk scarf on her hair, at the rings on her fingers, at the gold necklace around her neck. It was utterly implausible, impossible even, that this woman's sister lived in a slum.

"Is—is your family from Cairo?" she asked lamely. But as

she said it, she already understood the answer. There was nothing that held sisters together, no common destiny that bound them both to failure or success. Why should she be surprised?

Nasreen seemed to understand what she was actually asking, and answered the question behind the question. "No, but my brother-in-law was. He came to Alexandria to study."

This was even harder to believe. "To study? Study what?"

Nasreen sniffed, shaking her head and waving a hand, as if to say, none of this ever happened. Or never should have. "He was an educated man," she said at last, and Judith saw that she was suppressing a fury of her own. "That's what maddens me. He—their lives didn't have to be like this. Or perhaps they did. One cannot know God's will."

Judith felt Josie's presence now in her own body, in her chest, in her throat. Insolence rose to her lips. "Is—is your sister like you?" she asked. As she asked, she heard how ridiculous this was, how rude and also how pointless, how distant from anything she urgently needed to know. But the impertinent Josie within her struggled free, and won. "I mean, is she educated like you?"

"We went to the British academy together. My sister Zulaika had started studying at the university," Nasreen said. "Zulaika's English was as good as mine. Her husband spoke some English too. He was training to be an engineer."

Judith listened, astonished. She was no longer afraid of being bold. "How did they end up in a slum?"

She watched Nasreen hesitate, her face locked in a stern professional frown. A wall was going up, Judith saw, a stone face rising before her. But then she saw Nasreen pinching a corner of her lip between her teeth. Nasreen was caught.

"Zulaika married my brother-in-law against my father's wishes," Nasreen said simply. "As I see it, she was taken captive."

The words tightened Judith's skin. "What do you mean?"

Nasreen bit her lip again, paused again. At last she spoke. "She was pregnant," she said quietly. "Then she had no choice but to marry my brother-in-law, because she had nowhere else to go, and by then he had captured her mind too. My father would have put her on the street. I am sure my brother-in-law knew that when he seduced her. His only mistake was thinking that he could get my father's money too."

The evil of this story surprised Judith by making her physically ill. She shuddered in the frigid library air, tasting bile at the root of her tongue.

"Now she only contacts me when she needs money," Nasreen was saying. Judith swallowed, thinking of her own calls to her rich sister over the years, of her own pity-induced job. "He won't give her anything. She calls me about once a month, for money, to arrange for me to come to Cairo and give it to her in person. But only when she can manage it in secret. He keeps her confined there, like a dog."

Judith stared at the shining blond wood of the desk between them, ashamed to have asked anything, ashamed to be a woman, ashamed to be alive. Nasreen, too, bowed her head. Then she looked up, jutting her chin at Judith as she spun the paper back across the desk. As the paper slid on polished wood, the Egyptian woman said, "Last week he was elected to the new parliament."

Judith was struck dumb. Surely this was some sort of grammatical error, a mistake. "Your brother-in-law was elected?"

Nasreen sneered, an expression that on her angled face looked almost beautiful. "Of course he didn't tell me this himself. I saw it on television," she said, her voice holding back a smoldering rage. "I called this number then, but it was disconnected. I can imagine how he managed to do it. He must have been buying votes. Or threatening his neighbors. He does have many friends, as he calls them. There are all sorts of criminals there." Nasreen paused, frowned, continued. "The television said he became popular enough to win because he was distributing some kind of software for mobile phones just before the election, to memorialize the martyrs from Tahrir Square. He became a hero overnight among the families of the dead." Nasreen clicked her tongue.

The sound startled Judith, alarming her with its familiarity. "I see," she said. "That would make sense. You said he was an engineering student."

Nasreen clicked her tongue again. Judith knew what that sound meant: *No, and don't be stupid.* "He was studying urban engineering, not computers," Nasreen corrected. "In any case, he was failing. It isn't even slightly possible that he made that software. He's a thief, so he stole it from somewhere. And behold, here he is, leader of the people, sanctifying the martyrs' deaths, turning Egypt's misfortune into fortune. If one doesn't care to follow the rules, if one is willing to trample everyone in one's path, I suppose anything is possible. And this is our future. The country's future."

Nasreen shook her head with a slow, aching disgust, a gesture somewhere between anguished disappointment and an animal shaking off a restraint. She pushed the paper back toward the edge of the desk, visibly revolted. At last she looked at Judith. "Why do you have this number?"

Judith stared at the numbers on the paper. Her own evil rose before her like a column of fire, searing her lips. For a long time she couldn't speak. But then she knew what was possible. Judith raised her voice.

"My sister sent me a message from this number," she said.

Nasreen sucked in her breath. "Your sister, before she was killed?"

"No," Judith replied. "After that." The strange filth of truth rose to her lips. "Almost a month ago, in fact."

Nasreen's eyes widened. Her scarf slipped away from her hair, and she did not replace it. Orange glory blazed from her scalp, flaming up from dark brown roots. "From *this* number?" she said, in disbelief.

Judith nodded. "Your brother-in-law's number," she said. "She was asking to be rescued. Or at least someone pretending to be her was."

Nasreen said nothing. For a long time the room was silent, the air between them stretching through invisible strings.

"Do you think—do you think it's possible—" Judith stuttered.

"It did occur to me," Nasreen said softly. "In fact, it occurred to me months ago, when she was taken."

"What occurred to you?" Judith asked.

Nasreen paused, her motions suspended, like a statue. Then she stood, quickly, and rushed to the door. For an instant Judith thought Nasreen was running away from her, escaping. Then she saw her glancing down the corridor in both directions and softly, efficiently closing her office door. She returned in three long steps to her seat behind her desk.

"My sister knew I was hosting an important businesswoman," Nasreen said. Her voice had changed now. It was higher, more childlike, the faint outline of a wail. "When your sister came here, the library directors put me in charge of her. Someone was supposed to be minding her at all times while she was here, and I was the only woman at the library available to do it. I told Zulaika that that was why I couldn't go to Cairo that week to give her money like I had promised. I don't usually make excuses. I've never failed to visit her when she needed me, not once in many, many years. I know that if it weren't for my money, he might let her starve." She paused, pressing her lips together, then spoke quickly, as if she feared running out of nerve. "Zulaika asked me who this important woman was. I told her all about your sister. I didn't leave out any details, because I needed her to understand how important it was, and that I was only neglecting to visit her for a very good reason. I promised her I would come to see her after your sister went back to America. I remember how she paused on the phone, how her voice changed when she said goodbye. I assumed it was because she was angry at me, or because her husband had just come into the room. Later I felt guilty, as if I was reminding her of what her life could have been. But after it happened, it occurred to me that—that maybe I had given them an idea."

A deep pit of rage seethed in Judith's gut. The feeling was familiar. She imagined she was Itamar, suddenly knowing that she had been betrayed. "It occurred to you, but you never said anything to anyone about it," she said. Sarcasm burned her lips.

"No, I didn't say anything," Nasreen conceded. Her voice was still high, improbably innocent. "Because I wasn't certain. And then your sister was dead before I could say anything more."

"You never called the police, even just to suggest it?"

Now Nasreen laughed out loud. "You think like an American."

Judith grimaced. "You'll have to forgive me for that."

Nasreen sighed. "You do not understand Egyptian police," she said. "Before the revolution, the police killed Zulaika's son, when they wanted my brother-in-law for something else. My nephew was thirteen years old. They actually murdered him."

Judith tried, as she often did upon hearing of other people's disasters, to think of some excuse, of some reason why this particular world-ending catastrophe was completely fair and deserved. She had almost succeeded when she thought of Tali.

"One would think such things have changed with the revolution, but they haven't, or at least not nearly enough," Nasreen was saying. "Don't forget my sister is with her husband all the time. They have a daughter too. I knew what could have happened if I told anyone. I am not a fool. No one in this country can afford to be a fool."

Judith understood now. There was no recourse, no authority, no judge. Everything that happened here was based on no more than brute strength. But then how could one explain this stunning library, these new computers, this school of information sciences, this aggressive air conditioning, this—this—

"And now he was *elected*?" Judith asked.

Nasreen smirked. "Everything we thought was impossible for forty years suddenly happened. You thought that meant only good things, didn't you? No. It means everything. The impossible is now possible. Even for people like him. Especially for people like him."

Judith was no longer thinking about justice, but logistics. "I need to see him," she said.

Nasreen looked at Judith strangely, as though Judith had just announced that she, too, had been elected. A deep unease swelled in the frigid air around Judith, chilling her throat. "Could you give me his address?" Judith tried.

Nasreen laughed again. "You want to meet him? At his house? Brilliant. If you bring your own gun."

"You said you go to see them once a month."

"To see Zulaika," Nasreen clarified. "I arrange to meet her at home, when she knows he won't be there. Him I would never see."

Judith felt the churn in her stomach, and swallowed. "Would it be possible for you to give me her address in Cairo? I could go there in a taxi and just wait for him to leave."

Nasreen laughed once more, though this time she managed to control it, keeping her laughter to a few stunted breaths. "You cannot go to the City of the Dead alone," she said. Her voice was flat now, cold. "It is not like the rest of Cairo. There are no real streets there, no signs, no addresses, no taxis, no guides. An American like you, alone, would be eaten alive."

In the frigid air her sister once breathed, Judith inhaled a confidence she had never known. "Then take me there," she demanded.

THE CITY OF THE DEAD resembled nothing Judith had ever seen before. It was a maze, a warren of endless square stucco rooms and domed mausoleums stretching for miles in every direction. The alleys that passed for streets were narrow, carved from dust and trash. Old men lounged in doorways, cigarettes hanging from their toothless mouths. Occasionally the endless rows of squat boxlike homes would break into open plazas, full of tall carved tombstones arranged in neat rows. Hiding between these tombstones were dogs, cats, trash, and children. Several of the children spat at Judith's feet. Nasreen and Judith walked for over an hour, as Judith absorbed the glares and hisses of tired women who collected garbage in large fabric sacks. They were deep within the bottomless necropolis when Nasreen led her through an alleyway so narrow that Judith could touch both walls with her elbows. Then she turned another corner, which opened up into another burial plaza, this one marked by rows upon rows of free-standing sarcophagi, simple granite boxes with elaborate carved headstones lurching out of one end. Children were climbing on them, jumping from grave to grave. Judith followed Nasreen as she turned into a final alleyway, dodged a mound of dung, and knocked on a painted blue door. Judith stared as a tall woman opened the door. She looked very much like Nasreen, but older, with a thick creased forehead and dark folds of skin under her eyes. The headscarf she wore was pinned tightly beneath her chin.

"Nasreen!" the woman cried, and threw her arms around Nasreen's neck. The woman began to chatter in Arabic, pulling Nasreen into the house by the hand. But Nasreen's face was locked in a frown.

"I've brought a guest, from America," Nasreen said, in English, and nudged Judith forward. "This is Miss Judith Ashkenazi. She—she has come to see you too. Miss Ashkenazi, this is my sister, Zulaika Samir."

The woman considered Judith, cocking her head. Judith expected the woman to reply in Arabic, but when she finally spoke, English emerged from her lips. Her accent was almost as British as her sister's. "A pleasure to meet you," she said. She did not smile. "Please, come in." From the relentless sun outside they ducked in the door. For a few moments Judith's eyes failed her, as though she had just entered a cave. Only slowly did the outlines of objects in the space before her begin to emerge.

They were standing in a large room, Judith could see now, cluttered but strangely lavish. One corner seemed to buzz with bright new appliances, lined up as if in a store display: a refrigerator, a washing machine, a stove. Around the sides of the room were a variety of benches and chairs, each covered with an elaborately embroidered cloth or rug, some of which continued onto the swept stone floor. Along one wall, resting on a stone countertop, Judith was surprised to see a large flatscreen

TV. The walls were brown, with strange paint-peeling frescoes along their edges. In the center of the room were what appeared to be two kitchen islands, supporting large bowls of fruit and adorned with carved stone protrusions on their ends. A moment passed before Judith saw that they were sarcophagi, inscribed with Arabic lettering on their headstones. Nasreen's sister was setting out glasses of tea on one of them, motioning for Judith and Nasreen to help themselves from the coffins of the dead. Judith declined, and sat with Nasreen on a cushioned stone bench along one wall. Nasreen's sister sat down on a stool opposite them, her face grim.

"What brings you to the City of the Dead?" Zulaika asked. She reminded Judith of the receptionist at her hotel: *Business or pleasure?*

Judith considered what to say. "I am Josephine Ashkenazi's sister," she announced. The words were familiar; Judith had introduced herself this way, it seemed, for nearly all of her life. *Josephine Ashkenazi's sister.* For what else was she?

Nasreen continued for her. "Josephine Ashkenazi was the businesswoman who came to the library, the one who was kidnapped."

Zulaika's face showed no emotion. Her eyes narrowed as Nasreen continued. "She received a message from her sister, sent from Malek's phone."

"From Malek's phone?" Zulaika repeated.

"Yes, from Malek's old phone. The one that's no longer connected. I'm sure you know what I mean."

Zulaika seemed to hesitate, though perhaps that was just to translate her own thoughts. "Malek lost his phone a few weeks ago," she said. "I can give you his new number, if you like."

Nasreen had been sitting gingerly, balancing a hand on her

knee as she sipped hot tea. Now her nostrils flared. She put her tea down on the floor at her feet. "You want money from me, Zulaika," she hissed. "This time I cannot help you unless you help me."

Zulaika responded with a thick, blank stare. Judith watched the two sisters, wondering what was being said beneath the words. Then Zulaika rose from her seat and stepped away from them, bowing her head as she backed toward a door in the corner of the room.

"Excuse me for a moment. I must fetch my mother-in-law," she announced. Then she turned, opened the door onto what appeared to be a closet or a darkened hallway, entered it, and closed the door behind her.

Judith assumed they would wait for a minute or less. But soon she found that the moment had dilated, expanding to encompass the entire room, the entire day, the entire city. She and Nasreen tumbled into the silent void, eyeing each other with a suspicion bordering on fear.

"What is she doing?" Judith finally whispered. She hoped Nasreen would offer her some logical explanation, some reassuring words that would explain how no one but an irrational idiot would ever think anything in this situation could possibly be awry. Like Josie would have.

Instead, Nasreen whispered back, "This is dangerous."

"Why?" Judith asked. She didn't bother lowering her voice this time.

"I've never met her mother-in-law," Nasreen said softly. "This must mean her husband is watching her, through his mother. Be very, very careful what you say."

"But her mother-in-law wouldn't understand English, would she?"

Nasreen's eyes widened. "She would, in fact. Malek's mother worked as a tour guide, years ago, before she became religious. I thought she was dead. But of course everything here is a lie. Be careful."

"Careful?" Judith asked. "Careful how?" It occurred to Judith that she had no experience being careful, that as thick with disappointment as her life was, she had never in her entire life been in danger. Now the strange brusque woman from the library had become her closest relative, a paragon of sanity and intimacy in this strange shadowed room.

"Watch what you say," Nasreen whispered. And then Zulaika returned.

She came through the door slowly, escorting a stooped, frail-looking woman whose face and body were entirely veiled in black. The veil swathed her figure, with a narrow slit in black fabric that exposed, as if by accident, the slightest glimpse of the woman's dark eyes, which were cast to the floor.

The veiled woman moved with slow, deliberate gestures, and an anguished limp suggesting profound old age. When she turned toward Judith and Nasreen she appeared to straighten, heaving her ancient body upward as though alarmed. But when Zulaika shifted, the old woman faltered, stumbling until Zulaika steadied her and eased her onto a bench against a tapestried wall. The old woman lowered herself onto the bench in tandem with Zulaika and then breathed deeply, a sound that seemed to demand an audience. Judith listened to the woman's breath as it echoed through the room and sensed that she was in the presence of royalty, as though she had been summoned to an audience with an ancient queen. The old woman breathed heavily now. She seemed to be watching Judith, contemplating her from behind the safety of the thick black veil. Judith was surprised to find herself trembling. *Be careful,* Nasreen repeated in her mind. If only Judith knew how.

The veiled old woman raised a finger, barely exposing it from beneath her robe's immense dark folds. Her hand, Judith saw, was eerily pale and smooth, as if belonging to a corpse, one whose wrinkles had been embalmed away. Zulaika murmured something in Arabic and passed her a small notebook and a pen. The old woman took the notebook and pen in her strange pale hands. A metallic clicking announced the presence of bracelets beneath her robes.

"My honored mother-in-law has taken a vow of silence," Zulaika announced. "If she wishes to speak to you, she will write her words and I will read them."

Judith looked again at the strange dark figure. Nasreen opened her mouth to speak, but Judith spoke first, seized by a boldness that once belonged to Josie.

"I don't have anything to say to your mother-in-law," Judith said, her voice firm. "I—"

But already Judith had said too much. Nasreen leaned forward, jutting her chin at Judith. Nasreen was barely balanced on the edge of the stone bench, like a bird perched on a wire. She spoke quickly to her sister in Arabic. Her sister spoke back loudly, almost angered.

Nasreen sighed. "The mother-in-law will remain here," she said in English. Her tone made it clear: it was a concession. Zulaika now turned to Judith. Her face was calm, triumphant.

Judith glanced at Nasreen, who slowly nodded. Everyone was waiting for her. Judith turned to the old woman, who appeared to be squinting at her through the slit in her veil. "It is—it is an honor to meet you," Judith finally said, carefully choosing her words.

The old woman watched her, an intense watching that Judith could feel. "An honor," Judith repeated, looking directly at the old woman. As silence settled in the room, she felt the veiled woman waiting for more. Helpless, Judith rose slightly from her seat and bowed before her, a strange, deep bow. In this room, it felt natural. The gesture seemed to please the veiled figure in the armchair. The old woman leaned back, as if satisfied at last.

"How may we help you?" Zulaika asked in English. *We,* Judith thought.

Judith glanced again at Nasreen, but Nasreen was seething, refusing eye contact. Judith swallowed, and began. "You can help me find my sister," she said. "Josephine Ashkenazi. The woman Nasreen was hosting at the library in Alexandria. The woman who was killed—supposedly killed—after being kidnapped. Nasreen—I mean, Nasreen and I—we have reasons to believe that you might know where she is. As Nasreen mentioned, my sister sent me a message from your husband's phone number. Or at least someone did."

Was it too much, Judith wondered? Surely it was. But how long could this go on? What if the evil brother-in-law were to arrive? Or perhaps he was already here, in some hidden room, listening in? Surely he was the one who had the answers.

Judith turned and saw Nasreen shuddering, the tough, impenetrable professional façade suddenly shaken. Watching her sole guide in Egypt fluttering like a leaf frightened Judith. It occurred to her that she herself was trapped, that without Nasreen she could go nowhere, that she could never escape, never return home. But did she even have a home anymore?

Zulaika's eyes were on the old woman, who was writing something on a scrap of paper before passing it to Zulaika. She seemed to write for a long time, crossing things out and beginning again as she looked to Zulaika for an approving nod. The old woman's bracelets clicked again as she raised her hand. Zulaika's hand still rested at the small of the veiled woman's back, an intimate gesture. Judith noticed the old woman cringe at Zulaika's touch.

Zulaika read the note aloud, in a strange halting voice—as though she were translating, or having trouble reading the woman's writing. "My honored mother-in-law says she is sorry for your loss," Zulaika said.

This was maddening. Judith glanced at Nasreen, but there was no hope anymore from that quarter: Nasreen had become like a small child, tapping her feet against the room's stone floor. Zulaika looked again at the old woman's notebook, and once again spoke aloud.

"My honored mother-in-law would like to know why you have come alone."

"Alone? I'm not alone," Judith said, genuinely puzzled. She looked again at Nasreen, but Nasreen was staring at the floor.

The old woman scribbled again. Judith strained her neck, but could not see the woman's writing across the room.

"Alone, she says, without any other people from your sister's household," Zulaika said. "Did your sister have a husband? Children? Parents? Why were you sent alone?"

Judith breathed, startled. "Nobody sent me. I—I just came."

The ancient queen stared at her, waiting. Zulaika said nothing. The silence sat in the room like a person, watching Judith. At last, submitting, Judith spoke.

"My sister was married," she said. She was surprised by how much it hurt to say it. If only—she thought for the first time—if only it had been me, and not Josie! No one in the world would have missed me. "They have a little daughter," she added, bereft. "I was helping my sister's husband take care of her. Her daughter was the one who told me to come here, to find her mother. I came for her."

The old woman seemed to absorb this. Judith felt crippled by not being able to see her face. At last the woman scribbled on the notepad again, showing the paper to Zulaika. "Why didn't your sister's husband come with you? Or without you?" Zulaika read. "Why are you here now instead of him?"

Judith sucked in her breath, remembering Itamar's rage. "He couldn't believe that she might still be alive," she said. "I was the one who believed it. He—he just couldn't. I know it would have killed him to believe it and then to have it not be true. He couldn't bear to put himself through that again."

The old woman paused, her body straightening under her robe. After an interminable moment, she wrote another note. "How could you know what he believed? Do you know him so well?"

Now Judith shook, unable to control her body. The fire that had consumed Itamar on her last night in her sister's house burned her, tormented her flesh. There was nothing for her to do but let the words fly free.

"I have been living with my sister's husband since my sister's death," Judith said at last. *My sister's death.* She felt the deep pit opening at her feet again. This time it swallowed her into a bottomless, fathomless grief. No, she thought, as Itamar had surely thought when he first heard. Not the beautiful, talented, endlessly demanding radiance that once was Josie. It cannot be happening, it's impossible, it cannot be real.

Another note was passed. "What do you mean, that you are living with him?" Zulaika read.

This was more than strange. Judith glanced at the veiled woman again and felt herself being dragged into a deep dungeon in the earth, as though they were trying to bury her alive in her own shame. Was this what Nasreen meant when she warned her to be careful? She thought, selecting words. But there were no words to mask what she had done. "I mean living with him," she said.

The old woman breathed in slowly, and passed another note. "Why?"

Judith knew that this had gone too far. She did not turn to Nasreen, did not even look at Zulaika. Instead she stared at the slit in the old woman's veil. "She was dead, and he was alone. He couldn't live without her," she said. She paused. "And I knew it."

The old woman breathed again, a thick, swollen, nasal breath. How horrifying to grow old like this, Judith marveled, gasping for air in an ancient necropolis. But now the veiled woman had become a divine tribunal, putting her on trial in this courtroom in the city of the dead. *I can't be forgiven,* Judith knew. *I should never be forgiven.*

Nasreen clicked her tongue, a loud, echoing click like the report of a gun. "This is nonsense, Zulaika," she announced. "Complete nonsense. We don't have time for this. When is Malek coming home?"

Zulaika glanced at the floor, then at the veiled woman. The veiled woman shrugged her shoulders, her bracelets rattling underneath her robes. Then Zulaika spoke to Nasreen, her voice firing in rapid Arabic.

Nasreen stood, her feet in their ballet slippers firm against the floor. "No, Zulaika," she said loudly, in her perfect English. "I will not give you anything. No more money. Nothing more, unless you tell us what we need to know. This is your life, not mine. If you want to remain a prisoner here, that is your choice. I will not pay for your prison anymore." She stepped away from the stone bench, moving toward the door. "Miss Ashkenazi and

I are leaving now. Thank you, and may God be with you." She beckoned to Judith.

Judith remembered how she was chained to Nasreen, how without Nasreen there was no escape. But she couldn't leave now.

"I'll give them whatever they want," Judith blurted.

Nasreen, who had already turned toward the door, stopped short, reversed, gasped. "Don't be a fool," she hissed. "This is nothing but a trick."

It was what Itamar had said. Perhaps they both were right. But Judith had played her own tricks before. If there were more tricks awaiting her, she deserved them.

She turned to Zulaika, and to the old woman beside her. "What can I give you?" she asked. Her voice was meek, pleading. She bowed her head, groveling before them. "If you know anything about my sister, anything at all, I'll give you anything you ask."

Nasreen glared at her across the room. "No, Miss Ashkenazi. We must leave now."

But Judith was desperate, a swelling desperation that reverberated through her bones, through the air, through the invisible pit at her feet. "I have money. I have credit cards," she said. Her voice heightened, begging. She pulled a wallet out from a pouch in the waistband of her skirt and opened it wide, displaying cash and plastic. "I'll pay whatever you ask. I'll be indebted to my sister for the rest of my life. I already am."

Zulaika's eyes narrowed. The old woman leaned forward. There was something strange about the veiled woman's eyes, Judith noticed, an odd compassion in them, even through the slit in the cloth. But Judith no longer cared. The people in the room were irrelevant.

"She would never have forgiven me," Judith said aloud, her voice containing a cry. She was no longer speaking to the women in the room, but to God. And to Josie. "I don't deserve her forgiveness. I don't deserve her family. Please, take my money. Take everything. I only want my sister back."

Zulaika stood up slowly, her hand still braced behind the old woman.

"I do not want your money," she said.

This alarmed Judith. The danger that had hovered in the room suddenly thickened, as if the room were filling with dense smoke. Nasreen was standing by the door now, frozen. Zulaika began to raise her hands slowly into the air, but Judith's eyes were fixed on the woman in the veil.

The veiled woman, Judith noticed, was shaking. At first Judith assumed she was shaking out of fear, the way Judith herself was trembling. But now she saw that the woman was shaking intentionally, wriggling, visibly shaking her head with a vigor that belied her stooped body. At last she lifted her hands to her face, and as the sleeves of her robe slid back, Judith could see that the clicking metal bracelets were handcuffs around the woman's wrists. The woman pulled off her veil. Underneath the fabric was a long narrow face, sallow and gaunt yet somehow still beautiful, except for the square of duct tape over her mouth. It was Josie.

"What I want is you," Zulaika said, and pointed her gun at Judith's face.

"Josie?" Judith whispered.

"Zulaika, you're mad," Nasreen shrieked.

Zulaika turned the gun toward Nasreen, then back at Judith. Judith raised her hands, but did not take her eyes off Josie. Josie's face was thin. Her eyes shone with tears.

"Malek is coming soon," Zulaika was saying. "If he sees what I've done, I will die. Just take her out," she said to Nasreen, and gestured toward Josie. "Send her home, to her daughter."

Nasreen stepped toward her sister. "Zulaika, please. Let's all leave," she said, openly wailing now. "You can stay with me. You can—"

"No," Zulaika rasped. "He'll follow me to Alexandria, he'll know where I've gone. And Rana is coming home later. She needs me. I cannot go with you. Just—just go." She muttered more, in Arabic, and then turned back to Judith. "Don't speak," she said to Judith. "Get on the floor."

"Zulaika," Nasreen cried, and moaned more words Judith could not understand. Zulaika was still holding the gun at Judith's face. Judith bowed to the floor, pressing her forehead against warm stone.

"She will stay here," Judith heard Zulaika say above her. "If I veil her, he won't know. Then I will have time to think of something else. Go, now. Both of you. Go."

Judith turned her head and saw Nasreen, her horizontal profile rising against the stone walls as she tore the tape from Josie's mouth. Beside her, rising to her feet, she saw her sister Josie.

As Josie hovered, stooping slightly over Judith's groveling body, Judith remembered her as a child, towering above her. Josie had always towered above her, always would. Beyond her sister's face Judith imagined she could see the sky.

"Judith," Josie said, in a voice Judith recognized from many years before, when they once played together, in a time before memory. "I forgive you."

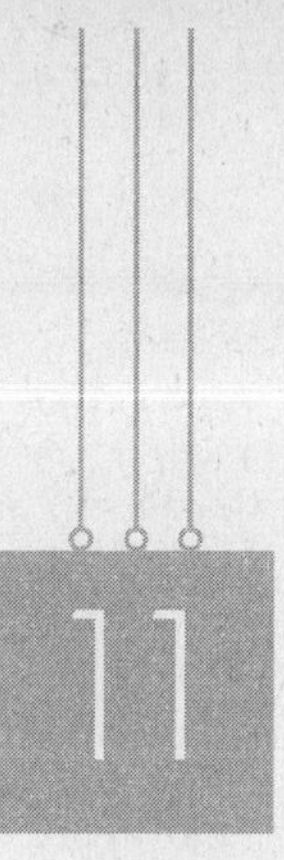

LONG AGO, JOSIE remembers, her mother had a jewelry box, a wooden case full of little doors and drawers. But her mother never wore jewelry. One day when Josie was thirteen, she sneaked into her mother's bedroom and opened all of the jewelry box's little doors and drawers. The tiny compartments, one after another, were filled with nothing but Judith's and Josie's baby teeth, resting on velvet like pearls.

She once imagined that when she was an adult she would have such a box herself, only better—with little compartments where you might open one and find your mother holding you, and then you would open another and find yourself holding your own child, and in a third drawer you might be opening a door for someone coming home, your face suddenly brushed with the scent of that person as that person leaned toward you. In her work she had almost succeeded in building such a box. But the elusive thing about the box she envisioned was that you could also see yourself in it, as if from the outside—even though when those moments had actually happened, you were only able to see the other person, not yourself. But for that, Josie had not managed to create the code.

Under the veil, in the room just beyond her private dungeon, she had seen her sister as she never had seen her before: abject, humbled, forced to her hands and knees. She wondered how her sister had seen herself, but she would never know. It had been too horrifying, the sudden clank of the lock and the woman pointing the gun at her, followed by the woman taping her mouth, muttering something hard to understand and even harder to believe.

"Someone is here," she murmured in Josie's ear. "She says she is your sister. I am sure she was sent by the police, to trap us."

Josie had choked, gagging against the duct tape as the woman continued. "I said I will let you go," the woman whispered. "But I cannot let you go now, not until I trust her. I cannot go to jail. My daughter needs me. You understand."

It was unfathomable, impossible. But Josie had no choices, no way to control her future. She didn't struggle as the woman covered her in a heavy fabric veil and pushed the gun into her back. And then she passed through the door for the first time and saw that it was true.

To see Judith in that room, but to be unable to speak to her, unable to do anything that might result in the gun being fired, was a greater agony than she could ever have imagined. To leave Judith behind was more terrible still. As they left the house, Nasreen had to clamp her hand against Josie's mouth to keep her from screaming. "He has friends everywhere," Nasreen had rasped in her ear. "No one can know. Not yet."

Josie hadn't walked in months; the journey to the edge of the ancient cemetery resulted in her collapsing from the exertion. She lay on the ground in a tiny alley, gulping at the air with her body pressed against a pile of trash, when Nasreen spoke again. "I couldn't believe it was you," she said.

"I—I—tried to tell you, and my sister," Josie gasped. "I wrote so many things on that paper, but I couldn't get her to read anything but the—"

But Nasreen was already looking away, pulling out her cell phone and lowering her voice. "I'm calling the police," she said.

Josie nodded, dazed, and then remembered what the woman in the dungeon had told her. "No, don't," she tried to shout. Her voice came out as a sob. "She—she said she can't be arrested, she—my sister—she—"

Nasreen paused, but only briefly. "Zulaika is completely paranoid; he's made her insane. Getting arrested would be the best thing that could happen to her. At least she would be away from him."

She placed the call as Josie passed out.

Many hours later, when Josie awoke in a makeshift hospital bed inside the American embassy, she saw Nasreen sitting before her. Through a veil of morphine, Josie heard Nasreen describe the arrival of the police at her sister's house—which had only happened after her brother-in-law returned.

"He was holding your sister in front of him, and he started shooting at the police," Nasreen said. Her eyes gleamed, but her voice was steady, as professional as Josie remembered it. "They had no choice but to shoot back. He survived, though. Zulaika did too." Nasreen sat back, silent.

"Is—is my sister—" Josie tried to ask.

Nasreen lowered her eyes, and Josie knew.

"He saw the police and became hysterical," Nasreen said through Josie's silence. "They told me he was screaming his son's name, over and over again."

"Musa," Josie whispered.

Nasreen stared at her. "How do you know his name?"

For the first time since she had arrived in the dungeon, Josie wept. Uncontrollable weeping, extravagant weeping, a bottomless wrenching weeping like nothing she had ever lived through before, not even when she was first locked into that tiny room. Two hours later, when she spoke to Itamar for the first time—when she saw his face and Tali's on the screen the embassy provided for her—she was still weeping. They thought she was weeping for them.

She was still weeping the following day, weeping in her sleep, when she awoke to see Itamar in the doorway.

"Yosefi," he whispered. "You came back."

He was taller than she had imagined him during those dark months—taller, and older. She hadn't remembered the bits of gray hair around his temples. *Was it a dream?* Josie wondered. *Or am I dreaming now?* He crumpled onto the bed beside her, on top of her, falling on her neck, covering her in his embrace.

"I did," she said, her voice small and still. She clutched his hard shoulders like planks in a shipwreck. She was afraid to look at his face. He was the first to pull away, to look at her, to smile.

"I should have known that the laws of mortality don't apply to you," he said. "Do me a favor and don't ever die again."

She was beginning to smile back when she was slammed by the memory, a physical three-dimensional force, of everything she had learned in the past twenty-four hours, of what Judith had said, what Judith had done, what had been done to her.

"Itamar," she said, "Judith—Judith is—"

She could see in his face that he already knew.

"Yosefi, I need to tell you—" he began.

"Judith told me everything," she said. "You don't have to say a word."

His grip tightened around her hand. "What do you mean?"

"When I saw her, she told me everything. Everything about you and her."

His face purpled. She squeezed his hand as he slid his fingers from her grip. "Don't be angry at yourself, Itamar," she said. "I'm glad she was with you. And with Tali."

Where was Tali? Josie suddenly thought. She glanced at the closed door of the room and understood that Tali must be right behind it, that Itamar had wanted to see her first, alone—to hold her himself, and to explain about Judith. But Josie already knew.

Itamar winced, and clutched the rail of the bed. Had she forgotten the wrinkles around his eyes, or were they new? "What she did to you—to us—was evil," he said. She could see that he had tried not to say it, that he couldn't help himself. His voice was shaking. "She was evil. I was an idiot not to know it."

Everyone thinks that someday there will be some large and cold and magnificent moment when they will confront the person who wronged them and wreak not revenge, but justice, the justice of seeing that person not punished, but shamed. Josie had long had such thoughts. You think it will happen, live your whole life with the understanding that it will happen, but it doesn't. Until one hard bright afternoon, it does. And only then do you understand that it wasn't what you wanted at all.

In a drumming rush of wind that burned through her lungs, Josie understood what Rambam had meant by absolute free will. *I am completely free,* she thought. Nasreen was right: it was impossible to control the future. But it was possible to control the past.

"No, she wasn't," Josie told him. "She saved my life."

Itamar scowled. She had forgotten, during those dark months, what Itamar's face looked like when he was angry. There hadn't been a reason to remember it. She touched his face, tracing his temples with her fingers.

"Yes, technically," he said, "but she—"

Josie swallowed, and dared. "No, Itamar, I mean it. She volunteered to take my place."

It wasn't true, of course. But the truth of the past was gone forever, Josie knew now, gone the instant a moment disappeared. What remained, always, was something new: creation, and redemption.

Itamar took her hand, and stared. "What do you mean?"

"She volunteered," Josie repeated. She leaned forward in the bed, straining her legs against the starched sheets. "When Judith saw that it was me under that veil, the woman who had me at gunpoint said that she couldn't let me go, that her husband was going to kill her if he saw that my room was empty. Then Judith asked the woman to cover her with the veil, so that she could stay there instead of me. So that I could escape."

Itamar lowered her hand to the bed, pressing her fingers between his. His mouth hung open. "The police said—"

"Forget what the police said," Josie interrupted. "I was there. They weren't."

"But that woman from the library—"

"Trust me," Josie said. It was a demand, not a request. Itamar understood. She waited until he slowly nodded. "Judith knew what was going to happen to her. She did it for me. For us." She paused, unsure of how far to go. "Her life was a gift to us. And to Tali."

It was done. In Itamar's face she saw what she had achieved. He was crying now, loud choking sobs. Josie knew then that he had loved her sister, and that now he was allowed to love her still, to love them both. She had given him that gift. Itamar saw her watching him, and buried his face in his hands. In the privacy before his covered eyes, Josie smiled. For the first time in her life, Josie loved her sister too.

He raised his head, and took her hands in his again. "Tali is waiting outside," he said.

"I know," said Josie, glancing past him. Already the door was dissolving, replaced by what she hoped to see.

"She doesn't know about Judith yet," he added. His voice was a whisper. "Should we tell her now?"

"Don't say anything," Josie told him. "I know exactly what to do." She swallowed, breathed, and then called, "Tali?"

The door opened. Behind it, framed in the doorway like an image on a screen, stood Tali. She was far more beautiful than Josie had remembered. The girl's eyes were full of pure joy.

Tali raced into the room and bounded onto the bed, laughing as she covered her mother with kisses. Her mother held the girl tight, enfolding her in her arms. "Mommy, you aren't dead! I'm so glad you aren't dead!" Tali shrieked, and laughed even harder, until Josie and Itamar were laughing with her.

"You aren't dead," Tali said again, as their laughter settled into happy breaths. Then Tali said, "Judith was right! Can we tell her?"

And then her mother told her what had happened.

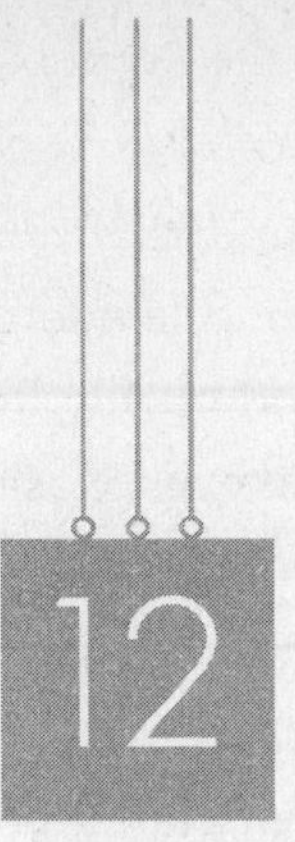

IT WAS THE DEPTH of the archive that disturbed him. Not the amount of material, but the depth. Solomon Schechter, who had committed sixty-three volumes of the Talmud to memory by the age of sixteen and who read every new humanities book the university library acquired on top of the 365 novels he read each year, wasn't afraid of having too much to read. What troubled him was not the vastness of what he had brought home from Egypt—it appeared that his two dozen large shipping crates had contained almost a quarter million medieval documents, all told—but the vertiginous bottomless pit of forgotten lives that each of those scraps of parchment managed to evoke. What frightened him was the thought—the shadow of a thought, really, since he did not quite allow himself to think it—that he would not live long enough to relive all of those buried lives. No one could. In which case the pile of parchments would remain exactly what it was: a heap of garbage, a destroyed city, an archive rendered pointless, if it had ever had a point at all. The tens of thousands of private letters and torn prayerbook pages and marriage contracts and business inventories in the heaps that now surrounded him in Cambridge had only reached this room because they were written in the same letters used to write the name of God.

Schechter enjoyed a fair amount of fame now, thanks to these piles of trash. Today he even had a letter in his pocket inviting him to become the head of a modern rabbinical seminary in New York. But Schechter was still searching, amid the garbage, for the material that actually mattered: the sacred words, the ancient poetry, the prophecies. He had discovered marvels, but for every hand-copied variation on Isaiah, there were a hundred medical prescriptions and a thousand sales receipts. They crowded his table, making it difficult for him to breathe.

And what was the point? What was the point of him reading the dowry list of the types of silk required for a bride named Hana's wedding dress, or the divorce papers for Abraham and Sarah, or the contract between Musa and David for the sale of some herbal remedy? More often than he would have liked as he searched for biblical works, he found himself distracted into imagining these people, picturing this Hana, that Musa, that David, trying to guess what sort of people they were, what they liked, what they hated, what they loved.

There was no point to it, he knew. Then why couldn't he stop? Sometimes he looked around the room and saw it filled not with papers but with people, people long dead, people he had captured on a fishing line dipped into the deep pit of Sheol, baited with a receipt for a medieval drug. But the idea that he could ever know who these people had really been was an illusion. There were no other people in Schechter's library room. Except for the twins.

"Mr. Schechter!"

"Mr. Schechter!"

By now Schechter could even—sometimes—tell them apart.

The sisters had joined him in Egypt, bringing a respirator to soothe his suffering lungs and reserving a beautiful hotel suite in which to clean the parchments. After another trip to the Sinai they had followed him home, meeting him daily in the room the librarians had set aside for him and his manuscripts, working through those that dealt with biblical Apocrypha, labeling and cataloguing them as best they could. Gaslights were inadequate for reading the darkened parchments, and a fire hazard at that; all the work had to happen in daylight. Now the day was turning, arcing toward night.

"Mr. Schechter, please, stop reading now. You'll damage your eyes," Margaret said. The sisters had risen from their own tables to hover over him like his parents once did when he was a small child, urging him to go to bed.

Schechter leaned back in his seat, reluctantly putting down a twelfth-century doctor's bill for imported pharmaceuticals. He hadn't noticed how much his eyes hurt. "Thank you," he said. It was odd to look up and see these two women in their modern widow's frocks, in this cold Gothic room. In his mind, he had been in Cairo in 1171.

"We need your eyes," Agnes added. "This archive is only a heap of dust without your eyes."

"It's actually the opposite of an archive, isn't it?" Margaret said as she sifted through a stack of dark leather scraps.

"Not quite," huffed Agnes. She pointed to a pile of brown dust on the table where Margaret had been working, the remains of a parchment accidentally crushed. "*That* is the opposite of an archive. And please be a bit more careful, or this entire room will become the opposite of an archive."

Schechter coughed, coughed again, sputtered. The heaps of dust had affected his health. He wasn't yet fifty, but he already resembled an old man. As he glanced at the dust that had caused his trouble—disintegrated animal matter that coated everything he touched and that floated in the air he breathed—it occurred to him that his body would ultimately become something just like it, that the bodies of every person alive would ultimately become something just like it, that every human being, in the end, becomes the opposite of an archive. But this was too disturbing to consider, and his living breathing body was coughing too hard for him to think it through.

On his way home from Egypt, he had spent a month in Palestine with his twin brother, Srulik. To his astonishment, his brother seemed barely to have aged at all in the thirty years since they had last met, despite the fact that Srulik was already a grandfather—to two girls the same ages as Schechter's daughters. Meeting another set of redheaded girls so similar to his own delighted and disturbed Schechter. Their Hebrew reminded Schechter of the rabbi in Cairo, and it occurred to him that his own daughters would have nothing to say to these girls, even if they had shared a language. There were far fewer misty moisty mornings here; the nursery rhymes weren't the same. But he and his brother had reverted immediately to their youth. They began arguing almost before Schechter reached the end of the pier. As they traveled from the port in Haifa to his brother's newly built town of Zikhron Yaakov, Schechter described the treasure he had collected in Egypt. Srulik laughed and called him a fool.

"You don't understand," Schechter had grumbled, still marveling at his brother's unwrinkled skin, and at the view from their rickety donkey-drawn carriage: biblical mountains, stumpy and bald and hideous, with their feet dipped in malarial mud. That night he would sleep in the three-room hovel his brother called home. His brother's house reminded him of their old house in Romania, except that here they slept under mosquito nets. "There are entire worlds in those sacks of papers. Even versions of the biblical books that no one has ever seen before. Forgotten prophecies! It's going to take decades just to read them all. Have you any idea what we might find?"

"No, I don't," Srulik grunted cheerfully, "and I also don't care. Forgotten prophecies don't interest me much. Who needs a prophecy if it's already come true?"

Schechter looked again at his brother's youthful face. Was it possible that he had aged while his brother had gotten younger? "Why live in a hole in a library?" his brother elaborated. "No matter how long you spend in that pit, you aren't going to resurrect the dead."

"But am I not obliged to try?"

Srulik laughed again. "Try something else," he said. Srulik had been smiling during their trip, but now his face turned thoughtful, grave. "Do you remember that night before you left for Vienna?" he asked.

The last time they had seen each other, Srulik meant. Schechter looked at his brother and remembered how he had last seen him, his final glimpse in the mirror of someone else's face. "Of course," he said softly.

"I'll always remember it," Srulik said. "It was a grand send-off, a don't-forget-where-you-came-from sort of thing. Father was going over the teachings of the rebbe Shneur Zalman, for whom he named you."

Schechter laughed. "As if I could forget."

"Well, I'm sure you'll remember what he taught us that night too. That night he read us some horrible passage from one of the rebbe's disciples, about how the rebbe's ideas are able to revive the dead." Srulik paused and deepened his voice, mimicking their father. "A corpse is something cold and unfeeling," Srulik quoted. Srulik's impressions of their parents used to send Schechter into hysterical laughter, but now Schechter was struck dumb as he heard his dead father's voice. "'And is there ever anything as frozen in self-absorption, as cold and unfeeling, as the mind?'"

The carriage was climbing one of the hideous bald hills now, providing an excellent view of several villages made of clusters of shacks and of the swamps leading down to the sea. Schechter had expected to gaze on the landscape here and see verses from the psalms and the sages come to life. But even he had to admit that these vast lakes of mud, occasionally interrupted by a row or two of carefully planted eucalyptus trees, were the very opposite of poetry. Language was pointless here, it seemed, and the mind even more so, the future as inscrutable as the past. There was nothing here but mud.

Srulik's own voice returned, jarred by the bumps in the dirt road. "Frozen in self-absorption, as cold and unfeeling as the mind," he repeated. "I couldn't get those words out of my own cold mind. It occurred to me then that I had been sinking deeper and deeper into a pit of snow all those years, every day, while I sat in that frigid study house next to you." Srulik was smiling now. "Father looked at me then, and he knew that I understood what he meant. He knew I wanted to leave, and not to live a life of learning like you. I know he aimed those words at me. Those words made it all right for me to close those books, as if Father was promising me that God wouldn't abandon me if I did. Everything I've done from that moment forward was because of what Father said that night. 'The cold and unfeeling mind.' I'll remember that for the rest of my life."

Around a cliff of gray rock, Srulik's town was emerging. To Schechter's surprise it was quite beautiful, with smooth streets lined by palm trees and several large stone buildings which Srulik would later identify for him (synagogue, enclosed water reservoir, hospital, and winery—or as Srulik put it, "everything a person could possibly need"). But as they passed the cemetery, full of children's graves from the town's first ten years of malarial plague, Schechter remembered something, and spoke.

"That wasn't what Father meant at all," he said.

Srulik looked up at him, and in his face Schechter saw their father. "What do you mean?"

"I mean that's not what that passage is about, and that's not why Father taught it to us. It does begin the way you quoted it—that the mind is like an unfeeling corpse. But the very next sentence says, 'And when the cold-blooded mind understands and is excited by a divine idea—is that not the revival of the dead?'" Schechter paused, glancing up at the stone buildings that had begun to emerge at the sides of the road, and at the people who had begun to gather at the roadside as their carriage approached. "Father was teaching me that passage intentionally, to remind me to continue serving God as I continued studying, even as I was studying in worldly universities," Schechter said. He could see that his chance to explain Srulik's mistake was disappearing; the door of the moment was closing, the carriage slowing, the pull of new possibilities impossible to resist. Srulik was already looking away, scanning the crowd for people he knew. "He was saying that reading and learning were ways to revive the dead," Schechter finished. "That's what I remember. Because that's what he said."

"That wasn't what he said at all," Srulik muttered.

Schechter felt the blood drain from his own face. The Mediterranean sun burned against Schechter's pale skin as he tried to think of something comforting to say, something to suggest that Srulik's entire life hadn't been built on a misunderstanding. But was it a misunderstanding? Perhaps Schechter was the one who had misunderstood. Why should his memories of their father be any less distorted than his twin's?

He was about to speak again when he was overtaken by a coughing fit, one that lasted a long time. His twin watched him with a sympathy Schechter hadn't seen on another man's face in many years.

"That old cough again," Srulik said. Schechter could feel his brother's relief as he changed the subject, and recalled what once had come to him unbidden: the ability to feel his brother's thoughts. "I had that stinking asthma for years after you left," Srulik added. "Here I don't get it much. When I do, there's a tea they sell in Haifa that helps. I'll have to remember to buy you some." And then the brothers disembarked in Zikhron Yaakov and greeted Srulik's children and grandchildren, native speakers of a language long dead.

Now Schechter was in the library, breathing in clouds of nostalgia and regret. He glanced at his notes for an essay he hoped to publish about this astonishing cache of forgotten lives: *Every discovery of an ancient document is, if undertaken in the right spirit—that is, for honor of God and truth and not for the glory of the self—an act of resurrection in miniature. How the past suddenly rushes in upon you with all its joys and woes! And there is a spark of a human soul like yours come to light again after a disappearance of centuries, crying for sympathy and mercy. You dare not neglect the appeal and slay this soul again. Unless you choose to become another Cain, you must be the keeper of your brother and give him a fair hearing.*

He had written those lines on the ship from Alexandria to Haifa, but now he wondered if they were true. The twins were at his side, exuding their aura of eternity. The hour was urgent, the light was fading, and Schechter decided to ask them.

"When you found the Syriac Gospel, I know it was a religious experience for you," Schechter said with hesitation. The twins nodded. "But I wondered," he continued. "Did you ever feel that its discovery was a religious experience not only for you, but for the person who had written it as well? That is, did you ever sense that by finding that forgotten book, you were bringing its author back to life?"

The two women looked at each other, as if unsure whether to tell him he was mad.

"I regret to say that it's impossible to resurrect the dead," Margaret replied. "Even Christ wasn't resurrected, according to the Gospel manuscript we found."

Agnes snorted. "Margaret, sometimes I think you will never forgive me for that."

"I only mean that people find what they wish to find, and remember what they wish to remember, regardless of the evidence presented to them," Margaret said.

Agnes frowned. "Are you suggesting that if you were the one who had learned Syriac, you would have managed to locate a Syriac manuscript that announced Christ's resurrection?"

"That is exactly what I am suggesting."

"But what if there were no such manuscript to be found?" Agnes asked.

"Look at this room," Margaret answered, waving at the heaps of parchment behind her. "Think of all the rooms in the world that might be like it. If one wants to find something, one finds it. Especially now. Our dear friend Mr. Schechter has brought back hundreds of thousands of documents, and he didn't even bother with the printed material. But just consider how much material there will be for historians in the future, now that we have printing presses, and telegraphs, and newspapers, and mail deliveries two or three times a day. For every book and letter we find in this genizah, the genizah of the future will surely have hundreds of thousands. It will be endless. The past will become a bottomless pit. In that kind of archive, one can find anything one wishes to find."

Schechter coughed again, and glanced at the piles on the table before him. "Putting Christ's resurrection aside," he began, "I'm referring to a much more earthly act of recovery. Just consider the letter I showed you yesterday, the one from Moses Maimonides when he was in mourning for his brother. Suddenly the great philosopher becomes human."

"He always was," Agnes pointed out. "It was merely a failure of imagination that made him otherwise."

"But when one reads that letter of his, about the death of his brother, one senses his—his—" Schechter faltered, coughing again. "His desperation. And then you see, in this stack"—he coughed more, then stepped over to the table behind him, where he had two weeks earlier labeled what he identified with wonder as a handwritten draft, by Maimonides himself, of his *Guide for the Perplexed*—"you see how deeply he believed that God was just. Listen to his words." Schechter picked up one of the parchments he had already sorted, and translated into English as he read aloud: "'The most marvelous and extraordinary thing about the story of Job is that Job is not said to be wise or intelligent, only morally virtuous. For if he had been wise, his situation would not have been obscure to him.' Maimonides has an entire chapter where he explains that Job's adversary is actually his own evil impulse, and that the story of Job is merely an allegorical description of Job succumbing to his own evil impulse and enduring its consequences. In effect, he claimed that Job deserved it."

"Poor old Job," Margaret murmured. "For thousands of years, no one has left him alone."

Schechter shook his head. "My point is about the letter

from Maimonides," he said. "It's impossible to imagine that the drowning of his brother wouldn't have changed his mind. There simply isn't any way he could have honestly believed that his brother's death at sea was something he or his brother had done anything to deserve." The light from the windows was growing dim; soon it would be impossible to read anymore. The remaining minutes were precious. But Schechter couldn't stop himself. "But then he writes his *Guide*, years later, claiming exactly that. Was he denying what he really believed? Or had he convinced himself that he was being punished for some obscure sin? Don't you think that if we dig through this pile for long enough, we might find out?"

"Don't you think that if Maimonides had dived deep enough into the Indian Ocean, he might have found his brother's body and resuscitated it?" Agnes asked.

Schechter looked up at her, startled. Before he could reply, Margaret looked at her sister. Schechter knew that they were sharing one mind now, the way he and Srulik once had, thinking each other's thoughts. "Or put it this way," Margaret said gently. "Mr. Schechter, would I be correct in assuming that your parents have passed away?"

"Yes," Schechter said. He thought of his father, and then remembered the argument with Srulik. What had his father tried to teach them? Did it matter what their father had said? Or did it only matter what each of them imagined he had said?

"Mr. Schechter, do you honestly think that your parents would want you to know everything about them?" Margaret asked.

"Or for that matter," her sister added, "would you want your children to know everything about you?"

The room had dimmed by now; the inked letters on the brown leather piles of parchments were no longer visible in the shadows. On the table before him lay stacks of dead animal hides, their words erased.

"Our mother died when we were two weeks old," Agnes said. "Can you guess what our father told us about her?"

Schechter looked up, weary.

"Nothing," Agnes said.

Schechter stared. He thought of his own parents and siblings, of the endless conversations that had raged through their three-room house at every hour of the day, on every subject, about every person any of them had ever met. "Nothing?" he asked. It was unfathomable.

The twins were looking at each other, shaking their heads. "He never spoke of her to us," Margaret confirmed. "Not one word."

"But weren't you—weren't you curious?"

"Of course we were," Agnes said. "But after so many years of that kind of silence, one gives up asking questions. Instead, one searches for evidence."

"We have a great deal of experience hunting for manuscripts, you see," Margaret added. "We'd been through our father's papers hundreds of times. That was where we found our first palimpsest."

The twins laughed. Schechter thought of the many palimpsests on the table before him, parchments where one text had been written over another. He had worked with palimpsests many times, enough to think of himself as one. "It was a letter to our father from our mother," Agnes explained. "Our father had written a draft of a legal brief over it. But underneath his handwriting we could make out hers."

Schechter breathed, relieved by their laughter. "What did it say?" he asked.

"There were only two phrases that were legible," Margaret answered. "The clearer of the two was the signature, 'With affection, Margaret.' I was named for her, of course."

"The other phrase was 'They strive with me,'" Agnes continued. "Or possibly 'They strive within me.'"

Schechter processed the words, hearing echoes of other twins within them. "Referring to the two of you, before your birth?" he asked.

"Of course," Margaret said.

"'Of course,' indeed," Agnes snorted. "Frankly, Mr. Schechter, it could just as easily have been about the farmers down the road. But you see, that was irrelevant to us. From those seven words we summoned an entire person into being, like the Lord creating the world. It's quite possible that the mother we imagined was better than the mother who actually existed."

"Probable, even," Margaret added. "Because we never troubled to imagine any flaws."

Agnes smiled. "I don't think either of us would entertain the thought that what we discovered wasn't exactly what she wrote," she said. "Even now that we are old women. We treasure that tiny discovery of a world that was. Even if it was a world that wasn't."

The library room was dark now, a deep pit of wordless shadows. Schechter rose from his chair and walked with the twins toward the door, to the dusk beyond it. He let the twins precede him through the door while he lingered at the threshold.

He looked over his shoulder at the dark shapes behind him, stacks of parchment and ink and dust. Someday, he had once dreamed, there would be a way of reading every word in that room, of searching through those hundreds of thousands of bits of trash to find anything one wanted. But for him, now, there was no point. Instead he patted his pocket with the letter from New York, turned around, and walked out the door. It was time to begin again.

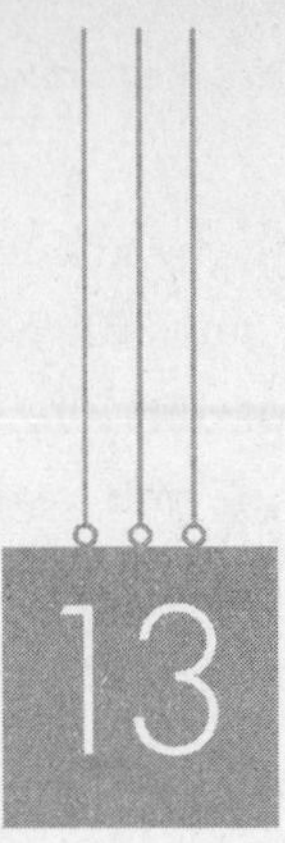

WHEN YOU OPEN a door for the first time, you imagine you have perfect freedom. You can enter through that door, or close the door and abandon it; you can proceed through the vestibule and into the hall, where more doors await your choosing; you can climb up the wide staircases to the upper floors or down the narrow ones to the underground rooms below. Each step you take is entirely your decision, each discovery behind each opened door entirely your own. The fact that the doors and the rooms behind them already exist, have always existed, does not interest you in the least. You imagine—you are convinced, despite all evidence to the contrary—that you have brought these rooms into being yourself, just by opening their doors.

Fourteen-year-old Tali knows what happened in that horrific year when she was six years old, knows what everyone knows happened. She has read the news reports about her mother's kidnapping; she has seen the broadcast interviews with local and international authorities; she has watched the initial cell phone video of her terrified, young-looking mother reading aloud, and then the second cell phone video—the astonishingly convincing one—of her mother's supposed execution. She has met Nasreen, the brave Egyptian woman who found her mother in her sister's house, and with Tali's aunt, rescued her. She has read the profiles of the kidnapper, a notorious ganglord who had apparently reformed himself enough to be elected to the new parliament, and of his wife, an abused woman whose elite family in Alexandria knew almost nothing of her squalid life. Tali has even read the translated articles from Egyptian bloggers claiming that the whole kidnapping was a hoax, that her mother was an Israeli spy who had invented the entire affair to smear the new government, that it was all an elaborate Zionist plot—a failed plot, presumably, since after an eighteen-month prison term, the ganglord returned to office.

And of course Tali has read over and over again about her aunt's great sacrifice, as her mother described it and as it was subsequently reported in every possible news outlet: how the ganglord's wife had hoped to set Tali's mother free, but hadn't thought through how to do it without her husband killing her; how Tali's aunt was the only one to believe her mother's secret message from the dungeon, and how she had come to Egypt to see what might be possible; how her aunt had valiantly volunteered herself as a hostage to replace her mother—and how her aunt had died in the raid that followed. This is the story—no, nothing so trivial as a story; it is the fundamental life-enabling fact—of her family, Tali knows: a family that could not exist but for the miraculous truth of her aunt's bottomless lifelong devotion to her mother. It is a truth whose bravery and commitment she knows she could never match.

She proceeds through her memories of these events the way she moves through the house where her family now lives in Israel, climbing the exterior stairs over the house built into the hill below it (it amazed her seven years ago, when they first moved to Israel after her American grandmother's death, how every house in Israel seemed to be built on top of another house) in order to arrive at her own future: entering through the front door with its half-lying family nameplate ("The Mizrahi Family," it announced, which seemed not to include her Ashkenazi mother), padding through the kitchen and hallway with their stone floors and continuing up the stone stairs, passing the closed door of the office where her mother often takes home work from her job running software systems for a digitized medieval archive, passing the closed door of her parents' bedroom where her father prepares for the university classes he teaches in computer science, passing the closed door of the bomb shelter where she keeps her bicycle, until she reaches the open door of her own little bedroom, where she drops her school bag and pats her pocket to check for her inhaler before turning around to leave again. It feels normal to her, casual, the initial strangeness of the family's move to Israel now engulfed by a new forgetfulness, by the impossibility of recalling her life before the move, like her old house in Massachusetts, whose halls and doorways and rooms she no longer remembers, although she occasionally tries. Her mother has password-protected the terabytes of photos and videos Tali would have loved to look through on her own. Her mother only occasionally shares them, while looking over Tali's shoulder. Often, now, Tali even forgets English words, as though the first seven years of her life were no more than a vanishing dream. But the things that happened that terrible year, thanks to the news reports, are familiar, intimate. The articles and broadcasts of every part of the story, from the initial kidnapping to her aunt's devotional death, seem like open doors, the rooms she passes through every day until she barely notices they are there.

At school she has to write a report about a philosopher. On her mother's suggestion, she chooses Rambam, and attempts to read parts of *Guide for the Perplexed*. It turns out to be much more difficult than she expects—the sort of thing her demanding and brilliant parents find simple, logical, even obvious, but when Tali actually tries to read the book in weird medieval Hebrew (which her mother claims is "perfectly clear"), or even in a heavily edited and modernized translation, it makes almost no sense. Skipping to the end, she comes across one of the only lucid passages in the entire book: a parable of a king in his palace, whose subjects stand with varying closeness to the palace's inner chambers. Those who are within the city, but who have turned their backs to the palace, Rambam wrote, are people who are smart enough to think for themselves, but who have adopted false ideas about the king. Those who seek to enter the palace, but never manage to see it, are people who believe in the law but lack the capacity to appreciate its source. Those who come up to the palace walls and walk around it are scholars of the law who do not question the fundamentals of their own beliefs. Those who enter the palace antechambers are people who have plunged into speculation about their beliefs, even if they have not yet answered their own questions. Only those who have mastered all there is to know of both the physical and the metaphysical world, to the extent possible for human beings, are able to enter into the innermost chamber of the king. But for most people, Tali understands, the gates of perception are locked against them. She counts herself as one who remains outside the palace walls.

For her school report, Tali has to include biographical facts. In Rambam's case, Tali discovers, the facts are largely drawn from the Cairo Genizah, the darkened synagogue storage room that a Jewish university professor from England discovered over a century ago—the room for which her mother once named the software program that made their family rich. From scraps of parchment in the genizah, Tali learns, it is known that Rambam was born in Córdoba, was trained as a physician in Fez, briefly lived in Crusader-occupied Israel, and then settled in Cairo. In Cairo he served as a personal doctor to royalty, first to a government administrator and later to the sultan Saladin. About his private life little is known, Tali discovers, beyond the fact that he had a merchant brother who drowned in the Indian Ocean along with much of Rambam's own money, that he married late and apparently had only one son, that he was overtaxed by his work, his community obligations, and his own genius, and of course that he published voluminous works on Jewish law, philosophy, and medicine—including, Tali notes with interest, a treatise on asthma written for an unidentified royal patient. The man was absurd in his brilliance, a gift to mankind. He reminds Tali, uncomfortably, of her mother.

Tali's mother now marvels over this original genizah professionally. After selling her company in the United States, she accepted a prestigious position as chief computer scientist for an Israeli institute that scans, uploads, transcribes, catalogues, and collates all of the quarter-million scraps of paper from that airless room in Cairo now kept in libraries around the world. It is a ridiculous job, Tali thinks privately, the height of irrelevance—the very opposite of what her mother once used her brains to do. But her mother is entranced by it, has been entranced since they moved. "Imagine, *metuka*, if someone tore up your school notebook and threw the pieces across the ocean," her mother says, explaining how the software she was creating could match handwriting and other characteristics, piecing together ancient manuscripts when one page was in Cambridge and another in New York and another in Kiev. The word *metuka* catches Tali's attention. Tali still recalls a time when only her father would address her with Hebrew endearments, when to her mother she was "baby" or "sweetie" or other English words. But that time seems submerged beneath the earth, buried in an underground room.

"It's almost impossible to reconstruct, but only almost," her mother continues. "Everything on every piece of paper in that room was perfectly preserved, just as it was when it happened. When scholars read through those papers, they can rebuild an entire city in their minds, exactly as it once was, with hundreds of thousands of details—everything from the stories of individual lives to the colors of the stripes on people's coats. It's like viewing the world through the memory of God."

The image haunts Tali, following her through the software her mother once invented as she explores the virtual rooms marked with a dungeon door. Because of the carefully preserved evidence, or at least the evidence that her mother's carefully encrypted passwords will allow her to see, Tali knows the truth of that time, can wander through it, relive it. What she doesn't know is what might have happened—what lies behind all the doors that weren't opened, how much of what happened was determined by people's choices and how much by some force of destiny beyond human perception. Often she imagines crawling through a small door high in an ancient wall, and entering the palace.

It is not a memory palace, like the ones her mother once created, though Tali often mistakes it for one. Memory palaces enshrine the past. But Tali's private mental palace contains only what has been excluded from both past and future: an imaginary past of what might have been.

She enters it first through the grand door of her mother's childhood, neglecting for now the twin portal beside it of her father's youth. Her father's is a crumbling Moorish arch containing a half-rotted wooden door, like the doors in her grandfather's old photos of his childhood in Marrakesh, while her mother's is a doubled screen door (the screen door preceding a wooden one), the sort that once felt unremarkable to her but which she now thinks of as loudly American. Behind this door is a long hallway, with rows and rows of interior doors.

Tali is practiced now at opening these doors. She chooses one painted pink, its smooth wooden surface soiled with half-scraped-off stickers. Behind it Tali finds a girls' bedroom, with two pink beds and a thick white carpet. Inside the room, two girls about Tali's age are seated on the floor, their expressions heavy with concentration and purpose. Tali recognizes them from the photographs that her mother has scanned into various computers and displayed around the house: they are her mother and her aunt. Theirs is an intense, deep, soul-embracing friendship, one that Tali cannot help but envy. Tali steps into their American bedroom, her feet sinking into a carpet as thick and indulgent as landscaped grass, and sees that they are playing chess. It has been a long game, judging by the intricate configuration of the pieces on the board and the collections of pieces lying uselessly in the carpet. As Tali watches, her aunt Judith picks up a bishop and deftly captures her mother's king.

"Checkmate," Judith announces. The smile on her face is kind, loving—the smile of someone who sees winning as a last resort, a smile of total trust.

"I was wondering why you were giving up your queen," Tali's mother says. Her voice is laced with laughter and admiration. The two sisters are laughing together now, the way Tali always envisions them. "Why do you always win, Judith?"

Tali is reluctant to close the door.

Up a flight of stairs, in a home office littered with electronic screens, Tali finds her mother as she looks now, engulfed in code. Tali enters the room cautiously, afraid to disturb her, because she knows how cold her mother can be to people who interrupt her work. But to her surprise her mother whirls around in her swivel chair, then jumps out of it to embrace her.

"Tali!" her mother calls—or at least this mother calls, for Tali has never heard her mother call her name with such enthusiasm, not even the first time they saw each other in Egypt. Then her mother was in a hospital bed, her smiles and laughter weakened. But this mother calls out "Tali!" and springs from her seat, grabs Tali's hands and dances with her, unable to confine her love to a mere embrace. What shocks Tali even more than this is seeing her mother do something she has almost never seen her do: her mother removes her phone from her pocket and drops it, unconsulted, on the desk.

"Let's go out and see the daffodils together," her mother suggests. "They'll only be in bloom for one more week. I don't want you to miss it." Her mother stretches out a hand to her, beckoning her to come along. But something in her mother's face seems forced, false. Tali drops her mother's hand, preferring, somehow, the version of her mother that sits facing a screen, unable to look up. Quietly, she leaves the room. As she closes the door, she notices that her mother seems relieved.

Back down in the main hallway, behind a heavy door decorated with frescoed paintings of ancient butlers and bakers carrying wine and bread to a long-dead king, a dark flight of stone stairs leads downward. Tali has often tried to avoid this staircase, but she finds that she cannot help herself. She follows it, for what seems like years, down into the depths of the earth. Deep in the basement of the palace, beyond the back of the furnace room, there is a tiny iron door that leads to the cell in which her mother was once held in Egypt. Tali arrives at the door's threshold, and stops. Behind this door, Tali knows, is her mother's dead body—a possibility that once, when Tali was six years old, was nothing other than real.

Tali knows this tiny door, knows what lies behind it. But she refuses to enter it, refuses even to imagine it. Instead she returns upstairs by a different staircase, a spiral staircase hidden behind a curtain alongside the entrance to the dungeon—a black velvet curtain that Tali would never have noticed if she hadn't approached the threshold of the tiny iron door. At the top of the spiral staircase she enters another door, this one a child's height and painted a thick red, like a door from a children's book.

Behind this door she finds her old kitchen in Massachusetts, alive with all the details that now feel as distant to her as Marrakesh must feel to her grandfather, down to the now unfamiliar brands of cookies in the pantry and the odd lack of a drain in the weirdly wooden floor (was the floor really made of wood?). Outside the kitchen window she can see the branches of deciduous trees, their leaves aflame in astounding colors she hasn't seen in seven years; she has been back to the United States five times since the move, but never in the fall. But strangest of all are the people seated at the kitchen table: not her mother, whose body she knows is in the dungeon below, but her father and her aunt Judith. It is a scene she remembers from when she was six years old, a memory as vague as if it had been a dream. What she doesn't recall from her dreams, though, is what she sees now: her father's smile, and her father holding Judith's hand.

"Come, Tali," her aunt calls to her, waving her free hand to beckon Tali to the table. A meal that Judith has made awaits her, composed of foods Tali has not eaten in years—pot roast, sweet potatoes, a salad made of enormous dark lettuce leaves. As Tali sits down in a strange wooden chair, Judith asks her about a test she has apparently taken in school about something called the Civil War, then tells her to hurry up and finish her dinner so she won't be late for field hockey—a sport Tali has heard of, but cannot actually describe. Her father smiles at her as she finishes her dinner, a strange smile she has never seen before. Tali finishes the meal, the flavors more than familiar on her tongue. She rises from the table, hesitant. Judith stands and embraces her. "I love you, Tali," her aunt whispers in her ear. As the door closes behind Tali, she catches a glimpse of her aunt kissing her father on the lips. It is here in this impossible room, for reasons that she will never understand, that Tali feels the most at home.

Tali spends lifetimes in this palace. As she masters the flow of its corridors, staircases, doors, and rooms, she begins to understand all that could have happened, all that might have happened, all that in fact did happen in a world beyond her own. Within the walls of this palace, she can see everything with perfect clarity: what was just, what was unjust, what could and should have been, when choices were possible, when choices were nearly—but only nearly—impossible, when a person could have squeezed through a half-opened door into a different life. She understands, as years pass within the palace walls, why her mother wanted to save every moment of everything that happened, why her parents have carved out their own palaces. Looking back at the past, no matter how false that past might be, allows a person to become like God.

The only person Tali cannot find anywhere in this palace—the one person who is excluded from it entirely, left outside the palace walls—is her sister Yael.

IT OCCURS TO TALI, often, that Yael is her aunt Judith's fault. If Judith hadn't gone to Egypt to save Tali's mother, her mother would have died—or as Tali thought of it, her mother would have remained dead—and Tali and her father would have continued living on their own. Or with Judith. Or perhaps there would have been another little sister, if Judith had stayed, a sister-cousin. But even if that were so, she wouldn't have been the sister Tali now had. She might have been someone Tali liked. Then Tali might have become what her aunt Judith once was: a champion among sisters, devoted to the very end. Or perhaps, if Judith had lived, Tali would have witnessed the love between Judith and her mother, would have known what it meant for sisters to live without envy. But that could never be true for Tali and Yael.

Tali is bright, or at least bright enough. Her aunt Judith taught her that, once. But Yael, whom Judith never met—beautiful, radiant Yael, six years old now and reading and writing fluently in Hebrew and English, already winning science competitions for children twice her age, already learning the fundamentals of code—Yael is not merely bright, but luminous. Tali's parents, especially her mother, love Yael embarrassingly, extravagantly. For while Tali is merely a survivor, a remnant of a forgotten life in an old country, a scrap of their former selves packed along with them to their new home, Yael is the true child of their hopes, the child who almost never was: the miracle child, the life that was saved by Judith's sacrifice, the gift of a benevolent God. Tali hates her sister with a passion that frightens her, and cannot speak to her in peace.

This is the beginning, as Tali sees it, and nothing else matters. All of the worlds before it might as well never have existed.

Author's Note: The Opposite of an Archive

UPON EMBARKING ON sorting the many thousands of documents discovered in the Cairo Genizah, the great twentieth-century historian S. D. Goitein declared the Genizah to be "the opposite of an archive." It's a label that some novels, including this one, might bear with pride. But readers who prefer their evidence more neatly organized can find many historical works addressing the ideas that appear in this book.

The story told in this novel of Solomon Schechter's discovery of the Cairo Genizah follows the outline of the tale as Schechter himself recounted it in a set of essays called "A Hoard of Hebrew Manuscripts." The lives of the twin "lady adventurers" Margaret Gibson and Agnes Lewis, discoverers of the Syriac Gospel of Mark, are beautifully recounted in Janet Soskice's *The Sisters of Sinai*. (I am grateful to Martien Halvorson-Taylor for pointing me toward Soskice's work.) Schechter's astonishing discovery earned him a fair amount of fame, but his frustration with Cambridge and his innate sense that the Jewish community's future lay elsewhere led him to accept the position of president of the Jewish Theological Seminary in New

York City in 1902. A critical biography of Solomon Schechter has yet to be written. For details of his personal life, including information about his parents, his health, and his twin brother, I drew from Norman Bentwich's *Solomon Schechter*, a hagiographic work published in 1938.

The story of the Cairo Genizah, its previous explorers, and the importance of the texts found within it is recounted thoroughly in *A Jewish Archive from Old Cairo*, written by Stefan C. Reif, the now retired director of the Genizah Research Unit and head of the Oriental Division of the Cambridge University Library. When I had already completed my research for this aspect of the book, two wonderfully accessible works on the Cairo Genizah's discovery and significance simultaneously appeared, and I was able to benefit from these as well. Amusingly, one is called *Sacred Treasure* while the other is called *Sacred Trash*. (The author of the former is Rabbi Mark Glickman; the latter was co-written by Adina Hoffman and Peter Cole.) Both, from slightly different angles, are marvelous entry points for any reader intrigued by the Cairo Genizah's history. They take the Genizah's story well beyond Schechter's discovery and right up to the Friedberg Genizah Project—an Israel-based digital enterprise to scan and catalogue every Cairo Genizah document in the world.

Guide for the Perplexed, written in Fustat (now part of Cairo) by Moses Maimonides (also known by his Hebrew acronym Rambam; d. 1204) as a series of letters to his student Joseph ben Judah in Aleppo, is a rich, dense, and complex philosophic work whose attempt to reconcile faith and reason inspired everyone from rabbinic leaders to Muslim philosophers to Christian theologians like Aquinas. The most accurate English translation available is that of Shlomo Pines, and Pines's edition is the indisputable entry point for English-language readers embarking on a philosophical study of this work. Quotations from the *Guide* that appear in this novel are drawn from an older translation by M. Friedlander due to that translation's greater accessibility, though I sometimes adapted the language or condensed the work's arguments for clarity. Maimonides' discussion of astrology in his letter to rabbis in Montpelier in France is adapted from a translation in Isadore Twersky's *A Maimonides Reader*. Another primary source for the ideas in this novel, though I did not quote it directly, was Maimonides' *Laws of Repentance*. Readers interested in Maimonides will find a lifetime's worth of secondary literature on every aspect of his work. I am not a philosopher or a Maimonides scholar, and I can only aspire to be one of those who glimpse the palace from its outside walls. For this reason I am all the more grateful to the many scholars who have provided pathways into his writings.

Maimonides was a royal physician, first to the grand vizier of Cairo al-Qadi al-Fadil and subsequently to the sultan Saladin. While in Saladin's service, he wrote a treatise on the treatment of asthma for an unnamed royal patient. (In this book I imagined the patient to be Saladin himself, though it is more likely to have been Saladin's son or nephew.) In the medieval Islamic world of Spain and North Africa where Maimonides lived, there were no effective treatments for asthma beyond lifestyle modifications. However, *ephedra sinica*—also known as *ma huang* or Mormon tea, and currently banned in the United States, though its synthetic version, pseudoephedrine, is familiar in decongestants—has been used in China and India to treat asthma for at least five thousand years. The ancient Roman physician Pedanius Dioscorides detailed its use in his pharmacopeia *De Materia Medica* (*On Medical Substances*). This book was available in Arabic translation during Maimonides' lifetime, though there is no reason to believe he was aware of it. Maimonides' brother David was a merchant involved in trade with India. Jewish physicians in Egypt in Maimonides' time often worked as pharmaceutical merchants as well as doctors, routinely commissioning the purchase of medications from other countries and selling them to patients. There is evidence from the Cairo Genizah that Maimonides was involved in this kind of work. Maimonides specifically mentioned that a great deal of his own money was also lost when his brother David drowned on his way to India. There is, however, no reason to believe that Maimonides sent his brother to India to acquire this medication or any other. In this aspect, my story is the opposite of an archive.

Much of what is known about Maimonides' life is drawn from documents in the Cairo Genizah, which contained draft copies of his *Guide* as well as personal letters. The letter Schechter finds in this novel about Maimonides' brother's drowning was indeed found in the Genizah, though not until Schechter returned to Cambridge. The letter from Maimonides' brother David detailing his journey to India was discovered in the Cambridge University Library among Genizah documents the library had previously purchased from Rabbi Shlomo Wertheimer of Jerusalem, a Genizah explorer who preceded Schechter. Material descriptions of medieval Fustat in this novel are gleaned from S. D. Goitein's magisterial *A Mediterranean Society,* his five-volume work on the "rubbish" found in the Cairo Genizah—that is, the documents that were not literary or religious texts, but rather the detritus of daily living: letters between non-famous people, civil records, business receipts, legal documents, children's schoolbooks, and the like. A discussion of Maimonides' relationships with his father and brother, and much else on life in Maimonides' time, can be found in Joel Kraemer's masterful and beautifully written biography *Maimonides: The Life and World of One of Civilization's Greatest Minds.* Many details in this novel are drawn from Kraemer's book, including aspects of Maimonides' personality and his rivalry with another physician in the royal court, his relationship with the grand vizier of Cairo, and the contents of his brother David's letter from the port of 'Aydhab.

Among the many classical and modern commentaries on the biblical Joseph story (and the seduction story within it involving Judah and Tamar) that I explored while writing this novel, Avivah Gottlieb Zornberg's interpretations in *The Beginning of Desire* and *The Murmuring Deep* were particularly inspiring to me. Each includes a Joseph-related chapter entitled "The Pit and the Rope."

The modern Library of Alexandria does exist, under the name Bibliotheca Alexandrina. Its breathtaking state-of-the-art facilities can be admired online as well as in person. While I was inspired by the reality of this library (and by my brief glimpses of it as it was being completed), the characters and context connected with it in this novel are drawn only from my imagination.

MANY PEOPLE HELPED ME to make this book much better than it might have been. The curator Jacob Wisse unwittingly got me started on this novel when he commissioned an original fiction piece from me to accompany an exhibit of contemporary art on Genesis at Yeshiva University Museum. I am also grateful to the Arabic literature scholar Ariel Moriah Sheetrit, whose reflections on contemporary Egypt were helpful to me in imagining several scenes in this book. Her generous reading of the manuscript also prevented me from publishing several outrageous gaffes. I am grateful as well to the software architect Rachel Elkin Lebwohl, who also graciously read the manuscript and steered me away from mistakes in another category entirely. All remaining errors are mine alone.

Alane Salierno Mason is as thoughtful and thorough an

editor as any writer could hope for, and Gary Morris is as insightful and persistent an agent as any writer could dream of. I am indebted to both of them for their years of dedication to my work.

I am grateful to my siblings, Jordana Horn (an accomplished journalist, marvelous writer, and blogger extraordinaire), Ariel Horn (author of the hilarious novel *Help Wanted, Desperately*, among other distinctions), and Zach Horn (an Emmy Award–winning animator), for decades of collective creativity—and especially to Ariel and her husband, Donny, in whose home I began writing this book. I am even more grateful to my parents, Susan and Matthew Horn, for taking me to Egypt years ago, and far more importantly for their active involvement as my family has expanded during the writing of this novel. This book and everything I write can be traced back to them, as well as to our family's teacher of Torah, Dr. Nathan Winter z"l, who first introduced me as a teenager to *Guide for the Perplexed*.

As always, I am most grateful to my most endlessly patient reader, my husband, Brendan Schulman, who first suggested that I reimagine the biblical Joseph story in a contemporary novel, and whose professional expertise in unearthing electronic legal evidence first inspired my thoughts on what a modern genizah might be. He is my first reader, and the recorder of our life.

And finally, I would like to acknowledge the four people who tried their hardest to prevent me from writing this book: our children, Maya, Ari, Eli, and Ronen. We have photographs and records of every occasion in their lives, but I hope they will grow to remember the many blessings in between. This book is for them.

A GUIDE FOR THE PERPLEXED

Dara Horn

READING GROUP GUIDE

A GUIDE FOR THE PERPLEXED

Dara Horn

READING GROUP GUIDE

AN INTERVIEW WITH AUTHOR DARA HORN

Your novel is about a software developer who creates an application that records everything its users do. Where did that idea come from?

When I was writing the book, it was fiction! (Six months later, it's called Google Glass.)

Since I was a child, I've had a fantasy of turning life into an archive, of writing everything down so that nothing could ever be lost. Now, of course, social media has made my dream come true—and turned it into a nightmare. We usually think of information overload as a modern problem. But because I moonlight as a professor of Hebrew literature (I have a doctorate in Hebrew and Yiddish), I know this has happened before.

A little over a century ago, a Cambridge professor named Solomon Schechter discovered a stash of medieval documents in a Cairo synagogue. Because of a religious law against destroying Hebrew texts, synagogues usually have a storage space called a "genizah"—a "hiding place" for damaged books and papers that can't be used but also can't be thrown away. This Cairo synagogue was a thousand years old. It had a genizah room containing a massive document dump—and no one had cleaned out the room in over nine hundred years. The Cambridge professor, in typical imperial British fashion, packed up more than 100,000 documents and brought them back to Cambridge. Some of them were priceless literary treasures. But most were things like sales receipts, ads, recipes, school projects. . . . This was not a library. This was the medieval Facebook, crammed with so much mundane

---

junk that you could reconstruct an entire world from it—except that merely cataloguing it took more than eighty years.

Memory is the foundation of identity, but the way we become who we are isn't through total recall. It's by curating our memories—by choosing, out of that bottomless well of information, what's worth saving.

Much of your book takes place in postrevolutionary Egypt, where your software developer winds up getting kidnapped. Did you set out to write about the Arab Spring?

No—I started writing the book before the Arab Spring, and then I had to change my plot! But it turned out to be very lucky, because it gave me a chance to write about an astonishing moment: when one of the oldest civilizations was suddenly forced to face a new world where everything is on the record.

Part of my book takes place in the Library of Alexandria, which you might remember from fifth grade social studies as the largest library in the ancient world (and which later burned to the ground). But what you didn't learn in fifth grade is that the Library of Alexandria was reconstructed ten years ago as a two-hundred-million-dollar complex, with servers that have archived every webpage ever created—sort of like how the pharaohs were buried with all their organs perfectly preserved.

The story inside the kidnapping plot is about the kidnapped woman and her jealous sister. Why are sibling relationships so important in this book?

The novel's plot is inspired by the biblical story of Joseph and his brothers—set in contemporary times, and with women instead of men. I think it's deeply important that some of the world's oldest stories are about sibling rivalry, because siblings are people who share a past but not a future.

For me, sibling stories are personal. I have two sisters who are published writers and a brother who just won his second Emmy. Luckily we are all very close, and none of the rivalries in this book are drawn from my own life. But I credit my siblings with teaching me the power of storytelling. When we were children, the four of us would torture our parents during dinner by talking endlessly about our days at school. One day our mother put a kitchen timer on the table and said, "From now on, each child gets five minutes to speak." My sisters and brother would then stand up and perform their days as five-minute comedies, five-minute tragedies, five-minute operas.

I think that today everyone worries about time disappearing—about missing opportunities, or about recording every moment online forever. But at those dinners, my siblings taught me what happens, if you're lucky, to days that disappear: they turn into stories.

What's a "Guide for the Perplexed"?

My book is named for a famous work of philosophy—a book whose rough drafts were found in that Cairo storage room. Its author, Maimonides, was a twelfth-century religious scholar, and also a doctor serving the Egyptian sultan. In his time, Egypt was the tech capital of the world. In his book, he tries to reconcile religious faith with a very modern high-tech life, and he asks the question we're still asking now: Are our lives determined by forces we can't control, or do we have the free will to determine our future?

Of course, as any parent knows, we definitely can't control the future. If we could, I wouldn't have spent last Tuesday stopping my four-year-old from climbing out the window and explaining to him that wearing a superhero cape does not actually mean he can fly. But I think the superpower we do have is our ability to control the past. In my book, the stories of the philosopher whose work was left in the storage room, the professor who found it, and the kidnapped software genius who stores every fragment of our lives—all their stories converge to reveal that ancient human power. Recording everything is the same as recording nothing, because it makes memories meaningless. It's the act of choosing what's worth saving that turns a lifetime's worth of memories into a story.

You have an academic career in Yiddish and Hebrew literature—languages that are rarely studied in the United States outside of religious communities. How did that affect your writing a novel about technology and memory?

When I was in graduate school, I noticed that many of my fellow humanities graduate students were plagued with doubts about their work—"Does the world really need another dissertation on Shakespeare?" But with my work, I had the opposite problem: If I don't read this stuff, who will?

In Massachusetts, there's a National Yiddish Book Center that collects Yiddish books from dead and dying Jewish readers around the world. They've gathered more than a million books, and now they're digitizing them. The same thing is true of the Cairo Genizah, that massive haul of medieval documents from the Cairo synagogue. There's an Israeli institute that's now scanning and cataloguing it all. But what's amazing about it to me is the greater question: who will read all these things? As a scholar, I've used those digital archives myself. But I look at the vast number of artifacts available and I'm also overwhelmed. It would take years to even begin to scratch the surface of the material there, and only a handful of people can even read them at all.

In the past few years as social media has exploded, I've seen this same problem emerge in people's personal lives. You used to get out your camera ten times a year, take twenty-four photos at a time, put them in an album, and you were done. Now I have photos of every second of my family's life, but I can't possibly look at them all. It creates a kind of paralysis because it makes it impossible to create a coherent story for our lives. I think my background in these languages has made me very aware of what it means to choose what matters from our personal past—which is what all of us have to do now, in a more conscious way than ever before.

Several characters in your book suffer from asthma—one in the twenty-first century, one in the twentieth, one in the nineteenth, and one in the twelfth—and the disease's treatment becomes a key point in the plot. Where did that come from? Why does the history of medicine matter in this book?

Three of my four children have asthma, so I've clocked many hours in the emergency room. My husband had it as a child, and his treatment was completely different from our children's—inhalers weren't available until he was twelve, so he had to get adrenaline shots. As I researched the life of Solomon Schechter, the Cambridge professor who revealed the Cairo Genizah to the world, I discovered that he had asthma—and when he was collecting these dusty medieval parchments, he kept collapsing and had to use a nineteenth-century respirator. And then as I read about the twelfth-century philosopher Maimonides, I found that he had written a book on asthma treatment for a member of the sultan's royal court. It was like a long chain of people who couldn't breathe.

What fascinated me about it was that everyone always thinks they're living on the cutting edge of science. We're convinced that we know the real facts and that the people who lived before us were superstitious idiots. The fact that we will someday be our own grandchildren's superstitious idiots is very humbling to me. My book is really about that weird and constant persistence of the unknowable—even in this information age.

You have four children, ages eight, six, four, and one. How do you find the time to write?

After my fourth child was born last year, I created an app that actually dilates time. If you buy my book, I'll give you one.

DISCUSSION QUESTIONS

1. Josie's Genizah software categorizes memories by themes like "entertainment" and "travel" and carefully curates what it records in order to bury the unpleasant and the ugly. Do our minds work this way? Would you subscribe to Genizah? How have other technologies already changed how you experience things and remember them?

2. What is the significance of dreams in the novel? Does it make sense to catalog them in Genizah along with daytime memories, as Nasreen wants to do? Do you think they are "mental garbage" or "a window to a world beyond what a waking person could perceive"?

3. Maimonides tried to reconcile faith and reason in his writings. What role do religion, rational thought, and intelligence play in how the characters see themselves and others?

4. Josie designed her software to record patterns in human behavior,

which she thinks can be used to predict future outcomes. Maimonides believed that, as the ancient rabbis expressed it, "Everything is foreseen, but freedom of choice is granted." Are their beliefs compatible? Do you believe that you are in control of the choices you make?

5. When Josie is putting together a Genizah of Tali from memory, she realizes that the Tali who emerges is very different from the one captured by the software at home. What does this suggest about Josie's feelings toward her daughter? How does their relationship differ from Tali's relationship with Judith?

6. One of Cairo's unique features is its vast necropolis full of living squatters, but Nasreen says, "All cities are really cities of the dead." Do you agree with her? Do you live in a place where you can feel the generations that came before you?

7. How do Josie and Judith and their relationship change over the course of the novel? Which of the sisters do you most sympathize with?

8. Schechter says, "Every human being, in the end, becomes the opposite of an archive." He also describes himself as a palimpsest—a piece of parchment on which one text has been inscribed over another. What does he mean by using these metaphors, and how do they apply to himself and others? Do they also apply to the novel itself?

9. The book is full of encounters between people of different backgrounds: Judith and Itamar, Schechter and the Scottish twins, Mosheh and the vizier, and Josie and Nasreen, to name a few. How do these people view each other? What cultural differences and worldviews come to light in their conversations?

10. There are four pairs of siblings in the novel: Judith and Josie, Schechter and Srulik, Margaret and Agnes, and Mosheh and David. How does the novel explore themes of jealousy, ambition, success, and love through the siblings? Did their relationships remind you of your relationships with your siblings?

11. In what ways does the novel's narrative parallel the biblical story of Joseph? Do you think this correspondence enhances the power of the novel? In general, are biblical stories relevant to the present or to understanding the challenges of modern life?

12. Did Judith deserve Josie's forgiveness in the end? Did Josie deserve Judith's? Did the final chapter about Tali change the way you felt about the outcome of the story?

13. Like historians piecing together the past, several characters wish to bring the dead back "to life" through bits of memory, writings, photographs, and recordings. Is this possible? How have you dealt with the death of someone you loved and the artifacts—such as letters and photographs—that were left behind?

14. How do the three stories—of Josie and Judith Ashkenazi, Solomon Schechter, and Mosheh ben Maimon—intersect and relate to one another? How does Maimonides's *Guide for the Perplexed* echo through all the layers of the novel?

BIBLIOGRAPHY AND RESOURCES

Joseph

Self, Struggle and Change: Family Conflict Stories in Genesis and Their Healing Insights for Our Lives, by Norman J. Cohen. LongHill Partners, 2000.

The Joseph Narrative in Genesis, by Eric I. Lowenthal. Ktav, 1973.

Joseph and His Brothers; Joseph in Egypt; Joseph the Provider, by Thomas Mann, translated by John E. Woods. Everyman's Library, 2005.

Coat of Many Cultures: The Story of Joseph in Spanish Literature 1200–1492, by Michael D. McGaha. Jewish Publication Society, 1997.

"The Book of Genesis (Part 2)," lecture on CD by Professor Gary A. Rendsburg. The Teaching Company, 2006.

Wrestling with Angels: What the First Family of Genesis Teaches Us About Our Spiritual Identity, Sexuality, and Personal Relationships, by Naomi H. Rosenblatt and Joshua Horwitz. Delta, 1996.

The Beginning of Desire: Reflections on Genesis, by Avivah Gottlieb Zornberg. Schocken Books, 2011.

The Murmuring Deep: Reflections on the Biblical Unconscious, by Avivah Gottlieb Zornberg. Schocken Books, 2009.

"The Pit and the Rope: Joseph and Judah," lecture on DVD by Avivah Gottlieb Zornberg. Infomedia Judaica, Limited, 2012.

"What If Joseph Hates Us?: Closing the Book," lecture on DVD by Avivah Gottlieb Zornberg. Infomedia Judaica, Limited, 2012.

Judah and Tamar

The Ladder of Jacob: Ancient Interpretations of the Biblical Story of Jacob and His Children, by James L. Kugel. Princeton University Press, 2009.

"The Book of Genesis (Part 2)," lecture on CD by Professor Gary A. Rendsburg. The Teaching Company, 2006.

Maimonides

Moses Maimonides: The Man and His Works, by Herbert A. Davidson. Oxford University Press, 2010.

Maimonides: A Biography, by Abraham Joshua Heschel, translated by Joachim Neugroschel. Farrar, Straus and Giroux, 1983.

Maimonides: The Life and World of One of Civilization's Greatest Minds, by Joel Kraemer. Doubleday, 2010.

The Guide of the Perplexed, by Moses Maimonides, translated by Shlomo Pines. University of Chicago Press, 1974.

Maimonides: A Guide for Today's Perplexed, by Kenneth Seeskin. Behrman House, 1996.

A Maimonides Reader, edited by Isadore Twersky. Behrman House, 1972.

The Cairo Genizah

Sacred Treasure: The Cairo Genizah, by Mark Glickman. Jewish Lights, 2012.

A Mediterranean Society: The Jewish Communities of the Arab World as Portrayed in the Documents of the Cairo Geniza, by S. D. Goitein. University of California Press, 2000.

Sacred Trash: The Lost and Found World of the Cairo Geniza, by Adina Hoffman and Peter Cole. Schocken, 2011.

A Jewish Archive from Old Cairo, by Stefan C. Reif. Routledge, 2000.

Solomon Schechter

Solomon Schechter: A Biography, by Norman Bentwich. Jewish Publication Society of America, 1938.

Solomon Schechter: Selected Writings, edited by Norman Bentwich. East and West Library, 1946.

Aspects of Rabbinic Theology: Major Concepts of the Talmud, by Solomon Schechter. LongHill Partners, 1999.

Margaret Gibson and Agnes Lewis

The Sisters of Sinai: How Two Lady Adventurers Discovered the Hidden Gospels, by Janet Soskice. Vintage, 2010.

The Brothers Ashkenazi

The Brothers Ashkenazi, by Israel Joshua Singer. Other Press, 2010.

Twins and Siblings

Self, Struggle and Change: Family Conflict Stories in Genesis and Their Healing Insights for Our Lives, by Norman J. Cohen. LongHill Partners, 2000.

When Brothers Dwell Together: The Preeminence of Younger Siblings in the Hebrew Bible, by Frederick E. Greenspahn. Oxford University Press, 1994.

Identical Strangers: A Memoir of Twins Separated and Reunited, by Elyse Schein and Paula Bernstein. Random House, 2008.

Technology

"The Visionary: A Digital Pioneer Questions What Technology Has Wrought," by Jennifer Kahn. *The New Yorker*, July 11, 2011. http://www.newyorker.com/reporting/2011/07/11/110711fa_fact_kahn

Who Owns the Future, by Jaron Lanier. Simon & Schuster, 2013.

Egyptian Political Scene

The Arab Uprisings: What Everyone Needs to Know, by James L. Gelvin. Oxford University Press, 2012.

Liberation Square: Inside the Egyptian Revolution and the Rebirth of a Nation, by Ashraf Khalil. St. Martin's Press, 2002.

SELECTED NORTON BOOKS WITH READING GROUP GUIDES AVAILABLE

For a complete list of Norton's works with reading group guides, please go to www.wwnorton.com/books/reading-guides.

Diana Abu-Jaber	*Birds of Paradise*
Diane Ackerman	*One Hundred Names for Love*
Alice Albinia	*Leela's Book*
Andrea Barrett	*Ship Fever*
Bonnie Jo Campbell	*Once Upon a River*
Lan Samantha Chang	*Inheritance*
Anne Cherian	*A Good Indian Wife*
Amanda Coe	*What They Do in the Dark*
Michael Cox	*The Meaning of Night*
Suzanne Desrochers	*Bride of New France*
Jared Diamond	*Guns, Germs, and Steel*
Andre Dubus III	*Townie*
John Dufresne	*Requiem, Mass.*
Anne Enright	*The Forgotten Waltz*
Jennifer Cody Epstein	*The Painter from Shanghai*
Betty Friedan	*The Feminine Mystique*
Stephen Greenblatt	*The Swerve*
Lawrence Hill	*Someone Knows My Name*
Ann Hood	*The Red Thread*
Dara Horn	*All Other Nights*
Pam Houston	*Contents May Have Shifted*
Mette Jakobsen	*The Vanishing Act*
N. M. Kelby	*White Truffles in Winter*
Nicole Krauss	*The History of Love**
Scott Lasser	*Say Nice Things About Detroit*
Don Lee	*The Collective**
Maaza Mengiste	*Beneath the Lion's Gaze*
Daniyal Mueenuddin	*In Other Rooms, Other Wonders*
Liz Moore	*Heft*
Jean Rhys	*Wide Sargasso Sea*
Mary Roach	*Packing for Mars*
Johanna Skibsrud	*The Sentimentalists*
Jessica Shattuck	*Perfect Life*
Joan Silber	*The Size of the World*

Mary Helen Stefaniak	*The Cailiffs of Baghdad, Georgia*
Manil Suri	*The Age of Shiva*
Brady Udall	*The Lonely Polygamist*
Barry Unsworth	*Sacred Hunger*
Alexei Zentner	*Touch*

*Available only on the Norton Web site